Cumbria
County Council
Libraries, books and more.........

H

Please return/renew this item by the last date due.
Library items may also be renewed by phone on
030 33 33 1234 (24 hours) or via our website

www.cumbria.gov.uk/libraries

Cumbria Libraries

CLIC
Interactive Catalogue

Ask for a CLIC password

r.

Also by Peter Murphy
Removal
Test of Resolve

The Ben Schroeder Series
A Higher Duty
A Matter for the Jury
And is there Honey Still for Tea?
The Heirs of Owain Glyndwr
Calling Down the Storm

Walden of Bermondsey
Judge Walden: Back in Session

ONE LAW
FOR THE
REST OF US

A BEN SCHROEDER NOVEL

PETER MURPHY

NO EXIT PRESS

First published in 2018 by No Exit Press,
an imprint of Oldcastle Books Ltd,
PO Box 394, Harpenden,
Herts, AL5 1XJ
noexit.co.uk
@noexitpress

ISBN
978-0-85730-140-6 (print)
978-0-85730-141-3 (epub)

2 4 6 8 10 9 7 5 3 1

Typeset in 11pt Minion Pro
by Avocet Typeset, Somerton, Somerset, TA11 6RT
Printed in Great Britain by Clays Ltd, Elcograf S.p.A.

For more information about Crime Fiction go to crimetime.co.uk

There is no scandal so serious that trying to cover it up won't make it worse.

Anon

PART ONE

1

Audrey Marshall

If it hasn't happened to you, I can't adequately explain what it feels like. You feel like you've been struck down without warning: like having a heart attack when you're young and in the prime of life, and going about your day of work and play and love, as young living people do; like a partner you trusted telling you he's leaving you for someone else, just when you've started to tell him about your day, and the plans you've made for dinner or the weekend or the summer, as lovers do. Everything stops. You can't comprehend it.

Nothing in your range of vision looks the way it did a few seconds before; nothing you hear sounds the same as it did. Your mind and your emotions have frozen, like drops of water on the tip of a stalactite in some sub-zero cavern that solidify before they can fall to ground. For a moment you're not sure who you are, or where you are: and when your mind and emotions slowly begin to thaw and you start to regain your bearings, you realise that your body has frozen too, and you're not breathing. You force yourself to breathe, and your body slowly begins to react to your commands; but then you feel like you're going to faint, so you find something or someone to hold on to; and when the fainting feeling subsides, you feel an urge to throw up; and when the urge to throw up subsides, you scream until you can't scream any more, a deafening primal scream that seems to last for ever. Then, if you're one of the lucky ones, you find that you can still cry.

The few experts who claim to understand it call it recovered memory. And this is what I've learned about recovered memory: you feel it's ambushed you and taken you completely by surprise; but in fact, that's not true. Once you make the connection, you realise that you knew all along. You feel that the memories have sprung from nowhere and have no origins or antecedents in your life. But at the same time you also have the contradictory sense that they have always been with you: like fragments of a dream hovering in the back of your mind as you're waking up, fragments that you can't define or identify, but that you somehow know are something more than a dream. That's when you put two and two together to make four. Four is the revelation that all those elusive grainy images flitting through your mind, images you could never quite hold on to, images so vague that you couldn't place them in time and space, but that somehow seemed real, were indeed real. And it all starts to make sense.

That sudden feeling of dread when you walked up some curved section of staircase, or entered a small room in someone's home, when there was nothing to fear.

That momentary panic when a male voice called to you unexpectedly when you were in your bedroom in your nightdress, even though the voice was one you knew and trusted.

That overwhelming urge to reject an approach from a man – even a man you fancied and who might have been just the kind of man you wanted to be with – because of the tone of his voice, or a phrase he used, or the colour of his tie, or a whiff of his cologne.

That feeling of bewilderment, embarrassment, and humiliation when you'd finally found a man you cared about: when you'd undressed each other, and you were lying on the bed together, and you were kissing him with closed eyes, and your hand was working on his cock, and you were feeling and hearing his passion increasing; and he gently slid his fingers inside you to reciprocate, which was what you were hoping he would do, which was what you wanted, because you were hot and wet for him; but when he actually did it, you found yourself closing your legs over his fingers; and then, without any warning, you felt your cunt tighten and slam shut against him, like the door of a bank vault.

You made any excuse you could: it felt painful, you were nervous, you were feeling ticklish that day. You'd even developed a silly giggle to represent feeling ticklish. 'It's not your fault,' you would say, 'it's just not working today. Let me...' And then, to compensate him for rejecting his attempt at intimacy, and to divert his attention, you would desperately transfer his cock from your hand to your mouth; or whisper a saucy invitation, as you licked an ear lobe, to put it in and fuck your brains out. And while you were fucking and while you were lying in his arms afterwards, you were hoping he wouldn't ask you: why, if you found his fingers so painful or ticklish, didn't that apply to his cock? Because you didn't have any answer to that question that made sense.

Later, when he was asleep, you would furtively masturbate, trying desperately to ignore your undeserved feelings of shame and guilt, and you would be faced with the inexplicable fact that there was nothing painful or ticklish about your own fingers touching you. And perhaps once or twice, when you'd had a few drinks and, to your surprise, fell nervously into bed with a woman friend, you found that you could accept the pleasure of her deliciously hesitant, exploring fingers without any contrary feelings at all: for which, when you reflected on the experience after the effects of the drink had worn off, you could also find no explanation.

When you eventually married a man you loved and trusted, you were finally able to allow him to do what no other male lover had been able to do for you. But even with your husband, there were nights when you couldn't – nights when you had to kick the old defence mechanisms into gear; nights when, yet again, you gave way to the silly giggle, and acted like a skittish teenager with an unpredictable phobia about being touched. And it was only his love and understanding that saved you from the misery that had haunted your love-making for as long in your life as you had been making love.

When I recovered my memories, any sense of mystery about all those experiences instantly vanished into thin air. I saw immediately, and with perfect clarity, that there was the most rational explanation in the world for every feeling of fear or dread I'd ever had in so many situations during my life. It was as if the floodgates had suddenly opened, and I was deluged by wave after wave of high-definition images from my past, images so clear and precise that the events I now remembered might have occurred the day before. They were all so clear that it was incomprehensible to me that I had not remembered at some much earlier time – indeed, it was incomprehensible to me that I had could ever have forgotten them.

But then, of course, I realised that my condition was not one of a simple loss of memory, or the result of any conscious effort on my part to suppress the images. It was a condition of the most profound amnesia, imposed on me subconsciously by my own mind for my protection, to save me from having to relive again and again the pain and humiliation I had endured at such an early age. It was an act of mercy, not a deprivation. But that thought brought little relief.

Worst of all, I felt a crushing, overwhelming guilt that my failure to remember had caused me to expose my daughter to the same horrors to which I myself had been exposed. Ironically, she was the same age then as I'd been when it happened to me. All it took for me to recover my memories was for Emily to speak two sentences, and for those two sentences to swirl around like acid in my mind for a few hours. The experience devastated me, and for hours afterwards I was incapable of rational thought. But, as soon as I recovered some semblance of composure, I swore by all I held sacred that I would protect her from that moment onward, and that I would bring those who had abused us both to justice, if it cost me everything I had.

2

'I asked the clients to come at four thirty,' Julia Cathermole said, glancing at her watch. 'I hope you don't mind, but I wanted to make sure that we had time to talk among ourselves first. We have forty-five minutes. I think that should give us long enough.'

'I'm sure it will,' Ben Schroeder replied.

They had gathered for the conference in Ben's chambers at Two Wessex Buildings, housed in the magnificent archway at the foot of Middle Temple Lane, from which the few remaining yards of the Lane lead down to the Embankment. Ben's junior clerk, Alan, had arranged the room so that they could sit as a group in chairs in front of Ben's desk, around a working table.

Ben was a handsome, dark-haired man, now in his mid-thirties, a rising star at the London criminal bar. His still thin, bony facial features had a way of forcing the observer to focus on his deep-set, piercing, dark brown eyes, eyes which had a discomfiting habit of seeming to bore into the witnesses and judges on whom he trained them in court. He wore an immaculate dark grey three-piece suit, with a light grey and white tie, over a pristine white shirt. The bar was a notoriously snobbish profession, and Ben's East End origins had been an obstacle earlier in his career; but they also offered intimate access to the best Jewish tailoring available anywhere in London, and he was known for taking full advantage of that craftsmanship. Now, after one or two turbulent years, he enjoyed the best of both worlds. The tailoring remained one of his trademarks, but his roots had long since become irrelevant to his professional success: he had more than proved himself in a series of high-profile cases, and his reputation was continuing to grow.

Julia had brought with her another barrister: Virginia Castle, Ginny to friends and colleagues, with Chambers in King's Bench Walk in the Inner Temple, who made up for a slight, will-o'-the-wisp figure with a forceful courtroom technique every bit the equal of Ben's, a sharp wit, and great personal charm, all used to good effect. She, too, favoured the barrister's dark suit, in her case, a two-piece suit worn over a well-starched white blouse; the effect, with her jet-black hair, tied neatly up at the back, was a striking one.

It was left to Julia to make up for the lack of colour with a light green suit and yellow scarf with matching shoes. The small firm of solicitors she had helped to found had had the confidence to forsake the City in favour of the West End, and her personal style reflected that same confidence. Her vivid outfits were becoming as familiar on the London legal scene as her sophisticated and occasionally outrageous dinner parties, invitations to which were eagerly sought, not only by lawyers and judges, but also by many of the capital's political and artistic names.

'It should be more than enough,' Ginny agreed. 'Has her husband come down to London with her?'

'He goes everywhere with her. With all she's been through, I don't think she could cope without him at the moment. He was the one who got in touch and asked me – well, my firm, Cathermole and Bridger – to represent them.'

'He's a solicitor himself, isn't he, up where they live, in Ely?'

'Yes. We had some dealings a year or two ago. He referred us a banking dispute his firm didn't have the firepower to handle, and we settled it for him. That's how he knew about us.'

'Julia, before we get started, do you mind if I ask why you've come to me?' Ben asked.

She laughed. 'Well, that's a new one, I must say. Most barristers want to know why it's taken me so long. It's rather refreshing.'

Ben smiled. 'I'm wondering whether you'd thought about a Silk? This is going to be a heavy case, and we're probably going to offend some powerful people. The only time our paths have crossed before, you'd instructed Ginny and I was on the other side – and you won.'

'I find that's the best vantage point from which to observe a barrister,' Julia replied, returning his smile. 'The fact that a barrister may lose a case doesn't interest me. Every barrister wins and loses cases: that's the nature of the game. It's how they do it that interests me.'

'What interested you about me?'

'The fact that you were determined to get to the truth, and you weren't going to let anything stand in your way. It can't have been easy in the case we had against each other.'

Ben laughed. 'It's not every day you start out with what you think is a cast-iron case, and then have to stand there and watch as it falls apart overnight.'

'You didn't know your client was another Kim Philby: how could you? Neither did the good Professor Hollander, if the truth be known. He *suspected* that Digby was up to no good, but he didn't *know* – and in the end he blew the whistle on Digby without a shred of real evidence.'

'We more or less begged Hollander to throw his hand in and publish a retraction,' Ginny smiled.

'We did everything except go down on bended knee,' Julia agreed. 'But, lo and behold, come the first morning of trial, Sir James Digby QC had been unmasked and was nowhere to be found. What happened?'

'Viktor Stepanov happened,' Ben replied.

Julia nodded. 'Exactly: but Stepanov happened because you and Ginny made him happen. But for that, Sir James Digby might still be one of the country's leading Silks, and Francis Hollander might have crawled back to America with his tail between his legs, with a huge bill for damages and costs in his pocket.' She paused. 'Not many junior counsel would have done what you two did, swanning off at short notice with a member of the Secret Intelligence Service to meet a Soviet defector in a foreign safe house, a couple of days before trial.'

'Stepanov turned the whole case on its head in a couple of hours,' Ginny recalled. 'He regaled us with the whole story: how he'd recruited Digby through their common interest in chess, and how they'd used chess symbols to swap secret messages.' She turned to Ben. 'I didn't tell you at the time, but I really admired the calm way you reacted. It must have been a hell of a shock, but you didn't give anything away.'

'There was nothing left to give away, was there?' Ben replied with a wry smile. 'The game was up – time to knock your king over and resign – and we told him so as soon as I got back to London; and the next day he took the Burgess and Maclean route to Moscow.'

'Here's the point I'm making,' Julia said. 'When you two went to The Hague with Baxter, neither of you knew what you would find. The stakes were sky-high, and you had no way of knowing what evidence Baxter had, or whose case that evidence would support. But you wanted the truth, and you weren't afraid to do whatever it took to get it. That's what we're going to need in this case too. Not to mention,' she continued, more quietly, after some moments, 'that you took quite a risk, professionally speaking – counsel aren't allowed to run around gathering evidence, are they? Strictly *verboten*, as I understand the rules. That's our job, as solicitors.'

'Baxter didn't give us much choice,' Ben observed.

'No, I know. He insisted that the two of you should be the ones to go.' She smiled. 'I was a bit miffed, I must say. I know it was Baxter's decision to leave me at home. I'm not sure I've forgiven him yet.'

'With your connections inside MI6?' Ginny said, smiling. 'I'm not surprised. You must have been furious.'

'I would have gone over his head, except that there wasn't time – we were on the verge of trial. But, looking back on it now, and much though it hurts my wounded professional pride to admit it,

Baxter was right. You two were the right choice, and you're the right choice for this case.'

'Does that mean we'll have to go digging for evidence again?' Ginny asked.

'Quite possibly: and we're certainly going to be ruffling some influential feathers, accusing some people in high places of some very nasty things – people who won't go down without a very hard fight. Audrey Marshall doesn't need a Silk, Ben. She needs counsel who are not afraid of a fight: and based on everything I've seen, the two of you fit that description to a T.'

3

Audrey Marshall
I was born Audrey Patterson in October 1933. I had a sister, Joan, who was almost exactly five years older. My dad, Jack, was a clerk in an insurance company in the City. My mum, Dorothy, had been a secretary before she got married, and she made a bit of extra money by taking in typing and editing. So, although we weren't exactly rich, we were pretty comfortably off. We lived in our own house in Stepney Way in the East End of London, and as far as I remember from so long ago, we were very happy together there. I remember going to the local primary school and playing in the street in front of our house with Joan; and I remember my seventh birthday party. Although the war had started by then, and some things we'd taken for granted before the war were in short supply, my mother somehow managed to bake me a cake and put seven white candles on it, and found balloons and ribbons to decorate the living room, and my friends from the street and school were all there. We played pass the parcel and hide-and-seek.

One reason I remember that birthday party so well is that it's the last real memory I have of my life in our house. The Blitz had been underway for about a month. The Luftwaffe was dropping its bombs on London by night and by day, inflicting as much damage as it could, and the East End bore the brunt of it because a lot of the bombing was aimed at crippling the docks. Then again, a lot of it was aimed simply at terrorising the city's population; and a good deal of it was probably random – bombs ditched to lose weight before attempting the flight home with damage inflicted by our anti-aircraft guns; or when short of fuel; or when the navigator had lost his way.

I was too young to understand the full extent of the danger. But at night, I remember hearing explosions and the wailing of sirens, and the rapid bursts of fire from anti-aircraft batteries; and, if I dared to peek out around the blackout curtains we had on the windows, seeing the red and orange glow of fires on the ground in the distance, and the white beams of searchlights in the sky. I remember my parents talking in whispered tones about people they knew who had been killed or lost their homes in the bombing, and about people sleeping on the platforms of the underground stations. For some reason, we never resorted to these obvious places of sanctuary from the nightly violence, even though Stepney Green and Whitechapel stations were close at hand. I've often wondered why. My parents never explained. Looking back on that time now with my adult understanding, I can only suppose that it was a case of denial. In common with many other Londoners, they couldn't bring themselves to accept that the assumptions of peace and security on which they had built their lives had been swept away so comprehensively and so suddenly: that in just a month, a hostile air force could have reduced their city to a state of such terror that people would abandon their homes and everything they had worked for, that they would leave everything they had defenceless in the dead of night. Perhaps, also in common with many other Londoners, they were clinging desperately to the delusion that it would never happen to them.

Whatever the truth, some sense of reality must have penetrated, because three days after my party, my parents packed suitcases for Joan and me. With no forewarning, they explained to us that we were being evacuated. That wasn't how they put it: what they said was that we were going for a short holiday in the country until the war was over, which would be any day now, so we wouldn't be away for long. What I'd seen, even through the eyes of a child, didn't suggest to me that the war would be over any time soon; and my mother was crying as she and my father tied our name-tags around our necks with white ribbon, and bundled us out of the house in the bleak hours of the morning, just before dawn. They walked us quickly to the corner of the street, where we boarded a dark, cold bus with a handful of other children. Our consignment would grow to twenty: one or two we knew, but most of them strangers; a few, from Bow and Whitechapel and Stepney, already on board or boarding with Joan and me; others picked up on our way, as we meandered through unfamiliar streets towards the north-eastern outskirts of London. Our parents kissed us as we left, and promised that they would see us soon.

I know they meant it. But on the third night after we left, the Luftwaffe scored a direct hit on our house, with my parents inside it.

The drive from East London to the country seemed to take forever. But, to a child who had never been out of the city, it was fascinating to see the change of scenery as the bus left London behind and emerged into a dawning world of green fields and trees: a world in which you could travel for miles without seeing more than one or two houses; and in which I saw, for the first time in my life, sheep and cows, and horses roaming free instead of pulling carts through the streets of Whitechapel for some wizened old rag-and-bone man. I gazed out of the window with my nose pressed hard against the glass for miles on end, and Joan had to remind me to eat the sandwich and biscuits we'd been given as a packed meal, before some greedy child could snatch it away from me.

Eventually we arrived at a huge mansion, which seemed to spring at us from nowhere as we were driving along a narrow country lane bordered by tall trees and hedges. It hasn't changed at all over the years. Today Lancelot Andrewes House looks exactly the same as it did when I first set eyes on it: an imposing six-storey construction of red brick, with austere bay windows formed of thin black panes and old wavy glass, set back from the road a hundred yards or so, with extensive grounds at the rear. It is a place I have come to know intimately, and which has played a huge role in my life, for good and for ill: and even now that I'm forty years of age and have seen it so often as an adult, I still remember how it looked for the first time through the eyes of a child; I still remember the sense of being overawed by its size and its unexpected presence, its ability somehow to spring at you suddenly from its hiding place behind the trees and hedgerows, the sense of its being unconnected to the world, certainly the world of my seven-year-old experience.

Lancelot Andrewes House is a Church of England boarding school situated in the Cambridgeshire countryside, about five miles from Ely. It is actually two separate schools, one for boys and one for girls; but the two are accommodated in the same building, with strict separation, girls on the left, boys on the right, as you see the building from the road. As a contribution to the war effort, the school had offered to take a limited number of children evacuated from the East End, and had agreed to waive its usual fees. The offer was a generous one, although it was meant to last only until it became safe for us to return to London; and most of the children who had arrived on the bus with me left to go home to Bow and Whitechapel and Stepney and Bethnal Green once our Spitfires had all but banished the Luftwaffe's bombers from our skies. But Joan and I were orphaned within three days of arriving, and out of sympathy, were immediately told that we could stay and complete our education at Lancelot Andrewes, come what may; and despite everything that happened subsequently, I am still deeply touched by that act of extraordinary kindness.

That same sympathy probably saved Joan and me from the worst of the nastiness many of the East End evacuees experienced at the hands of snobbish school mates, girls who came from richer homes and whose parents could afford the fees. Joan and I seemed to get off relatively lightly. But the richer girls found it fun to laugh at our lack of sophistication, at our Cockney accents and poor diction, at our ignorance of life outside the East End, and at our more shabby clothes: until Matron – a lovely, plump, forty-something, caring but no-nonsense woman called Molly – supplied us with second-hand school uniforms, red blazers and grey skirts, grey stockings and black shoes that looked exactly the same as everyone else's. That wasn't Matron's only kindness, by any means. Somehow – looking back on it, I'm pretty sure she must have had a whip-round among the staff – she found us some weekly pocket money: not as much as the richer girls had, of course, but enough to allow us to patronise the school tuck shop; and to hold our own when we were allowed to go for tea and cakes in the High Street after our monthly school service in Ely cathedral. As we all got used to each other, and as most of the London children returned home, the worst of the childish prejudices faded away. Joan and I made friends, some of whom I'm still in contact with today, and we were sometimes even invited to their homes for school holidays.

I'm grateful, too, despite everything, for the education I received at Lancelot Andrewes. I settled without too much restlessness into the daily routine of prayers, classes and games, and the discipline did me good. I think it did Joan good, too. It structured our grieving for our parents, and it gave form to our new life without them, without the only home we had ever known; it enabled us to avoid the temptation of clinging exclusively to each other, of erecting barriers against the rest of the world to defend ourselves from the pain. The staff were dedicated teachers, who, unusually for the time, expected the same high academic standards of the girls as they did of the boys, with the result that the school was continually breaking national records for the number of girls gaining university places.

Joan left Lancelot Andrewes at the age of eighteen to study History at Edinburgh, and I followed in her footsteps five years later, to read English. After graduation, as a twenty-one-year-old woman with no other plans for her life, I decided to stay with Joan in Edinburgh. By then, she already held a responsible administrative position with the Royal Bank of Scotland, where she was highly thought of; so much so that at her request, her manager offered me a job too, on a similar career path. We shared an upstairs flat in a lovely old Georgian town house in the New Town district.

We lived and worked together, happily as far as I could tell, for almost four years: until one Saturday afternoon, when I got back from the shops and the library, I found her lifeless body hanging from the staircase on the attic floor above our flat. I'd had no idea, not the slightest indication, that she'd had any thoughts about taking her own life. She was always quiet, and could be rather reserved, even with me. But she was doing well at work and there was a young man she seemed to like who was paying attention to her. I hadn't detected any change in her mood. But there she was, hanging there. Dead.

She'd left me a note. It said: 'I'm sorry, Audrey. I wanted to stop it, but I couldn't.' At the time, I didn't understand what she meant. If I had, I might perhaps have saved her: and, in a sense, and to some extent, myself.

4

'I suppose the first question I have,' Ginny said, after Julia had introduced Audrey and Ken Marshall, and they were comfortably settled around the table with cups of tea, 'is why you haven't been to the police? What you're saying is that this Father Gerrard has been enabling a network of paedophiles to molest young girls at Lancelot Andrewes School for two generations, and that you and Emily are both victims. Why haven't you been to the police? For that matter, why hasn't *anyone* been to the police before now?'

Audrey nodded. 'We've been trying to decide what to do ever since Emily told us what happened to her, and my memory came back. I know it's the right thing to do, to tell the police. But... well, we're not sure we'd be taken seriously if we reported it in Ely.'

'The school has a lot of influence locally, Miss Castle,' Ken added. 'You'd be surprised. And with Audrey having worked for the diocese of Ely for so long, we just don't feel confident about going to the police at home.'

'Is the school under the control of the diocese?' Ben asked.

'Not now,' Audrey replied. 'It was originally, but the Church suddenly cut all ties to the school in the early 1950s. No one seems to know exactly why, but it was quite abrupt. Since then, Lancelot Andrewes has been an independent school with its own charitable status. It still describes itself as a Church of England school, and the headmaster's a priest, but there's no formal connection with the Church. Obviously, with the school being so close, there are still contacts with the diocese; they still hold regular services in the cathedral, and so on.'

'Why should that affect the police?' Ben asked.

'Because of Father Gerrard,' Ken replied.

'Desmond Gerrard has a national reputation, Mr Schroeder,' Audrey added. 'Lancelot Andrewes is one of the most respected schools in the country. He's been headmaster since before my time – and I started there in 1940. The Queen gave him the CBE for services to education. The Church gave him a special title, the Most Reverend Father Desmond Gerrard. Desmond Gerrard is a legend in Ely. He's untouchable.'

'Nobody's untouchable,' Ginny said.

'No, I know,' Audrey said. 'But… I'm the deputy administrator for the diocese. I've been in my job for the best part of fifteen years, so I've had ample time to see how these things work…'

'Go on,' Ginny said encouragingly.

'The diocese is represented by the same solicitor as Lancelot Andrewes, a man called John Singer. Singer is ruthless when it comes to protecting the Church. I report to the administrator, and he reports to John Singer. Believe me, I know.'

'That's why we asked Julia for advice,' Ken added. 'We needed an outsider, someone with some contacts, someone who won't be intimidated by the Ely mafia.'

Ginny laughed. 'Julia's taken on more sinister characters than the Ely mafia in her time, Audrey. She won't be intimidated, I can promise you that.'

'Amen to that,' Julia smiled.

'I know John Singer,' Ben said, 'or, at least, I worked with him for some time on a case, not long after I'd started out in practice.'

'What? In Ely?' Ken asked.

'No. St Ives. The defendant was a vicar there. He had a very unusual name, Ignatius something. This would be ten years ago, 1964.'

'Ignatius Little,' Audrey said immediately.

'That's the man.'

Audrey scoffed. 'I remember Ignatius Little. Don't I just? He was bad news from the day we ordained him: couldn't keep his hands off his choir boys. But he wasn't one of the obvious ones – he looked the part, you know. He was a real blighter to pin down. Finally, he was arrested and charged.' She smiled ruefully. 'But then you went and got him off, didn't you?'

Ben nodded. 'Sorry. I'm afraid I did. We went for trial at Quarter Sessions in Huntingdon, and we got the right jury. And he had a really nice fiancée, who made a good witness. But some time later…'

'Some time later, we shipped him off to the diocese of Chester,' Audrey interrupted, 'where he distinguished himself by getting himself arrested for importuning in a public place; following which he hanged himself in a police cell. But that was typical Singer: anything to protect the diocese. We should never have sent Ignatius to Chester – not without telling them what we knew about him. I argued against it, but I was overruled. By the time it all finally came out, it was Chester's problem, not ours. Singer was happy with that, needless to say. I wasn't happy, and neither was my boss. But we had no say in it.'

'It sounds to me,' Julia suggested, 'that you may have been right not to go the police in Ely – not as a first step, anyway.'

'But she must go to the police, Julia,' Ginny insisted. 'There's been a long history of child sexual abuse at Lancelot Andrewes, and it has to be investigated.'

'There's something else, too,' Audrey said after a silence.

'Go on,' Ginny said. 'Don't be afraid. We're on your side.'

'She's worried no one will believe her,' Ken said quietly.

'Why?'

'I sent Emily to Lancelot Andrewes after I'd been molested there myself, didn't I? The school still gives employees of the diocese a special rate on the fees. When she reached the age to start school, I'd been working for the diocese long enough to qualify, and it was a huge, huge reduction. To be honest, we couldn't have afforded it otherwise. At the time, it was too good to turn down. But now I'm afraid they will use it against me.'

'You had no memory of being molested then,' Ginny pointed out. 'You had no way of knowing.'

'No, but...'

'And they can't hold that against Emily. There's no question of recovered memory in her case. Her memory is as fresh as a daisy.'

'Yes, Ginny,' Ben agreed. 'But she's a child, claiming to be the victim of sexual assault. Any evidence she gives would need corroboration from an independent source.'

'So they could say that Audrey's trying to provide Emily with corroboration,' Julia asked, 'by pretending to have memories of being molested herself?'

'Exactly,' Ben replied.

'That's what scares me,' Audrey said quietly.

'Other witnesses will come forward,' Ginny insisted. 'They're bound to, once word of this gets out. Emily will have all the corroboration she needs. So will you, Audrey.'

'Perhaps,' Ben said, 'but it's a problem we can't just ignore. There's no reason why you shouldn't be believed, Audrey, and it's no reason not to go forward. But the first step is to find a way to report to the police, in such a way that John Singer can't obstruct us.'

'The question is: how to do it?' Julia mused.

'I dealt with a capital murder committed in St Ives,' Ben said, 'at about the same time as Ignatius Little's case. There were two senior officers from Cambridge dealing with it, a Detective Superintendent Arnold and a Detective Inspector Phillips.'

'I know Ted Phillips from Rotary Club,' Ken said. 'Arnold has retired, and there's a Detective Superintendent Walker who's taken over now. Ted's still there, though. I've always thought of him as somebody you could trust.'

Ben nodded. 'He struck me as a good man. We have to start with the Cambridgeshire police. There's no way around that. It's their jurisdiction.'

'Let's contact Phillips, then,' Ginny said. 'Singer may have the ear of the police at Ely or St Ives, but I find it hard to believe that he's going to have much clout in Cambridge – certainly not in a case like this.'

'One would hope not,' Ben replied. 'But just in case, let's get Scotland Yard involved too, just to make sure that we can snuff out any local interference before it even starts.'

'How will you do that?' Julia asked.

'I'll talk to Andrew Pilkington,' Ben replied. 'Andrew is senior Treasury counsel, one of the prosecutors at the Old Bailey. Andrew can talk to the Director of Public Prosecutions, and the Director can make sure that the Yard gets involved.'

He took a deep breath.

'There's a way to do this, Audrey. It's not going to be easy, and none of us is going to pretend otherwise. But if you want justice for yourself and Emily, it's something you're going to have to face up to. What you and Ken have to decide is whether you can live with what you know if you don't come forward. Remember, this is for Emily too, not just yourself.'

'And for many, many others,' Ginny added, 'including those Father Gerrard is allowing to be abused even now, as we speak.'

Audrey and Ken looked at each other for some time.

'We've come too far to go back now,' Ken said.

'Yes, I know,' Audrey replied. 'I just want to make sure Emily is all right.'

5

'So: what about names?' Ben asked.

Julia opened her briefcase and took out a number of documents. She laid them out in front of her on the table.

'Do you want to start with the girls, or the men?'

'Let's start with the girls.'

'Girls, it is. Obviously, Emily's case is easier, because it's so recent and she remembers everything. Emily told Audrey that it had happened to four or five girls she knew, but we haven't spoken to anyone as yet. We didn't want to throw the cat in among the pigeons until we had our strategy in place. Once we approach her school friends or their parents, there's likely to be pandemonium, and we need to be prepared.'

'We shouldn't approach them,' Ben said. 'We should leave that to the police.'

Julia nodded. 'All right. Here's Emily's list of names.' She handed a sheet of paper to Ginny. 'And this,' handing her another sheet, 'is Audrey's list, going back to her time at school. And, of course, this is where we enter the world of recovered memory.'

'Father Gerrard was always very careful,' Audrey said. 'He would leave it until about eight thirty to nine o'clock, when there would only be one member of staff on night duty. What I remember is: he never came for more than one girl at any given time, so I was taken on my own, or another girl was taken on her own, and we only ever knew for sure if she spoke about it later. Often, we didn't talk about it. Most of the time, we just went straight back to bed and cried our eyes out. That's a general impression. I can't remember specifically everyone I talked to. I know I would have told Joan and my best friend, Mary Forbes.'

'Where were you taken to?' Ben asked. 'And where from?'

'Father Gerrard would come to our dorm. It started not long after I got to the school, so I was seven. All the sleeping accommodation was upstairs, on the fifth and sixth floors. At that age, we slept in dorms of twelve girls. When you got older, fourteen or fifteen, you shared a bedroom and study with one other girl, but until then it was always dorms of twelve. Father Gerrard would take you downstairs to a room next to his study, and that's where the men would be waiting for you.'

'What kind of room was it?' Ginny asked.

'As I understand it now, from having seen plans of the school we keep at work, it's his private library. It's a room you would never normally see as a pupil. You might go into his study, but there'd be no reason to go into his library. It was like something from a gentleman's club in Pall Mall, you know, with book cases all around the walls, filled with old books and busts of God knows what Greek philosophers and what-have-you, and a long cherry-wood table in the middle of the room and heavy red leather armchairs. I remember, there was always a smell of tobacco, cigars or a pipe.'

'So, you do remember some of the other girls who were taken?' Ginny asked.

'I gave Julia that list you have, with five names.'

'These are girls who told you they'd been taken?'

'That's what I remember now. The girls I knew from the East End went back to London once the Blitz died down. There were two girls from that group I know it happened to, but they got out pretty quickly. I've included their names, but even if they remember, I'm not sure they would want to talk about it.'

Ben scanned the list. 'So, Betty Friedman and Sylvia Marks were the two from the East End?'

'Yes. They're both in London still. Betty's married to a furniture

importer and she's still living in the East End. Sylvia married a
stockbroker and they live in Islington, or they did when I last
heard from her.'

'And the other three?'

'Jenny Hamilton, I added to the list because I have a memory
of her. But she died a year or two ago, from cancer of some kind.
Mary Forbes was a good friend to me. Her parents were well off,
from the Guildford area, but they weren't snobbish at all. Joan and
I spent several school holidays with them. Mary became a solicitor,
and married an international lawyer, a Canadian. They live in
Toronto. Then lastly, there's Alice Hargreaves. I'm not sure where
she is now. I heard she'd gone travelling after she left university.
There was talk three or four years ago that she'd come back and
settled in some remote corner of Ireland. But...'

'We will find her if we need her,' Julia said in a matter-of-fact
tone. 'Those are the only girls you have specific memories of?'

'Yes. Of course, the school would have a complete record of all
the girls who were there in my time, and they will have contact
information for most of them. The school relies heavily on old
girls and boys, and their families, to fund its endowments and
scholarships, so they're pretty keen on keeping in touch with us.
They pester us to update our contact details all the time.'

'That would be one strategy,' Ginny said. 'To approach all of
them and ask them point blank whether they were ever taken to
the private library. I bet we'd get a good response.'

'Again,' Ben replied, 'I think we have to let the police do all that.
This has to be an official investigation, with the police in charge,
not us. I don't want it to look as though we're trawling for victims.
With any luck these women will find us, or the police, without our
having to approach them.' He replaced the list on the table. 'What
about the men?'

Julia delved into her briefcase again. 'You're going to love this.'

She took out a number of newspaper clippings, and handed them
to Ben, who perused them in silence, with Ginny looking on over

his shoulder. It was some time before anyone spoke.

'You took these clippings after your memory returned?' Ginny asked.

'Yes. As soon as I saw their pictures in *The Times*, I recognised them as men I'd seen in his library – men Father Gerrard invited there to molest me.'

'Thirty or more years ago,' Ben observed quietly.

'I remember them as they were, Mr Schroeder,' Audrey insisted. 'They haven't changed that much. I'd know them again anywhere.'

'She reacted instantly, Mr Schroeder,' Ken confirmed, 'as soon as she turned to the page and saw them. She must have seen these men hundreds of times – they're in the papers and on TV all the time, aren't they? You see them every day. But she'd never reacted to them like that before her memory returned: never. But she did once the memories came back, believe you me. She screamed and jumped right out of her chair. She looked like she'd seen a ghost.'

Ben nodded. 'That's exactly what will worry a judge or jury,' he replied.

'These men are public figures, Ben,' Julia pointed out. 'Why pick on these three? If Audrey intended to pick names out of a hat, or out of *The Times*, what guarantee would she have that they don't have cast-iron alibis?'

'I'm not suggesting that you're making anything up, Audrey,' Ben said. 'Please understand that. I'm playing devil's advocate.'

'I know,' Audrey replied.

'And as devil's advocate, I would point out that it's difficult to produce an alibi if all you're told is that you're accused of having done something some time in 1940, by someone who saw your face in a newspaper more than thirty years later – an image she'd seen many times in the intervening years, and said nothing.'

'That's not fair…' Ken began.

'Yes, it is,' Audrey replied, cutting him off. 'That's what they're going to say, and we may as well face up to it now.'

There was a long silence.

'So now you know what I was referring to when I said we would be ruffling some influential feathers,' Julia said, at length.

'One member of the House of Lords; one former cabinet minister, still an MP; and one…?' Ben concluded inquiringly.

'Retired bishop, currently serving as Master of an Oxford college,' Julia replied.

'I don't suppose any of them were still getting up to their tricks with Emily?' Ginny asked. 'We couldn't be that lucky, could we?'

'Emily says the men wear masks now,' Julia replied. 'Apparently, they've got more self-conscious over the years.'

'It wouldn't help anyway, would it, if they were the same men?' Audrey said. 'That would just give me more motive for identifying them, wouldn't it?'

Ben smiled grimly. 'You're developing a good instinct for how this works.'

'I'm developing a bad case of paranoia – and a bad case of cynicism,' she replied.

6

Audrey Marshall

Finding my sister hanging there from the staircase of the house in which I thought we were happy was a moment of utter devastation. I never saw the scene of my parents' death, the bombed-out ruins of the other house in which I'd been happy. I found out about their death in a detached setting, when Father Gerrard called Joan and me into his study, with Matron in attendance weeping into her handkerchief, and told us that we were now orphans, in much the same tone he used to read out the daily notices in morning assembly. It was a moment of fear and bewilderment and wondering what would become of us in the world. But at least I didn't have to see the results of the Luftwaffe's work up close, and I still had Joan.

Now I had to see the results of her desperation for myself, and I no longer had anyone. She had asphyxiated, the procurator fiscal explained, in the course of reporting that Joan had committed suicide while the balance of her mind was disturbed. No further enquiry into her death was necessary, he concluded. It would have taken her some time to die, because she'd positioned the knot to the right of her jaw, causing it to move down to her throat and effectively strangle her; instead of to the left, from where the knot would have turned up behind the back of her neck, causing an immediately fatal fracture of the second and third vertebrae and severance of the spinal cord – a technical nicety, the procurator fiscal added thoughtfully, well known to public executioners. As it was, the effects of her death struggle were obvious. I have often wondered whether, once she knew she had passed the point of no return, she regretted what she was doing; and would have given everything she had for a second chance; and whether she would have liked to talk to me once more, to tell me why she thought she had to leave me, to give me the chance of talking her out of it. 'I'm sorry, Audrey. I wanted to stop it, but I couldn't.' Stop what? Was the balance of her mind disturbed, or had she finally found the balance of her mind again? She couldn't tell me now.

I remember that, on discovering her body and the note she had left, I sat down on the top stair, staring helplessly at her and at the note in turn, finding it all completely inexplicable. It was almost an hour before I stood up again, strangely calm by then, in the way that only people devoid of all consciousness of hope are calm, and made my way downstairs, almost as an afterthought, to tell anyone who might for any reason be interested in the information that my sister was hanging from the staircase on the attic floor upstairs.

I remember very little about the ensuing weeks. I think they kept me sedated for at least three or four days, the first two in hospital, the second two back at home with a nurse at my bedside day and night. After that, with the procurator fiscal's investigation pending, they allowed me, still under supervision and medicated, to go through her things and decide what I wanted to keep and what could be donated to some charitable cause. Eventually the supervision stopped and I was left with a supply of a tranquilising drug, my discretion whether to take it or not. After the procurator fiscal had presented his report, I returned in my mind – a police officer had seized it as evidence and had to retain it for some period of time – to her note. 'I'm sorry, Audrey. I wanted to stop it, but I couldn't.' Stop what, Joan, for God's sake, stop what? Was there some scandal at work I didn't know about? Had you got yourself involved with drugs? Surely I would have noticed? Your boyfriend didn't impregnate you or pass on some terrible disease – the procurator fiscal would have explained that as helpfully as he had explained the mechanics of an efficient hanging. What in

God's name brought you to this? What in God's name was too terrible for you to confide in me: in your sister who had shared the experience of being orphaned and exiled from the home we had loved; in your sister who, after we had survived those irreversible losses, had chosen to make a home and a new life with you in Edinburgh? In God's name, Joan, what is it you couldn't tell me?

Two weeks after the inquiry was complete, I returned to work. The staff at the bank were incredibly kind to me. They never once hurried me, or even hinted that my job depended on my coming back by a given date. They were genuinely sad to lose Joan, and within a month of my return I was asked to move up to her job as a senior administrator. Out of gratitude and loyalty I would have liked to accept: but everything about the place, everything about Edinburgh, reminded me of Joan; there was no respite, and I knew I couldn't move on while I stayed there.

Matron, from school, to whom I had reported Joan's death and who must have been reading my mind, sent me by post, special delivery, an advertisement taken from the *Cambridge News*. The diocese of Ely urgently needed to fill a vacancy for a deputy to work alongside the diocesan administrator: experience of administrative responsibility highly desirable, but willingness to learn and the ability to work efficiently without supervision more important; prior knowledge of church affairs not essential; salary commensurate with experience. I applied at once, enclosing an embarrassingly effusive reference from my manager at RBS. The diocese paid for my travel south for an interview with the administrator, Bill Hollis, who became my boss, and the diocesan solicitor, John Singer. They offered me the job without even asking me to leave the room, and I accepted similarly.

Two weeks after that, I said a tearful goodbye to Edinburgh and to my friends at the bank, and to my friends from university who were still in the city; and for the second time in my life, made a life-changing journey to Cambridgeshire. It was 1958. I was approaching the age of twenty-five.

7

I met Ken at a reception given by the bishop after a service in the cathedral. Like me, he was a university graduate who had fallen in love with the setting and atmosphere of his university, and so had never wanted to leave the Cambridge area. After graduating with a law degree he qualified as a solicitor, and set up on his own in practice in Ely. He was doing well by the time I met him in 1960, and was a generous benefactor of the diocese; and after our first meeting, we ran into each other on a regular basis.

There had been an immediate attraction between us, but it was some time before I agreed to go out with him on our own for an evening. It was an area of my life that wasn't working, and I was scared. There had been no opportunity for dating while I was still at Lancelot Andrewes. There were known instances of boys and girls defying the rigidly enforced apartheid between the boys' school and girls' school: romances happened, and one or two girls even managed to get pregnant during the years I was there. But to say that fraternisation was frowned on would be an understatement: as often as not it resulted in, at least an extended suspension, and in some cases expulsion from school; and I had nowhere else to go. In any case, I never had sufficient interest in any of the boys to consider battling against such overwhelming odds to pursue him.

That changed when I became a student at Edinburgh. I wasn't exactly making up for lost time, but like my contemporaries I began to go out with boys I met in class or at social gatherings, and everything seemed to be going normally: until Alistair. Alistair was a year ahead of me, reading medicine. He was handsome and sporty, and I really fancied him. One evening when we knew each other pretty well, I went back to his place with him after a few drinks. We started kissing, and one thing led to another, and suddenly there I was: naked on a bed with a naked man. Oddly enough, perhaps because of the drink, I didn't feel unduly nervous. We lay down together and kissed using tongues, and I took his cock in my hand as if I'd been doing it all my life, and stroked him until he started to get hard. Then – and it was really the most natural thing in the world – he put his hand on my knee and very gradually moved it up my leg and thigh until he was ruffling my pubic hairs. At which point my legs, in fact my entire body below my waist, seemed to freeze. I started to say something, but before I could, two of his fingers ventured very gently just inside me. I felt a moment of intense excitement, but then, without any conscious decision on my part, I remember my cunt snapping shut as if someone had slammed the door of a vault, and I remember pulling his hand away quite roughly, and saying no.

I don't know which of us was more surprised. I was flabbergasted. I very much wanted him to do what he was about to do, and I had no way of explaining my body's reaction to his touch. He began to ask me something, but I had no answer to offer. In desperation, or out of sheer embarrassment, I quickly laid him on his back, moved down, and took his cock in my mouth, which served to distract him. I think he had a good time, but something had happened that neither of us understood, and as a result of whatever it was, I wasn't ready to take our relationship any further. We broke up a week or two later.

It was months before I gathered enough courage to go out with another man. His name was Brian, and he was a geographer, and the first time we undressed each other, the same thing happened. By then, I'd thought a great deal about what I was going to do if I couldn't persuade my body to unfreeze. The strategy of sucking the man's cock had worked once, but there was no guarantee that it would work again. After some reflection I persuaded myself that my reaction was caused by feeling ticklish when I was touched, and that was something I could explain rationally. Not only that, I'd practised what I thought was a pretty convincing giggle to illustrate the ticklishness. The problem was, I knew better.

I wasn't in the least ticklish when I masturbated, or when one evening I ended up in bed with my friend Susan after a party, and found that I welcomed her fingers enthusiastically without any hint of freezing at all. For a short time I even thought I'd found the real explanation: I was a closet lesbian; and at one point I seriously considered adopting that way of life as a compromise solution. But reality prevailed. My real interest has always been in men, and I went back to dating them. But it had become a nervous experience, one that made me feel insecure, and I didn't do it very often. There were one or two men less sensitive than Alistair and Brian, who didn't much care about my pleasure and were more than happy with a quick, uninvolved fuck: and to my distress, and occasionally despair, I found that I actually preferred those shallow encounters – I could get through them without any problem. For the others, I had the giggle and the enhanced attention to fall back on: but nothing brought me any satisfaction or pleasure.

The first time I was naked with Ken, at my place after a nice dinner, I was so anxious that I felt ready to burst into tears at any moment. I'd found someone I really cared about, and I was so afraid that I would mess it up between us because of something I couldn't control. And sure enough, right on cue, as his hand made its way up my leg, my body froze. He looked at me, and I tried in vain to activate the giggle. But I just wasn't in a giggly mood. Instead, I collapsed on to my back and rolled away with my back to him, crying my eyes out. I was sure he would get dressed and leave. I wouldn't have blamed him. But instead, he did something really remarkable. Very gently, he turned me again on to my back. He went down far enough to kiss my feet, which he did for some time, unhurriedly, as though time were unimportant; and as his tongue did its last turn around my left ankle, he allowed it to drift slowly up my leg, followed by a hand. Predictably, I started to freeze again. He stopped immediately, but left the hand in place.

'Look at me,' he said. I couldn't, immediately.

'Look at me,' he said again. I did, wiping away a tear.

'It's me,' he said. 'Ken. You're safe. It's OK. You're safe.'

He kissed my leg, and repeated his words several times, like a mantra: 'It's me. Ken. It's OK. You're safe. You're safe.'

Then he told me to take a deep breath, one at first, then several deep breaths in succession. I did, and to my amazement, I felt my body start to relax. His tongue and fingers moved up my leg very slightly. I froze again. He repeated the mantra and told me again to breathe. How long this went on, I have no idea: it felt like hours. All I know is that eventually, I was able to relax long enough for his fingers to be inside me, and once he made contact and I felt myself being turned on, I gave a deep sigh, raised my arms above my head and held on to the headboard, and finally allowed a man to do what I had allowed myself and Susan to do – to give me pleasure and a wonderful orgasm. As I was unwinding from the orgasm, I felt him ease his cock into my cunt, and we had the most wonderful gentle, loving, intimate fuck.

It wasn't a magic cure. But it was a breakthrough. The freezing continued to happen, but it became less frequent, and while there were occasions when we had to give up – about which he was always very understanding – there were also many occasions when the mantra worked and we had wonderful sex. I knew, of course, that I hadn't found any explanation for the freezing, but somehow that mattered less now. Ken and I had fallen deeply in love, and it wasn't long before he asked me to marry him. I accepted without hesitation. This was in 1963.

8

'I think the best way to start,' Andrew Pilkington began, 'would be to go around the table and let everyone introduce themselves. Let's start with the right-hand side, shall we?'

Andrew was senior prosecuting counsel to the Crown at the Old Bailey, and he had not hesitated when Ben Schroeder asked him to become involved in the emerging story of Lancelot Andrewes School. Quite apart from the fact that he and Ben were friends – a by-product, often found at the bar, of having fought each other vigorously as opponents in a number of difficult cases – Andrew saw immediately what would be at stake when the revelations about the school's history became public. Without delay, he dropped what he was doing, called in the people he needed, and booked a conference room at the Old Bailey.

'My name is John Caswell,' the man sitting to Andrew's immediate right said. 'I'm deputy director in the office of the Director of Public Prosecutions.'

'DI Steffie Walsh, currently attached to the Met Police Vice Unit, based at West End Central Police Station,' the woman to Caswell's right said.

'DI Ted Phillips, from Cambridge.'

'Thank you,' Andrew said. 'Left-hand side?'

'Julia Cathermole, Cathermole and Bridger. We act for Mr and Mrs Marshall.' Julia smiled to her right and nodded to give her clients their cue.

'I'm Audrey Marshall, from Ely.'

'Ken Marshall: I'm Audrey's husband.'

'Ginny Castle: I'm instructed by Julia on behalf of the Marshalls.'

'Ben Schroeder, also instructed by Julia.'

Andrew nodded. 'All right, thank you. Let me see if I can summarise where we are at the moment. Audrey, you've made a detailed witness statement today to DI Phillips and DI Walsh, in which you allege a pattern of sexual abuse against young girls at Lancelot Andrewes School over a long period of time, apparently instigated and managed by the school's headmaster, Father Desmond Gerrard. Is that right?'

'Yes, sir.'

Andrew smiled. 'You don't have to call me "sir". I'm just a barrister, like Ginny and Ben. Let's use first names, shall we?'

'All right… Andrew… Yes, that's true.'

'Your time at the school goes back to the early 1940s, but you also say that your daughter Emily has been a victim of abuse, more recently?'

'Yes.'

'I interviewed Emily this morning, sir,' Steffie Walsh added, 'in the presence of her father, Ken. I found her to be an intelligent, articulate girl, clear and focused, and very specific about what happened to her, remarkably so for her age. I think she's easily mature enough to give evidence under oath, so I took a witness statement from her.'

'Good,' Andrew replied. 'That alone should give you and DI Phillips enough to arrest Father Gerrard on suspicion of conspiracy, or inciting acts of indecent assault and indecency with a child. But Emily couldn't identify the men who committed the offences, could she?'

'No, sir. She says they all wore black masks that covered their faces, apart from the eyes. They all wore suits and ties, but that's about it. We don't have any way to identify them unless Father Gerrard gives them up, or there's another witness we don't know about yet. But she identifies Father Gerrard: no problem there.'

'Audrey, you make allegations against three men who all have a high profile in public life. These allegations are mainly of acts committed against you, but some involve other girls, based on what they told you at the time, in the 1940s. Yes?'

'Yes.'

'All these allegations – correct me if I'm wrong – are based entirely on memories you recovered spontaneously after Emily had told you what happened to her?'

'Yes, that's correct.'

'And that's what will make the Director nervous,' John Caswell said.

'Her allegations are very specific, John,' Ginny intervened, 'and she has no motive whatsoever to implicate any of these three men.'

'I accept that,' John replied, 'but – forgive me, Audrey, I'm not saying I doubt your word – but unless Father Gerrard implicates them, any case against them would depend entirely on your recovered memory, which is controversial as far as the experts are concerned.'

'It's not controversial as far as we're concerned,' Ken reacted angrily.

'No, of course not; nor should it be. But please try to understand our concerns, Ken. Once Father Gerrard is arrested and all this becomes public knowledge, the press is going to have a field day. I'm not concerned about Father Gerrard. We're on solid ground with him. But the other men are also going to be pilloried in the media. They can protest their innocence all they like, but they won't be able to prevent some mud sticking to them: which means that the Director must be very careful to ensure that the evidence is sufficient for an arrest, and sufficient to justify a prosecution.'

'Some of her allegations involve other girls,' Ginny pointed out.

'Based on what those girls told her, which is hearsay.'

'Not if the girls – women, as they are now – confirm what Audrey says,' Ben replied. 'And actually, even if they don't, I think it's admissible in evidence: provided that Audrey can confirm that the woman concerned was making a complaint about what happened to her, shortly after the event, and while she was distressed about it.'

'I agree with that,' Andrew added.

'Another positive,' Ginny said, 'is that Emily provides corroboration for Audrey, and *vice versa*.'

'Only against Father Gerrard,' John pointed out. 'Not against the other men.'

'Fine. But once the press gets hold of the story and Lancelot Andrewes becomes a household name, other women are bound to come forward. We just need to interview the women Audrey's named; if only one of them confirms what she says, we have more than enough.'

'I'd be happier if Father Gerrard gave them up,' Ted Phillips said.

'Do you know Gerrard at all?' Andrew asked. 'Audrey and Ken do, of course, but have the Cambridge police had any dealings with him?'

'Not as far as I know, sir,' Ted replied. 'I've never met him. He may have some history with officers at Ely and round that way, but not on our patch. I'm not worried about him, though. Once we confront him, I'm betting that we, or his solicitor, will persuade him that cooperation is his only hope of avoiding a long sentence.'

'Well, any court that sentenced him would be impressed if he saved the victims from having to relive the horror in the witness box,' Ben pointed out.

'That was my thought exactly, sir,' Ted replied. 'Let's invite him to turn Queen's evidence. My money says he'll give up the men he entertained at the school.'

Andrew turned to Audrey and Ken. 'What's your take on him?'

'That's not the Father Gerrard I know,' Audrey said. 'He's always struck me as a hard man, and I never detected any compassion in him for the likes of us.' She shrugged. 'But I'm not exactly a neutral as far as he's concerned, so perhaps I'm not the right person to ask.'

'I can't add anything to that,' Ken said.

'Well, we will just have to see,' Andrew concluded.

'Andrew,' John said after a silence, 'the Director's bound to be a bit nervous about this. I think I can talk him into following your advice: but he can't stop Cambridge from prosecuting, can he? At the end of the day, the Chief Constable is free to arrest anyone he thinks he has a case against, and to prosecute them accordingly. That's a matter for the Chief Constable. The Director may ask me why he should stick his neck out.'

'Because the Director's involvement would make all the difference,' Andrew replied immediately. 'Once this starts, we're looking at massive, unrelenting publicity, deep local feeling, and, very likely, unwelcome local pressure on the police. It would be a hard case for Cambridge to handle without the Director's support.'

'And, with all due respect, sir,' Ted added, 'even without the pressure, this will be a very big case. It would really stretch our resources to try to manage it without the Yard's help. I'm not sure how we'd do it, to be honest, not if we have to approach all the girls who were at school all those years ago, and goodness knows what other witnesses may come out of the woodwork once word gets out.'

'John, my advice to the Director would be this,' Andrew said. 'He should take over the case against Father Gerrard as soon as DI Phillips has arrested him. I'd be happy to take responsibility for the case, as long as I can bring Ben and Ginny in as counsel to work with me. I'd need help anyway: with my present trial schedule, it's not something I can handle on my own.'

'And if I may, Andrew,' Ben added, 'we should ask the magistrates to commit the case for trial here at the Bailey, rather than Cambridge: there's too much risk of local feeling poisoning the jury pool at Cambridge.'

'Agreed,' Andrew said. 'Then, depending on developments in the case against Father Gerrard, we'll consider whether there is enough evidence to arrest the three men in public life. Until we reach that stage, we won't refer to them publicly by name. We will call them Lord AB, Sir CD, and the Right Reverend EF. Inspector

Walsh, we'll need to prepare a redacted version of Audrey's witness statement, so that we protect their identities.'

'Right you are, sir.'

'Why should they have special protection?' Ken demanded. 'They've brought all of this on us. Why should they get special treatment?'

'Because the Director has a duty to protect people in public life to a certain extent,' John replied. 'I'm sorry, Ken; I have to insist on that. But it's a limited protection. It ends once they're arrested. We're only talking about the period before their arrest.'

'But their names are withheld while ours are dragged through the mud. That's what it comes to, isn't it?'

'Ken, we can't protect you and Audrey from all publicity: but we can – and will – protect Emily's identity, and those of her friends. Children who are the victims of criminal offences are entitled to anonymity.'

'I wouldn't put money on anyone remaining anonymous for long,' Julia said quietly, 'not once the press wakes up and realises the extent of the scandal. It won't be long before everyone knows exactly who did what to whom.'

'If they go too far, it will be at their peril,' John insisted. 'The Director takes his responsibilities very seriously, and the court will support him when it comes to publicity.'

'Does that mean that you will be advising the Director to take over?' Ginny asked, smiling.

John nodded. 'I will advise him to take over – in accordance with Andrew's advice.'

Ted smiled happily at Steffie.

'In that case, I'll make my way back to Cambridge and make arrangements to introduce myself to Father Desmond Gerrard. Would you care to accompany me on behalf of the Met, Detective Inspector Walsh?'

She returned the smile. 'I'd be delighted, Detective Inspector Phillips.'

9

Audrey Marshall

Emily was born in June 1965. She's an only child, though not for want of trying. We did our best to provide her with a little sister or brother, but for whatever reason, I didn't, or couldn't, get pregnant again; and I'm not sure there's enough of me left for another child now, even if I could. Emily is a bright girl, curious and articulate, but like Joan, she can sometimes hide away silently within herself for hours, as if she's communing with some higher power. Actually, she reminds me a lot of Joan, both physically and mentally. There are days when the resemblance makes me happy; but there are also days when it makes me cry, and I can't explain the tears to her properly until she's older.

As she was approaching her seventh birthday, I was chatting to Bill Hollis one day about schools, and he suggested that we apply to have Emily admitted to Lancelot Andrewes. It had never occurred to me. I'd somehow made the assumption that we would never be able to afford the fees – even though Ken and I weren't badly off, and we lived close enough to the school for her to attend as a day girl, which would have been significantly cheaper. But Bill pointed out that the school had a special rate for senior employees of the diocese, which reduced the fees to a level we could manage, even with Emily boarding. He'd sent his own two sons to Lancelot Andrewes as boarders. Besides, he added, as an old girl myself, surely I would want Emily to have the same excellent education I'd had myself. Well, of course I did. I told Ken as soon as I got home, and we fairly jumped at the chance. Not long after that we received a warm note from Father Gerrard, in which he said how much he was looking forward to seeing Emily in the new term, once she turned seven.

We left the choice of whether or not to board to Emily. She chose to board, secure in the knowledge that we would never be far away, because boarders have much easier access to sports and other extra-curricular activities. She entered the school in the autumn term of 1972.

I hope that, at some point during the very public discussion of my recovered memory that is about to take place, someone will acknowledge that, if I'd had the remotest recollection at that time of what had happened to me while I was a pupil there, I would never have let Emily come within a hundred miles of Lancelot Andrewes school, much less let her board there. I really do hope that someone will allow me that much.

She'd been at the school for a little over a year when we first noticed some signs of disturbance. We'd got into the habit of taking her home for a day on some weekends, school activities permitting, and sometimes for an evening here and there. The school didn't like the idea particularly, because they didn't want to be seen to be giving some girls extra privileges just because their parents happened to live within easy reach. I understood that. But we couldn't ignore her and pretend she wasn't there when it was so easy to see her. Besides, with my history I understood very well the feelings of any girl whose parents were far away, or worse; and we encouraged Emily to befriend girls in that kind of situation, so that we could invite them to come home with her. At first, she was very excited to be at school, proud to wear the same uniform I'd worn all those years ago, enthusiastic about the games she could play, the friends she was making, full of talk of everything she was learning. And then she suddenly went quiet.

I didn't pay much attention to it at first. As I said before, she's always been the kind of girl who retreats into her own head from time to time, and it's something we'd got used to. It would pass, and she would return to her usual self. But now it didn't pass. Even then, I couldn't bring myself to worry unduly at first. But it didn't pass for three weekends, and on the third Sunday evening Ken and I decided that I would ask her, while I was putting her to bed, whether anything was wrong: which was when she told me, in much the same injured tone she might have used to complain that another girl had hit her with a hockey stick during a games period, that men came to the school in the evenings to touch her, and she didn't like it.

I didn't recover any memory immediately. I recall feeling, as any mother would in the circumstances, horrified and shocked and angry and sick to my stomach, and at first disbelieving. As I questioned her as gently as I could, all those feelings, with the exception of disbelief, grew stronger. The disbelief melted away. I told her that she didn't have to go back to school; she was safe at home now; and she should go to sleep while her father and I discussed what to do. She nodded, and climbed into bed without protest, asking me to leave her night-light on. I really don't know how I made it downstairs in one piece, physically or emotionally.

We decided within the first five minutes that we would withdraw Emily from the school immediately. We didn't make much progress in deciding what else we should do. We knew we should go to the police. That sounds obvious enough, I know. But in a small community like Ely, nothing is as straightforward as it seems in a big city like Edinburgh or London. In places like Ely, it's easy for men like Father Desmond Gerrard and John Singer to acquire power out of all proportion to their true importance in life, and to have the ear of the police and the authorities. I worked for the diocese, and I'd caught glimpses of what happened when we had the odd priest who didn't quite live up to his vows. Things had a way of getting covered up or vanishing into the fenland mists. We couldn't take it for granted that Emily would be believed outside our home: and once we breathed a word of what she had said, my employer, the diocese, became my enemy – not only

Desmond Gerrard, but my friend Bill Hollis, and, by inevitable extension, our community, and the Church itself. Those were not good enemies for someone in our position to make.

Then there was the question of other girls to whom this might have happened, and their parents. It seemed unlikely that only one girl would have suffered abuse: based on what Emily told us, it all seemed too well organised, too persistent and systematic for that. But we had no way of knowing the scale of the abuse. We hadn't asked Emily about other girls: she had enough on her plate with what had happened to her. Later, it turned out that she didn't know everything, any more than I'd known everything in my day: Father Gerrard was too cunning for that. But she'd talked to some other girls, and once word of Emily's complaint got out, whether to the police or to other parents, it wasn't hard to imagine the storm that would descend on us.

I woke up screaming at three o'clock that morning. We hadn't been in bed very long. We were exhausted, having spent hours in increasingly inconsequential exchanges about the situation, which had not even begun to point us in the right direction. When I awoke, it took Ken almost an hour to calm me down to the point where I could speak coherently enough to tell him what I'd remembered – in between bouts of further screaming, and bouts of not being able to breathe, and bouts of vomiting, and bouts of uncontrollable sobbing, with him running from bedroom to bedroom periodically to check on Emily, who, bless her, was gallantly pretending to be asleep throughout. I think the process of confiding my memories in him took about two hours, after which he called our friend and GP Linda Gallagher, who with great kindness came straight round to the house, and shot me up with something that made me go numb at first and then made me relax a little and breathe more easily; and left me boxes of tablets that she assured me would have the same effect; and promised to come back to check on me twice every day; and told Ken that if he didn't take Emily out of 'that' school immediately, he would have her to answer to.

We'd already decided that: we knew we had no choice. But in addition, Ken made an inspired decision. He saw, long before I did, that we were hopelessly out of our depth, and needed guidance about where to go and what to do next before we jumped into the terrifying unknown. He remembered having worked on a case with a high-powered London solicitor called Julia Cathermole, who had close connections to people in high places, and was used to dealing with them. She sounded like just what we needed, and he contacted her that same morning.

10

This is what I remembered.

Not long after my arrival at Lancelot Andrewes, I had noticed that Father Gerrard would come into our classroom from time to time, while class was in progress, for no apparent reason. He would stand just inside the door and watch. I didn't pay much attention to it at the time. Our teacher would carry on with the lesson without interruption, so I concluded that it was nothing out of the ordinary, nothing to be concerned about. After watching quietly for some time he would leave.

I'm vague, to say the least, on dates and times. Apparently, the preferred age range for Father Gerrard's guests was seven to twelve. I was never called on after my twelfth birthday, and I don't remember any of my friends telling me about being touched after that age. But on what days it happened, and how often it happened, I couldn't say. It wasn't every week; often, I was left alone and another girl was taken. I remember that it wasn't unusual for him to come for someone. But I couldn't begin to say how often, or when, it happened. It just became a part of our life.

Father Gerrard would come into our dormitory at about eight thirty at night, by which time the only other member of staff left in our side of the building would be the night duty teacher, who wouldn't stir from the staff common room unless summoned in case of illness. He would pause at the door and then select a girl – only one – to come with him. We went with him as we were, wearing our regulation nightdresses and nothing else, and in bare feet, regardless of the time of year and the temperature. We walked down familiar staircases, and I remember thinking, the first time it happened to me, that Father Gerrard must be taking me to his study, and assuming I was going to be punished for some transgression or other, and being unable, for the life of me, to think what it could have been. Father Gerrard was known for sometimes beating girls who had transgressed in a serious way with a cane in his study. It had happened to Joan; she had told me about it; but I'd always understood that the beatings were administered during the day, with Matron present.

When we walked past his study into a room I didn't even remember being aware of, and had certainly never been in, I was taken aback, and somewhat relieved that, apparently, I was to be spared punishment. The relief didn't last long. There were three men in the room, smartly dressed in dark suits and ties, as if they'd just come from the city. They were standing around the long table in the middle of the room, talking and laughing, and drinking what from my memory, from its colour and the size of the glasses, I think must have been whisky – I couldn't have known that at the time. One – the man I'm told I have to call the Right Reverend EF, to protect his reputation – was smoking a cigar. When Father Gerrard brought me into the room, they turned towards me, and I heard mutterings, something like, 'Yes, very good.' Sir CD walked over to me, took my hand, and led me to where they were standing at the table. 'What's your name, my dear?' he asked. I told him. 'Audrey,' Lord AB repeated. 'What a nice name. I had an aunt called Audrey.' I remember pulling my nightdress tightly around me.

The Right Reverend EF was the first to touch me. Father Gerrard never joined in the touching, never once, but he also never left the room. He stood quietly in the far corner of the library, watching. The Right Reverend EF gently prised my fingers away from my nightdress, which he then lifted up to expose my body. The other two men gathered round to watch. I see what happened next in my memory through the eyes of a grown woman. I can't imagine what thoughts I had of it as a child, or even how, as a child of seven or eight, I tried to describe or explain it to myself. I don't know how a seven-year-old child could make sense of having a grown man kneel in front of her, put two fingers inside her cunt, and fondle her, destroying what was left of her hymen, if there was anything left of it after so much hockey and gymnastics; while two other men stood on watching, rubbing their cocks through their trousers, or sometimes out of their trousers. I don't know whether I even tried to make sense of it then. My memory is that I detached from what was going on, looking around me, doing my best to read the titles of the rows of books on the shelves that covered the walls, trying to count how many books there were in the nearest section of bookcase; anything to take my mind away from what was happening to my body. When the Right Reverend EF had satisfied himself, Lord AB and Sir CD took their turns with me. I'm describing, as a grown woman, my memory of what was done to me as a child. As a woman I understand what was going on. It doesn't make it any easier.

As far as I remember, those were the only three men who ever touched me, and they weren't always all there together. I was never raped; and I was never asked to touch any of their cocks. I don't remember any of my friends saying they'd been raped, though one or two told me that they'd had their hands placed on a cock and been told to rub it; whether by these same men or others, I have no way of knowing. I remember, to my horror, that after I'd been taken to the men a number of times, there came to be a routine, a regularity, almost a monotony, about it. There was a numbness in me, too. They would ask me questions about how school was going, how many goals I'd scored at hockey, and sometimes they brought me chocolate, for which I thanked them politely and mechanically, before turning my attention to the books on the shelves.

And at three o'clock on that morning, it all came flooding back. Reflecting on it later, I asked myself how I could have suppressed the memory for so long. I come back to the conclusion that my mind had taken pity on me, and had wiped the slate clean so that I didn't have to torture myself with those images. There was a culture of silence at school, too. I don't think I ever spoke to a friend, or she to me, about it more than once. But because my memory banks had been wiped clean, I'd allowed Emily, my daughter, to follow in my cold bare footsteps down those chill staircases to that clubby private library. It was a thought that broke my heart. I thought it had been broken completely. But later, another thought came to me, which found another piece of my heart to destroy, a piece that must still have been intact until then.

I'd confided in Joan, I realised, more than in my friends. Joan was never taken; she was already past the preferred age when we first arrived at school. But Joan had been beaten in Father Gerrard's study. At the time, I never understood why, and she never told me. It hadn't made sense at the time. Joan wasn't the kind to misbehave; she was an obedient, responsible girl. But I'd told her what happened to me. And suddenly, in the early hours of that day, it all made horrific sense. 'I'm sorry, Audrey. I wanted to stop it, but I couldn't.' She'd known what was happening to me at school, and later she'd seen the scars I still carried when I grew up: when we lived together in Edinburgh, I'd confided in her about the intimate problem I was having with my boyfriends. She'd tried to stop it. It could only mean one thing. She'd confronted Father Gerrard, told him to leave her sister alone, perhaps even threatened to expose him. She was a determined girl. It wouldn't surprise me at all if she had threatened him. She hadn't misbehaved. She was trying to save me. We had no parents to protect us. As my older sister, it had been up to her. I never knew what a toll it had taken on her. But now I saw it all too clearly. When she thought she'd failed, she couldn't live with it. She couldn't even talk to me about it.

And that's when I swore, by all I held sacred, that I would make them pay for what they had done, all of them: Father Gerrard, and all those high-profile bastards to whom he loaned the bodies

and souls of his pupils for their entertainment, while he stood in
the corner and watched; all those high-profile bastards who were
now hiding behind the initials of their names to protect their
reputations. I would make them pay, if it took me the rest of my
life and cost me everything I had.

11

Tuesday 12 February 1974

'Today is the twelfth of February 1974, and it's now eleven fifteen in the morning. We are in an interview room at Parkside police station in Cambridge. Present are: myself, DI Phillips, of the Cambridge police; DI Walsh of the London Metropolitan police, who is making a note of the interview; Father Desmond Gerrard, headmaster of Lancelot Andrewes school; and Mr John Singer, the solicitor for Lancelot Andrewes School. Mr Singer, I understand that you are also representing Father Gerrard for the purposes of this interview, is that correct?'

'It is. In the unlikely event that this matter is taken further, I will ensure that Father Gerrard is represented by a solicitor with more experience of criminal matters, but, confident as I am that it will go no further, I shall represent his interests today.'

'I assume, Mr Singer,' Steffie Walsh intervened, 'that you have explained to Father Gerrard that you have a possible conflict of interest, given that you represent the school?'

'I don't know what you mean.'

Steffie and Ted exchanged a smile. Before they left the Old Bailey conference room, Ben Schroeder had taken them aside and quietly suggested dropping this spanner into the works – and to judge from John Singer's reaction, it was having the desired effect. Steffie noted that Father Gerrard had also reacted, with a quick glance in Singer's direction. Gerrard was an imposing man, dressed in a long black cassock, a large silver crucifix hanging down from his neck over his chest, his black hair interrupted only intermittently by grey flecks, making him look younger than his seventy years of age. There was also a quiet, a reserve, about him. It was the first time he had raised his head to look at anyone since they had seated him in the interview room.

'I understand from our counsel,' Steffie continued unhurriedly, 'that the school and its trustees may be legally liable to victims of the assaults and their parents. So, in the highly likely event of parents taking legal action against Father Gerrard and the school, Father Gerrard's interests and those of the school would not be the same. Counsel suggested that Father Gerrard might prefer to have independent advice.' She shrugged. 'It's up to you.'

As if irritated by the interruption, Singer pulled his chair alongside Father Gerrard's and whispered frantically in his ear for some seconds, after which he turned back and shot Steffie a look of defiance.

'I am a churchman, Inspector,' Father Gerrard said, 'and as such I look to the Church to safeguard my interests. I am perfectly content to be advised by Mr Singer.'

Steffie nodded and resumed her note-taking position.

'Father Gerrard, you are here today voluntarily, at our request, so that we can put questions to you about alleged events at Lancelot Andrewes School,' Ted said. 'You are not under arrest, and you are free to leave at any time. Do you understand that?'

'Yes, I do.'

'Thank you, sir. And I'm sure that Mr Singer has explained this to you, but I must begin by cautioning you. You are not obliged to say anything unless you wish to do so, but what you say may be put into writing and given in evidence. Do you understand the caution?'

'Yes, I do.'

'Thank you.' Ted rummaged through a small pile of documents he had in front of him on the table and selected one. 'If I may, Father Gerrard, I'd like to begin by making sure I understand the layout of the school. Can you confirm that what I am showing you is a plan of the school, floor by floor?'

Father Gerrard glanced at the document briefly. 'Yes, it is.'

'Six floors in all?'

'Yes.'

'And we understand that, as we look at it from the main road, the girls' school is on the left, and the boys' school on the right?'

'Yes.'

'What separations are there between the two?'

'Separations? I'm not sure I understand.'

'Our understanding is that the boys and girls are not allowed to mingle.'

'That's partly true, Inspector, but we enforce that with rules, not locks and keys. I'm not running a prison. The only doors between the two sides kept locked are on the fifth and sixth floors, where pupils and some of the staff have their living quarters. Except for that, everyone can move freely. They have to – the school couldn't work, otherwise. We have facilities such as the assembly hall, the gymnasium and the science laboratories, that are used by both boys and girls, so everyone has to have access across the building.'

'Where are your own living quarters?'

'I have living quarters on the sixth floor, on the boys' side. Of course, I also have my study on the ground floor, where I see parents and other visitors.'

'And, looking at the plan, it seems that your study is next to the business office: is that right?'

'Yes. My secretary and the other administrative staff work in that area, so that they can deal with members of the public, tradesmen, and so on, who may have business with the school.'

'Yes, I see. And what is this room here, on the other side of your study?'

'That is my private library. The school has its own library, of course, which takes up about half of the fourth floor. This room houses my own collection, mainly theological and philosophical works, and provides me with a place to work in peace during the few moments I can find to do anything in peace.'

'Are pupils ever allowed to use your private library?' Steffie asked.

'Pupils? No. Certainly not. I may invite a member of staff to use it from time to time if they are doing some research for which I may have relevant books. In the highly unlikely event that a student needed something – a sixth-former preparing for a scholarship examination, perhaps – they would ask the school librarian, and she would come to me to borrow it. But the school library should have everything they need.'

'Do you ever use your private library for meetings?'

'Yes: sometimes, if I want to make sure I won't be interrupted. My secretary is in and out all the time when I'm in my study, and there are times – for example, if I'm with someone who's considering making a substantial donation to the school – when I need to be able to talk to them without people barging in and out of the room.'

'So, your secretary knows that she has to leave you alone when you're in the library, does she, Father Gerrard?' Steffie asked.

'Yes, she does.'

'Does that go for other members of staff, too?'

'Yes. Unless there's some emergency, obviously. But that would be very rare.'

'Thank you.' Steffie nodded to Ted, to hand back to him.

'Father Gerrard, I think you're aware that a girl we're going to call Girl A – and you've been told who Girl A is, but you understand why we're not using her name, is that right?'

'Yes.'

'A girl we're calling Girl A has alleged that on three or four occasions over the past year to eighteen months, you took her from her dormitory down to your private library, where a number of men wearing masks to cover their faces indecently assaulted her in your presence. I remind you of the caution, Father Gerrard. Is her allegation true?'

John Singer leaned forward, his arms fully stretched out towards the officers on the table.

'Father Gerrard will exercise his right not to answer any questions relating to these false allegations,' he said.

'If they're false allegations, Mr Singer, I would expect Father Gerrard to tell me so himself.'

'I'm here to represent Father Gerrard, and I'm telling you.'

'Are you telling me that as the solicitor for Father Gerrard, or the solicitor for the school?'

'We've already been through that once, Inspector, and I've explained as clearly as I can that I'm representing Father Gerrard today.'

'That doesn't satisfy me, sir.'

'Doesn't satisfy you, Inspector?' Singer snapped. 'It doesn't satisfy *you*? Who do you think you are? You are a police officer, and I am a solicitor. Are you questioning my professional judgement? This is nothing less than an... an impertinence.'

'Is it, sir? Well, I'm sorry if you think that. My only concern is that Father Gerrard should have a fair opportunity to respond to the allegations.'

'And I say that he should have a fair opportunity *not* to respond to them, if he so wishes. I'm his solicitor. I am looking after his interests, and if I deem it necessary to protect his interests, I will terminate this interview. May I remind you that Father Gerrard has come here voluntarily?'

'We can easily change that situation, Mr Singer. If you'd prefer me to arrest Father Gerrard, I'm quite happy to do so.'

With a huge effort, Singer controlled himself. There was a silence.

'Mr Singer,' Steffie intervened, with a brief diplomatic touch of her hand on Ted's, 'all DI Phillips is saying is that Father Gerrard must be given a fair chance to say whatever he wishes. If he cooperates with us now, it may be to his benefit in the future. I'm sure you understand what I'm saying. If there's anything he wants to bring to our attention that might help him, we want to hear it.'

'We are doing our best to cooperate, Inspector. But in my view as his solicitor, Father Gerrard's interests are best served by saying nothing at this juncture.'

'Father Gerrard's best interests, sir?' Ted asked. 'Or those of the school?'

'Once again, Inspector,' Singer replied, 'this is an intolerable interference with my professional duty to my client. It is also a gross impertinence; and if you continue in this way, I shall have to report the matter to the Chief Constable – who, I may say, I happen to know quite well.'

'In this instance, Mr Singer,' Steffie intervened, 'we don't report to the Chief Constable. The Director of Public Prosecutions has taken over the conduct of this case, and we report to him. The gentleman dealing with it in the Director's office is Mr John Caswell. I'd be happy to put you in touch with him, if you wish.'

John Singer opened his mouth as if to speak, but did not. Father Gerrard raised his hands slightly.

'It's all right, John,' he said. 'I'm quite capable of speaking for myself.'

'Desmond...'

'No, John, let's get on with it. If we keep on arguing like this, we will be here all day. On the advice of my solicitor, Inspector, I have nothing to say at this time.'

'You have nothing at all to say to this little girl or to her parents?' Ted asked.

'I have nothing to say at this time.'

'Has she made all this up, Father Gerrard, this little seven-year-old girl? Has this seven-year-old wickedly invented these stories about men touching her, lied to her parents, and lied to my colleague DI Walsh?'

'I have nothing to say at this time.'

'Her mother has also alleged that she was assaulted in much the same way, Father Gerrard. This was many years ago, when she came to the school as an evacuee from London during the war. She says she was assaulted in the same way on several occasions. Is she making it all up, too?'

'I have nothing to say at this time.'

'She also says that some of her friends at school complained to her of being assaulted in exactly the same way. We will be interviewing these women, Father Gerrard. Are you sure you don't want to say something now?'

'I have nothing to say at this time.'

'I'm showing you a photograph,' Ted continued, reaching down again into his pile of papers. 'Do you recognise the man shown in this photograph?'

A brief glance and nod of the head. 'Yes, of course.'

'Is this the man we are calling Lord AB?'

'Of course it is. He's a well-known public figure, and a trustee of the school, which makes it all the more reprehensible that his name is being dragged –'

'Desmond –' John Singer interrupted.

'Please continue if you have something to say, Father Gerrard,' Ted said.

Father Gerrard shook his head. 'I have nothing to say.'

'Has Lord AB ever visited the school?'

John Singer put his hand on Father Gerrard's arm, but the priest pushed it away in frustration.

'Of course he has. He's one of our trustees. He's also an old boy of the school, and his son was a pupil too, in the late forties, early fifties. I can't remember exactly when, but you can find out from the records. Since then, he's been a generous benefactor: he's given Lancelot Andrewes a lot of money. So, yes, he has visited the school on many occasions.'

Ted nodded. 'Did he ever visit the school for the purpose of indecently assaulting young girls in your private library?'

'That is a… I have nothing to say at this time.'

'I'm showing you another photograph. Do you recognise the man shown in this photograph?'

'I believe he is, or was, a Member of Parliament. I've never met him, as far as I remember.'

'As far as you remember?'

'I don't believe I've ever met him. Please, Inspector, try to understand. I meet Members of Parliament all the time. I've sat on advisory panels on education for both Houses of Parliament for many years, and I've been to the House of Commons many times; so, I can't exclude the possibility that we've said good day to each other at some time, but if so, I don't recall it.'

'We're calling him Sir CD, but you've been given his real name, haven't you?'

'Yes. But I don't recall any dealings with him. I don't recall him as a member of any House committee I worked with.'

'Did this man ever indecently assault young girls in your private library?'

'I have nothing to say at this time.'

'One more photograph, please, Father Gerrard.'

'Well, yes, he's one of our trustees also, and a colleague in the Church – or at least he was, until he went off to Oxford. I know him very well, of course.'

'We're calling him the Right Reverend EF. Did he ever indecently assault young girls in your private library?'

Father Gerrard made a huge effort to control himself before replying. 'I have nothing to say at this time.'

'Does the Right Reverend EF smoke cigars?' Steffie asked suddenly.

'Yes,' Father Gerrard replied, before John Singer's hand arrived on his arm. 'It's something of a trademark, an affectation...' His voice trailed away.

'Is there anything else you wish to add?' Ted asked.

'No. And I have nothing else to say at this time.'

Ted and Steffie looked each other. She nodded.

'In that case, Father Gerrard,' Ted said, 'I am arresting you –'

'What?' John Singer exclaimed. You can't – !'

'I am arresting you on suspicion of an unknown number of indecent assaults and acts of indecency with young children committed between the year 1940 and the present time. I must caution you that you are not obliged to say anything unless you wish to do so, but what you say may be put into writing and given in evidence. Do you understand the caution?'

'Yes, and I have nothing to say.'

'This is ridiculous,' John Singer said.

'As and when you've found Father Gerrard a solicitor with more criminal experience, sir,' Ted replied, 'have them get in touch with me. I'll make sure they're brought up to date with everything.'

12

Monday 22 April 1974

Julia Cathermole smiled as Mary Forbes opened the door of her room at the Savoy and invited her in with a gesture. Mary was dressed casually in a light green shirt and brown slacks, barefoot, her hair tied casually back with a large butterfly clip, and wearing a minimum of makeup. But the pile of papers on the desk at the side of the room, and the number of empty cups and plates on the coffee table, dispelled any idea that she was at the Savoy to relax: this was a busy woman.

'Thank you for seeing me, Mary,' Julia said. 'You're obviously up to your neck in it. I know the feeling. Your desk reminds me of my office.'

Mary smiled thinly, waving Julia into a chair. 'Complicated commercial case involving a Canadian plaintiff and a City investment bank. I have to report my conclusions to Toronto by tomorrow evening.'

'I won't keep you long,' Julia promised.

'Julia,' Mary said, 'I agreed to see you because you're representing Audrey, and I'm grateful that she has you to help her. But I may as well be honest with you: if you're going to try to persuade me to give evidence, you're wasting your time. The police have already interviewed me. DI Walsh was very persuasive, but I'm not going to do it.'

'I hear you,' Julia said. 'But I'd appreciate a few minutes, just to present it in a slightly different way from DI Walsh.'

'Yes, of course… I'm sorry, I'm being very impolite. I think I'm out of coffee, but I'd be happy to order some up from room service.'

Julia held up a hand. 'No, thanks, I'm fine; I had some earlier. Look, your time is valuable, so I'll come straight to the point. I know you and Audrey were close friends when you were at school. She and her sister Joan came to stay with you and your family during the holidays sometimes. And you've kept in touch since.'

She nodded. 'Yes. That's true.'

'You know that Father Gerrard has been charged with offences relating to Audrey being molested in the 1940s. What you may not know, because I don't know how much DI Walsh told you, is that he's also charged with identical offences relating to Audrey's seven-year-old daughter Emily during the last couple of years.'

Mary sat back in her chair and placed a hand over her mouth. She did not respond for some time.

'She told me there was a girl involved from the present student body, a girl they were calling Girl A… but I didn't know…'

'No, well, DI Walsh was right not to go any further. Like any child in her position, Emily's entitled to have her identity protected. But that's the truth of the matter, Mary. Emily is Girl A. Unlike you, Audrey didn't have a continuous memory of what had happened to her at school.'

'She'd blanked it out.'

'Yes. And having no reason not to put her trust in Lancelot Andrewes, she sent Emily there as a boarder at the age of seven – the same age she herself was when she arrived from London during the Blitz. When Emily told her that she was being treated in exactly the same way Audrey herself had been treated, Audrey's memories came flooding back.'

'Oh, my God… that's awful,' Mary said. 'She must feel terrible.'

'Mary, I'm in exactly the same position as DI Walsh, which means I shouldn't have told you what I've just told you. I'm going to have to rely on your discretion not to let it go any further. I hope you understand.'

'Yes, of course. You don't have to worry. I won't say a word.'

'Thank you.'

Julia paused for a few seconds.

'I don't mean to pry, Mary, but would you mind telling me why you don't want to give evidence?'

Mary stood and walked across to the desk, leaning on it, her back to Julia. Slowly, she turned back. Julia stood and walked over to her.

'I told my parents what happened to me when I was about nine. I remember it was when I was at home for the Christmas holidays. But I've never told anyone else. Never. And now… Julia, I have a husband and two children…'

'Your husband doesn't know?'

She shook her head. 'It was difficult enough telling my parents. I never felt the need to expose myself by telling anyone else. I'm a fairly resilient person. As I said, it stopped when I turned nine – which made me one of the lucky ones, I suppose, because from what I understand, some of the girls were still being molested when they were eleven or twelve. So I decided to put it behind me and move on.' She smiled. 'I even made use of the experience in a perverse kind of way.'

'Oh?'

'It gave me some inside knowledge of the male anatomy, and a certain amount of technique, when I started dating. I'm sorry to be so crass, but that's how I rationalised it to myself; that's how I got through it.'

'No apology needed. Everyone reacts differently. The important thing is to remember that none of it was your fault. You were a victim, just like the other girls.'

'Also, my parents encouraged me not to talk about it,' Mary said. 'Actually, "encouraged" is something of an understatement. I wasn't going to anyway, but they went on and on about it until I swore to keep it to myself. I know today, children are encouraged to speak out, and I do agree with that approach. But it wasn't like that in our day.'

'Tell me about it,' Julia replied quietly.

'My parents were embarrassed by it all. They said it would bring shame on the family if I ever told anyone; no one would believe me; we'd be ostracised; none of our friends or relatives would have anything to do with us; my father might lose his job; they just went on and on. So I swore I would never say anything, and I never did.' She was silent for some time. 'I think their feelings of shame rubbed off on me. I know it wasn't my fault. I get that intellectually. But emotionally, I would feel – I don't quite know how to say, it – but I would feel... dirty, somehow.'

'It's very common for victims to feel like that,' Julia replied.

'I know. But it doesn't make it any easier. I don't know how I could land on Steve with this now.'

'Why would he think of it as landing on him?' Julia asked. 'He's a lawyer, isn't he? Don't you think he'd understand?'

'My mother is still alive, too,' Mary added, returning to her chair.

'I hear you,' Julia said. 'Look, Mary, I didn't tell you about Emily to try to make you feel bad. I told you because, unless you give evidence, there's every chance that Father Gerrard will walk away from this case.'

Mary looked up sharply.

'Walk away? Why should he walk away? Audrey and Em – Girl A – give you a history of sexual assault going back thirty years, and they provide corroboration for each other. You've got a solid legal case.'

'Well, yes and no,' Julia replied. 'Audrey's evidence consists entirely of recovered memory, and that's something not all experts support. There are those who think a witness in that position, even if she's being honest, is creating memory, not recovering it. There are some judges who wouldn't allow it to go to a jury. And Emily is eight, going on nine. Technically, a nine-year-old is a child of tender years. She's legally capable of being a competent witness, but it's up to the judge to decide. The judge will have to examine her to see how far she understands the duty to tell the truth in a court of law. In front of the wrong judge, we could lose her evidence too. So, yes: on paper, the case is legally sufficient, but the reality is another matter.'

They were silent for some time.

'But you must have other evidence. There must be other girls who've come forward...' Mary's voice trailed away.

'I'm afraid not. We assumed that we would have a lot of women and girls coming forward, especially with all the publicity. But it hasn't happened. It's as though everyone is taking the same line as your parents did. DI Walsh and DI Phillips, and other officers, have spoken to everyone Audrey and Emily identified, or their parents, but it's almost as if there's a conspiracy of silence.'

Mary held her head in her hands for some time.

'There is,' she replied.

13

'Is there something you want to tell me?' Julia asked.

Mary did not reply for some time.

'If I tell you this, you have to agree that you didn't hear it from me.'

'Agreed,' Julia replied at once.

'I've never told anyone about this, and I wouldn't say anything now, except for the fact that you're representing Audrey.'

'I understand.'

'All right.'

There was another lengthy silence. Julia watched as Mary wrestled with herself.

'Those three men, the three who've been in all the papers...'

'The men we're calling Lord AB, Sir CD and the Right Reverend EF?'

'Yes. Those three men molested me, in the same way they molested Audrey. But in my case, once or twice, there was also a fourth man...'

'Go on,' Julia encouraged, quietly.

'He was German.'

Julia caught herself holding her breath. It took her a moment or two to speak.

'German? Are you sure, Mary? Remember, this was 1941, 1942; it was wartime.'

'Yes, I know. It seemed strange to me at the time.'

'How do you know he was German?'

'I heard him speak German to Bishop EF. My father was a German scholar, and even before I went to school, I'd heard the language spoken at home often enough to recognise it. My father had even taught me a few basic words and phrases. I didn't understand what this man and the bishop were saying, but in fairness, I was rather distracted at the time.'

'Distracted?'

'I was rubbing the German man's penis.'

Julia nodded. 'I see.'

'But I'm sure he was German. I have no idea who he was, but I know he was German.'

'Did you tell anyone about this?' Julia asked after some time.

Mary nodded. 'I told my parents at the time. But it was never mentioned again until last year, when my father was dying. I'd made the trip over from Canada to see him, because we knew he didn't have long to live. And one evening, when there were just the two of us, he suddenly brought it all up again. I tried to stop him, to tell him it didn't matter, that it was water under the bridge; but he insisted that there was something he had to say to me.'

She took a sip of water from a glass on the table.

'My father had worked for the Home Office during the war, doing God knows what, secret work of some kind – I'm sure his knowledge of German was useful to them. Anyway, after I'd told my parents about the abuse, apparently my father went to see someone high up in the Home Office – I have no idea who – and reported it to them. He had never told me until that night.'

'What happened?' Julia asked.

'He said the Home Office had ordered him to drop it, and never mention it again to anybody.'

'What?'

'They said the security services knew all about what was going on at Lancelot Andrewes, and had some kind of interest in it. It was a matter of national security. He was to drop it and say nothing to anyone.'

'The security services?'

'Yes.'

'Which service? Did he say? Domestic, MI5? Or foreign, the Special Intelligence Service, MI6?'

She thought for a moment. 'MI6… or was it MI5? MI6, I think… but I'm not absolutely sure whether I'm remembering that, or whether that's what I assumed because the man was German.'

'Please, Mary, try to remember. It may be important.'

'MI6. Yes, I think it was MI6.'

Julia sat down and leaned back in her chair.

'And did your father do what he was told, and drop it?' she asked.

'Yes. So he said… but that wasn't the end of the story.'

'Oh?'

'They promised him that I wouldn't be molested again.'

'The Home Office promised that you wouldn't be molested again? And you weren't?'

'And I wasn't. And that wasn't even the end of it. After that time, my parents never received a single bill for my school fees: not once, even though I stayed at the school until I went to university at eighteen.'

Julia's jaw dropped.

'They bought your father off by giving you a free ride at school?'

She nodded. 'Apparently. And I don't suppose I'm the only one, Julia, do you?'

Julia got to her feet again and stood behind her chair, leaning against it, her hands in front of her.

'So,' she said quietly, as if to herself, 'it's really no great surprise that no one's coming forward, is it? Many victims, or their parents, would react in the same way yours did. They would feel embarrassed, ashamed.'

'And even if they came forward,' Mary added, 'at the end of the day, it would be their word against the word of Father Desmond Gerrard, wouldn't it? Father Desmond Gerrard, education guru to the government, who has the ear of some very powerful people.'

She shook her head. 'Most people would keep their heads down, wouldn't they? They would think they were on a hiding to nothing: easier just to let it go.'

'And those who did complain, they bought off,' Julia said quietly.

'Yes.'

'How did your father feel about that?' Julia asked.

'He sounded ashamed of himself. I tried to reassure him; I told him that it was all right, that I was OK, but I think it had been on his conscience all those years. I think he felt as if he'd sold me to pay my school fees. It wasn't like that at all, but...'

Julia advanced to stand in front of Mary, took her hand, and gave her a light kiss on the cheek.

'I won't keep you any longer, Mary,' she said. 'Thank you for confiding in me. I know it wasn't easy.'

Mary smiled. 'Is there anything else you want to say to try to persuade me to give evidence?'

'No,' Julia replied. 'I've said all I can.'

On her way back to the office, Julia stopped off at her house, where she made a phone call. The person she wanted to speak to was in a meeting. Julia left a message asking that person to return her call as soon as possible.

14

Thursday 25 April 1974

It was a familiar routine, a staple of service practice, which was why he had chosen it: the walk was a proven safe route. But if the truth be known, the choice was made mainly out of habit. After so many years with the service, his tradecraft had become as much a part of him as the suit and tie he selected from his wardrobe each morning. Another advantage was that she knew the routine also. They met as if by chance and started walking along the Embankment, opposite Temple tube station, towards Charing Cross.

'This is a pleasant surprise, Julia,' Baxter said. 'I haven't seen you since the Digby case.'

'Has it been that long?' Julia smiled.

'And, according to the newspapers, you've got Mr Schroeder and Miss Castle, who were also involved in that case, prosecuting the unfortunate Father Gerrard for you. A coincidence, I wonder?'

'The *Director of Public Prosecutions* has them prosecuting Father Gerrard, *on behalf of the Crown.*'

He smiled. 'Of course. Well, whoever chose them made a good choice. You learn a lot about people when you spend a couple of days with them in a foreign safe house. I would say the case is in good hands.'

They stopped to look out over the river.

'I assume I'm right in thinking that you want to talk about Lancelot Andrewes?'

She smiled again. 'Are you reading my mind, or have you been intercepting me?'

He returned the smile. 'Let's try not to get too paranoid, Julia, shall we?'

'I'm sorry, but just at the moment I feel that a healthy dose of paranoia isn't necessarily a bad thing.'

He nodded. 'Fair enough, but the answer to your question is: neither. I read newspapers, not minds; and no, we haven't been bugging you – well, not as far as I know, and I probably would know.'

They were silent for some time.

'Are you authorised to talk to me?'

He hesitated. 'Pass. Let's say I'm prepared to answer some questions – probably not all the questions you'd like me to answer – but some.'

'All right.'

'Without attribution, of course.'

She nodded. 'Of course. All right: the prosecution is having difficulty in getting witnesses to come forward. Part of that seems to be related to – well, let's call it compensation, shall we? – paid out covertly by the Home Office to some of the victims and their families.'

He smiled. 'I'm glad to see you haven't changed. You're still your father's daughter – never one to beat about the bush, either of you.'

'The compensation being related in part to the activities of a German man who visited the school while we were at war with Germany – which is odd, to say the least. I've heard whispers that the service may have had something to do with that. Is there anything you can you tell me?'

Baxter nodded, but did not reply immediately.

'If you can't answer, you can't answer.'

Baxter resumed his walk, and Julia fell in at his side.

'His name was Hansdieter Köhler – Father Hansdieter Köhler, actually; he was a priest.'

'Lutheran?'

'Roman Catholic. From Stuttgart originally, but he'd been over here, in London, since the mid-1930s.'

'Doing what?'

'Ostensibly just being a priest, but there was something about him that didn't quite fit, and somewhere along the way he attracted the attention of our friends at Five.'

'Because of his proclivity for little girls?'

'That, and his close friendship with the man the newspapers are calling Bishop EF. I'm sure you know his real name as well as I do, so I won't make you dance around that – just as I'm sure you know that he has the same proclivity.'

'Yes,' Julia nodded.

Baxter stopped again, to watch the river. She stood by his side.

'That alone would have been enough for Five to keep an eye on him, but they soon discovered that there was more to Father Köhler than they'd first thought, and they told us about him. By early 1939 we already suspected that he was passing valuable information to Berlin. Sources we had in place there reported that Köhler had high-level contacts within the Reich's security apparatus, and his friendship with EF had opened a lot of doors for him in the higher echelons of government here. Alarm bells were ringing. So we put him under close surveillance, and towards the end of 1939 we duly caught him at it.'

'How was he doing it? Was someone handling him?'

'No. It was the good old wireless set, no less, tucked away in the attic of his priestly residence. Madness, really. He must have known we had all the wavelengths covered; we were bound to catch him eventually.'

'What did you do with him?'

'We almost didn't get the chance to do anything. The Home Office wanted to intern him as an enemy alien. We told them that would be a wasted opportunity. We asked them to give us a chance to turn him: they agreed, and turn him we did.'

'How?'

Baxter smiled. 'In the traditional way. We explained to him that he had a choice: he could either work for us, or we would have him shot as a spy. He chose to work for us, and he spent the rest of the war supplying Berlin with a lot of highly misleading information that we fed him; in addition, we took immediate possession of whatever he got from Berlin. We made him tell Berlin he'd been spared internment in return for acting as a chaplain for our internment and POW camps. It was a brilliant cover. Berlin never worked it out.'

Julia nodded. 'You had a very valuable asset.'

'You have no idea,' Baxter replied. 'But that's under wraps for several generations. Suffice it to say that he was like gold dust. We were with him night and day, never let him out of our sight. Well, the Home Office insisted on that, as a condition of not interning him, but we would have done it anyway. We also gave him a British identity, by the way, so that he didn't attract suspicion.'

'Name?' Julia asked.

'Pass.'

They resumed their walk.

'Where does Lancelot Andrewes come into the picture?' Julia asked.

'Five told us that Köhler visited Lancelot Andrewes from time to time with EF,' Baxter replied. 'They didn't know why, at first, but when they started to suspect him of passing information to Berlin, they called on EF one day and persuaded him to spill the beans about what was going on.'

Julia smiled grimly. 'Did they threaten to shoot him, too?'

'No. They just explained to him that they knew all about his interest in little girls, and gave him a choice between, on the one hand, scandal and imprisonment, and on the other, working with them to make sure Köhler never left their radar. He chose to work with them.'

'So Five recruited EF?'

'In a manner of speaking, yes. That was before they made him a bishop, of course. I can't say any more about that.'

'What happened to Köhler after the war?'

'Ah, well, that's an interesting question. I don't know. His file is less than specific about it. It just says that arrangements were made for him to assume a new identity somewhere abroad. I assume it wouldn't have been safe to return him to Germany, and it wouldn't have been a good idea to let him stay here. But beyond that, I have no idea where he went, or what name he's using there.'

'And you wouldn't tell me even if you knew?'

'Correct.'

This time, it was Julia who stopped.

'So, the service knew all along what was happening to those little girls.'

'Yes,' Baxter replied after staring into the river for some time.

'And you let those men keep on going to Lancelot Andrewes, knowing what you knew? In the eyes of the service, those little girls were expendable?'

Baxter paused again. 'I would like to think that we would handle him differently today,' he replied at length. 'But try to understand, Julia, we were at war, and Köhler was giving us direct access to the nerve centre of the Wehrmacht –'

'But –'

'I understand what you're saying, and I only wish I could tell you how much Köhler gave us, how many lives he saved, how many enemy agents he betrayed, how many of their operations he sabotaged for us; but I can't – none of that will be in the public domain in our lifetimes.'

'But surely to God, there must have been a way to handle him without letting him loose on those little girls?'

'We didn't let him loose on them. He was doing that long before we knew about him.'

'Even so: you could have stopped it.'

'With the benefit of hindsight, and in the calm of peacetime, yes, I'm sure you're right. But at the time, we had to do whatever we could to survive. A judgment was made, for security reasons, that he should be allowed to continue the way of life he'd established.

You know the service, Julia, and you know that there are times when we have to work with the dark side, embrace it, even. It's always been that way, and always will. You're family, Julia. You know that.'

'What do you know about Lord AB and Sir CD?'

'Pass. Nice try.'

'Was my father involved with Köhler?' she asked suddenly.

'Pass.'

'Come on, Baxter, you can't do that to me. You just said I was family.'

'He wasn't involved in decision-making about Köhler,' Baxter replied after some time, 'or if he was, there's nothing on the file to that effect, and he never suggested anything like that to me. In any case, as you know, he was stationed in Vienna until just before war broke out, so he couldn't have been involved in the early days.' He paused again. 'But he was involved in handling Köhler and EF at various times. Most of us were, Julia. That level of handling is very labour-intensive, and we had limited resources. A lot of us had to pitch in when we weren't involved in other operations.'

Julia bowed her head and remained silent. Baxter put a hand on her shoulder. After a few moments they resumed their walk.

'Is there anything else you wanted to ask?'

'I suppose,' she replied, looking up, 'it would be useful to know what attitude the service is going to take to the prosecution?'

He nodded. 'May I ask you a question?'

'Yes.'

'Why are you going after Father Gerrard on his own? Why haven't you brought charges against the other three men you know about?'

'No attribution?' she asked.

He laughed. 'No attribution.'

'We're not sure how much of a case we have against any of them. Counsel thought it was best to test the evidence against Gerrard first. If Audrey's evidence stands up, and if we can get some corroborative evidence in, then we have a good shot of potting Gerrard, and we might have a realistic chance against the others. We're also hoping that Gerrard might give us something we can use against the other men. He hasn't said a word so far, but once the reality of the trial kicks in, we're hoping he may name a few names to try to talk his way out of it.'

'That makes sense,' Baxter replied.

'But that's not what Ben's going to tell the jury in his opening speech.'

'No, I daresay not. Julia, I have to ask you this: your witnesses aren't going to talk about the service, are they?'

'No.'

Charing Cross was coming into view.

'We don't care about Gerrard,' Baxter said.

'Really?'

'We don't think he knows much, if anything, about Köhler, except that he was a friend of EF. He would have met Köhler from time to time, but there's no reason to think he knows about our involvement.'

He paused, and they stopped again.

'There's something else I'd like you to know, Julia. We weren't totally unconcerned about the girls. Once the war was over, we sent an officer from Special Branch to interview Gerrard. That officer delivered a clear message: that the police couldn't turn a blind eye any more, and it was time to put his house in order. We hoped that might have some effect. Apparently, it hasn't. But we gave him his chance, so as far as we're concerned, do whatever you want with him. He's of no interest to us. And personally, off the record, I hope they lock him up and throw away the key.'

'Thank you. I'm glad to hear that.'

'But it may be different with the others,' Baxter added. 'EF knows all about the Köhler operation, quite possibly including where he is and what he's calling himself now; and I'm sure he's never forgotten the warning Five gave him all those years ago. He has even more to lose now, doesn't he, as a bishop and Master of an Oxford college? If he has his back to the wall, he may be desperate enough to start saying things he shouldn't.'

'We can't let them get away with it, Baxter,' Julia said, 'not when so many vulnerable girls were abused over so many years, so many lives ruined for the entertainment of those paedophiles. Those men must be held to account for that. If we have evidence against them, we will have to proceed, and, given its record on Lancelot Andrewes, I would sincerely hope that the service would not try to stand in the way.'

Baxter offered his hand.

'It's been good to see you again, Julia,' he said. 'You're your father's daughter in so many ways. Are you sure you wouldn't like to come and work for us? The offer is still open. A woman with your talents could go very far in the service today.'

She took his hand.

'I know,' she replied. 'But I'm very happy doing what I'm doing. And I'm not sure I could bring myself to get as close to the dark side as others can.'

'You would protect your country if you had to,' he replied, 'just as your father did.'

'I think I'm already doing that,' Julia said.

PART TWO

15

'May it please your Lordship, members of the jury, my name is Ben Schroeder, and I appear to prosecute this case with my learned friend Miss Virginia Castle. My learned friend Mr Anthony Norris appears for the defendant, Father Desmond Gerrard.'

It was an opening speech, and indeed a trial, that had given Ben some sleepless nights. Neither he nor Ginny Castle had prosecuted before, and although they were both seasoned trial lawyers, the prospect of taking the lead and carrying the burden of proof, arguing a case from the other side, was a new one. As Andrew Pilkington had predicted, his trial schedule was too heavy to let him remain active in the case. He had been embroiled in a fraud in an adjoining court that had already run for three weeks and had at least another three to go, and he had delegated the trial to his colleagues with a smile that said, 'Now you can see what it's like on my side.' 'Nothing to worry about,' he had added, 'John will be sitting behind you. He's done hundreds of cases sitting behind counsel. If there's anything you need, just ask him.' John Caswell's presence was indeed reassuring, Ben reflected, but he also noticed that the Deputy Director couldn't resist the occasional grin at the expense of his nervous prosecutorial neophytes.

More disturbing was the choice of Anthony Norris to represent Father Gerrard. Although John Singer had handed the case over soon after his client's arrest, he had handed it over to Thomas Watson and Co, an aggressive firm of South London solicitors.

Thomas Watson had instructed Anthony Norris, but Ben suspected that he had been Singer's suggestion. If so, Ben could not help seeing it as a deliberate provocation. Anthony Norris was a senior member of Ben's chambers, who had a reputation at the bar for arrogance and a painfully direct style of advocacy, a barrister who paid little deference to clients, witnesses, or judges. When Ben had applied to join chambers, Norris had openly opposed him, giving as his reason Ben's Jewish origins. Norris was possessed of a malicious, wanton sense of humour, and was quite capable of saying such grotesque things with a straight face, as his idea of a joke; and no one ever knew how seriously to take him. Norris had relented only when fate left him little option: as fate would have it, Ben had won his first jury trial, a rape case at the Old Bailey, instructed by the firm of solicitors that was the source of most of Norris's work at the bar – while Norris was away on a skiing holiday. Norris had good reason to be very grateful to Ben; and indeed, he had since apologised and behaved in a civilised way towards him. But Ben would always remain wary of him, and in a sensitive case such as this, Anthony Norris was the last person he wanted on the other side.

Fortunately, there was also one ray of light: the judge assigned to the trial, Her Honour Judge Rees, a lifelong friend of Ben's head of chambers, Gareth Morgan-Davies QC, and a fellow Welsh exile. It was not unknown for the two to be seen together at Cardiff Arms Park on international days. Delyth Rees had recently been appointed a judge at the Old Bailey after a career as a London stipendiary magistrate. In that capacity, she had gained a reputation as a competent, plain-spoken, no-nonsense tribunal, a reputation she was already consolidating as a judge. The case cried out for a woman judge, and if there was one judge who would not be intimidated by Anthony Norris, Ginny suggested to Ben with a smile when her assignment to the case was announced, it would be Delyth Rees.

Nonetheless, a hard road lay ahead, and Ben was relieved when Judge Rees's previous trial overran, and she was unable to start the trial of Father Gerrard until two o'clock. There would be ample time for Ben's opening speech, but he was hopeful that he could persuade the judge not to make Emily Marshall, Girl A, begin her evidence that afternoon, with the strong probability that she would have to return the next day to complete it. With any luck, and a prompt start the next morning, they would have her evidence finished in one session of the court.

'This will be a distressing and difficult case, members of the jury. There's no way around that fact, and we may as well confront it immediately. I'm sure that was obvious to you when the learned clerk read the indictment to you just a few minutes ago. You have it in front of you. It contains four counts. Count one alleges that between 1972 and 1974 the defendant conspired with others unknown to commit indecent assault against young girls, girls between the ages of seven and twelve, including a girl we shall be calling Girl A. Count two is an almost identical charge. It alleges a conspiracy, during the same time period, to commit acts of gross indecency with children, again girls between the ages of seven and twelve, including Girl A. Counts three and four allege exactly the same kinds of offence as counts one and two, but they relate to events which occurred long ago, between 1940 and 1946, and they include reference to a girl who has since grown up to become our Woman A. You will notice also that counts three and four differ from counts one and two in one other way. Counts three and four identify three individual co-conspirators, named in the indictment as Lord AB, Sir CD, and the Right Reverend EF, in addition to the others unknown.

'In a nutshell, members of the jury, the Crown say that this defendant, Father Desmond Gerrard, over many years, abused his position as headmaster of a boarding school, by facilitating access to his female pupils aged between seven and twelve for men who derived sexual satisfaction from touching little girls in that age group indecently. From at least the early 1940s, the Crown say, Father Gerrard made available young girls entrusted to his care to be molested by members of a paedophile group which he sponsored and facilitated on the premises of his school. He caused those young girls to suffer an unimaginably terrifying and humiliating ordeal, the consequences of which haunt them to this day, and will no doubt remain with them for the rest of their lives.

'The school concerned was the Lancelot Andrewes School, a boarding school open to both boys and girls, situated near Ely in Cambridgeshire. Father Gerrard, an ordained Anglican priest, was its headmaster between 1936 and his arrest, earlier this year. The group of men for whom he provided this service included men prominent in public life, including those named in counts three and four.'

Ben looked across to the bench. 'My Lady, I'm told there is no dispute. With your Ladyship's leave, I will provide the jury with a plan of Lancelot Andrewes School.'

'No objection,' Anthony Norris said in a disinterested tone, without looking up.

'I'm obliged. With the usher's assistance...'

Geoffrey, the tall, silver-haired usher, wearing a black gown over a pristine charcoal-grey suit, a starched white shirt, and a dark blue tie emblazoned with the coat of arms of the City of London, collected six copies of the plan from Ben and distributed them to the jury, one between two.

'As you will see, it is a very large building, consisting of six floors. The first page of the plan shows the front of the school. You will notice that the left of the building, as we look at it, houses the girls' school – with which we are mainly concerned – while the right side houses the boys' school. Moving on, the plan then devotes one page to each floor. If we go through it quickly, you will see that the first floor consists of what we might call the school's public rooms – the business office and the headmaster's study. You will see those areas marked. Next to the headmaster's study, off to the right as we look at it, is a room which will feature a good deal in this case. That is the headmaster's private library, and it is the room, the Crown say, in which the indecent assaults and acts of indecency occurred.

'The second, third and fourth floors house the classrooms, and, towards the centre of the building, so as to be readily accessible to both, some facilities shared between the two schools, the assembly hall, the gymnasium and the science laboratories. The fifth and sixth floors house the living quarters for pupils who board – some, of course, are day boys and girls, but if they board, this is where they live, in dormitories of twelve for the younger girls, and study bedrooms for the older girls, those in the sixth form. Some members of the teaching staff also live in, as did Father Gerrard, and the staff living accommodation is also on the sixth floor.'

He paused for a sip of water.

'You will hear, members of the jury, that on certain evenings, Father Gerrard would select one girl from one of the dormitories, at about eight thirty in the evening, after lights out, when the only member of staff available would be the duty staff member, who was expected to remain in the staff room on the fourth floor in case she was needed if a girl became ill. How often this happened, and over what period of time it went on, the prosecution cannot say with any real certainty. Because only one girl was taken at a time, from only one dormitory at a time, that is not something we can be absolutely precise about. And because the events in relation to counts three and four occurred some thirty years ago, I'm sure you will understand that our witnesses cannot be expected to remember every detail. But we do expect to prove that this went on with some frequency over the years, at least from the early 1940s onwards.

'You will hear that Father Gerrard would make the girl accompany him, dressed only in her nightdress and in her bare feet. He would lead her down the staircases between the boys' school and the girls' school, to his private library on the ground floor. In this windowless room, with book cases around the walls, and furniture that would not be out of place in a gentleman's club, men – two or three at a time – would be waiting, drinking and smoking, for the girl Father Gerrard had selected for them. When Father Gerrard brought her into the library, these men would reach under her nightdress, fondle her private parts, and insert their fingers into her vagina. While doing so, the men would touch their penises, either through their trousers, or having taken their penises out of their trousers.'

He paused, and allowed the jury a moment or two, taking another sip of water.

'Members of the jury, in law, the Crown say, those acts amounted to acts of indecent assault, and acts of indecency with a child. Her Ladyship will direct you later in the trial about the law, and about the verdicts you will be asked to return, and you must take the law from her. So, I will not dwell on it now. But I do wish to make this clear: we do not suggest that Father Gerrard himself ever touched the girls in a sexual way. The Crown say that his role was as the broker and facilitator of the offences. He provided the service. He provided the girls, the drinks, and a private place, in which the men he invited were free to molest the girls without being disturbed. He was present throughout the molestation.

'But I hope you will agree, members of the jury, that even if he did not touch the girls himself, Father Gerrard's role was just as central to the commission of these offences as if he had; and it is for that reason that he is charged with conspiracy to commit the offences. Her Ladyship will explain to you that a conspiracy is no more than an agreement between two or more persons: either an agreement unlawful in itself, or an agreement, the performance of which necessarily involves the commission of a criminal offence. We say that Father Gerrard was undoubtedly a party to at least one conspiracy, as set out in the indictment.

'Who were the other men involved, and what, if anything, did they give Father Gerrard in return for facilitating this paedophile ring, of which they were part? In relation to counts one and two, members of the jury, the Crown is unable to identify any of the men involved in touching the girls. The reason for that is quite simple. The men involved with Girl A, on whose evidence the Crown's case depends, wore masks to hide their faces – a sensible precaution on their part, you may think, but one which must have made the girl's experience even more terrifying. In relation to counts three and four, you will hear that Woman A is able, despite the passage of time, to recognise the three men who were involved in molesting her. These are the men named in the indictment as Lord AB, Sir CD and the Right Reverend EF.

'You may be wondering, members of the jury, why those three men are not before you today, together with Father Gerrard. The answer is very simple. While they are involved in the conspiracies relating to the 1940s, counts three and four, they are not said to have been involved in the more recent offences, or in activities after the 1940s. The Crown has taken the view that it would be unfair to those men to try them together with Father Gerrard, and the Crown will make a decision at a later date about whether to try them, and when to try them.'

To Ben's left, Anthony Norris gave an audible snort. Ben ignored him.

'Members of the jury, Woman A is the mother of Girl A, and she will tell you that she had repressed her memories of what happened to her in the early 1940s. For many years, she simply didn't remember those events. And, not remembering, she saw no reason not to send her daughter, Girl A, to Lancelot Andrewes as a boarder when she reached the age of seven. Woman A will tell you that it was only when her daughter told her what had happened to her, that she recovered the memory of her own treatment at the hands of Father Gerrard and his guests so many years before. She will tell you, members of the jury, that it was a terrifying and hugely distressing experience to have those memories suddenly come flooding back, and with them, of course, the knowledge that she had unwittingly exposed her daughter to the same abuse.

'Members of the jury, the Crown bring these charges against Father Gerrard, and the Crown must prove them beyond reasonable doubt if you are to convict. Father Gerrard does not have to prove his innocence. Indeed, he doesn't have to prove anything to you at all. But we say, when you have heard the evidence, you will agree that the case is proved, and that the only proper verdicts you can return in this case are verdicts of guilty on all counts.'

Ben turned to the judge.

'My Lady, the prosecution will be calling Girl A first. Because of her age, your Ladyship will have certain preliminary questions to ask her, and if we were to start today, inevitably we would have to bring her back tomorrow. I am hoping that your Ladyship will allow us to start her evidence tomorrow morning, so that we can finish her evidence within one session of the court.'

The judge nodded.

'I quite agree, Mr Schroeder. Ten thirty tomorrow morning, please, members of the jury.'

'Nicely done, Ben,' John Caswell said as they left court. 'Good opening. We'll make a prosecutor of you yet.'

Ben laughed. 'Let's see how we go before you draw any conclusions.'

'Is there anything you need before we get to Emily tomorrow?'

'I don't think so,' Ginny replied. 'As long as you have someone to look after her, and we have the screen ready to go.'

'All done,' John replied.

In the silence that followed, a woman approached.

'Excuse me,' she said hesitantly, 'but are you dealing with the prosecution of Father Desmond Gerrard?'

'Yes, we are,' John replied. 'How can we help you?'

'My name is Mary Forbes,' the woman said. 'I want to give evidence for the prosecution.'

16

'My Lady, the prosecution will now call Girl A. But before I do, I have an application, and I've asked that the jury remain out of court for now.'

'Yes, Miss Castle.'

'My Lady, Girl A is now almost nine years of age. Assuming that your Ladyship finds her to be competent, she will be giving evidence about events that occurred when she was aged seven and eight. Under any circumstances, that is bound to be an ordeal for her. There's no need to make it any worse than it has to be. My application is that she be allowed to give evidence while screened in such a way that your Ladyship, the jury, and counsel can see her, but the defendant cannot. The usher has been kind enough to bring a screen into court, and I understand that she can be brought into court via the judicial corridor, without being seen.'

Judge Rees nodded. 'Any objection, Mr Norris?'

Norris stood at once. 'My Lady, I most certainly do object. It is a basic principle of our law that a man accused of crime should be able to see and confront his accuser. He can't do that if she's concealed behind a screen.'

The judge stared at him.

'Mr Norris, it's my understanding that the right of confrontation is satisfied when the defendant is given the right to cross-examine the witnesses against him. You will be able to cross-examine in the usual way, and you will be able to see the witness. I fail to see how the defendant would be disadvantaged just because he can't see her personally, and I must say that I think his appearance may well be intimidating to a young child.'

Norris turned briefly to look at his client in the dock.

'Forgive me for pointing this out, my Lady, but Father Gerrard is in fact properly dressed as a priest. He is wearing a black cassock.'

'And a massive crucifix.'

Norris positively threw his notebook down on to the bench in front of him.

'It's not proper for your Ladyship to criticise a defendant for attending court properly dressed,' he insisted.

'Sit down, Mr Norris,' the judge replied.

'Before I sit down, my Lady, I wish to add that if the courts start to travel down the path of allowing witnesses to hide from defendants, just because they may feel nervous about giving evidence, it's not going to be long before we have secret courts in this country.'

'Sit down, Mr Norris,' Judge Rees repeated, in a tone that suggested that she meant to be obeyed. Norris obeyed.

'Your application is granted, Miss Castle,' she said. 'I will ask the usher to erect the screen, show the witness into the judicial corridor with the court officer assigned to look after her, and then bring the jury down to court. I will rise for a few minutes to allow that to be done.' As she was getting to her feet, she added, 'And I very much hope, Mr Norris, that you will bear in mind the age of the witness you are going to cross-examine.'

Norris gave her his most insincere smile. 'Of course, my Lady. I wouldn't dream of being mean or unpleasant to a child. I've been doing this long enough to know that juries don't like it.'

After the judge had risen, Ginny shook her head and turned to Ben.

'What is his problem, for God's sake?'

'I wish I knew,' Ben replied.

Emily was brought into court with judge and jury already in place, by a female usher. The usher sat Emily in a chair behind the screen and took her own seat next to Emily.

Judge Rees smiled.

'As you know, we're going to call you Girl A. That's not as pretty as your real name, is it?'

Emily, and the jury, laughed.

'No.'

'No, of course not. It won't be for long, just long enough for you to give evidence, and then you can have your name back again.'

'Thank you.'

'Girl A, do you know the difference between telling the truth and telling lies?'

'Yes.'

'Can you tell me in your own words what the difference is?'

'Telling the truth means telling someone what really happened.'

'I see. Whereas telling lies means…?'

'Telling lies means making something up, that didn't really happen.'

'And if someone asks you to tell them about something important that happened, what's the right thing to do? Would it be to tell the truth, or to tell lies?'

'To tell the truth.'

'Why?'

'Because it's important to know what really happened.'

'Very good,' the judge said. 'Girl A, you know you're in a court of law today, don't you?'

'Yes.'

'Do you understand why you're here?'

'Yes. To tell you what Father Gerrard did at school.'

'*Allegedly* did,' Norris muttered, just loudly enough to be heard.

Judge Rees fixed him in her gaze and pointed a warning finger.

'That's quite right,' she replied. 'And do you understand why it's especially important to tell the truth in a court of law?'

'Yes, because somebody might be punished, and they shouldn't be punished for something they didn't do.'

'Very good, Girl A. Do you know what happens to people who don't tell the truth in a court of law?'

'They can be punished, too.'

Judge Rees nodded. 'Does either side wish to address me?'

'My Lady, I submit that Girl A is plainly a competent witness,' Ginny replied, 'and that she ought to be permitted to take the oath.'

'I note,' Norris said, 'that your Ladyship omitted to ask the witness whether or not she believes in God, in relation to being punished for breaking the oath. Given that we have a priest as a defendant, I would have thought it might be pertinent.'

The judge looked at both counsel in astonishment. Ginny stood.

'I believe that practice went out of fashion at some time during the late eighteenth century,' she observed.

'It's certainly out of fashion in my court,' Judge Rees replied, with some venom.

Norris had resumed his seat with a smirk on his face.

'I do,' Emily said quietly.

'I'm sorry, what was that?' the judge asked.

'I do believe in God, my Lady.'

'Thank you, Girl A,' Judge Rees said. 'I am more than satisfied that the witness understands, not only the difference between telling the truth and telling lies, but also the particular importance of speaking the truth in a court of law. She is, therefore, competent to give evidence. There is a further question of whether she should give evidence under oath, or unsworn under the Children and Young Persons Act 1933. In this case, it may make little difference in practice: as she is complaining of sexual offences, her evidence will require corroboration in any event. But as I am fully satisfied that she is capable of giving evidence under oath, I shall permit her to do so.'

17

'Girl A,' Ginny began after Emily had read the oath faultlessly from the card handed to her by Geoffrey, 'I must ask you this, first. Will you look at the card the usher is going to show you? Is that your name written on the card? Is it correct? No one else will see it. It's just for the court's use, so that the judge knows who you are.'

'Yes. It's right.'

'Thank you. How old are you now?'

'I'm eight, almost nine.'

'And do you live with your mum and dad, not very far from Lancelot Andrewes School?'

'Yes.'

'When you were seven years old, did you start at Lancelot Andrewes as a boarder?'

'Yes.'

'Was it your idea to be a boarder, or your mum and dad's? You live near enough to be a day girl, don't you?'

'Yes. I said I wanted to board.'

'Why was that?'

'There are a lot of games and activities after school, and it's easier to join in if you board.'

'What kind of games do you like?'

'I like running, and I want to learn to play tennis.'

Ginny smiled. 'Was it fun being away from home, too?'

She returned the smile, shyly. 'Yes – quite fun.'

'Are you still a boarder?'

'My parents took me away from the school.'

'When was that? Do you know?'

'A few months ago: when I told them about Father Gerrard.'

'Tell us about what life was like as a boarder. Where did you sleep and do your homework?'

'We slept in dorms, and there was an area by your bed where you could do homework.'

'How many girls were in a dorm?'

'Twelve.'

'All about the same age?'

'Most of the girls were the same age, but there would be one or two a bit older, who were sort of in charge.'

'To make sure you didn't get too noisy?' Ginny asked with a smile.

'Yes.'

'I'm sure that was just as well.'

She laughed. 'Yes.'

'And was there a particular time for lights out at night?'

'They rang the bell at half past seven for girls my age. That meant that you had to have finished your homework. Then you could read or write letters until quarter past eight, but you had to be washed and in bed by half past eight. It was later if you were there at weekends. Then you could stay up until nine, or even a bit later, and no one minded.'

'I see. But during the week, bed by half past eight?'

'Yes.'

'All right. Now, did anyone ever come into your dorm after lights out?'

She hesitated and replied more quietly. 'Yes.'

'Louder, please,' Norris intervened.

'Mr Norris,' Judge Rees replied, 'kindly address any remarks you may have to the court, not to the witness.'

'All I'm saying is that I can't hear her,' he persisted.

'And all I'm saying is that you will address yourself to me.' She turned away from him. 'Girl A, I know it's not easy, and you can have a break any time you like – just let me know. Try to keep your voice up as much as you can. Imagine yourself cheering on your hockey team at school.'

Emily smiled. 'Yes, my Lady,' she said, louder and more confidently, this time.

'Who would come into your dorm?' Ginny asked.

'Father Gerrard.'

'And who is Father Gerrard?'

'He's the headmaster.'

'How did Father Gerrard dress?'

'He always wears a long black... like a dress... I don't know what the word for it is...'

'That's all right: don't worry...'

'And a big silver cross, with Jesus still on it.'

'Yes, I see. What time would it be when he would come? Was it always about the same time?'

She thought for some time.

'It was always after lights out... but...'

'You don't know the exact time. Of course you don't. That's my fault for asking a silly question. You weren't wearing your watch in bed, were you?'

'No.'

'No. But it was after lights out?'

'It was usually before I fell asleep.'

'Do you fall asleep quite quickly once you're in bed?'

'Usually, yes.'

'Good. Thank you, Girl A. How often did Father Gerrard come to your dorm at that time, after lights out?'

She hesitated. 'I don't know.'

'I don't mean exactly: but was it every week, more often than that, less often?'

'Less often.'

'Let me try another way,' Ginny said. 'Between the time when you started boarding and the time when your mum and dad took you away from the school, how often did Father Gerrard come to your dorm?'

She thought for some time, apparently counting on her fingers. 'About twelve times.'

'About twelve. All right. And when he came, what would he do?'

'He would choose a girl to go with him.'

'Just one girl, or more than one?'

'Just one.'

'Girl A, were you ever that girl?'

She did not reply immediately. 'Yes.'

'How many times were you chosen?'

Again, not immediately. 'Four, I think.'

'Take your time. If you can't remember exactly, that's all right: just tell us you don't remember.'

'I think it was four... my Lady, could we stop for a few minutes, please, so that I can go to the toilet?'

'Of course,' Judge Rees said. 'Let's take fifteen to twenty minutes.'

'Is she going to be all right?' John Caswell asked, from behind Ginny, after the judge had left the bench.

'She'll be fine,' Ginny replied. 'She's doing fine.'

18

'Are you all right, now?' Ginny smiled.

'Yes, thank you.'

'Good. Girl A, I was asking you about the times when Father Gerrard came to your dorm after lights out, and chose a girl to go with him. Do you remember?'

'Yes.'

'And you said he chose you – you can't be absolutely sure – but about four times?'

'Yes.'

'Try to remember, if you can, the first time that happened – when you were chosen. Can you do that?'

'Yes.'

'Where did you go with Father Gerrard?'

'We walked all the way downstairs.'

'When you say, "all the way", what do you mean?'

'My dorm was on the sixth floor, and we walked all the way down to the ground floor, to his study.'

'Did you go into his study, or where did you go?'

'No. We went into a room near his study.'

'Was it a room you'd been to before?'

She shook her head.

Ginny smiled, and indicated the court reporter. 'Girl A, I'm afraid you have to answer out loud, so that this lady can make a note of what you're saying.'

'No. I'd never been there before.'

'Just before I ask you about the room, what were you wearing?'

'Just my nightdress. Nothing else.'

'What did you have on your feet?'

'Nothing.'

'I see. Did you and Father Gerrard go into the room?'

'Yes.'

'What did you notice about it? What was the room like?'

She thought for some time. 'It wasn't a big room – not like this. But there were books all around the walls, and red chairs, and a big table.'

'So, a bit like a library of some kind?'

'Yes.'

'All right. When you went in, was there anyone else in the room?'

'Yes. There were two men.'

'Can you describe these men?'

'I couldn't see their faces.'

'Why not?'

'They were wearing masks.'

'Really? What kind of masks? Can you describe them?'

Emily thought for some time. 'You know, like the Lone Ranger.'

'Oh, yes,' Ginny replied. 'He wears a black mask, doesn't he, and you can see his eyes, but the rest of his face is covered?'

'Yes, that's what they were like.'

'Hi-ho, Silver,' Judge Rees said, to loud laughter, including from Emily.

'Yes, my Lady.'

'What can you tell us about them, apart from their faces?' Ginny asked.

'They weren't very old,' Emily replied.

'How do you know that?'

'They both had thick black hair. When you're older, you lose some of your hair, don't you? At least, my dad has. But they still had theirs.'

More laughter from the jury. Ginny joined in.

'I'm sure he won't mind your telling us. What were they wearing?'

'Suits. Black or grey, I'm not sure, and a tie, and black shoes with laces.'

'Did you hear them call each other by name?'

'No.'

'What were they doing when you and Father Gerrard came in?'

'They were having a drink and talking.'

'Do you know what they were drinking?'

'No.'

'All right. Girl A, what happened next?'

'Father Gerrard told me to stand in front of the table where the men were standing, and not to say anything unless they asked me something.'

'Did Father Gerrard ever tell you who these men were, or why you were there?'

'No.'

'Then, what happened?'

'One of the men – he was a bit taller than the other man – asked me my name. So I told him.'

'Did he say anything else?'

'He said I looked very nice. The other man said, yes, I did look nice.'

'Did either of the men do something?'

She hesitated for some time.

'Girl A, do you need a break, or...'

'No. I'm all right.'

'I was asking –'

'The taller man was standing close to me. He loosened my nightdress and pulled it up.'

'Then, what did he do?'

'He pulled it almost all the way up, so that they could both see me.'

'Girl A, what were you wearing under your nightdress?'

'Nothing.'

'What did he do then?'

'He... touched me...'

'The taller man?'

'Yes.'

'How did he touch you? Can you tell us?'

She nodded. 'He put his fingers in my...'

'Don't lead her, please,' Norris whispered. Ginny shot him a look of contempt.

'Do you know the grown-up word for it? If not, use whatever word you would use at home.'

'My... vag...'

'Your vagina?'

'Yes.'

'I told you not to lead,' Norris snarled in a whisper.

Ginny took two steps to her left and bent down close to whisper back.

'For God's sake, Norris. This isn't the time to get technical. You'll get your chance to cross-examine.'

Norris laughed quietly. 'Technical? Oh dear, we are getting fraught, aren't we? Have I caught you at the wrong time of the month?'

She got right in his face. 'Why don't you just fuck off?'

'I only wish I could. This isn't my idea of fun.'

'Is there a problem, Miss Castle?' Judge Rees asked.

'No problem at all, my Lady,' Ginny replied, returning to her side of counsel's row. 'I'm just explaining the rules of evidence to Mr Norris. If you remember, Girl A – and I understand that you may not remember exactly: but can you tell us how many fingers the taller man put inside you?'

'Two, I think,' she replied.

'Could you see whether either of the men was doing anything else?'

'I couldn't see much because my nightdress was pulled up.

But I could see that the shorter man was doing something.'

'What was he doing?'

'I don't know, really: rubbing himself by his private parts.'

'Could you see that clearly?'

'Yes.'

'Could you see his private parts, or were they covered by his trousers?'

'They were covered by his trousers.'

'I see.'

'But another time when I went to the room, and there were two different men, they did take their private thing out of their trousers, and I had to touch them there.'

'I see,' Ginny said. 'Well, let me ask you about that time, then. How long was that after the first time?'

'Two or three weeks.'

'In between your first and second times, were there times when Father Gerrard chose another girl to go with him?'

'Yes, once or twice.'

'And when you went the second time, the two men weren't the same men as the first time?'

'No.'

'Could you see their faces?'

'No. They were wearing masks again.'

'The same Lone Ranger masks?'

'Yes.'

'Can you tell us anything about them?

'They were a bit older than the first time. One was quite fat.'

'And was the second time different from the first time, or did the same things happen?'

'The same thing happened. But also…'

'Take your time,' Ginny said encouragingly.

'I had to touch one of the men's private thing – not the fat man, the other one.'

'Touch it with your hand?'

'Yes.'

'And what happened?'

'I rubbed it for a while, and it got all sticky, and then he took it away.'

Ben was moving closer, to say something.

'I'm sorry, my Lady, would you give me a moment?'

'Of course, Miss Castle.'

Ben whispered for some time. Ginny nodded.

'Girl A, I'm not going to go through all the four times with you. I just have a few more questions. First, when the men were touching you, where was Father Gerrard?'

'I don't know exactly. Somewhere in the room.'

'He didn't leave the room?'

'No. He had to take me back upstairs to the dorm when they'd finished.'

'Did Father Gerrard ever touch you himself, or did he ask you to touch him?'

'No.'

'All right. You mentioned other girls who were chosen by Father Gerrard. I don't want you to tell us their names, but did you give the names of the other girls to the police when they asked you?'

'Yes.'

'How many names did you give the police, do you remember?'

'Three. They were –'

'That's all right, Girl A. I don't want to ask you anything else about that. I only have one more thing I want to ask you. How did it make you feel when the men did those things to you?'

Finally, her composure melted away in a flood of tears.

'Twenty minutes,' Judge Rees said, as the female usher led Emily out of court along the corridor behind the bench.

After the judge had left the bench and the jury had retired to their room, Ginny walked quickly over to Norris.

'If you ever speak to me again like that in court, you shit,' she said, 'I'll put my knee somewhere where it will make your eyes water and make it very hard to breathe. And then I'll report you to your benchers and have you disciplined. Do I make myself clear?'

She walked away without waiting for a reply.

'Is everything all right?' Ben asked anxiously when she joined him at the door of the court on his way out.

'Everything's fine,' she replied, perfectly calmly. 'I just had to sort something out with Norris.'

'I was very frightened,' Emily said. 'I didn't understand what they were doing, and I thought they might really hurt me. And I thought it was wrong.'

'And I'm sure the masks must have made it even more frightening for you?' Ginny asked, with a look in the direction of Anthony Norris that dared him to object to her leading the witness. He remained silent, staring straight ahead of him.

'Yes.'

'After the four times, or about four times, when Father Gerrard took you to the library, did you tell your parents what had happened?'

She nodded. 'I told my mum when I went home for a weekend.'

'Why did you tell her?'

'Because I didn't want it to happen any more. I was frightened.'

'Yes, I'm sure,' Ginny replied comfortingly. 'What did your mum say?'

'She told me not to be frightened, and she said I didn't have to go back to that school. Ever.'

Ginny glanced at Ben, who nodded.

'That's all I want to ask you, Girl A,' she said. 'You've been very brave. Thank you very much.'

'Yes, Mr Norris,' the judge said.

To Ginny's surprise, any trace of aggression in Norris seemed to disappear as he stood to cross-examine. He suddenly adopted his quietest and most charming manner.

'My name's Anthony Norris, Girl A. I'm one of those older men who doesn't have much hair left,' he smiled. 'That's why they make me wear this silly wig.'

She laughed with him.

'I've only got a couple of questions for you. I won't take long. Before the first time when you say Father Gerrard took you, had any of the other girls been taken from your dorm?'

'Yes.'

'I don't want you to say their names, but can you tell me how many?'

'Two,' Emily replied.

'Two. All right. So, you weren't the first?'

'No.'

'And before you say you were taken, did those two girls tell you what had happened to them?'

Emily nodded.

'I'm sorry, Girl A, the court reporter has to make a note...'

'Yes.'

'They told you they'd been touched, and they'd had to touch a man?'

'Yes.'

'Thank you. And, if that's true, you must have known what to expect when you were taken: isn't that right?'

'I suppose so, yes.'

'I'm sure it must have worried you – in fact, I'm sure it must have worried all the girls in the dorm?'

'I didn't think it would happen to me. I hoped it wouldn't.'

'No, but it must have worried you?'

'Yes.'

'Before you say you were taken the first time, had you ever heard your mum talking about anything that happened to her while she was at school?'

'What do you mean?'

'Well, you know now, don't you, that your mum says the same thing happened to her, many years ago, when she was at school?'

'It did happen to her.'

'What I'm asking is, whether you ever heard your mum talking about it, before the first time you say you were taken?'

'No.'

'Are you sure? Are you sure that what you've told us today isn't just something you heard from someone else?'

'Something someone told me?'

'Yes, exactly. And perhaps you got confused and thought it had happened to you? It's quite understandable. Is that what happened?'

'No… it did happen.'

'Is it fun to have a mysterious name like Girl A, and say things from behind the screen where Father Gerrard can't see you?'

'No…'

'My Lady…' Ginny protested.

'That's enough, Mr Norris,' Judge Rees said.

'I have nothing further,' Norris replied.

There was a silence for some time. Then there was the sound of a chair falling over, and the witness pushed her way past the screen into open court. The usher tried to stop her, but Emily was too quick for her. Emily stared into the dock at Father Gerrard.

'I'm not Girl A, Father Gerrard,' she said. 'My name is Emily Marshall. And it did happen. You know it did.'

19

'My first point, my Lady,' Anthony Norris said, when they resumed at two o'clock, 'is this: there's no point in keeping the names of the witnesses from the jury, now that Girl A has publicly identified herself in open court.'

Emily's sensational revelation had taken everyone in court by surprise. Witnesses who were entitled to withhold their identity rarely proclaimed it in the courtroom, and they certainly didn't proclaim it as dramatically as Emily had. It was a novel experience for judge and barristers alike, and Judge Rees had adjourned until after lunch to allow everyone to recover from the shock, and to decide what, if anything, should be done about it. Before adjourning, she had warned the press not to report Emily's identity; but she was not even entirely sure that she was right to do that, and she knew that a lunch hour of work in chambers or the court's library lay ahead.

'My Lady,' Ginny replied, 'it's a matter that each of the witnesses must decide for herself. I will ask Mr Caswell to speak with them in the light of what has happened. It may be that in the circumstances, they will agree to their names being used; but equally, they may not.'

'The jury already know that Woman A is the mother of Girl A,' Norris pointed out. 'My learned friend Mr Schroeder opened that fact to the jury – as he had to: it's an essential part of the prosecution's evidence. So it's particularly pointless in her case.'

'That doesn't mean she automatically forfeits the right,' Ginny replied.

Norris scoffed. 'In that case, my Lady, can we call Father Gerrard "Priest A" for the rest of the trial?'

Judge Rees shot him a disapproving look, but then turned to Ginny.

'Mr Norris does have a point, Miss Castle, doesn't he?'

'Anonymity is a matter of law, my Lady. It doesn't come to an end because my learned friend or I – or, I venture to say, with respect, even your Ladyship – may think that it's no longer necessary. But, as I have said, I will cause inquiries to be made. We shall have to see what the witnesses decide.'

'Yes, very well,' the judge replied. 'But that must be done before you call the witnesses, Miss Castle. I must give the press directions that make some kind of sense about what they are, and are not, allowed to report.'

'I see Mr Caswell leaving court now, my Lady,' Ginny replied. 'Both witnesses are in the building, and I would anticipate that we will have an answer quite quickly.'

'What else, Mr Norris?'

'My Lady, I'm very concerned about the evidence the prosecution proposes to put before the jury. It's unreliable and dangerous.'

'In what way?'

'Well, let's take Woman B. She's come forward at the last minute, saying that she wants to give evidence, despite having told the investigating police officer on a previous occasion that she wouldn't. I've been provided with a statement she's made, which suggests that, like Woman A, she's claiming to have been abused in the early 1940s. The two women were at school at the same time. Unlike Woman A, she says that her memory has continued uninterrupted throughout the long period between the 1940s and the present time, and that obviously raises the question of why she would choose this particular time to come forward.'

'Which you will no doubt ask her about when you cross-examine, Mr Norris,' the judge smiled.

'Yes, my Lady. I can deal with it in that way, but it's hardly satisfactory.' He paused. 'And then when we come to Woman A, there are even greater problems.'

'How so?'

'My Lady, Woman A says that she had no recollection whatsoever of the abuse she now says she suffered, until her daughter told her what she has told the jury today. She was so blissfully unaware of what these men had done to her in the 1940s that she didn't think twice about sending her daughter to the same school as a boarder in the 1970s. But – lo and behold, abracadabra – as soon as her daughter utters the fateful words, she instantly remembers everything in excruciating detail – including the identity of her three abusers, whose photographs conveniently appear in *The Times* soon afterwards.'

'Again, Mr Norris, those are matters you can ask her about in cross-examination, aren't they?' Judge Rees suggested, but not without some hesitation.

'Well, I *can* ask her, of course. But there comes a time when that is not sufficient. If evidence is so thin that it's little more than speculation, it's dangerous to leave that evidence to a jury; and if it's dangerous to leave evidence to the jury, your Ladyship has a duty to exclude it. There's no other way to ensure that Father Gerrard has a fair trial.'

'I can direct the jury to treat her evidence with great caution and analyse it carefully. We do that all the time in criminal trials.'

'With respect, my Lady, that's rather like letting a rat loose in the jury box and then telling the jury to ignore it. It's asking too much of them.'

Judge Rees smiled, but did not reply.

'The problem,' Norris continued, 'is that there can be no guarantee that Woman A's memories are accurate. What if it's her imagination at work, rather than her memory? What if none of this ever happened, except in Woman A's mind? What if her memories have been created, rather than recovered?'

'Created by what?' the judge asked.

'By what her daughter said; by something she once heard

Woman B – or Woman C or Woman D or Woman E – say at some time in the 1940s; by something she read somewhere in the course of the last thirty years; or by suggestion of any kind: that's the point – there's no way for the jury to know.'

Judge Rees nodded. 'Miss Castle, I'm not entirely unsympathetic to Mr Norris's concerns. We are in uncharted waters here.'

'In my submission, your Ladyship's first reaction was correct,' Ginny replied. 'These are all matters my learned friend can ask about in cross-examination, but at the end of the day, they are matters for the jury to decide. There is no reason not to trust the jury to weigh up the evidence and form their own view about it.'

The judge was silent for some time.

'With some reservations,' she concluded, 'I think that the justice of the case requires me to allow the evidence to go before the jury. So that's what I'm going to do.' She looked at both counsel in turn. 'But – and I emphasise this, Miss Castle – I'm going to see how the land lies after she's given evidence. If at that stage I feel uneasy about it, I will discharge the jury and order a retrial – without the evidence of Woman A. I hope that's clear.'

'Perfectly, my Lady,' Ginny replied. 'I'm much obliged.'

20

Audrey Marshall

After Emily's humbling, shaming display of courage this morning, I can no longer be Woman A. I am Audrey Marshall; I am Emily Marshall's mother; I am Joan Patterson's sister; and I am Ken Marshall's wife; and I'm proud and honoured to play, and to have played, all of those roles. My daughter has made herself the conscience of the case. By stepping out of the shadows, she has shown me the way, and I will no longer hide behind a screen or an anonymous letter of the alphabet.

Even before this morning I hated being Woman A. It felt less like a gift of anonymity than a wilful suppression of my identity: like an army recruit, or a prisoner, who must submit to being defined by a number instead of a name. It felt like one more violation, one more assault on my identity as a person. I was anonymous in the same sense I'd been anonymous when I stood before those men in that impersonal grey school nightdress and my bare feet. They didn't know, or care, who I was. If they'd known, I don't think they could have behaved in that way towards me. In certain circumstances anonymity is, if not a necessary condition, a kind of permission for the most dehumanising and shameful treatment to which men and women can be subjected. In a sense, it's the ultimate license to abuse. That's why you have identically dressed enemy prisoners starving behind the barbed wire fences of prison camps; identically naked victims marching slowly towards gas chambers; and identically featureless houses in the dead of night waiting for the bombs to fall and wipe out all trace of the lives that once inhabited them. If you stop to think of the victims as people, even for a moment, you couldn't do it.

I like Ben Schroeder and Ginny Castle: I admire their knowledge and skill; and I'm grateful for their compassion. Their preparation and reassurance have made the ordeal of giving evidence easier than it would otherwise be, as has Emily's courage. But nothing can prepare you for the experience of entering this most formal of settings, in which it is decreed that the ritual of public judgment shall be performed. The barristers you've had coffee with are now wearing wigs and gowns and grave expressions; there is a solemn judge, similarly attired; and there is another barrister, one you don't know, whose job it is to tear you apart, to destroy you if he can – nothing personal, you understand, he's just doing his job, all part of the ritual. Nothing can prepare you for the sight of the jury, twelve men and women – in my case men, by a clear majority of nine to three – to whom you have to speak in excoriating detail of events you have remembered but wish you could forget; to whom you have to speak of things that, if compelled to speak of them at all, you would choose to whisper in the dead of night, over a shared pillow, to your most intimate partner. These twelve of your fellow citizens, who do not know you, but before whom you must stand as naked as if you had to leave every stitch of clothing at the door of the court: which I think, in some odd way, might actually make the ritual of public judgment easier to endure.

I am not on trial. I must remember that. I am not on trial. I repeat the words Julia has whispered in my ear as a mantra, as the usher escorts me to court from the small, claustrophobic room in which I've been contained ever since returning from a lunch my stomach is struggling to keep down. There were some legal issues, the usher explains, without explaining. The judge had to hear from counsel without the jury; but they're ready for you now. Hear about what? Legal issues? About me? I am not on trial. Am I?

Once I'm in the witness box and I've taken the oath, I dissociate by using my mind to analyse Ben's approach to my examination-in-chief. I do this to avoid the gaze of the jury and opposing counsel, and to alleviate my anxiety as far as I can. I'm not anxious about my ability to give evidence, as such. Barristers aren't allowed to prepare witnesses in detail, Ben tells me, in case there's a suspicion that the witness is being coached. But I've had my witness statement to read as often as I've needed to; I know he's using the statement as a guide, and so I have a good idea of what to expect. Most importantly of all, I know I'm telling the truth, which is the best reassurance any witness can have. So it's not a matter of worrying about the evidence itself. It's far more to do with the hostile, adversarial atmosphere in which the ritual demands that my evidence shall be presented.

I release my mind to study intellectually how Ben presents my story to the jury. The first analogy that comes to me is that he's like an accomplished film director, who knows how to use colour and black-and-white, light and shade, long shots and close-ups, and how to increase or decrease the pace of the dialogue, so as to draw attention to the landscape and events he wants us to understand. For example, we skate quite quickly through my early childhood, school and play, my relationship with Joan and my parents. But with the outbreak of the war, we slow right down. He takes me at leisure through my recollection of the nightly air raids, the devastation of the East End I saw all around me, and the curious circumstance of our determination to ride it out at home instead of seeking the safety of the underground stations. When we reach the moment at which Joan and I are evacuated, and (cleverly skipping forward in time slightly to complete the scene) the moment when we receive news of the death of our parents and the destruction of our home, we don't skip a single detail, either of the events or of my feelings about them. I start to wonder whether the camera will ever move on to another subject. But then, suddenly, we've left the war and London behind, and we're in a sun-filled bus rolling though a bucolic landscape towards a new life in a strange place.

Ben wants to make use of me to give the jury a more detailed sense of Lancelot Andrewes School, so he asks the usher to hand me a copy of the plan and a black marker. We begin with the layout of the building, which we take quite briskly, with me marking various points of interest on my copy of the plan, which will shortly be given to the jury. My dissociating mind notes how wise he is to get me physically involved in preparing a piece of evidence like this. For the few minutes it takes, my attention is completely focused on the task I've been allocated, and I forget to be anxious. I find that I can even glance at the jury to make my points, while I'm putting an X here and a label such as 'gymnasium' there. We also move quickly through the daily school routine of uniforms, assemblies, classes, games, meals, homework, and bedtime. But when we come to the arrangement of the dormitory, the girls I shared it with, especially those like Mary Forbes who became close friends, we're taking our time again, no rush at all, making sure the jury has every chance to take it all on board.

Mary, Julia told me before we started, has chosen to remain Woman B. I understand. She has a husband and children in Canada who have only just found out that she was molested as a child, and that she is about to give evidence about it in a court of law in England; and quite apart from the emotional fallout from that new reality, both she and her husband have high-profile legal careers to worry about.

I assume that from there, we may be going straight to the molestation; but Ben understands that every great film has an unforgettable climax, and he's not going to waste his most dramatic scene by screening it too soon. So we accelerate again through my academic and sporting achievements at school, such as they were, and my leaving school to continue my studies at Edinburgh. This necessarily includes my experiences with my boyfriends, and my resistance to their fingers.

My dissociating mind speculates that the jury must be wondering what on earth Ben is up to, asking me to reveal such intimate details of my early relationships. But, of course, every film needs a touch of mystery to baffle the audience until the final climactic revelation, as when Hercule Poirot gathers the protagonists together in the library, or the dining car of the Orient Express, to take tea while he reveals the truth about the dastardly deed. Ben knows this, and towards the end of his film he will step effortlessly into the role of Poirot, and reveal all to the jury. I'd been dreading this part of my evidence. But when it comes, to my immense surprise and relief, I find that these details of my sexual encounters actually have a funny side. It's the language that does it. I have to relive those humiliations using the correct anatomical terminology, instead of the blunt Anglo-Saxon vocabulary I use when I reflect on them in the privacy of my own mind. My experiences sound comical to me when related in the stilted formal language of the courtroom, and that helps me to get through it; though I don't see anyone laughing, or even smiling.

Ben's camera moves on pitilessly to a house in Edinburgh, and to the lifeless body of a young woman hanging from a staircase, as her sister looks on, holding a hand-written note. The visual impact of the scene is considerable, and Ben allows it ample time to linger before the jury. The scene requires little in the way of dialogue, but Ben makes sure that the jury hear my feelings, and my interpretation of my sister's last words; and for the first time, the jury are given a glimpse of the evidence they are going to hear when the scene shifts back, for the last time, to Lancelot Andrewes School in the 1940s, to the evidence that will unlock the mystery.

My final close-up, and the film's drawn-out climax, depicts those long nights when I was taken by Father Gerrard to his private library for the amusement of his highly-placed friends, Lord AB, Sir CD, and the Right Reverend EF. When my memory returned, I regained a clear picture of four occasions when this happened. I can't say on what dates I was abused, and I have a clear sense that the four occasions of which I have total recall are only examples of something that happened to me more often, between the ages of seven or eight and eleven or twelve. I know this because

I recovered fragments of those other occasions, occasions when something distinctive caught my attention: perhaps the aroma of a different cigar or cologne; an unusual brightly coloured tie; or some odd phrase someone used when they asked me about school – which they were wont to do before they touched me, presumably to suggest an air of normality, to suggest that in some sick, perverted way, we were having the kind of normal, civilised conversation adults and children have with each other in a clubby drawing room.

But the four occasions of which I have total recall I remember in glorious Technicolor, and Ben slows the action down, not quite to slow motion, but to a frame-by-frame exposure of this casual obscenity: so that the jury can't help but see the sense of entitlement of those participating in it; so that they can't help but see the gradual wilful destruction of any sense of safety, any sense of innocence, any lingering sense of physical and emotional integrity the child in the close-up may once have had.

By the time Ben decides it's a wrap, I'm a basket case, and I'm sure I look it. Mercifully, by then, we've reached the end of the court day. Anthony Norris's assault on me will have to await tomorrow. Judge Rees warns me in strong terms not to discuss my evidence with anyone overnight, including my nearest and dearest. I'd already heard that from Ben, and I've made arrangements to stay in a hotel overnight, while Ken has taken Emily back home to Ely. I don't sleep well, and it seems no time at all before the judge is inviting Norris to do what he can to discredit me.

21

'Thank you, my Lady. Mrs Marshall, you told the jury that you recovered your memories in the early hours of the morning, after your daughter Emily had complained to you of having been molested?'

'Yes. That's correct.'

'You recovered memories of four occasions when you claim to have been molested, but you believe you were also molested on other occasions, of which you have no clear memory: is that correct?'

'I have impressions of other occasions: fragments of memory.'

'Yes. Please understand, Mrs Marshall, that I'm using the word "recovered" because that's the word you used. You understand that I don't accept that your so-called memories are real?'

'You're entitled to your opinion.'

'Thank you. I hope you would agree that the members of the jury are also entitled to theirs?'

'Yes, of course.'

'So I would like to explore this process of recovery with you: and my first question is, not when you *recovered* your memories, but when you *lost* them?'

'Lost them? I don't understand the question.'

'Well, you can't recover something unless you've first lost it, can you? I'm asking you when you *lost* your memories of being molested?'

'I don't know.'

'Well, let's see if we can reconstruct it, shall we? As I understand your evidence, the molestation stopped, at least in your case, when you reached the age of eleven or twelve?'

'Yes.'

'And from conversations with other girls, you have concluded that seven to eleven or twelve was the preferred age range for this group of paedophiles?'

'Yes.'

'But you didn't leave school at eleven, did you?'

'No.'

'No. In fact, you stayed at school until you left to go to Edinburgh University at the age of eighteen?'

'Yes, that's correct.'

'And because you and your sister had been orphaned during the war, you spent a good deal of time at school even during the holidays, didn't you?'

'Our friends were very kind and we were often invited to their homes; and we sometimes went to stay with an aunt in Northumberland. But yes, we were at the school during some holidays, or parts of holidays.'

'After the molestation stopped in your case, for how long did you continue to sleep in the same dormitory?'

'Until I was fifteen and went into the lower sixth form. We had study-bedrooms after that.'

'So, that's between three or four years, of being in the same dormitory?'

'Yes.'

'With much the same group of girls?'

'Yes. Well, one or two girls would have left for various reasons, and sometimes a new girl arrived.'

'Yes, I'm sure. But you were in a dormitory for three to four years with other girls – girls who had told you that they had also been abused?'

'Yes.'

'Including the girl we're calling Woman B?'

'Yes.'

'During those three or four years, did Father Gerrard continue to come in after lights out and take one of the younger girls, in the same way he'd taken you – before, presumably, you got too old?'

She thought for a long time.

'I don't remember,' she replied.

'Really? Because if he was still coming in and taking girls away, that would be bound to remind you of what had happened to you, wouldn't it?'

'Yes, I suppose it would.'

'It would make it difficult to forget, wouldn't it?'

'Yes.'

'In your time at school between the ages of eleven and eighteen, how many times did you walk up and down the staircases to get from one floor to another?'

She smiled. 'I couldn't begin –'

'No, of course you couldn't. How could you? It was a silly question, wasn't it? But that's my point. It must have been thousands of times, mustn't it?'

'Yes.'

'Thousands of times, up and down the same staircases you used when Father Gerrard took you downstairs to be molested, and took you back upstairs after you had been molested, wearing nothing but your nightdress and in your bare feet?'

'Yes.'

'It wouldn't be possible, would it, for you to walk up and down those staircases without remembering the times when you were molested?'

'I don't remember.'

'In those same three or four years, were there occasions when you went to Father Gerrard's study for one reason or another?'

'Yes.'

'Were there times when you went to the business office for one reason or another?'

'Yes.'

'And on those occasions, you would pass Father Gerrard's private library, wouldn't you?'

'I suppose I must have.'

'Yes. Did you ever go into the private library for any reason, other than when you were taken there to be molested?'

'No.'

'So you never went inside, but you passed by the door many times?'

'I assume I must have, yes.'

'It wouldn't be possible for you to pass by that room without remembering what had happened to you while you were inside, would it?'

'I don't remember.'

Norris paused for some time.

'What I'm putting to you, Mrs Marshall, is that you could not possibly have passed another three or four years in that dormitory, another six or seven years at school, after you reached the age of eleven, without being reminded constantly of what had happened to you in the private library – if you're telling the truth, that is.'

'I *am* telling the truth,' she replied angrily.

'Then, please answer my original question: when did you lose your memories of being abused?'

'I can't answer that. But I'm telling the truth.'

'All right. Let's come to your life after you left school. You gained a place at Edinburgh University?'

'Yes.'

'Your sister Joan had already graduated from the same university; she'd decided to stay in Edinburgh; she was living and working in the city: yes?'

'Yes.'

'Joan, of course, was quite a bit older than you, wasn't she?'

'About five years older.'

'Yes. In fact, when the two of you first arrived at Lancelot Andrewes, she was already twelve?'

'Yes.'

'Beyond the age of interest to this group of abusers?'

'Apparently so, yes.'

'Well, did Joan ever say that she had been abused?'

'No.'

'Did you ever complain to Joan about what had happened to you?'

'Yes.'

'When?'

'When?'

'Yes: when? While you were at school? When you were how old? Or was it later, when you were both in Edinburgh?'

'No, while we were both still at school.'

'How often did you talk to her about it?'

'I can't remember.'

'More than once?'

'Yes, I'm sure it was a number of times.'

'And we can assume, can't we, that if you could talk to her about being abused, you must still have had memories of being abused?'

'Yes.'

'Was Joan also about eighteen when she left school and went to university?'

'Yes.'

'At which point you would have been about thirteen?'

'Yes.'

'After university, you also decided to stay in Edinburgh, didn't you?'

'Yes.'

'In fact, like your sister, you went to work for the Royal Bank of Scotland, and the two of you lived together?'

'Yes.'

'Yes. And one day...' Norris paused. 'And I hope you'll believe me, Mrs Marshall, when I say that I'm truly sorry to have to bring this up again – but as you told the jury yesterday, you came home one day to find your sister's body after she had taken her own life?'

Audrey took her handkerchief from her handbag and wiped away her tears.

'Yes,' she whispered, barely audibly.

'Would you like a break, Mrs Marshall?' Judge Rees asked.

She shook her head. 'No, I'm all right, thank you. I'd prefer to continue.'

'Your sister had left a note for you, hadn't she?'

'Yes.'

'Saying that she was sorry that she couldn't stop it?'

'Yes.'

'Which you, at some point, came to interpret as meaning that she was sorry she couldn't stop the abuse you had told her about?'

Audrey nodded.

'I'm sorry, Mrs Marshall, but the court reporter –'

'I'm sorry. Yes.'

'At that moment, Mrs Marshall... is it your evidence to this jury that, at that moment, at the moment when you found her body and her note, you had no memories of being abused at Lancelot Andrewes School?'

Audrey turned to Judge Rees.

'I think I would like a break after all,' she said quietly.

The judge nodded.

'Let's take twenty minutes. If you need longer, Mrs Marshall, let me know.'

22

'Mrs Marshall,' Norris said when court resumed, almost half an hour later, 'you're just not telling the jury the truth, are you?'

She slapped her hands angrily on the edge of the witness box.

'Yes, I am. Why wouldn't I tell the truth?'

Norris nodded. 'I'm coming to that,' he said. 'Let's go back to the time when Emily told you she'd been abused at Lancelot Andrewes, shall we?'

'All right.'

'Wouldn't you agree with me that most parents, on being told by their daughter that she had been sexually abused, would immediately call the police?'

'I've explained why –'

'I mean, all right, if it was late at night, you might leave it until the next day: but wouldn't any normal parent be standing at the door of the police station first thing the next morning?'

'I've already explained that Ken and I thought we needed legal advice.'

'You've *told* us that,' Norris said. 'I'm not sure you've *explained* it.'

'My Lady, perhaps my learned friend would ask questions rather than making comments,' Ben intervened.

'I'd be obliged if my learned friend would refrain from interrupting my cross-examination,' Norris replied. 'I understand his instinct to protect his witness when she's in trouble, but I'm entitled –'

'That will do, Mr Norris,' Judge Rees said. 'Mr Schroeder is quite right. Ask a question.'

'As your Ladyship pleases. Mrs Marshall: what kind of legal advice did you need before going to the police?'

'We didn't know what to do for the best.'

'Really? Your husband is a solicitor, isn't he?'

'Yes. He is.'

'And you're telling the jury that he didn't know what to do?'

'Ken is also Emily's father. He was emotionally involved.'

'Too emotionally involved to know that it was a matter for the police? Is that really your evidence, Mrs Marshall?'

She did not reply immediately.

'You knew perfectly well that the right thing to do was to go the police, didn't you?' Norris continued, with a glance towards the jury.

'It wasn't that simple,' she replied. 'I was working for the diocese of Ely.'

'Yes, I know,' Norris said, 'and I'll come to that in a moment...'

'You don't know what it's like in a small town like Ely.'

Norris laughed out loud. 'What on earth do you mean by that? Do you mean there are no police officers to report things to in Ely?'

'No. We have police officers. But the powers that be have a way of covering things up. I've worked there long enough to know that.'

Norris paused, leaning forward on the bench in front of him.

'Covering up what, exactly, Mrs Marshall? Covering up abuse at Lancelot Andrewes School? Is that what you're suggesting?'

'No,' she said. 'Other things. Nothing to do with the school. But I've watched it happen.'

'And when you say the "powers that be", who are you talking about? The bishop?'

'No, of course not... Look, there are people associated with the diocese who have a lot of influence. That's all I'm saying. We were worried that those people would put pressure on us not to harm the school's reputation, to make this go away.'

Norris shook his head. 'Is there a police station at Cambridge that you know of, away from all this local intrigue and corruption in Ely?'

'Yes. That's where we went to report it.'

'Yes, you did,' Norris agreed. 'But that was almost a week later, wasn't it?'

'Yes.'

'And by that time, you'd already consulted your solicitor, Julia Cathermole, hadn't you?'

'Yes.'

'And Miss Cathermole had instructed no less than two barristers on your behalf – who happen, by an extraordinary coincidence, to be the same two barristers prosecuting Father Gerrard today, Mr Schroeder and Miss Castle: yes?'

'Mr Pilkington would have prosecuted, but he's tied up in another case.'

'Indeed so, Mrs Marshall. You also got senior Treasury counsel involved, didn't you, not to mention the Director of Public Prosecutions and Scotland Yard? You made good use of your week to recruit a whole army to support you, didn't you?'

'My Lady...' Ben intervened.

'Let's move along, Mr Norris, shall we?' Judge Rees said. 'Is there something of relevance you would like to put to the witness?'

'Indeed, my Lady, yes. Mrs Marshall, when you delayed going to the police, it wasn't because you were afraid that the powers that be might cover it up, was it? Quite the reverse, in fact: you were *counting on them* to cover it up, weren't you?'

She stared at him. 'What do you mean?'

'I mean that, as soon as Emily told you she'd been sexually abused at school, you and your solicitor husband saw the possibilities.'

Audrey's jaw dropped.

'What? I don't understand what you're getting at,' she replied.

'Neither do I, my Lady, frankly,' Ben added.

'Do you not, indeed?' Norris replied. 'Then, let me explain. There you are: a faithful employee of the diocese of Ely for any number of years. You get a reduction in the fees to send your daughter to Lancelot Andrewes. The school induces you to entrust it with the care of your seven-year-old daughter. But instead of taking care of her, the school allows her to be sexually abused by a group of paedophiles, invited to the premises for that purpose by none other than the headmaster. Any school that gets sued for something like that is looking at a huge bill for damages, isn't it?'

'What?'

'You said it yourself, Mrs Marshall: you'd seen them cover things up in the past. Did it really not occur to you that this time, you could name your price for helping the school to cover this up?'

Audrey stared at Norris blankly for some time.

'Are you... are you saying,' she asked eventually, 'that I would use what happened to my daughter to... to somehow make money?'

'I'm suggesting that you and your solicitor husband are both intelligent people, Mrs Marshall, and you saw the potential straight away. You thought the school's trustees would probably cave in at the mere threat of being sued. You thought they would pay you any amount of money to prevent a case like that from going to trial.'

Audrey looked at the judge.

'My Lady, do I really have to answer that?'

'In my submission, my Lady,' Ben intervened, 'no, she doesn't. My learned friend has no basis for making such an outrageous suggestion. It's speculation at best: in addition to which, whatever conversation Mrs Marshall may have had with her solicitor is privileged – as my learned friend knows very well.'

'I haven't asked her what conversation she had with her solicitor,' Norris replied, 'and I don't intend to. I do, on the other hand, intend to ask her what her own plans were. There's nothing privileged about that – as my learned friend knows very well.'

'All right,' the judge said. 'Mrs Marshall, don't tell us what you said to your solicitor, or what she said to you. But Mr Norris is suggesting that you delayed reporting the matter to the police as part of a plan to persuade the school to pay you damages in settlement of any claims you might have against it. That's what you're suggesting, Mr Norris, isn't it?'

'That's exactly what I'm suggesting, my Lady.'

The judge nodded. 'It's a proper question, Mrs Marshall. Please answer it.'

Audrey shook her head.

'I don't believe this,' she said.

'The jury are waiting, Mrs Marshall,' Norris said.

'That is completely untrue,' she replied. 'Such a thing never occurred to Ken or myself.'

'Thank you,' the judge said. 'Next question, Mr Norris.'

'As a point of interest,' Norris said. 'May I ask why not?'

'Why not what?'

'Why it didn't occur to you or your solicitor husband to sue the school?'

'Move on, Mr Norris,' Judge Rees said.

'Yes, my Lady. The problem you had was this, Mrs Marshall, wasn't it? Before you could sue the school, Father Gerrard would have to be convicted in a criminal court.'

'As I hope he will be,' she replied.

'Yes, I'm sure you do,' Norris said. 'Tell us, Mrs Marshall: are you familiar with the term "corroboration"?'

'Yes,' Audrey replied after a pause.

'And before anyone jumps up to scream privilege, I'm not asking you what your solicitor or counsel may have told you. I'm asking for your own understanding. What do you understand corroboration to mean?'

'Then I am going to jump up,' Ben intervened. 'If my learned friend is asking for a legal definition, he is necessarily asking for what she has heard from a legal adviser.'

'Not at all,' Norris replied. 'I'm not asking for a formal definition. I'm asking for her own understanding of the word: if she has one; if she doesn't, she can tell us.'

'Mrs Marshall,' Judge Rees said, 'you're not obliged to reveal any conversation you may have had with any of your legal advisers. If you think you have an understanding of the term "corroboration" from your own knowledge, please tell us. Don't worry about whether it's right or wrong. On the other hand, if you don't have any such understanding, just say so.'

'I believe it means that in certain cases, it can be dangerous for a person to be convicted on the unsupported evidence of only one witness. There should be evidence from more than one witness.'

'Excellent. I couldn't have defined it better myself,' Norris smiled.

'Ask a question, Mr Norris,' the judge said.

'Is it your understanding that the cases in which it's dangerous to convict on the evidence of a single witness include: cases where the witness is a child; and cases involving sexual offences?'

'Yes.'

'Both of which apply to Emily?'

'Yes. Obviously.'

'Obviously. But when Emily came to you, you didn't know whether her story would be corroborated or not, did you?'

'Yes, we did,' Audrey replied quickly. 'Emily gave us the names of some other girls.'

'Who might or might not come forward to support her,' Norris rejoined, equally quickly. 'But they haven't, have they?'

'Not yet.'

Norris laughed again. 'Not yet – and here we are on the third day of trial. You didn't want to take a chance on that, Mrs Marshall, did you? You thought you'd take matters into your own hands, and create your own corroboration.'

'I don't understand what you mean.'

'You know exactly what I mean –'

'Mr Norris –'

'Yes, my Lady. What better corroboration could there be, Mrs Marshall, than for Emily's own mother to suddenly remember that she had been abused in exactly the same way, thirty or more years ago, in the 1940s, when she was a homeless orphan?'

'What?'

'My Lady…' Ben was on his feet in a flash.

Norris ignored him. 'Not only does it provide Emily with corroboration, but it also provides the jury with a fantastic story, doesn't it? Two generations of abuse: mother and daughter, both victims of the same heartless headmaster and his paedophile friends? How could any jury resist that?'

'My Lady, I must protest in the strongest terms…'

Norris laughed. 'Protest about what?'

'That will do, Mr Norris,' Judge Rees said.

'My Lady,' Ben said, 'may the jury please retire, so that I can mention a matter of law?'

'No, Mr Schroeder,' the judge replied. 'What's going to happen is that we're going to deal with this in a calm way. Mr Norris, ask the witness a question, and spare us the emotive language.'

'Yes, my Lady. Mrs Marshall, I put it to you: that you have not recovered any memories – if indeed such a thing is even possible; that you have made up a story designed to correspond in great detail with what Emily told you; and that you have done this in the belief that, with such compelling corroboration, the jury would be driven to convict Father Gerrard – clearing the way for you to sue Lancelot Andrewes School.'

Audrey had turned white, and was staring straight ahead of her.

'Answer the question, please, Mrs Marshall,' Judge Rees said.

Audrey looked at her. 'What question?' she asked.

'Is the suggestion Mr Norris has made true or false?'

She shook her head. 'It is false,' she replied, 'completely false.'

'Anything else, Mr Norris?' the judge asked.

'I've almost finished,' Norris replied. 'Mrs Marshall, not only do you say that you recovered memories of being abused, but you say that you were abused by three men in particular, namely: the men we have been calling Lord AB, Sir CD, and the Right Reverend EF. Is that correct?'

'Yes, it is.'

'And you know that because, rather conveniently, photographs of all three men were published in *The Times* within a short time of Emily telling you that she had been abused.'

'I did see their photographs, yes. There was nothing convenient about it. I had no control over it. Fragments of my memory returned to me over a number of days, and when I saw them in *The Times*, I remembered that they had been there in the library when I was molested, and they were the ones who did that to me.'

'Did your friend Woman B ever tell you that she had been abused by these three men?'

'I can't remember. She told me she'd been abused, but no, I don't think she ever told me their names.'

'So, it was just the happy coincidence of seeing them in *The Times*?'

'There was nothing happy about it, I assure you.'

'Really? But you must suddenly have realised that at least you'd been abused by a very good class of abuser – a peer of the Realm, a Member of Parliament, and a bishop. At least Father Gerrard wasn't giving you to the riff-raff, was he?'

'My Lady...' Ben protested again.

Judge Rees leaned forward. 'That's enough, Mr Norris. I'm losing patience. This is not an appropriate forum for sarcasm.'

'I do have a tendency towards sarcasm, my Lady,' Norris replied with a smile. 'It's a weakness I freely own up to. But on this occasion, I assure your Ladyship, it wasn't my intention to be sarcastic.'

'If you have a question, Mr Norris, ask it. If not, sit down.'

'Yes, my Lady. Mrs Marshall, it could do no harm to your strategy to accuse three men in the public eye, could it – especially when two of them are trustees of the school? It puts the school in an impossible situation, doesn't it?'

'What situation?'

'The school would have no choice but to settle any case you might bring, would it? With the reputations of these three men on the line, two of whom are its own trustees, what else could they do? You'd have them exactly where you want them.'

'That is a disreputable suggestion,' Audrey replied.

'With the usher's assistance,' Norris continued, 'I'd like you to look at three sets of photographs. There are two photographs in each set. My Lady, I will have formal proof of these at a later stage, but I don't think there will be any dispute about them. There are two photographs of each of the three men, Lord AB, Sir CD, and the Right Reverend EF. In each case, the first photograph is one taken in the early 1940s, while the second is taken from *The Times* within the past year.' He waited for Geoffrey to hand them to the witness. 'Please take your time, Mrs Marshall. Look at these photographs, and tell us whether you can swear, under oath, that you recognise the faces in the more recent photographs as being those of the men you saw in a recovered memory from the early 1940s.'

Audrey looked at them carefully.

'Those are the men who abused me.'

'If they may please be shown to the jury, my Lady,' Norris said, 'I have nothing further.'

23

'Mrs Marshall,' Ben began. 'It's been suggested to you that this is all a wicked plot, cooked up by you and your husband to enable you to sue Lancelot Andrewes School and make a lot of money. Is that why you're giving evidence today?'

'No,' she replied. 'It's not.'

'Tell the jury why you are giving evidence.'

She bowed her head and was silent for some time.

'I'm here because, when Emily told me what had happened to her, my memories of being abused returned to me; and I suddenly understood what my sister had been trying to tell me in her suicide note. I realised then how much Emily had been abused, and how much I'd been abused – and how much countless other girls had been abused, and were still being abused at Lancelot Andrewes School. And I resolved then that it would stop with me: that I would do whatever I could to bring the abusers to justice, to hold them to account.'

'Thank you, Mrs Marshall,' Ben concluded. 'Does your Ladyship have any questions?'

The judge thought for some time.

'Just this, Mrs Marshall. Have you ever received counselling, or have you ever spoken to a psychologist or psychiatrist about your recovered memories?'

'No, my Lady.'

'Have you ever been made aware of the possibility of recovered memories being false memories? Not that you're not telling the truth as you see it, let me make that clear: but that the mind can play tricks on us, and create false memories. I wondered if you've ever had that conversation with a professional – or with yourself?'

'Yes, I have. I haven't consulted anyone, but I'm well enough informed to know that there are such things as false memories.'

'That's what I wanted to ask you about. Let me say again, I'm not questioning the sincerity of your belief. But how can you be sure your memories are genuine? Is it possible that, in your imagination, you put yourself in Emily's place when she told you what had happened to her?'

'I have asked myself that, my Lady. But my memories are so clear, so detailed – right down to the layout and furnishing of Father Gerrard's private library, a room I would never have entered if I hadn't been abused – and I've since verified that my picture of that room is exactly right. I couldn't have imagined that.'

'I don't want to repeat matters Mr Norris asked you about, but do you have any explanation for having your lost your memories so completely for so long?'

'I believe that my mind suppressed the memories for many years to spare me the pain of them, my Lady. But when the same thing happened to Emily, it was too much, and the memories returned to me.'

The judge nodded.

'I understand. And as you examine your conscience today, as a witness giving evidence under oath, you have no doubt that the memories are real?'

'No doubt at all, my Lady,' she replied.

'Thank you very much, Mrs Marshall,' Judge Rees said. She glanced up at the courtroom clock. 'You can call your next witness after lunch, Mr Schroeder.'

'How did I do?' Audrey asked. 'I feel discouraged, as though I've let everyone down.'

They were standing outside court as everyone filed out for the lunch hour. John Caswell had excused himself to check on the progress of Andrew Pilkington's case.

'I was watching from the public gallery,' Julia replied, 'and I thought you did very well. To me you came across as honest and believable.'

Ben nodded. 'We knew it was going to be a rough ride, but you didn't let Norris get to you. You stayed calm, and your evidence was clear. I couldn't have asked for any more.'

'I'm not sure anyone believes my memories are genuine,' Audrey replied quietly. 'Even the judge was questioning them.'

'She has to,' Ginny pointed out. 'The jury have to be sure they can rely on your evidence, and it's the judge's duty to make sure they understand the point. That doesn't mean they won't believe you.'

'Do you need to rush off home? Or are you staying to hear Mary and Ken?' Julia asked.

'I'd like to stay, if it's all right. Emily's with friends. As long as I can get back to Ely tonight, she will be fine. Can I sit with you?'

'Of course,' Julia replied.

'Thank you,' Audrey said. 'Would you excuse me, please? I feel exhausted. I'd like to go outside for a few minutes and get a breath of fresh air.'

'So, what do you really think?' Julia asked, as they watched Audrey make her way out of the building.

'She came across as honest,' Ginny replied, 'and I don't think the jury will buy the idea that she's just in this to take the school for everything she can lay her hands on. But we've got a problem with the recovered memory. It's not her fault: there are real doubts about people suddenly remembering such dramatic events; that's just the way it is.'

'But she made a good point about the detail of the library,' Julia pointed out. 'How else could she know that?'

'Yes, she did,' Ben agreed. 'The real test is whether the jury believe her identification of the Three Musketeers. We've got Mary

Forbes coming to back her up this afternoon, but I'd be happier if we had some independent evidence to put at least one of those men at Lancelot Andrewes during 1940, 1941, 1942.'

Julia leaned against one of the large pillars outside the door of the court.

'Since it's just the three of us here,' she said, 'and I know you will understand what I'm about to say: there is evidence to put the Right Reverend EF at Lancelot Andrewes on any number of occasions during the early to mid-1940s. But it's not accessible to us.'

Ben nodded. 'You mean, we'll never get a witness to give evidence to that effect.'

'Not during our lifetimes.'

They were silent for some time.

'That doesn't mean we can't take a flyer,' Ginny suggested. 'Look, we've always known that the key to this case is what Gerrard has to say when he gives evidence. We have a reasonable basis for believing that EF was there. There's no reason we can't press Gerrard hard about it in cross-examination. He doesn't know we have no access to the evidence. He may give EF up.'

'That's fine in theory, Ginny,' Ben replied. 'But I don't think he's going to give evidence.'

'Why do you say that?' she asked.

'How could Gerrard not give evidence?' Julia demanded. 'By the end of the afternoon, the jury will have heard three witnesses say that he took them down to the library and watched while his guests abused them. How can he not offer the jury some answer to that?'

'What would he say?' Ben replied. 'Beyond a blanket denial – that the whole story is a pack of lies, cooked up by vicious former pupils hell-bent on taking the school for a lot of money. And the price of giving evidence is that he opens himself up to cross-examination – when he has no idea what ammunition we may have against him.'

'But he'd be taking a terrible risk, Ben,' Ginny pointed out. 'This man is one of the stars of the Church of England. He'd be giving up the opportunity to tell the jury all about his good character, and his stellar record as a priest and a teacher over God knows how many years. The jury are bound to wonder why. The judge can remind them as often as she likes that he's not obliged to give evidence, but it's not going to matter. They're very likely to convict.'

'All perfectly true,' Ben agreed. 'But Anthony may have advised him that it's his best chance.'

'I can't see it,' Julia said.

'Look at it this way,' Ben replied. 'Anthony's floated the idea that this is all a cover for a planned civil action for damages against the school. But he doesn't have to go that far – at least as far as Audrey's concerned. The judge has already floated an alternative view: she's telling the truth as she sees it, but she may well be drawing on her imagination rather than her memory. So now, Anthony can say, "You don't have to call her a liar after all. You can simply find her evidence to be unreliable".'

'That's true,' Julia agreed. 'It's easier for them to go with him if they don't have to brand her as a liar.'

'Add to that,' Ben continued, 'the suspicion that Audrey and Mary have been talking about this and feeding each other's imaginations for years, and Audrey's dead in the water. You've still got Emily, of course, but if you can't believe Audrey and Mary, Emily's evidence is uncorroborated. So it's not a bad choice if you want to play the odds, and you don't want to risk betraying your high-profile paedophile friends, who may have their own ways of taking revenge if you give them up.'

He paused.

'It's a strategy Anthony will have considered, I guarantee you that: and I'm not sure it isn't his best option.'

24

'Woman B,' Ginny began. 'Please tell the jury when you were born and how old you are now.'

'I was born in 1932, so I'm now forty-two.'

'Are you a solicitor by profession, and are you married with two children?'

'Yes, that's correct.'

'Thank you. I'm not going to ask you any more about your personal details. But as a child, where did you go to school?'

'From the age of seven, my parents sent me as a boarder to Lancelot Andrewes School, near Ely.'

'For how many years were you a boarder at the school?'

'Until I left to read Law at Cambridge when I was eighteen, in 1950.'

'I imagine there weren't very many women doing what you did at the time?'

Mary smiled. 'That's the truth,' she agreed. 'The university didn't even award degrees to women until 1948, and we were still very much second class citizens in 1950.'

'And it hasn't changed all that much since, has it?' the judge asked sourly, to chuckles from the jury box.

'Not as much as one would have hoped, my Lady,' Mary replied, still smiling.

'Woman B, the jury have heard a good deal about the school from another witness, so I needn't ask you in detail about your life there,' Ginny continued. 'But when you first went to Lancelot

Andrewes as a seven-year-old, did you sleep in a dormitory of twelve girls?'

'Yes.'

'And was one of those girls Audrey Patterson, as she then was – Audrey Marshall, as she is now?'

'Yes, Audrey and I shared a dormitory until the lower sixth, and then a study-bedroom. We were – and are – good friends.'

'Yes, I want to ask you about that. Did you become friends early on?'

'I was already at school when Audrey arrived. She came in March and I'd arrived the previous September. She was one of about twenty girls who'd been evacuated from London during the Blitz. We were told to expect them, and make them welcome.'

'Did all the girls do that?'

'Sadly, not. Most of us came from fairly well-off families who could afford the fees, and there were some girls who resented the fact that the evacuees got in without paying. It was only until it was safe for them to go back to London, but some girls still held it against them: that and their Cockney accents.'

'Of course, we know that Audrey stayed on at school until she left for university.'

'Yes: that was because she and her sister Joan lost their parents in an air raid, just after they arrived. That was how I got to know Audrey, really. She didn't know what to do with herself. She seemed so lost and bewildered, and I tried to take her under my wing and introduce her to other girls I knew. That was when I found out what a sweet, kind girl she was, and we became very good friends.'

'I understand that Audrey and Joan would come to stay with your family during school holidays?'

'Yes, quite often. They had nowhere else to go. Well, there was a distant relative, who they called an aunt, up in Northumberland or thereabouts, if I remember rightly. But I got the impression they weren't very happy up there. They used to call her "the witch". I couldn't stand the thought of Audrey and Joan being stuck with her in the middle of nowhere or locked up at school throughout the holidays, so I pestered my parents to invite them all the time. They were pretty good about it, actually. I think they really grew to like them, Audrey especially.'

'Let me turn to something else,' Ginny said. 'Were there ever times when someone came into your dormitory after lights out?'

Mary nodded. 'Yes. Father Gerrard.'

'The headmaster? The gentleman in the dock at the back of the court?'

Mary glanced at the dock with distaste. 'Yes.'

'Woman B, I want to ask you this before I go any further. Is your memory of what happened on those occasions a recovered memory, or has it been continuous?'

'There hasn't been a day in my whole life since those days,' Mary replied, 'when I haven't remembered exactly what those men did to me. I've never forgotten it, and I don't expect ever to forget it.'

'Give the jury your recollection, then, please, Woman B. What would happen when Father Gerrard would come to your dormitory?'

'He would select a girl – apparently at random, although I'm sure it wasn't at all random – and he would take that girl with him just as she was, in the grey school nightdress we all wore.'

'Did he ever select you?'

'Yes, a number of times.'

'Can you give the jury any more detail about that?'

She shook her head. 'I can't give you exact dates. But I can say that it happened to me roughly once every couple of months, starting soon after I arrived at the school at the age of seven, and continuing until just after my ninth birthday.'

Ginny paused, and looked at Ben for a moment.

'Do you know why it stopped when you were nine?'

Anthony Norris had leapt to his feet. 'My Lady, would my learned friend please make sure that she's asking matters of which the witness has personal knowledge? I'm concerned that she's calling for hearsay, if not rank speculation.'

'I'd be glad to,' Ginny replied. 'Woman B, you understand the point, I'm sure. What, if anything, can you tell us from your own knowledge?'

'It stopped after I told my parents about the abuse while I was at home for Christmas. I have a good idea why, so I could go on, but everything else would be what my father told me – it would be hearsay.'

Ginny glanced at Ben again. He shook his head.

'All right. I'll leave that for now. But are you saying that, in your case, the abuse stopped once you had told your parents about it?'

'Yes, that's correct.'

'Tell the jury, please, what would happen when Father Gerrard took you from the dormitory on those occasions.'

'He would walk me downstairs to a room near his study on the ground floor, a small library. There would be two or three men – three usually – waiting for us there, smoking and drinking.'

'What would these men do?'

'One at a time, they would put their hands under my nightdress, as I was standing in front of them, and they would insert fingers – two usually – into my vagina. The man doing this would leave his fingers there for some time, moving them up and down. At the same time, he would be playing with his penis, either through his trousers, or after he had taken it out of his trousers. Actually, all three of them would be doing that, almost the whole time.'

'Did they do anything else?'

'Sometimes, one of the men would take my hand, put it on his penis and tell me to rub it.'

'Would you do that?'

'Yes. I would rub it until he achieved a climax. I'm describing that as an adult, obviously. At the time, as a seven-year-old child, I didn't understand what was going on. All I knew was that at some point, his penis would shrink and my hand would feel sticky. Usually, I was left to wipe it off on to my night dress, though sometimes someone would give me a handkerchief.'

'I know this is a difficult question,' Ginny said, 'but how did that make you feel?'

Mary shook her head. 'I'm not sure how to answer that. I was very afraid, because it was such a strange experience, and I could never understand why Father Gerrard would be sitting there watching while all this happened, without doing or saying anything; and sometimes I would imagine that the men were just inspecting me, testing me, to see if they wanted to take me away somewhere else, somewhere where they could do whatever they wanted to me and no one would ever find me. That's how you think, when you're seven. Looking back now, as an adult, I would say that it made me feel insecure; I hated it, but I felt powerless to stop it.'

'Was Audrey ever taken from the dormitory?'

'Yes, on a number of occasions. I honestly couldn't tell you when or how often. There were other girls being taken as well. But it went on longer in her case, until she was eleven or thereabouts.'

'Did you and she talk about your experiences afterwards?'

Mary thought for some time. 'Yes, we did. But I'm not sure how often, or in what kind of detail. I think I was more able to talk about it than she was. She always seemed rather reserved. She seemed very intimidated by it all, and I can't remember her telling me in as much detail what happened to her. But she said enough for me to know that it was much the same as what happened to me.'

'Woman B, are you able to identify any of the men who abused you in the library?' Ginny asked.

'Yes.'

'Before I ask you to name them, I need to ask you two other things. First, are you aware of the form in which we're using their names during this trial?'

'The initials they're using to hide behind? Yes, I'm aware of them.'

'There are reasons for that,' Ginny said.

'Yes, I'm sure there are.'

'My second question is: how are you able to identify them? You've told us that your memory of the abuse is continuous from those days to the present time.'

'Yes. Actually, I was able to identify Lord AB at the time. I should explain, my parents raised me to take an interest in current affairs. I think they put a copy of *The Times* in my hands before I could even read, and they paid for a subscription for me until I'd graduated from Cambridge. So I've always been very aware of people in the public eye. Lord AB was mentioned quite often.'

'From which I take it that he was one of the men who abused you?'

'That's correct.'

'Who were the others?'

'One was Sir CD. He was a Member of Parliament, and I think a minister at some point, but not one of those who's always in the news. I probably read his name in *The Times* long before I saw a photograph of him. But I saw his photograph, if not during the period of the abuse, certainly within a year or two after it stopped.'

'And the third man?'

'The third man was the Right Reverend EF. I didn't identify him until he became a bishop, which was just after I'd qualified as a solicitor, but I recognised him the first time I saw his photograph.'

'So, this would be in…?'

'I was admitted as a solicitor in 1956, so somewhere in that period.'

'Was there any particular reason why you would remember Bishop EF?'

'He was one of two men who made me rub his penis.'

'The other being…?'

'A man I can't identify. He was present with EF sometimes. They seemed to be friends. All I remember about him is that he was German. I heard him speaking German, which I was used to hearing at home, because my father was a German scholar. But

I've never seen a photograph of him, and I have no idea who he is, or was.'

'Thank you, Woman B,' Ginny said. 'That's all I have. My learned friend Mr Norris will have questions for you. Please wait there.'

25

'Woman B,' Norris began, 'I don't mean to ask you any questions simply in order to embarrass you.'

'You won't embarrass *me*,' she replied. 'I'm not the one in this courtroom who should be embarrassed.'

Norris nodded. 'The abuse you claim you were subjected to must have taken place between 1940 and 1943, is that right?'

'That's correct.'

'You told Audrey about it at the time?'

'Yes.'

'Did you tell her that you knew the identity of at least one of the men who'd been abusing you?'

'I'm not sure. I might have – in Lord AB's case, quite possibly. Not the others.'

'And you told your parents about it during the Christmas holidays. Would that have been 1942 to 1943?'

'I think it must have been: yes.'

'Who was the next person you told, after your parents in 1942 to 1943?'

'Detective Inspector Walsh.'

'DI Walsh? The officer in charge of this case?'

'Yes.'

'And when did you tell DI Walsh?'

'About a week ago.'

'Just before this trial was due to start?'

'Yes.'

'In other words, after telling your parents in 1942 or 1943, you waited for thirty years to tell anyone else: is that right?'

'That's correct.'

'You had never told your husband?'

'I told my husband just after I'd spoken to Detective Inspector Walsh. I would have preferred not to, but as there was going to be a trial I didn't think it was right to risk his finding out from some other source.'

'Why didn't you tell your husband before now?'

'I think that's a personal matter.'

'Father Gerrard thinks it's a personal matter that you're giving evidence against him.'

'Oh, really, my Lady...' Ginny objected, throwing her notebook down on top of the bench in front of her.

'I'm not going to keep telling you, Mr Norris,' Judge Rees said. 'I will not have you making that kind of snide remark in my court. If it happens again, I will consider taking further action.'

'I'm not making snide remarks,' Norris insisted. 'I'm dealing with a witness who's quite content to answer the questions she wants to answer, but is keen to avoid questions she doesn't want to answer. The question of why she was silent on this subject for thirty years, but has suddenly come forward now, is relevant to the issues the jury have to consider.'

'Then ask her about that,' Judge Rees replied. 'Whether or not she told her husband has nothing to do with it. That's a matter for her.'

'As your Ladyship pleases. Woman B, what was it that persuaded you to break cover after all these years, on the eve of trial?'

'I didn't want to. In fact, I told Detective Inspector Walsh, the first time she interviewed me, that I wouldn't give evidence. But then I spoke to someone who persuaded me that it was my duty to speak out, to support Audrey and her daughter.'

'And who was the person who had that magical effect on you?'

'Julia Cathermole,' Mary replied.

'Julia Cathermole?' Norris said, turning to look in the direction of the jury. 'That wouldn't by any chance be Audrey's solicitor? It wouldn't be *that* Julia Cathermole, would it?'

'You know perfectly well who she is,' Mary hit back.

'Indeed I do. Where did this meeting take place?'

'In my hotel room in London.'

'Who initiated the meeting?'

'Julia did. She called me at the Savoy.'

'And what did Miss Cathermole say to you in your hotel room at the Savoy that persuaded you to change your mind, and break your silence after thirty years?'

Mary hesitated. 'I don't want to get her in trouble...'

'You won't,' Judge Rees replied encouragingly, with a pointed glance at Norris.

Mary nodded. 'She told me that Emily was Audrey's daughter.'

'And why would that make a difference?'

She shook her head. 'I'd always assumed – naively, I suppose now, looking back – but I'd always assumed that the abuse stopped with my generation of girls. I'd told my parents and it stopped with me, and I suppose I assumed that other girls would do the same and it would stop with them. When Julia told me about Emily, I couldn't believe it. It had been going on all this time, and no one had stopped it. I was heart-broken, and ashamed that I hadn't spoken out. And I knew then that I couldn't leave Audrey and Emily to face this on their own. I had a duty to speak out, even though it was the last thing I wanted to do.'

'So, it's a matter of principle, is it?'

'Yes, Mr Norris, it is. And if I'd known what was happening, I would have done it long ago. But I decided, after Julia had left, that I had to do something now, even at this late stage.' She turned to the dock, and pointed a finger. 'You don't get to hurt little girls any more, Father Gerrard, you or your friends. This stops with me, here and now. It's over.'

'My Lady,' Norris said, 'would you kindly advise the witness that she is to address the jury, not the defendant?'

The judge shot him a withering look.

'Please address the jury, Woman B,' she said kindly, with a smile.

'I'm sorry, my Lady.'

'Anything further, Mr Norris?' Judge Rees asked.

'Yes, my Lady. Woman B, you're a solicitor, aren't you?'

'I am.'

'So I don't have to explain to you what corroboration means, do I?'

'No, you don't.'

'You understand perfectly well that your evidence corroborates the evidence of Emily Marshall and Audrey Marshall?'

'And their evidence corroborates mine.'

'Indeed so. And they were in need of corroboration, weren't they?'

'I'm aware that the judge must direct the jury to look for corroboration of the evidence of children and that of complainants in sexual cases.'

'And that it's dangerous to convict in the absence of corroboration in those cases?'

'Yes.'

'Did Miss Cathermole tell you that no other witness, either from Emily's generation or yours, has come forward to provide corroboration?'

'She did tell me that: yes.'

'So you were well aware of how important your evidence would be in the context of this case.'

'I was aware that it could make a difference, of course, and that is my intention.'

Norris nodded, smiling. 'Tell me, Miss Cathermole – as a solicitor: what, in your professional opinion, would be a reasonable award of damages against Lancelot Andrewes School for the systematic sexual abuse of two generations of boarders?'

'I'm a commercial lawyer. I don't know...'

Ginny was on her feet. 'My Lady, that is a grossly improper question.'

'It's a perfectly proper question,' Norris insisted.

'The witness has explained that she's a commercial lawyer,' the judge pointed out. 'It's not within her expertise.'

'My Lady –'

'Move on, Mr Norris –'

'My Lady –'

The judge picked up a heavy legal tome and banged it down on the desk, startling everyone in court.

'Move on, Mr Norris. Now.'

'I was going to say, my Lady,' Mary said, 'that I don't know the range of awards of damages in such a case, but I would hope it would be very substantial.'

'I'm sure you do,' Norris continued, 'because you would be one of the beneficiaries, wouldn't you?'

'What?'

'Woman B, has it really not occurred to you, as a solicitor, that, if Father Gerrard is convicted in this case, Audrey's next move will be to sue the school for damages?'

'As a matter of fact, it's not something I'd given any thought to,' Mary replied. 'But now that you mention it, it seems like a very good idea. I hope she does.'

'In which case, you would be the first to jump on the bandwagon, wouldn't you?'

Mary stared at Norris for some time.

'Are you suggesting that I'm giving evidence to facilitate some civil action from which I might benefit?'

'Well, you're claiming to be one of the school's victims, aren't you?'

'I am a victim.'

'Then why wouldn't you join in the action?'

'I find that suggestion to be beyond contempt.'

'That's a "no", is it?'

'I don't think I need to add to what I've said.'

'My Lady, would you please instruct the witness to answer my question?'

'She's answered your question, Mr Norris,' Judge Rees said.

26

'My full name is Kenneth Marshall.'

'And you are the husband of Audrey Marshall, who gave evidence yesterday and this morning?'

'Yes, that's correct.'

'Are you a solicitor by profession?'

'Yes.'

'Tell the jury briefly about your practice,' Ben continued. 'Are you based in Ely?'

'Yes. We're a two-man firm. We do family law, and small- to medium-range civil work, in and around Cambridgeshire. My partner, Greg Berman, also does a bit of crime in the local magistrates' courts.'

'In addition to your practice, have you been involved with the church in Ely?'

'Yes. I was brought up in the Church of England, and I've always been quite involved with the cathedral and the diocese of Ely. I've done some fundraising for the cathedral. That's how I met Audrey, as a matter of fact. She's an administrator for the diocese, and we met at an event at the cathedral. After that, we ran into each other quite often, professionally and socially. We started seeing each other and one thing led to another.'

'Yes,' Ben said. 'I may come back to that later. But for now, I want to move ahead. I think you and Audrey married in 1963, is that right?'

'Yes.'

'And Emily was born in 1965?'

'Yes.'

'How did Emily come to be a boarder at Lancelot Andrewes School?'

'We'd talked about the kind of education we wanted for her. Of course, as an old girl of the school, Audrey had a preference for Lancelot Andrewes. But we didn't see any way we could afford the fees, certainly not without putting a huge strain on our finances. So we were looking at various schools at the time. But then, Audrey's boss at work told her about the special rates available for employees of the diocese, and when we looked into it, we found it had suddenly become affordable. The school had an excellent reputation, so I was quite happy about it.'

'You live just a few miles from the school, don't you? Couldn't Emily have been a day girl?'

'Yes, and if they hadn't given us the special rate, that would have been the only way we could have managed it. But as it turned out, we were able to give her the choice. We left it up to her, and she chose to board. It surprised me a bit, to be honest, because she was always a bit shy, the kind of girl who kept herself to herself a lot at home. But the boarding really brought her out of her shell. It did her the world of good in terms of her self-confidence, and we were very happy about it.'

'How old was Emily when she started at Lancelot Andrewes?'

'She was seven. She started in the autumn of 1972.'

Ben paused.

'Mr Marshall, did there come a time towards the end of January of this year when Emily was at home, and said something that alarmed you and your wife?'

'Yes, it was a Sunday evening. She came home for weekends sometimes. Actually, it was Audrey she told. Emily hadn't been her usual self for some time. Something was off. We couldn't put a finger on it, but we'd been worried about her for a while; so Audrey and I agreed that she would speak to her as she was getting ready for bed. When Audrey came back downstairs, she was crying uncontrollably and shaking like a leaf. It took me ages just to calm her down enough to find out what was going on.'

'What did Audrey tell you?' Ben glanced over at Anthony Norris. 'I take it there's no objection?'

Norris shook his head. 'The jury have heard it all before.'

'I'm obliged. You can answer, Mr Marshall.'

'Emily had told Audrey that men were touching her at school. How much detail she gave, I really can't say because I wasn't there. But it was obvious from Audrey's reaction that by touching, she meant something sexual.'

'Mr Marshall, it's already been pointed out to the jury that you didn't go to the police for almost a week after Emily had told Audrey about being touched. Please explain to the jury why that was.'

He smiled and nodded. 'I know it seems strange. I would like to say that it was always our intention to go to the police. But Audrey has a senior position in the diocese, and it occurred to me immediately that we would be in a very delicate position if we reported it locally.'

'What do you mean by a "very delicate position"?'

'She worked for the diocese and I was a financial supporter. And... Ely is one of those places where everyone knows everyone else. I've had experience dealing with the diocese professionally, and their people have a reputation locally for taking a hard line when it comes to defending themselves against potential claims. I'm not saying they would do anything illegal, but they know how to put pressure on you.'

'But the diocese isn't responsible for Lancelot Andrewes School, is it?'

'No. But it's the same cast of characters. The diocesan solicitor, a man called John Singer, also represents Lancelot Andrewes, and I'd had dealings with Singer before.'

'Can you give us any examples of that kind of pressure from your own knowledge?'

'Once or twice I represented families whose child had been victimised when a priest in the diocese, shall we say, went off the rails. Before I could even interview them they would receive a visit from Singer – as I said, nothing illegal, but his message was always: don't rock the boat; think of the Church; we'll take care of it in-house; leave it to us; Father so-and-so won't be a problem again, we promise. It's surprising how effective that kind of thing can be in a small tight-knit community based around a cathedral. We thought we would be particularly vulnerable, given the close relationship we both had with the diocese.'

'In the light of those concerns, Mr Marshall, what did you decide to do?'

'I decided that we should get legal advice about how to proceed, specifically about how to go over the heads of the local police. I'm not a criminal lawyer, and it's not the kind of thing I felt comfortable trying to do on my own.'

'Did you contact a solicitor?'

'Yes. I called Julia Cathermole. Greg and I had referred a case to her some time before, because she had the reputation of being well connected. Her firm did an excellent job with the case, and I thought, even if she didn't know how to advise us herself, she would know someone who could.'

'And soon after you called, did Miss Cathermole arrange a conference with Miss Castle and myself, during which we met you and your wife, and discussed the questions you had?'

'Yes. And a day or two after that, we also met Mr Pilkington, and two senior police officers.'

'DI Walsh of the Met, and DI Phillips, who is based at Parkside police station in Cambridge?'

'Yes.'

'And did you report Emily's complaint to those officers?'

'Yes, we did.'

'Mr Marshall, did any of that – your contact with Miss Cathermole, Miss Castle and myself, and the officers – have anything to do with any plan to sue Lancelot Andrewes School?'

'No, not at all. It never occurred to us. Our first concern was to protect Emily, and our second concern was to make sure that there was an investigation, to find out what was going on at Lancelot Andrewes. We were completely in the dark. Our only purpose was to find the best way of getting an investigation started. Our main focus was on taking care of Emily. Suing the school wasn't in our minds at all.'

'Now,' Ben said, 'I want to go back to the time when Emily told Audrey that she had been touched. What happened in the early hours of the following morning, at about three o'clock?'

Ken shook his head, and did not respond for some time. 'I've never experienced anything like it,' he replied quietly, 'and I hope I never will again.'

'Take your time,' Ben said.

'Audrey and I were in bed. She had cried herself to sleep, eventually. I checked on Emily, and then I went to sleep myself, and everything seemed normal – as much as anything could be normal, in the circumstances. And then I heard this terrible scream, almost as if someone was taking a knife to her. She was sitting up in bed, screaming, and telling me that men had touched her. To be honest, at first I thought she was having a nightmare, and I was trying to calm her down. But she wasn't having it. She kept on and on, saying, "I remember now". She said that she remembered now that men had been touching her.'

'She told you she had remembered something about being touched?'

'Yes.'

'Did she give you any more detail about what she had remembered?'

'Not that night. She was too distressed. She was making herself ill. She had to run to the bathroom once or twice. In the end, I had to call our doctor to come round and sedate her. There was nothing else I could do. As time went by, and she calmed down, she did gradually tell me what she remembered. She said that –'

'Whatever she may have said,' Norris objected, getting to his feet, 'is hearsay and inadmissible.'

'It may be hearsay,' Ben replied at once, 'but it's not inadmissible. My learned friend has specifically accused Mrs Marshall of fabricating evidence in an effort to create corroboration for Emily, get Father Gerrard convicted, and then sue the school. The jury should hear what she said before she'd had any opportunity whatsoever to concoct such a devious plan.'

Judge Rees nodded. 'I agree, Mr Schroeder. You may answer, Mr Marshall.'

'Over the next day or two, she described in some detail what she'd remembered when she'd been a pupil at the school herself in the early 1940s.'

Norris stood again. 'If it was a day or two later,' he objected, 'she'd had every opportunity to think about corroboration, as had this witness.'

'That will be a matter for the jury to decide, Mr Norris,' the judge replied. 'You will have your chance to cross-examine. Continue, please, Mr Marshall.'

'My Lady, she told me that she remembered at least four occasions when Father Gerrard had taken her from her dormitory to another room, where she was touched in a sexual way by two or three men.'

'And did she, on later occasions,' Ben asked, 'tell you that she had identified one or more of the men who had touched her?'

'Yes. I know this was as a result of seeing some photographs in *The Times*. I wasn't present when she first saw the pictures, but she showed each of them to me later, and in each case, she told me that she remembered that man in the photograph as one of the abusers.'

'Who did she identify to you in this way?'

'Lord AB, Sir CD and Bishop EF.'

'Thank you, Mr Marshall. Finally, I would like to return to the time when you and Audrey were dating, between 1960 and 1963. I'm sorry if you find this embarrassing, but it may be of some importance.'

'I understand.'

'Thank you. In the course of your getting to know each other sexually, did anything happen that struck you as strange?'

He smiled. 'I think it struck both of us as strange. Neither of us had any particular sexual inhibitions; we were quite open and free with each other. But there was something she couldn't bring herself to let me do for her – not at first, anyway.'

'Would you mind telling the jury what that was?'

'She wouldn't let me put my fingers inside her.'

'I'm sorry to press you, Mr Marshall, but it may be important. When you say, "inside her", what do you mean?'

'I'm sorry. Inside her vagina. Anything else wasn't a problem; it was just that one thing. I couldn't understand it, and she couldn't understand it any more than I could. Looking back on it now, it all seems so obvious... but at the time, as I say, it was a bit of a mystery.'

'How did her unwillingness to allow this one thing manifest itself?'

'She would push my hand away, tell me no, she didn't like it. Sometimes, she would giggle and complain that I was tickling her. There was nothing I could do, at least at first. She just couldn't bring herself to let me touch her in that way.'

'You say, "at first". Were you able to overcome the problem?'

'Sometimes, yes, but not every time. Often, we just moved on, a bit awkwardly, to another activity. She could only let me do it if I asked her to keep her eyes open the whole time and look at me, so that she knew it was me, and she would feel safe. There were times when that made her relax, and I was able to touch her, and she had an orgasm. I can't believe we didn't work out what it was all about. It seems so obvious looking back now, but –'

'Let's not have too much speculation, please,' Norris muttered without getting up.

'Thank you, Mr Marshall,' Ben said. 'That's all I have. Wait there, please.'

'Mr Marshall, when your wife woke up screaming, you thought she was having a nightmare, did you?' Norris asked.

'That was my first reaction, yes.'

'Thank you,' Norris replied. 'Nothing further, my Lady.'

'That's as far as we will go this afternoon, members of the jury,' Judge Rees said, after the court had adjusted to the abrupt conclusion of Ken Marshall's evidence. 'Please be back in time to resume at ten thirty tomorrow morning.'

She waited for the jury to file gratefully out of court.

'Where do we stand now, in terms of the evidence?'

'My Lady,' Ben replied, 'tomorrow morning I will call DI Walsh as the officer in the case. DI Phillips is also available. Those two officers can deal with the investigation generally. There are other officers who played a role in interviewing potential witnesses. If my learned friend would like to indicate which officers he would like me to call, I will make sure they are available.'

'My Lady,' Norris replied, 'it may be that we can save some time. All I'm really interested in is, how many potential witnesses the officers interviewed. If my learned friend and I can agree the number, I have no reason to call the officers.'

Ben nodded. 'My Lady, I'm sure my learned friend and I can agree on that if we can put our heads together outside court for a few minutes now; and in those circumstances, I will be in a position to close the prosecution case more or less first thing tomorrow morning.'

'As I'm sure your Ladyship will have anticipated,' Norris added, 'I will have a submission of no case to answer.'

'I can't say that I'd anticipated it, Mr Norris,' Judge Rees said. 'But I will look forward to hearing it. I will rise until tomorrow morning.'

27

'My Lady,' Anthony Norris began, 'now that my learned friend has closed his case, and in the absence of the jury, may I come to my submission of no case to answer?'

'Yes, Mr Norris.'

'My Lady, I don't say that there is *no* evidence on which the jury, properly directed, could convict. But I do say that it would be extremely dangerous to leave the case to them as the evidence stands. There would be a real potential for a miscarriage of justice.'

'In what way?'

'My Lady, let me begin with the historic charges in counts three and four. The prosecution has presented the jury with two witnesses, Mrs Marshall and Woman B. The evidence of both is open to serious doubt. In Mrs Marshall's case, she asks us to believe that she spontaneously recovered memories of being abused, some thirty years earlier, in circumstances identical to those related by her daughter. We don't even know whether this so-called recovered memory is memory at all, or simply an exercise of the imagination – and I'm sure your Ladyship remembers her husband saying that even he thought it was a case of a nightmare, very understandable, given what her daughter had just told her.'

'He said that was his first reaction,' the judge pointed out. 'He seemed to be quite clear that he later came to believe that she had recovered the memories.'

'He changed his mind subsequently. Of course, he did. He had to support his wife. But first reactions are telling, and your Ladyship must bear in mind the rather obvious motive both of them have to provide corroboration for the evidence of their daughter. Getting Father Gerrard convicted in this court is an essential step in preparation for their action against the school.'

'They both denied in the strongest terms having any intention of suing the school,' Judge Rees interrupted.

Norris smiled. 'They did, my Lady, and that in itself is suspicious.'

'In what way?'

'Well: why wouldn't they sue the school?'

'Excuse me?'

'My question was rhetorical, my Lady. Why wouldn't they sue the school? It's the logical thing to do, surely. If they truly believe that Father Gerrard has exposed their daughter to this horrendous sexual abuse, why wouldn't they sue? It doesn't make sense not to: and for Mr Marshall, a solicitor who practices in the field of civil litigation, to tell the jury that the idea never occurred to him, is simply absurd. But even without that, they would naturally want to support their daughter, and providing her with corroboration is the best way they could possibly support her.

'And then, your Ladyship must consider what it is Mrs Marshall is claiming. She can't say when she lost her memory. But how could she have forgotten during those six or seven long years after she became, as she believes, too old to interest the molesters anymore? During those six or seven long years when she was living at Lancelot Andrewes School, trudging up and down those staircases every day, walking past the door of Father Gerrard's library? How could she have forgotten when she discovered her sister's body, and that sad note her sister left for her to find? Could she really have had no memory of the abuse at those times?'

'She suggested that her mind suppressed her memories, to protect her; and that a traumatic event later led to their recovery,' Judge Rees said. 'That can happen, can't it? These things can be very unpredictable. That seems to be the state of scientific opinion, doesn't it?'

'The jury haven't heard any evidence of the state of scientific opinion, my Lady, so they are in no position to judge. But that just goes to prove my point. If it's all so unpredictable, how can the jury be sure they can trust her evidence? Mrs Marshall is asking the jury to believe that she had such a vivid and complete recollection that she could later identify the three men who abused her – from photographs of them taken thirty years later and published in *The Times*. But the fact that the prosecution hasn't charged any of those three men speaks for itself. How could they, on that evidence? And by the same token, how could they charge Father Gerrard?'

'But they have Woman B too, don't they?' the judge asked. 'She's not claiming to have recovered her memory.'

'Another witness who comes forward after thirty of years of silence,' Norris replied, 'in her case, after a meeting with Mrs Marshall's solicitor, and after telling the police that she wouldn't give evidence. It's not hard to imagine what was said between her and Miss Cathermole, is it?'

'You're suggesting that she's part of the conspiracy to sue the school, too?'

'I haven't called it a "conspiracy", my Lady, and I do not call it such. A conspiracy is an unlawful agreement. There's nothing unlawful about suing the school. Why are they all being so coy about it?'

'It's unlawful to commit perjury, Mr Norris, to give false evidence to this court: and you've certainly suggested that.'

'Indeed, I have, my Lady. But it's an extraordinary coincidence, isn't it: after thirty years of silence, not even telling her husband, Woman B comes forward now, after talking with Mrs Marshall's solicitor? Yesterday afternoon, my learned friend and I agreed between us that the police interviewed five other girls from Emily's intake, and their parents, and four women who were contemporaries of Mrs Marshall at school: yet with the solitary exception of Woman B, not one of them has come forward to offer corroborating evidence.

'Lastly, my Lady, I come to Emily and counts one and two. Emily was, your Ladyship may think, by some margin the best witness the prosecution has called, a very intelligent, articulate, and brave young girl. And I confess freely that, but for the fatal weakness in their other evidence, she would be enough to doom my submission to failure. But your Ladyship is required to direct the jury that it would be dangerous to convict on her uncorroborated evidence, both because she is a child and because she is a complainant with respect to sexual offences. It would be dangerous in the extreme to allow the jury to consider the evidence of her parents and Woman B as corroboration, when that evidence is so plainly unreliable.

'In those circumstances, I respectfully submit that your Ladyship has no alternative but to withdraw this case from the jury.'

Norris resumed his seat. Ben stood, but after some seconds the judge shook her head.

'I needn't trouble you, Mr Schroeder. Mr Norris, you've made some points which the jury will have to consider very carefully, and, as you rightly say, I will have to give the jury a very careful direction on the danger of convicting without corroboration, and explain to them what corroborating evidence there may be. But, at the end of the day, the strength of the evidence is a question for the jury to decide. You've raised some classic jury questions about the credibility of the witnesses, and the jury will have to answer those questions. But that's why we have juries, and I'm not persuaded that it would be in any way dangerous to allow them to do their job. I shall, therefore, leave the case to them.'

'As your Ladyship pleases,' Norris said, rising to his feet again. 'Before the jury return to court, I should tell your Ladyship that Father Gerrard will not be giving evidence, nor will he be calling any witnesses. I will open and close the defence case when the jury come back, and we can proceed without further delay to closing speeches.'

Ben stood slowly.

'In that case, my Lady, may I please have half an hour to regroup?'

'Take an hour, Mr Schroeder,' Judge Rees said. 'We all need to regroup.'

28

'Members of the jury,' Judge Rees began, 'you've now heard all the evidence you're going to hear in this case. You've heard closing speeches for the prosecution and the defence delivered by polished English voices, and now you have to listen to a rougher voice from the South Wales valleys for a while.'

She smiled, and the jury chuckled.

'I won't take too long, I hope, but I have to sum the case up to you. Let me begin with two important matters. Firstly, what is your job, and what is my job in this case? As the judge, members of the jury, my job is to deal with the law: to decide what principles of law apply, and how they should be applied; and then to direct you about the law. That's my job. You, on the other hand, are the judges of the facts. It's your job to say what evidence you accept, what evidence you don't accept, and what weight – in other words, what significance – any given piece of evidence has. You must then draw such conclusions as you think should be drawn from the evidence, and based on those conclusions, you must say where the truth lies, and you must return verdicts accordingly. No one else's opinion about the facts matters at all – including mine. I don't intend to express any opinion about the facts. But even if I did, or if I seemed to, it would be your duty to disregard it, because that's not my job – it's yours.

'The second matter is what we call the burden and standard of proof. Members of the jury, in this case, as in all criminal cases, the prosecution bring the case, and the prosecution must prove it, if you are to convict. The defendant, Father Gerrard, doesn't have to prove his innocence. In fact, he doesn't have to prove anything to you at all. Therefore, the fact that he has decided not to give evidence or call witnesses is of no significance at all. The prosecution has the burden of proof. If you are to convict, the prosecution must prove the case beyond reasonable doubt. Nothing less than that will suffice. If you have any reasonable doubt at all about Father Gerrard's guilt on any count, you must find him not guilty on that count.'

'Now, members of the jury, please find your copy of the indictment, and let's look at it together. As you know, there are four counts. Counts one and two relate to recent events, based on Emily's evidence, and both allege a conspiracy. Counts three and four relate to older events, based on the evidence of Audrey Marshall and Woman B, and each of these counts also alleges a conspiracy. What is a conspiracy?

'A conspiracy, members of the jury, is an unlawful agreement. The prosecution must prove that Father Gerrard entered into an unlawful agreement with one or more other persons, and that he played some active role in giving effect to the agreement. Those other persons do not have to be before the court, and indeed, in this case, they are not. In relation to counts three and four, the prosecution say they know who some of the others were – the men we are calling Lord AB, Sir CD, and the Right Reverend EF. The prosecution have chosen not to include them in this case. It makes no difference: as long as you are sure that Father Gerrard entered into an agreement with one or more of them, or with other men whose identity we don't know, and that he played some role in giving effect to the agreement. In relation to counts one and two, the prosecution say they are unable to identify any men, because those men who were involved in the offences against Emily wore masks to conceal their faces. Again, that makes no difference. The question is whether you are sure that Father Gerrard entered into an unlawful agreement with any such men and played some role in giving effect to the agreement.

'The agreement must be such that, if carried out in accordance with the intentions of the parties who enter into it, would necessarily involve the commission of a criminal offence. What, then, are the offences the prosecution say Father Gerrard conspired to commit? In counts one and three, the offence is indecent assault. An assault, members of the jury, simply means the unlawful use of force against another person. Touching that person in the genital area and inserting fingers into her vagina may, in law, amount to an assault. In law, no person under sixteen can consent to an assault; and it follows, therefore, that if you accept the evidence of the three witnesses that they were touched between the ages of seven and eleven, there can be no defence based on consent. The prosecution must also prove that the intended assaults would have been carried out in circumstances of indecency. Indecency, members of the jury, means what you, as reasonable and right-thinking persons, decide it means. You would certainly be entitled to find that touching a young girl in the way alleged would be indecent. Indeed, although it's a matter entirely for you, you may feel that you could hardly reach any other conclusion.

'In counts two and four, the offence is gross indecency with a child. That, the prosecution say, refers to ordering or persuading a child to touch the penis of any of the men in the room. Again members of the jury, because of the age of the girls, there can be no question of a defence based on consent; and again, it is for you to say whether causing such young girls to touch a man's penis constitutes an act of gross indecency. And again, you would certainly be entitled to find that such an act would be grossly indecent. Indeed, and again I stress, it's a matter entirely for you; but you may feel that you could hardly reach any other conclusion.

'The fact that Father Gerrard may not have touched the children himself in a sexual way doesn't matter. If he conspired to facilitate the commission of the offences, by providing the girls and a safe haven for the other offenders to commit the offences, knowing what was intended and intending to give effect to the agreement, that is enough to make him guilty of conspiracy.

'With that in mind, members of the jury, let me come to the evidence on which the prosecution rely.'

29

'Let me take counts one and two first. As you know, both counts relate to Emily. Her evidence was that she was taken from her dormitory by Father Gerrard on various occasions between the autumn of 1972 and early in 1974. She was taken after lights out, and was walked down the staircases to Father Gerrard's private library, where men wearing masks inserted their fingers into her vagina, and sometimes told her to touch their penis with her hands. Your first task, of course, is to say whether you accept her evidence. Mr Norris invites you to say that her evidence may be the result of childish imagination, perhaps based on some conversation she had heard at home; or perhaps the result of ill-feeling of some kind towards Father Gerrard. Mr Schroeder, on the other hand, paints her as a thoroughly reliable girl, who was composed and sure of herself in the witness box, and even had the courage to leave her cover behind the screen and confront Father Gerrard in person.

'Members of the jury, it is for you to say where the truth lies. But I am obliged to warn you that it would be dangerous to convict Father Gerrard based on Emily's evidence in the absence of corroboration. You've heard the word "corroboration" used quite often during this trial, and I must now explain to you exactly what it means. There's no magic in the word "corroboration", members of the jury. All it means is this: evidence is corroborated if there is some other evidence, independent of the evidence that requires corroboration, which supports that evidence by tending to prove that the defendant committed the offence charged.

'Because corroboration must be independent of the evidence to be corroborated, what Emily told her parents on that Sunday evening cannot corroborate her evidence. That doesn't mean that what she said is irrelevant. Indeed, the defence suggests that it is very relevant, because it may have affected her mother's claimed recovery of memory. The prosecution also say that it's relevant as what we call a "recent complaint" that confirms the evidence she gave in court. But what you can't do – even though it's an obvious temptation – is to treat her statement as corroborating the evidence she gave in court; it's not independent evidence.

'I must make it clear that, when I say it would be dangerous to convict on the basis of Emily's uncorroborated evidence, I don't mean that you aren't allowed to do so. It's your job to decide where the truth lies, and if you are sure that you can rely on her uncorroborated evidence to convict, you may do so. But again, the experience of the courts over many years, indeed centuries, is that it is dangerous to convict based on the evidence of children of tender years, especially those complaining of sexual offences, without some corroboration. What corroboration does the prosecution offer? For this, we have to turn to the evidence of the adult witnesses, which relates to counts three and four. Some of you may be tempted to ask: but how can their evidence corroborate Emily's evidence, when they gave evidence about events that occurred about thirty years ago, in the early to mid-1940s?

'The answer, members of the jury, according to the prosecution, is this: if you find that the way in which Audrey Marshall and Woman B were treated in the 1940s is strikingly similar to the way in which Emily was treated in the 1970s, you would be entitled to conclude that it couldn't possibly be a coincidence, and that the evidence shows a pattern of conduct. It would be wholly unreasonable, they say, to believe that two witnesses could, quite independently, have fabricated stories so strikingly similar to each other. The prosecution say that the evidence shows a systematic course of conduct, which continued during that long period of time between the 1940s and the 1970s, whereby Father Gerrard would select girls to be touched by men he invited to the school for that purpose; and that the details of what occurred were remarkably similar in points of detail. The prosecution point to the way in which, in each case, the girl was taken from her dormitory to the library; the fact she was dressed only in a nightdress, and was barefooted; the fact that the men were waiting in the library; and that they touched the girl, and induced her to touch them, in exactly the same way. So the prosecution say that if you accept the evidence of Audrey and Woman B, it will convince you that Emily must be telling the truth also, and *vice versa*. There can really be no other explanation, the prosecution say, other than that Emily is truthfully describing her part in a long-standing pattern of sexual abuse at Lancelot Andrewes School, in which Father Gerrard played a central role.'

'Now, of course, evidence cannot amount to corroboration unless you accept it as truthful and reliable. Mr Norris invites you to say that the evidence of Audrey Marshall and Woman B is neither truthful nor reliable. As to Audrey Marshall, he reminds you that she claims to have recalled being assaulted when she was at school, between the years of 1940 and 1945. She never made any claim of being abused until she recovered her memory during that night in January of this year when Emily told her what had happened to her. Members of the jury, you must bear in mind the possibility that rather than recovering memories, Mrs Marshall was creating memories, so that what she claims to "remember" may in fact be no more than her imagination, fuelled by what she had heard from Emily. Mr Norris goes further. He suggests that Mrs Marshall and her husband, a solicitor, immediately saw the potential for a civil action against Lancelot Andrewes School, realised that Emily's evidence would need corroboration, and provided that corroboration accordingly.

'Members of the jury, you don't have to go that far to question Mrs Marshall's evidence. Mr Norris suggests that it is not to be believed that she spent six or seven years at Lancelot Andrewes

School after the assaults had stopped, without having any memory of them; or that even her sister's suicide, and that terribly sad note her sister left, failed to bring back any memories at all. He suggests that, even if you reject the idea that this is all a plot to enable the family to sue the school – even if Mrs Marshall is doing her best to be truthful – you simply can't rely on her evidence. How, he asks, can you account for her ability to identify Lord AB and the other two men from photographs in *The Times*, taken thirty years later, when they had aged and looked different compared to the photographs he provided you showing them in the 1940s?

'You will also, no doubt, ask yourselves whether you can exclude the possibility that Mrs Marshall's recovered memory, in particular her identification of one or more of the three named men, owed something to her discussions with Woman B in the early 1940s. On the other hand, you should also bear in mind the question Mr Schroeder posed to you: is it conceivable, he asked, that Audrey Marshall would have sent her daughter Emily to Lancelot Andrewes School if she'd had any memory of being the victim of sexual abuse there herself?

'Members of the jury, those are matters which you must consider extremely carefully. If you are not sure you can rely on Mrs Marshall's evidence, then two things follow, don't they? Firstly, unless there is other evidence that you do find reliable, you can't be sure that the prosecution has proved the case on counts three and four beyond reasonable doubt. Secondly, you can't use Mrs Marshall's evidence as corroboration of Emily's evidence.

'You must take the same approach to the evidence of Woman B. Firstly, is her evidence truthful and reliable? Again, Mr Norris suggests that it is not. He points out, quite correctly, that at the time she came forward, Woman B had not mentioned having been abused as a child for more than thirty years. It is true that she reported the abuse to her parents at the time, and that it then stopped, in her case, at the age of about nine. But she has since married, and she had not even told her husband about it. Mr Norris also notes that, having refused to give evidence when asked to do so by Detective Inspector Walsh, Woman B agreed when approached by Miss Cathermole, Mrs Marshall's solicitor, who, Mr Norris says, is presumably involved in the plot to sue the school. I think there was some suggestion that Woman B might join in that civil action for her own benefit – a suggestion she strongly denied. I should add, in fairness to Mr Norris, that the word "plot" is my word. Mr Norris did not suggest that there would be anything wrong with suing the school if there is a valid ground: indeed he says it would be the logical thing to do. Fabricating evidence in support of such an action, on the other hand, would obviously not be right, and indeed, would be a serious criminal offence in itself.

'Again, members of the jury, if you are not sure that Woman B's evidence is both truthful and reliable, two things follow. Firstly, you can't rely on it to convict Father Gerrard on counts three and four. Secondly, her evidence can't be used as corroboration of Emily's evidence. So, the evidence of Audrey Marshall and Woman B is of the greatest importance: not only in relation to counts three and four, in which they claim to be the victims of the abuse; but also in relation to counts one and two relating to Emily.'

30

'Some of you may ask: what was Father Gerrard's motivation in all this? No one suggests that Father Gerrard touched these girls in a sexual way himself. The case against him is that, for whatever reason, he made young girls available in the secure setting of his private library to a group of paedophiles – the composition of the group perhaps changing over the years. The prosecution has offered no evidence about what Father Gerrard's motive was in acting in this way. Members of the jury, you may not speculate about matters about which no evidence has been given. No evidence has been placed before you about motive. But the prosecution are not obliged to prove what a defendant's motive may have been for committing an offence. It may assist a jury to know what a person's motive was, or may have been, but it's not essential for the prosecution to prove motive. If the defendant's guilt is proved beyond reasonable doubt, your duty is to convict, even if the motive remains unclear.

'There are, however, two further matters you must consider. Firstly, as I said earlier, you may not draw any inferences from the fact that Father Gerrard has decided not to give evidence or call witnesses. The prosecution has the burden of proof, and no defendant in our courts is ever obliged to give evidence. You may not draw any conclusion against him because of his decision not to give evidence, and you must not speculate about the reasons for that decision. He was fully entitled not to give evidence, for any reason, or for no reason.

'Secondly, it is agreed that Father Gerrard is a man of previous good character. Indeed, not only is he a man of good character in the narrow sense of having no previous criminal convictions, but he is also a man of good character in the wider sense: he is a clergyman of the Church of England who has occupied a responsible position as headmaster of Lancelot Andrewes School for many years, and has a reputation as a knowledgeable figure in the world of education. Members of the jury, it is not a defence to a criminal charge that the defendant is a man of good character. If it were, no one would ever be convicted of anything, because we all start life as persons of previous good character. But good character is important in this way: you are entitled to consider whether it is likely a man of Father Gerrard's character and background would commit a criminal offence, especially an offence of the kind charged in this indictment. You must take Father Gerrard's good character fully into account in that sense, when you consider whether the case against him has been proved beyond reasonable doubt.

'Members of the jury, I'm not going to send you out to begin your deliberations this afternoon. I'm going to wait until tomorrow, so that you are fresh, and then you will have as long as you need to reach your verdicts. I will conclude my summing-up tomorrow and I will adjourn now until ten thirty tomorrow morning.'

Anthony Norris waited for the jury to leave court, then stood.

'My Lady, Father Gerrard has been on bail throughout, and he has appeared at court in good time whenever called upon. Given that record and his good character, I would invite your Ladyship to say that he may remain on bail until the jury has reached a verdict.'

Judge Rees nodded. 'In the circumstances, I will extend Father Gerrard's bail until delivery of the verdict,' she agreed. 'In the event of a conviction, you can address me further at that time.'

'I'm much obliged, my Lady.'

Ben made his way back to chambers and put his head around the door of the clerk's room to announce his return. It was almost four thirty, the busiest time of the afternoon. The senior clerk, Merlin, and his junior, Alan, both had a phone in each hand, arranging work with solicitors and court listing officers, while keeping track of when their barristers returned from court, and when they expected to be available for a new case.

'Part heard, jury out tomorrow morning,' he said quietly, trying to provide the necessary information without being too disruptive.

Merlin nodded, and put his hand over the speaker of the phone on which he had been talking to a solicitor.

'Free next week, then?' he asked. 'Mr Davis has a GBH for you.'

'Yes, shouldn't be a problem.'

On the way out, he bumped into his head of chambers, Gareth Morgan-Davies QC, on his way in.

'How are you finding prosecuting, Ben?' Gareth smiled. 'Going well?'

'The jury's still out,' Ben replied, 'metaphorically speaking, that is. The literal jury will go out tomorrow.'

'Are you going to get him?'

Ben shook his head. 'I don't know, Gareth. It's in the lap of the gods. We might, but it's a close-run thing.'

'It often seems that way from the Crown's side,' Gareth observed. 'Didn't your witnesses do well?'

'The witnesses did fine. Without the corroboration rules, I'd be pretty sure of potting him on at least two of the four counts. But as things are, it's touch and go.'

'It's about time they did away with the corroboration rules, or at least made them less technical,' Gareth said. 'I think they will, eventually. But that doesn't help you in this case, does it?'

'No, it doesn't,' Ben replied.

31

Ben sank wearily into the chair behind his desk. Merlin had left a number of phone messages, all marked 'urgent', in the centre of the desk, where he could hardly miss them; together with several requests from solicitors for an opinion, all marked, 'For Counsel's urgent attention'. He ignored them for some time, turning his chair around to gaze out over the Middle Temple gardens, their colourful beauty rapidly fading from view in the darkening gloom, and the lights from surrounding buildings and the traffic on the Embankment. Eventually he scanned the messages. His wife, Jess Farrar, had called from her chambers, and would he please call her back. Jess had a busy family law practice, and had been in the High Court for the past two days, arguing about the division of matrimonial assets as trivial as the kitchen table, in the case of two people who had enough money to go their separate ways in great comfort: the kitchen table, and other similar items, simply excuses for venting their spite on each other in court.

'Hello, darling,' she said. 'Good day? Did your jury go out?'

'No. It got too late. They'll go out first thing tomorrow morning.'

'How's it looking?'

'I'm not sure. Delyth Rees was depressingly fair and balanced.'

She laughed. 'Well, it hasn't taken you long to turn into a prosecutor, has it? Not long ago you would have been praising her to the heavens for a fair, balanced summing-up.'

He laughed too. 'True. I haven't been able to think of what I'm doing as prosecuting yet. I'm still looking at it more as representing Audrey and Emily Marshall.'

'That's what prosecutors are supposed to do, isn't it: represent the victims?'

'I suppose so. I'm sure I'll get used to it. How was your day?'

'More of the same. We've now got down to arguing over the ironing board and such like. But the reason I called is that I'm going to have to stay late in chambers. Duncan Furnival wants closing speeches tomorrow morning. I think he's as sick of the case as we are, and he's desperate to give judgment and get it over with. Leaving aside the furniture, there's a lot of money involved, and I want to go over the bank records again.'

'No problem, darling,' Ben replied. 'Thanks for letting me know. Take care. I'll see you later.'

'But I wanted to ask if I could book you for dinner tomorrow evening?'

'Yes, absolutely. Are we going out?'

'No,' she replied. 'I thought I'd cook at home.'

'That would be great,' Ben said. 'What's the occasion?'

'I want to have dinner with my husband.'

After she had hung up, Ben turned his attention to a set of papers from Barratt Davis, introducing a new client, a retired surgeon caught trying to import a substantial quantity of cannabis from a Belgian port into Folkestone harbour, aboard his private yacht. His reading of the papers was interrupted by a knock on the door. Anthony Norris entered without waiting for an invitation.

'Got a minute?' he inquired.

'Of course,' Ben said, waving him in.

Norris seated himself in an armchair in front of Ben's desk and lit a cigarette.

'Thank you for agreeing to let the jury hear so much about his good character,' he said.

'Don't mention it,' Ben replied.

'Most prosecutors will let the jury know he has no previous

convictions, but you went a lot further than that: much appreciated.' He drew deeply on the cigarette. 'Which way do you think it's going?'

'I'm not sure,' Ben replied. 'Until your client decided not to give evidence I thought he was probably going down, at least on counts one and two. Now, I think it could go either way.'

Norris laughed. 'I couldn't let him anywhere the witness box,' he said. 'You'd have crucified him on cross-examination – sorry, bad turn of phrase in the circumstances, but you take my meaning, I'm sure.'

'From which, I take it, you don't think he has much of a defence?'

'As far as I can see, he doesn't have *any* defence. But fortunately for him, this case isn't about defences. It's about the rules of evidence, and the science of recovered memory. If Audrey Marshall's memory had been intact from 1940 until today, the only thing I could do for Father Gerrard would be to find him a berth in a prison with a decent library – and away from the general population, who are not greatly enamoured of child molesters, I'm told.'

'You think so?'

'God, yes. Audrey would have him stone cold on counts three and four; and Emily, duly corroborated, would have him stone cold on counts one and two. If Gerrard walks away from this, as I think he will, it will be because of scepticism about recovered memory, and the rules of corroboration.'

'I don't think the jury is buying your theory that this is all a plot to take Lancelot Andrewes School for all it's worth.'

Norris smiled. 'Neither do I. But I've got them worried about whether they can trust her memory. Can I ask you something? Do you think she's right about Lord AB and the other two?'

Ben thought for some time. 'About the Three Musketeers? Yes, I do, actually. Woman B identified them too, remember.'

'All those girls talked to each other, Ben; they were talking in the 1940s and, if you want my opinion, they're still talking in the 1970s.'

'I think Audrey honestly believes she's right,' Ben replied.

'You should have indicted all of them together, you know. You'd have a much better chance with all four in the dock. Whose idea was it to go after Gerrard on his own? Pilkington's?'

'We would still have the same problems with the evidence.'

Norris nodded and extinguished his cigarette, extracted another cigarette from his silver case, and lit it.

'There's something I would like you to think about,' he said. 'It is my considered opinion that there's something going on at Lancelot Andrewes – and it's something much bigger than Father Desmond Gerrard.'

'Oh, yes?' Ben asked, looking at him closely.

'This is off the record, understood? Gerrard is my client, after all. You know what I'm saying.'

'Understood.'

'Just step back and look at it objectively for a moment. You've made a pretty convincing showing that a paedophile ring has been operating at the school, on a continuous basis, or at least on and off, since 1940. You may not succeed in proving it in this case; the rules of evidence may bring you down. But if you leave the rules of evidence out of it, if you concentrate on the facts, it's as plain as the nose on your face. Now, I ask you this: how many girls have been molested during that time?'

'Who knows? A lot.'

'Exactly. A lot. But when Gerrard is arrested and charged, with all the attendant publicity, how many women come forward to assist in putting this evil man, this cassock-wearing godfather of paedophiles, behind bars, where he belongs? Woman B, and only Woman B. And she only surfaces at the eleventh hour. That's it.'

'We were surprised by that, too – and frustrated, obviously,' Ben admitted.

'It doesn't make any sense. There should be women coming out of the woodwork – unless the allegations are a total fabrication, which I don't believe; or there are other forces at work.'

'So, you conclude that there's something rotten in the State of Denmark?'

'There has to be. But let me come to the point. To be perfectly frank, I don't give a damn about Lancelot Andrewes School. What concerns me is the effect this case could have on chambers.'

'What on earth do you mean?'

'We've got into a good rhythm recently, Ben. Our last two heads of chambers, Duncan Furnival and Bernard Wesley, have gone straight up to the High Court bench. The word is that Gareth is going to follow them in a year or two; and everyone who's applied for Silk has got it at the first time of asking.'

'What has that got to do with this case?'

'This case involves people in high places. We don't want to make enemies in high places, Ben. This is not the time. When Gareth leaves, Aubrey Smith-Gurney becomes head of chambers. Kenneth Gaskell and I will apply for Silk. Smith-Gurney makes us vulnerable. He was, or is, a close friend of Conrad Rainer: a High Court judge proved to have stolen money from members of his former chambers to fund his gambling habit; and who killed his mistress and stuffed her body into a closet in his flat in the Barbican, before doing a runner to God only knows where.'

'Yes, I'm well aware of that, Anthony. I was doing a murder in front of Rainer at the Old Bailey at the time.'

'Then you'll remember that there was a strong suspicion that Smith-Gurney gave his Lordship a helping hand to flee the jurisdiction.'

'There's no evidence of that, as far as I know.'

'Two police officers came to chambers to interview him, Ben. Here, in *chambers*, for God's sake: *police officers*.'

'Yes: and three years later, nothing has come of it. Look, Aubrey was quite open about his friendship with Rainer, and he admitted that he tried to find him a way out of the mess his gambling had got him into. But there's no evidence that he went any further than that.'

'They don't need evidence to take chambers off the approved

list for Silk and judicial appointments,' Norris said. 'All they need is a hint of doubt. And, as if Smith-Gurney isn't bad enough, Gaskell had an affair with a client and caused a scandal that nearly brought chambers down – would have done, if Bernard Wesley hadn't worked some of his magic.'

'That was more than ten years ago, Anthony. Kenneth and Anne have been happily married ever since then.'

'That doesn't change the fact that the next two heads of chambers are suspect, at least in terms of the quality they expect for the High Court bench. It could destroy the rhythm we've managed to establish by dint of a lot of hard work.'

Ben sat back in his chair. 'And you're worried that the establishment might somehow be involved with Lancelot Andrewes, and that the case may draw more attention to chambers?'

'I am.'

Ben laughed. 'Well, it's a bit late to worry about that now, isn't it? You and I are both in the case, and the trial's almost over – the judge is about to send the jury out.'

Norris shook his head. 'This phase of the case, with Gerrard, will come and go. It's the next phase that worries me. If you go after the Three Musketeers, you'll be going after men with some seriously powerful friends inside the establishment. Remember, Ben, you have no idea who else may be involved in this ring. If it's been operating since 1940, there could be quite a collection of household names, and the chances are they have the same powerful friends. Lord AB and the other two may be just the beginning: which means that you have no idea what lengths the establishment may go to, to protect them.'

He looked at his watch and put out his cigarette. 'Well, I've said my piece. I must be off. Pleasure calls: cocktail party, followed by dinner at the Athenaeum.'

'Anthony,' Ben said, 'why are you telling me this?'

Norris shook his head. 'Gerrard is a sanctimonious bastard,' he replied. 'I have a feeling he's going to get off – which means I've done my job. But I don't have to like him, and if he does go down, I'm not going to lose any sleep over him. Either way, I'm out of it. I would prefer to see you hand it over too, if it's likely to go any further.'

'I see,' Ben said.

'I'm not suggesting it only for my own sake, Ben. You're going to be up for Silk yourself before too long, the way your practice is going. You're getting to the stage where you have to consider these things.'

'So, I should tell my client I've lost interest?'

'You're prosecuting, Ben. Your only client is the Crown, and you've represented the Crown very ably.'

'Audrey and Emily deserve more.'

'Hand them over to Miss Castle,' Norris suggested. 'She's the type to tilt at windmills, so one hears.' He grinned. 'Spirited girl, too, Miss Castle, isn't she? She gave me a real piece of her mind when I was giving her a hard time in court. I'm sure I richly deserved it. She doesn't mess around, you've got to give her that.'

'Are you finally admitting that there may be a place for women at the bar after all, Anthony?' Ben asked.

'I wouldn't go quite that far,' Norris replied, standing and making his way to the door. 'But credit where credit's due, and all that kind of thing.'

32

Friday 10 May 1974

'Members of the jury,' Judge Rees began, 'I only have one or two more things to say to you. I won't be long, and then you'll be able to start work. First, you may know that, because of a very recent change in the law, a court may now accept a majority verdict from a jury in certain circumstances. If those circumstances should arise, I will bring you back into court and give you a further direction. My direction at this time is that you must reach a unanimous verdict on each of the four counts before you: and when I say "unanimous", what I mean, of course, is a verdict on which all twelve of you are agreed.

'I suggest that the first thing you should do, on retiring, is to appoint one of your number to be the foreman of the jury. Although we use the word "foreman", I'm sure you understand that the foreman may be either a man or a woman. The foreman's main job is to preside over your discussions, and to return the verdicts when you return to court; but in addition, if you have any questions or concerns while you're deliberating, it's the foreman's job to write a note setting out whatever the question or concern may be, and give it to the jury bailiff, who will bring it to me.

'Members of the jury, on any view, this has been a distressing case, and you would be less than human if you didn't feel distressed about the evidence you have heard, and indeed, if you didn't feel some empathy for some of those involved in the sad story you have listened to so patiently. But it is your duty now to put any feelings of that kind aside as you begin the work of reaching your verdicts. You must set aside all feelings of empathy for anyone, and any feelings of prejudice against anyone, so that you can assess the evidence dispassionately and impartially. It's not an easy thing to do, members of the jury, even for those of us who sit in these courts every day; and for jurors who come here so seldom, it is even more difficult. But you are judges now – the judges of the facts – and as judges, your duty is to be fair to both sides. You can only be fair to both sides if you put your feelings aside as you analyse the evidence.

'Now lastly, members of the jury, like all criminal cases, without exception, this is a serious case. There is no deadline for returning your verdicts. By the same token, there is no length of time for which you are expected to be out. Take your time. Because of another very recent change in the law, I don't have to keep you together throughout your deliberations, which means that we will work the same hours we work during trial. If you haven't finished work by the end of the court day, you will be able to return home and come back on Monday morning to resume your discussions. So don't rush it. Let everyone say whatever they want to say. When you're sure you have the right result, and not before then, come back to court and return true verdicts in accordance with the evidence.'

Geoffrey, the usher, walked briskly to the clerk's desk and took the New Testament in his right hand.

'I swear by Almighty God that I will well and truly keep this jury in some private and convenient place. I will not suffer any person to speak with them, neither will I speak with them myself concerning the trial this day, without leave of the court, unless it be to ask them whether they are agreed upon their verdict.'

He returned the book to the clerk's desk and walked over to the jury box.

'Come with me, ladies and gentlemen, please.'

The jury followed, and retired to begin their deliberations at ten forty-five.

'Come on, Audrey,' Julia said, as they gathered outside court. 'It's going to be a long day. Let's head up to the canteen.'

'How is Emily?' Ginny asked.

'Ken says she's fine,' Audrey replied. 'We've finally agreed on a local day school we're going to send her to – for now, anyway. She seems to like it, and it's got a good reputation, so Ken registered her there yesterday, and she can start whenever she feels ready. She's missed so much school because of this case. I just hope we can put it behind us soon.'

'You both did very well,' Ginny reassured her. 'Whatever verdict the jury may return, there was nothing more you could have done.'

'And Emily's a bright girl,' Ben added. 'She'll catch up on school in no time.'

'I hope so.' She raised her hands to her face; there were tears in her eyes.

'Of course she will,' Julia said, putting an arm around Audrey's shoulder. 'Coffee. Come on. It does no good to hang around, endlessly discussing the case, while the jury's out. They could be out for hours.'

'Whichever way it goes,' Ben said, 'we'll get together once they've returned the verdicts and decide what comes next. Just don't leave the building, unless you want to go for lunch between one and two. The judge won't take a verdict during the lunch hour.'

'What do you think?' Ginny asked, once Julia and Audrey had turned the corner.

'Touch and go. What do you think?'

'I don't know.'

'Norris thinks he will get off. He came to see me when I got back to chambers yesterday afternoon.'

'Did he? That was nice of him. Did he also reveal what explanation Gerrard would have offered us if he'd given evidence?'

'No: quite the reverse, actually. He seems to think that Gerrard was up to his neck in it, but he also thinks we have too many problems with the evidence to convict him. He may be right.'

'Do you want to go up to the bar mess and get some coffee?'

'Good idea,' Ben replied. 'I've brought some papers to read. I always do when I'm waiting for a jury, but I don't usually read much of them.'

She laughed. 'I'm the same way. What have you brought?'

'A retired surgeon smuggling cannabis into Folkestone on his private yacht.'

'For medicinal purposes, presumably?'

'Presumably,' Ben replied. 'Either that, or he didn't know it was there.'

'We are such cynics,' she said, smiling.

Judge Rees had started a new trial, a case of fraud involving a number of managers at Smithfield Market. It was not until just after four o'clock that Geoffrey called for all parties in the trial of Father Gerrard to return to court. He brought the jury back into court only after everyone else was assembled. They looked haggard and frustrated: the men had loosened their ties, and both men and women looked dishevelled.

Lewis, the retired barrister who served as clerk of court, stood. He wore his wig and gown, and his manner was formal. He bowed to the judge before turning to the jury.

'Would the foreman please stand? Would the defendant please stand? My Lady, approximately five and a half hours have elapsed since the jury retired. Madam foreman, please answer my first question either yes or no. Has the jury reached verdicts on all four counts of the indictment on which they are all agreed?'

The foreman was a tall, distinguished-looking woman in her fifties, dressed in a dark grey business suit. By convention, once elected foreman, she sat in the front row of the jury, in the place nearest to the bench. She turned to look at the judge.

'No, my Lady.'

Lewis bowed to the bench again and resumed his seat.

'Very well,' Judge Rees said. 'Then, I will release you for the weekend in just a moment. Before I do, madam foreman, is there anything I can help you with, any point of law you're unclear about?'

The foreman smiled thinly. 'No, I don't think so, my Lady. We just haven't been able to agree yet.'

The judge nodded. 'In that case, I will now formally release the jury bailiff from his oath to keep you together. Members of the jury, I must make it clear that all discussion of the case must stop now, and must not resume until the jury bailiff has renewed his oath on Monday morning and you are all twelve together in the jury room. Is that clearly understood?'

She scanned the jury box. The jurors nodded.

'Thank you. You are free to go. I wish you a pleasant weekend. Please be back in time to resume work at ten thirty on Monday.'

Norris turned to Ben as the judge rose for the day.

'Told you,' he said.

33

'Anthony thinks the case is damaging chambers. He wants me to pull out of it.'

They were at home, in their quiet upstairs flat in a huge old Canonbury house. Ben had cleared away the remains of the shrimp cocktail Jess had prepared as a starter, and watched as she took the Dover sole out of the oven and served it with new potatoes and green beans. They each carried a plate back into the dining room, and Ben poured them both another glass of the white Burgundy he had chosen to accompany it.

'Damaging chambers?' she smiled. 'Where does he get that from?'

'He thinks that if we rock the boat too much, the "establishment" – whoever they may be – will stop appointing our heads of chambers to the High Court bench, and sabotage him and Kenneth Gaskell when they apply for Silk.' He tasted the fish. 'This is wonderful. Thank you.'

They raised glasses and toasted each other. She shook her head.

'Ben, the only thing that will stop Anthony Norris getting Silk is Anthony Norris. Doesn't he realise how obnoxious he is? Is he really so arrogant that he doesn't see the effect he has on people?'

'He thinks he's God's gift to the bar.'

She snorted. 'If he's that delusional, I hope he doesn't get Silk. That might really damage chambers. Does his practice justify Silk?'

'I'm not sure. Perhaps: but he's not in the same league as Gareth or Aubrey.'

'You'd have a better chance than Anthony in a year or two.'

Ben shrugged.

'You would,' she insisted. 'And people know what Anthony's like, Ben. You know what a rumour mill the bar is. People know how he treated you and Harriet when you applied to join chambers. The bar is changing, and that kind of prejudice isn't acceptable any more. It's bound to come up when he applies.' She paused. 'You're not thinking of bowing out of the case, are you?'

'Absolutely not.'

'Good.'

'That's what the bar is supposed to be about, isn't it,' Ben replied, 'representing clients who may have cases the authorities would prefer to bury? What's the point, if we drop a case because we think it may upset somebody? We might just as well give the whole thing up. But obviously, Anthony doesn't see it that way.'

'Well, don't listen to him,' Jess said. 'I feel sorry for Audrey. Let's hope she gets a good result on Monday.

'Yes.'

Dessert was a chocolate mousse with coffee. Afterwards they sat together on the sofa in candlelight, finishing the wine.

She kissed him. 'I'm glad we're married,' she said. 'I want it to last forever.'

He kissed her. 'So do I.' He grinned. 'But if it doesn't, I promise you that I will never fight you over the ironing board. It's yours.'

She pushed his arm gently. 'I'm being serious.' She turned towards him and held both his hands in hers. 'I've been thinking quite a bit about the future recently, and I'm just glad we're sharing it together. We're very lucky, you know. A lot of couples don't make it. I see so much of that in my line of work, and I don't want it ever to happen to us.'

He looked at her closely. 'Neither do I. But what's brought this on? There's something you're not telling me.'

'Yes.'

'Well?'

She nodded. 'Well... You know I've been feeling a bit queasy in the mornings for a while, now...' She allowed her voice to trail away.

'Yes... Jess, you're not...? Are you telling me...?'

'We're going to be parents, Ben,' she replied quietly.

He looked at her for a long time, then took her in his arms.

'Really?'

'Really. Are you pleased?'

'Pleased? Jess, I'm ecstatic. Are you sure?'

She nodded. 'I went to see the doctor a couple of days ago.'

He held her for a long time.

'We may need to look for somewhere bigger to live,' he said.

'This will be fine for a while. But we should start thinking about it.'

'Have you told your parents?' he asked.

'I haven't told anybody. You had to be the first to know. But I will, now. And we must tell your family, too.'

'They'll go crazy,' Ben said, 'especially my mother. You know Jewish families and children: they won't talk about anything else. It will be all over the East End by next week.'

She laughed. 'I'm so glad your grandfather is still with us,' she smiled. 'I can just picture him now. He'll be so happy.'

Ben laughed. 'Joshua's always said that I'm the family's Rufus Isaacs, the Jewish boy who's destined to overcome his humble beginnings to end up as Viceroy of India – or at the very least Lord Chief Justice.'

She smiled. 'I know. He will be glad you're carrying on the Rufus Isaacs line. If it's a boy, we should call him Joshua.'

They kissed again, then sat in silence for some time.

'It's such a responsibility,' Ben said. 'There's going to be so much to think about.'

'Yes,' Jess replied, 'including education. Before you know it, we will be the ones thinking about schools.'

'Well, I know one school that's not going to be on our list,' Ben replied.

34

At ten thirty-five Judge Rees sent the jury back out to continue their deliberations, before resuming her fraud trial. At just after twelve thirty, she adjourned the fraud for an early lunch and called the case of Father Gerrard back to court.

'It's about time they made their bloody minds up,' John Caswell muttered from behind Ben. 'What the hell are they doing in that jury room?' Ben nodded. Norris gave them both a smug grin.

The scene was solemnly enacted once more. Lewis bowed to the judge before turning to the jury.

'Would the foreman please stand? Would the defendant please stand? My Lady, approximately seven and a half hours have elapsed since the jury retired. Madam foreman, please answer my first question either yes or no. Has the jury reached verdicts on all four counts of the indictment on which they are all agreed?'

'No, my Lady,' the foreman replied.

Judge Rees nodded.

'Very well, members of the jury. I am now going to give you a further direction. In a few moments I am going to ask you to retire again and do your best to reach unanimous verdicts on all four counts. But the time has now come when, if you are unable to reach a unanimous verdict as to any or all counts, I can, and will, accept a majority verdict. But I must first explain what majority the law allows the court to accept. The court may accept a majority verdict only if it is one on which not less than ten members of the jury agree. I'm going to say that again. The court may accept a majority verdict only if it is one on which not less than ten members of the jury agree. Is that clear to you all?'

The jurors nodded. 'Yes, my Lady,' the foreman replied.

'Thank you,' the judge said. 'Then please retire and continue your deliberations. Do your best to reach unanimous verdicts; but if you are unable to do so, the court will accept verdicts on which at least ten of you are agreed. Go with the jury bailiff, please.'

There was silence from the jury room until four o'clock, at which time the jury asked to return to court. It took several minutes after the case of Father Gerrard had been called back on for the jury to make their way from their retiring room to the courtroom. Once again, they looked tired and tense: ties and scarves had been discarded now, and their faces were drawn and pale. John Caswell sat behind Ben and Ginny, and behind them sat, Julia Cathermole and Audrey Marshall, holding hands. No one spoke. Yet again, the formal ritual of judgment was played out.

'Would the foreman please stand? Would the defendant please stand? My Lady, approximately eleven hours have elapsed since the jury retired. Madam foreman, please answer my first question either yes or no. Has the jury reached verdicts on all four counts of the indictment on which at least ten of you are agreed?'

'No, my Lady,' the foreman replied.

Caswell cursed silently. Ben bent forward and rested his forehead briefly on the bench in front of him.

'Madam foreman,' the judge said. 'I'm not allowed to inquire about how the jury may be divided, and you are not allowed to tell me. But let me ask you this: if I were to allow you further time to deliberate, is there a realistic – and I stress the word "realistic" – is there a realistic chance that you may be able to reach majority verdicts that the court can accept?'

The foreman shook her head. 'I'm afraid not, my Lady.'

Judge Rees bit her lip. 'Very well,' she said. 'Thank you, madam foreman. In that case, members of the jury, I discharge you from returning verdicts in this case, and you are free to go, with the thanks of the court for your work in what I know has been a difficult and distressing case. I want you to know that your work has not been wasted simply because you have been unable to agree, and in recognition of that work, I will excuse you from further jury service at this court for a period of five years. You are free to go.'

No one spoke as the jurors filed wearily out of court.

'Mr Schroeder,' the judge said, 'I will give the prosecution seven days in which to decide whether or not you wish to proceed with a retrial. I will extend Father Gerrard's bail until that time.'

35

'I know we've all had a long day,' Andrew Pilkington said. 'But we only have seven days to decide whether we're going to retry the case, and John has to give the Director time to reflect; so it would be good if we could reach a consensus this evening. Who wants to start?'

They had gathered around the table in the conference room after court had risen for the day.

'I should probably go first,' John replied. 'I'm sure you want to have another crack at him, Audrey. I know I do. But…'

'I'm not sure I know what I want yet,' Audrey replied quietly. 'I'm exhausted. I feel completely deflated, numb. It feels like the roof has caved in. How am I ever going to explain this to Emily?'

'I think Emily will understand,' Ben said.

'It seems like we've climbed an enormous hill, and now we have to do it all over again. I don't know whether I can do this again.'

'You don't have to climb it today, Audrey,' Julia pointed out gently. 'And let's not forget that they didn't find him not guilty. He's not off the hook, and he knows it. We have that to hang on to.'

'I understand, Audrey,' John replied. 'It's infuriating that he's been able to hang up the jury, despite refusing to give evidence. But I know what the Director is going to ask me. He's going to ask me why we think we have a better chance of convicting this man the second time round than we did this time. What's our answer to that?'

There was silence for some time.

'Perhaps we should call an expert witness to deal with recovered memory,' Julia suggested eventually, 'a psychiatrist or psychologist, to explain to the jury how it works. I'm not saying they doubted your word, Audrey, because I don't think they did. But they may have felt that they couldn't rely on recovered memory in general. If we can reassure them about that, it might make all the difference.'

'But then, the defence will call their own expert to say how dangerous it is,' Ginny replied. 'Apparently, even the experts don't really know what to make of it, and if the experts can't agree, the jury might just think: "If *they* don't know, how can they expect *us* to know?" That might push them towards a not guilty.'

'Plus,' Andrew added, 'it's too defensive. I don't want to apologise for evidence before anyone even attacks it. If I don't have confidence in the evidence I put before the jury, why should they? If the defence called an expert first, I'd be happy to call one to hit back; but I don't want to give the jury the impression that we're running scared.'

'Just a thought,' Julia replied quietly.

'There's another problem, too,' Ben said. 'It's a point Norris made to me the evening before the jury went out, and much as I hate to admit it, I'm afraid he may be right. Where are all the women who were abused between the 1940s and the present time? Why aren't they lining up to make sure Gerrard goes down?'

'We don't know that it went on continuously from the 1940s,' Ginny insisted. 'Actually, we don't have a very precise idea of how many women were assaulted, or when.'

'It would be very strange if it was happening in the 1940s, then suddenly stopped happening, and then started to happen again spontaneously in the 1970s,' Ben replied.

'Not necessarily, Ben. The men who assaulted Emily were not the men who assaulted Audrey. The ring could well be ephemeral: it disappears from sight from time to time if interest wanes, then it becomes active again when the right people come together.'

'In any case,' Ted Phillips suggested, 'you're never going to get every woman who was assaulted to come forward. Woman B is the perfect example. Yes, what happened to her was terrible: but that was then, and this is now; and now she has a husband and children, and she wants to get on with her life. The last thing she wants is to get involved in a scandal. I've seen it happen in other cases.'

'I also have a life, Ted,' Audrey said. 'So, are you saying I'm wrong to stand up against Gerrard? Should I be getting on with my life, too, and allowing my daughter to get on with hers? Perhaps you're right. Perhaps that's exactly what I should do.'

'No, of course not –'

'None of us think that,' Ben insisted. 'Besides, it can't be as simple as that, can it? Yes, you will always have some who don't want to get involved. But statistically, there must be some women who want to do what Audrey's doing – if only to protect the girls who are at Lancelot Andrewes now. Where are they?'

'Maybe some of them don't want to fight the Church,' Steffie Walsh suggested. 'The Church still has a surprising amount of influence in people's lives.'

'All right,' Ben agreed. 'Subtract some to allow for that. That still leaves us with a number greater than one. Where the hell are they?'

'I think I may know where some of them are,' Julia said quietly. 'But there are things I can't tell you. I'll tell you what I can. Perhaps it will be enough.'

Every eye turned to her.

'Mary Forbes – our Woman B – told the jury that she reported the abuse to her parents during the Christmas holidays, when she was nine, and that the abuse stopped after that. What she didn't tell the jury was that something else stopped at the same time: her parents didn't receive a single bill for her school fees during the nine years she spent at the school after that Christmas.'

Total silence engulfed the room.

'Julia…' Ginny said after some time, 'that's dynamite. If that's true, it's as good as an admission. They were buying the parents off.'

'*Someone* was buying the parents off, yes,' Julia agreed. 'I can't say any more about that, and I asked Mary not to say anything about it to the jury.'

'You asked...? Julia, that could have...?'

'There was other information I had – not from Mary – that I couldn't risk being exposed.' She smiled. 'Besides, she couldn't have told the jury about it anyway. The judge wouldn't have allowed it.'

'It was hearsay?' Ben suggested.

'Total hearsay. She was nine at the time, and knew nothing about the fees until her father told her recently on his deathbed. It's not admissible.'

'Then why does it matter now?' Steffie asked.

'I only found out about this a few days before trial. There was no time to do any further investigation. Now there is.'

'What kind of investigation?'

'I'm thinking that Mary probably wasn't the only girl who had her fees waived as a bribe to her family not to rock the boat,' Julia said. 'I'm thinking that some of those other girls have parents who are still alive, and could give evidence about it. And I'm thinking that Lancelot Andrewes has records stashed away somewhere that would corroborate their evidence.'

'Of course,' Audrey said. She suddenly sounded engaged again. 'The school has complete records of fees for all the girls.'

'Would it be clear why a girl's family wasn't paying fees?' Ben asked.

'Absolutely,' Audrey replied. 'Almost all the girls are fee-paying. Payments are made quarterly, and their files should contain records of all payments, and any missed payments. Non-fee-paying girls are either on scholarship, in which case their file is marked with a capital S, or charity cases, like my sister and me, whose files are marked with a C. What we'd be looking for are cases where payments for fee-paying girls stopped abruptly for no obvious reason.'

'All we need are two or three instances where that happened,' Ginny said. 'It would turn the case around.'

'How can we get our hands on these records?' Ben asked.

'Records of current pupils are kept at the school, together with records for pupils who have left within the last five years,' Audrey replied. 'All the earlier records are housed in the diocesan storage facility, an old warehouse at Impington, just outside Cambridge. It shouldn't be difficult to find what we need.'

'We'll need a subpoena to produce documents, and a search warrant for the storage facility,' Andrew said.

John Caswell and both police officers nodded.

'We're on it,' Steffie said.

'What about the Three Musketeers, sir?' Ted asked.

'It's time to invite them to the party,' Andrew replied. 'Give them the opportunity to come in voluntarily for interview. Do it as quietly as possible. I don't want anyone complaining that we're exposing them to unnecessary publicity. Let John and myself know what they have to say before you charge them.'

'Andrew, do you think we have enough?' John asked, tentatively. 'They are men in the public eye. The Director is going to be nervous about it. What can I tell him?'

'Remind him that we have two victims who positively identify all three of them,' Andrew replied. 'That ought to do it.'

'What about the indictment?' Ben asked.

'We can't just add them to the original indictment at this late stage,' Andrew replied. 'I'll ask a High Court judge for a fresh bill of indictment, so that we can join all four of them.'

'Will that be a problem? We've already had one trial.'

Andrew smiled. 'Shouldn't be. We keep one or two tame judges for such occasions. Audrey, go home and see Emily, and regroup. We'll keep you up to date.'

'I'm on my way,' she replied.

36

Audrey Marshall

I told Ben I didn't know how I was going to explain the hung jury to Emily. But now, on the train back to Ely with time to reflect and nowhere to hide, I am forced to admit to myself that Emily isn't the problem. I am. Emily has overcome any fears she had about the case and the courtroom. She will get up and do it again fifty times if she has to. I'm not afraid of explaining it to Emily. I'm afraid of explaining it to myself.

Ben and Ginny told me over and over again that the hung jury isn't a personal rejection, and so I shouldn't take it personally. It doesn't mean that I wasn't telling the truth in their eyes. Intellectually, I understand that. I understand what corroboration means, and I understand that there are experts who don't accept that what I experienced can be real. But for me, this is not an intellectual exercise. I'm not standing where Ben and Ginny are standing. I'm not watching this game from the side-lines. I'm a player. I'm one of the people whose lives this case is going to change forever, and beyond recall. Twelve people I don't know, and who don't know me, found that they couldn't rely on my evidence. To me, that is personal – very personal.

It's personal that the law regards my evidence as inherently suspicious just because it concerns sexual abuse, as opposed to burglary or fraud. It's personal that the law regards my daughter's evidence as inherently suspicious for the same reason, and doubly so simply because she's a child. It's personal that the rules of evidence make it so easy for somebody like Anthony Norris to turn a trial into a forensic game of chess, instead of a search for the truth. It's personal that experts can analyse my memory as nothing more than a scientific speculation. You can't do that, I want to scream at them: not if you haven't been where I've been; not if you haven't stood as a terrified seven-year-old, barefoot in a flimsy nightdress, in Father Gerrard's library, waiting for men to put their fingers inside you; not if you haven't found your sister hanging from the staircase because she was sorry she couldn't stop it; not if you haven't listened to your seven-year-old daughter telling you that she has suffered the same abuse, after you've sent her to the same school, because you had no inkling that anything was amiss. If you haven't had those experiences, I want to scream at them, don't fucking tell me that my recovered memories aren't real. And you, Anthony Norris: don't tell me that I'm in this because I want to sue Lancelot Andrewes School for money – as if any amount of money could begin to make up for what has happened to me. Don't you dare. Don't you fucking dare.

The men who abused me, those cowardly men hiding behind the protective shield of false initials, don't have to worry about rules of evidence. They don't have to worry about corroboration, or the opinions of experts. It's personal that the law places no such obstacles in their path; that it's apparently so easy for them to walk away.

I want desperately to give it all up and hide away in some hole for the rest of my life. But I can't. I can't: because I have a little girl at home who had the courage to come out from behind a screen and confront the man who abused her in front of the whole world; and I can't let her down.

PART THREE

PART THREE

37

'Good morning, everyone,' Steffie began. 'Sorry you all had to get up so early, but it's in a good cause.'

'I hope so, ma'am,' a female voice replied from the back of the room, to general laughter. 'I'm missing all my beauty sleep.'

Steffie joined in the laughter. 'It doesn't show, Ruthie.'

'It does from where I'm standing,' DS Steve Harris commented.

Ruthie punched him hard in the arm, to more laughter. 'Cheeky bugger.'

'Now, if everyone's got coffee to keep them awake, let's get started. I think you all know me by now. I'm DI Steffie Walsh from the Met. You've just been introduced, in typical Met fashion, to two of my colleagues, DS Ruthie Foster and DS Steve Harris, who both have forensic accounting training. I've asked them to spend a few days with us here at Parkside, to assist with the inquiry into the records of Lancelot Andrewes School. Do you all have the notes I typed up yesterday?'

There were nods around the room.

'Good. This information comes from Audrey Marshall, one of our victims, who works for the diocese as an administrator, so there's every chance she's right about what we're going to find on the ground. The general idea is this: we have reason to believe that the school has been paying off the families of victims of child sexual abuse by waiving their child's school fees if the child complained. This comes from another witness, Mary

Forbes. We couldn't use Mary's evidence at the trial because it's hearsay: her father knew about it, but he died some time ago. But we don't think Mary's family was the only one this happened to.

'So, what we're looking for is evidence that a girl's family suddenly stopped paying fees for no obvious reason, after a particular date. The problem is that we have no way of estimating how many such cases there are, and they could be cases of girls at the school at any time between 1940 and the present.'

'"Obvious reason" meaning that the girl was on a scholarship?' Ruthie asked.

'Either on a scholarship, or the fees were waived for charitable reasons, such as in Audrey's case – she was an orphan and an evacuee from London during the war. In a few cases, fees may have been waived temporarily if the family fell on hard times, with an understanding that they would resume payments when they could.

'The school starts an administrative file for every girl on the date of her entry. That file contains two sets of records. The first part consists of her academic records: her marks for school exams; extracurricular achievements – sports, music, and so on; scholarships awarded; what O-levels and A-levels she got; university entrance; and any disciplinary actions taken against her. There may be some interesting stuff in there if the girl's history isn't clear, but the second part is more directly relevant.

'The second part consists of her financial records. There should be a record of each quarterly payment of fees, and of any reason why fees were not paid. If it was a scholarship or charity case, the file should be marked with a capital S or C, and it should be obvious that fees were not being paid from the relevant date. What we're looking for are girls who started off paying, but whose payments stopped without any evidence of a valid reason. I need complete copies of all such files, including current contact details. Then we're going to interview as many of them, and their parents or guardians, as we can.'

'They were admitting roughly forty girls a year?' Steve Harris asked.

'Yes.'

'And would all of those be boarders?'

'No, but there were very few day girls, and we have no evidence that any day girls were abused; so don't worry too much about that.' She paused. 'Any other questions?' There were none.

'All right. Now, we're going to divide into two teams. Team A, led by DI Phillips, will have Steve, plus DC Woolley and PCs Martin and Kelly. Steve is very experienced in inquiries with masses of documents, so he will be your guru. If you have any questions – any questions at all – about a file, he's the man you go to.'

'Don't be nervous about it; I'm a very nice bloke,' Steve said. 'Ruthie will tell you: won't you, Ruthie?'

'No comment,' Ruthie replied, to renewed laughter.

'So don't be shy about it.'

'Thank you, Steve – or Mr Nice Guy, as we all call him down in London,' Steffie said. 'I will lead Team B, with Ruthie, DC Lund, and PCs Everett and Shaw. Ruthie has the same experience as Steve, and she will be our guru.

'Team A, DI Phillips's team, will be visiting the school itself, where they keep records for current pupils and any who've left school in the past five years. So the files you'll find there are relevant mainly to our inquiry into more recent abuse, including Audrey's daughter, Emily.'

'Though they may be helpful more generally, depending on the picture they form. They may suggest that the abuse has been going on consistently over the years,' Ted added.

'Absolutely,' Steffie agreed. 'Treat everything as important. In Father Gerrard's absence, the diocesan administrator, Bill Hollis, will be the man to show you round. Bill is Audrey's boss, and she says he's a reasonable enough fellow; but she also says that the diocesan staff are all fiercely loyal, so how he will react when you confront him remains to be seen. Don't take anything for granted, but don't take no for an answer.

'Team B, my team, is going to the diocesan storage facility at Impington, where they keep all the older records – or so we hope. We currently have no reason to believe that they've destroyed any records; but this scandal has been all over the papers recently, so it's not beyond the realm of possibility that someone may have been tempted to dispose of some embarrassing documents. If so, they probably weren't very subtle about it, and they will have left clues. Keep your eyes open – any suspiciously low number of files for a particular year, any files that are suspiciously light on documents, any hesitancy or nervousness on the part of the staff. You all know what I'm talking about.'

'Who's the man in charge?' Ruthie asked.

'Donald Terrence,' Steffie replied, 'your typical jobsworth, according to Audrey, but nothing else known. Now, look: timing is important. If it hasn't occurred to anyone yet to start disposing of documents, it might once they get word that there's a search warrant on the way. We've kept very quiet about it. Superintendent Walker is going to serve the warrants for both places on John Singer, the school's solicitor, at nine o'clock precisely, at his office. If he's not there at nine o'clock, the Super will let us know: in that case we go into both buildings anyway at that time, and the Super will serve Singer as soon as he can. DI Phillips and I will keep in regular radio contact, to make sure we're on the same page.

'Both teams will have plenty of copies of the warrants. The warrants are valid, so we're not going to let anyone hold us up. They may try to fob us off, saying they want to call Singer. We will tell them they're welcome to call anyone they want, but we're starting the search immediately.'

'Protocol?' Steve Harris asked.

'One officer to be designated exhibits officer, to be in charge of any files you decide to seize, and those files to be removed and brought to Parkside when you finish at the end of each day. Work as long as you like; tell the staff you'll lock the place up for the night. Remember, this is going to take more than one day, maybe three, or even four – it's hard to say until we get a feel for what we're dealing with: so some poor bugger will have to be elected night watchman, to make sure the place is secure overnight, including over the weekend.'

There were moans around the room. Steffie smiled.

'I know. I'm sorry. Maybe I'm being paranoid, but I'm hearing things about John Singer that are making me nervous. We can't take any chances with these files. Our prosecuting counsel say they may make all the difference between winning and losing when the case comes to trial.

'So: let's synchronise our watches. Mine says it's eight fifteen. If there are no more questions, let's hit the road and get into position.'

Donald Terrence, manager of the diocesan document storage facility at Impington, had had a premonition that he was going to have a bad day. He had slept through his alarm, and had woken up feeling stiff, unrested, and out of sorts. His stomach was upset, and he had a vague headache. He'd had to rush his morning routine in the interests of making it to work on time. He'd cut himself shaving, and had no time for breakfast. He knew that his worst fears were to be confirmed when a group of five people, obviously police officers, pushed past his receptionist at the main entrance to the building, just as a spluttering John Singer was trying to explain something to him, over an indifferent phone line, about a search warrant. The woman who led the party approached his desk, produced her warrant card, and gestured to him, making it clear that she expected him to complete the call without delay. Terrence told Singer that he would call him back as soon as he could and replaced the receiver. He stood and tried to appear as defiant as he could.

'Can I help you?' he asked her, brusquely.

'Yes, you can,' Steffie replied. 'I am DI Steffie Walsh, and, as you can see, I have four other police officers with me. We're here to execute a search warrant. This is your copy.' She gave him a few seconds to run his eyes over it. 'We will be here until further notice, which may be several days. We expect your full cooperation.'

Terrence shook his head. 'I don't know about this. I'll have to ask Mr Singer. I can't just let you –'

'Mr Terrence,' she interrupted, 'in case I didn't make myself clear, I'm here to execute a search warrant, of which I've provided you with a copy. Unless I'm very much mistaken, you've just been speaking with Mr Singer, and I would sincerely hope he's explained to you that you have no alternative but to cooperate with us. If you refuse to cooperate, I will ask DS Foster here to arrest you for obstructing us in the execution of our duty.'

Any appearance of defiance in Terrence evaporated.

'So,' Steffie said, 'I would be grateful if you would show us where the historic files for girls at Lancelot Andrewes School are kept, and make sure we have full and unrestricted access to them.'

'Anything else?' Terrence demanded sullenly.

'Yes. Once you've done that, gather your staff together, and make it clear to them that anyone who tries to obstruct us, or interfere with the records in any way before we're finished with them, will be arrested and prosecuted.'

Terrence took a deep breath and placed his hands on his hips.

'And, just as a point of interest, Mr Terrence,' Steffie added, 'has anyone removed any of those files, or interfered with them in any way recently?'

Terrence recoiled and put his hands in his pockets.

''No… no, of course not. Why would anyone do that?'

'I'm just asking.'

'No.'

'Good. I'm glad to hear that, Mr Terrence, because if you or your staff were to do anything like that, or if anyone were to ask you to do anything like that, we'd be out of the realm of obstructing a police officer. We'd be in the realm of perverting the course of justice – and believe you me, you don't want to be involved in perverting the course of justice: does he, Detective Sergeant Foster?'

'No, ma'am,' Ruthie confirmed. 'In my experience, that would be a very bad thing for Mr Terrence to be involved with.'

'I told you,' Terrence protested weakly. 'Nothing like that has happened.'

'Good,' Steffie replied. 'If I were you, I would do my very best to ensure that it stays that way.'

38

The two men in the interview room stood as they entered.

'DI Phillips, DI Walsh, good morning. May I introduce the man you've been calling the Right Reverend EF? You know his real name, of course, but if you don't mind, shall we just call him "Bishop" for the purposes of today's proceedings?'

'Fine with me, Mr Singer,' Ted Phillips replied. He nodded politely. 'Bishop.'

He and Steffie Walsh shook hands with both men, and Ted invited them to resume their seats. Steffie was immediately struck by the bishop's bright blue eyes, which in contrast to Father Gerrard's, engaged her fully without any attempt to avoid her scrutiny. He was a tall man, with distinguished-looking silver hair, a short and neatly trimmed moustache and pointed beard, wearing a light grey suit and a blue tie; and he gave the impression of being at peace with himself. 'I bet he would make quite an impression on a jury,' she found herself thinking.

'I will be conducting the interview this morning,' Ted continued. 'Today is the twenty-second of May 1974, and it's now ten o'clock in the morning. We are in an interview room at Parkside Police station in Cambridge. Present are: myself, DI Phillips of the Cambridge police; DI Walsh of the London Metropolitan police, who is making a note of the interview; Bishop EF; and Mr John Singer, the solicitor for Lancelot Andrewes School. First of all, Bishop, thank you for coming. Can you confirm for me, please, that you have attended voluntarily this morning for interview?'

'That's correct.'

'Do you understand that you are not under arrest, and you are free to leave at any time?'

'I understand.'

'Because of the nature of our inquiries, I must caution you that you are not obliged to say anything unless you wish to do so, but what you say may be put into writing and given in evidence. Do you understand the caution?'

'Yes, I do.'

'Before we start the interview proper, Mr Singer, will you please confirm for the record that you are acting as the Bishop's solicitor for the purposes of the interview today?'

'I can confirm that.'

'In that case, as we did on the occasion of Father Gerrard's interview, I'm going to note once again my view, and that of DI Walsh, that there is a possible conflict of interest, given that you are also the solicitor for the school.'

'You raised that question last time,' Singer replied, 'and I thought I'd explained quite clearly that I was representing Father Gerrard only for the purposes of the interview. I said I would hand the case over to a solicitor with more criminal experience when it came to the trial, and that's exactly what I did.'

'You did, Mr Singer,' Ted replied. 'But by that time, Father Gerrard had opted not to answer our questions about the alleged offences, presumably on your advice.'

'That's none of your business,' Singer replied, 'as I believe I made abundantly clear at the time. Besides, it doesn't appear to have harmed his interests, does it, having regard to the result of the trial?'

'The *first* trial,' Ted pointed out. 'And this may be a good moment for me to point out for the record that the Director of Public Prosecutions has decided to retry the case against Father Gerrard –'

'I'm fully aware of that, Inspector –'

'And to apply to a High Court judge for a voluntary bill of indictment, to add the Bishop's name to the present indictment, together with the names of Lord AB and Sir CD.'

'The Bishop and I are quite aware of all that, Inspector. We wouldn't be here otherwise, would we?'

'I'm going to repeat what we said to Father Gerrard,' Ted continued, 'because I believe it to be important for the Bishop to hear this also. We understand from our counsel that the school may be legally liable to victims of the assaults and their parents. So, in the highly likely event of their taking legal action against Father Gerrard, the school, the Bishop, and the other men involved, the Bishop's interests and those of the school would not be the same. Counsel suggested that the Bishop might prefer to have independent advice.'

'Oh, not again: this is outrageous –' Singer began, but Bishop EF placed a hand on his arm.

'I understand what you're saying, Inspector. I have discussed the situation with Mr Singer, and I have agreed that he should represent me today.'

'And you're aware that there may be a conflict of interest?'

'The Church doesn't see it that way,' Bishop EF replied, 'so neither do I. Now, Inspector, your time is valuable, as is mine, so if you have questions to ask me, may I suggest that you get on with it?'

Ted exchanged glances with Steffie.

'Very well, sir. Do you know Father Desmond Gerrard?'

'Yes, of course. I've known Desmond for years.'

'How did you first meet?'

'We were ordained at about the same time, and we were both assigned to the diocese of Ely; so we saw each other at retreats, conferences, gatherings of various kinds, and we came to know each other quite well. Later, when Desmond joined the teaching staff at Lancelot Andrewes, and subsequently became headmaster, I saw him in connection with the school. I had become a trustee of the school by then. I've also had an interest in education during my career, although I didn't take the teaching route as he did.'

'What route did you take?'

'I started out in parochial work, then became an archdeacon and adviser to my bishop – about education, as well as many other matters – and in due course I became a bishop myself. I'm now at Oxford, as Master of my college, as you know.'

'Do I take it from what you've said that you've visited Lancelot Andrewes School fairly frequently?'

'Of course. I've been there many times.'

'When was the first time?'

'I don't remember the exact date. It's too long ago. But it was before the war, not long before Desmond became headmaster, if my memory serves.'

'What was the purpose of that visit?'

'I'm sure it was connected to my work there in some way. I can't remember precisely after so long. I became a trustee when Desmond took over as headmaster, and I would have visited any number of times over the years.'

'Bishop, I would like to ask you about the war years, specifically about the years 1940 to 1945.'

'Very well.'

'Did you visit Lancelot Andrewes School during those years?'

'Yes, of course. The war caused us all sorts of problems – the safety of the children; making arrangements for shelter in the event of an air raid; what we would do when a child lost a relative as a result of enemy action, and so on. As a matter of fact, I was involved in advising Desmond about the decision to accept a limited number of boys and girls who were being evacuated from London; and I was involved in the decision to tell Mrs Marshall and her sister that they were welcome to stay at the school and complete their education after their parents were killed.'

'Bishop, were you ever there in the evenings, let's say between eight and eleven?'

Bishop EF sat back in his chair and exchanged looks with John Singer.

'I was, on occasion, but that raises some issues.'

'Issues?' Ted asked, with a glance towards Steffie. 'What do you mean by that?'

'What I mean, Inspector,' Bishop EF replied, 'is that I will answer your questions as far as I can, but I'm afraid there will be some I'm not allowed to answer.'

'You're going to have to explain that to me, sir, if you don't mind,' Ted said. 'You do understand that we are inquiring into certain very serious offences?'

'I understand that, Inspector. But there are some things that must take precedence, I'm afraid.'

39

'I'm having some difficulty in understanding what would take precedence over an investigation into sexual offences against children at a boarding school,' Ted said.

'Inspector, you asked me whether I had visited the school in the evening in the period between 1940 and 1945. During the period you're referring to, I went to Lancelot Andrewes a number of times in the evenings. I went there on behalf of the government. It was wartime, and there were certain things I was asked to do.'

'Asked by whom, sir, specifically?'

He paused. 'The security services.'

'Which service would that be?'

'I'm not at liberty to say.'

Ted nodded. 'All right. I think I understand what you're saying, but for the record –'

'What the Bishop means,' Singer intervened, 'is that much of the information he might otherwise give you is covered by the Official Secrets Act.'

'That's correct, Inspector,' EF agreed. 'They made me sign a form when my work was finished. I can't talk about it, even now.'

'I suggest you take it one question at a time, Inspector,' Singer said. 'He will do his best to assist you.'

'All right,' Ted said. 'In general terms, what was the purpose of the evening visits you made to the school?'

'I was asked to accompany a man in whom the security services had an interest.'

'Who was this man?'

'I'm not at liberty to say.'

'What was the purpose of this man's visiting Lancelot Andrewes School?'

'As it turned out,' EF replied, 'he was there to molest little girls, pupils at the school.'

Ted sat back in his chair and stared at the man. No one spoke for some time. Eventually, Steffie touched his hand with hers and raised her eyebrows questioningly. Ted nodded.

'Bishop,' Steffie said, 'in view of your last answer, I must remind you of the caution. You are not obliged to say anything unless you wish to do so, but what you say may be put in writing and given in evidence. Do you understand the caution?'

'Yes, as I said before, I understand the caution.'

Steffie turned to Ted, asking with her eyes whether she should continue. Ted nodded, and took his pen from his jacket pocket to continue the note of the interview.

'How do you know that this man – shall we call him X...?'

'Yes, all right.'

'How do you know that X was going to Lancelot Andrewes to molest girls there?'

'Because I was present and saw it for myself.'

Steffie suddenly felt her heart beating faster.

''Bishop,' she asked, speaking slowly and deliberately measuring her words, 'are you saying that you personally witnessed children being abused at the school?'

'I witnessed it on a number of occasions.'

'"A number" meaning...?'

'Over the period we are discussing, at least once a month.'

'Where were you based at that time?' Ted intervened.

'In London.'

'So, did you travel to the Ely area with X, or did you meet him there?'

Bishop EF thought for some time. 'I'm not at liberty to say.'

'Did the abuse occur in one particular place in the school, or more than one?' Steffie resumed.

'It always occurred in the room next to Desmond's study – he called it his private library. It was where he kept his theological and philosophical books.'

'Had you been to this room before?'

'Yes. Desmond often held meetings there. I'd been there many times.'

'Let me take you back to the first occasion when you witnessed abuse in that room,' Steffie said. 'Can you describe what happened?'

EF sat up in his chair. 'I'd been asked to accompany X during his visit to the school. This would have been early in 1941. I don't know the date, obviously, but I remember being glad to get out of London: the Blitz was in full cry, and it was a terrible time. Anyway, there I was, at the school. Desmond asked us to wait in the library. He didn't say why, but when we went into the library, there were drinks waiting – water and a decanter of whisky. One of Desmond's indulgences,' he added with a smile.

'What were you expecting to happen?'

The Bishop shrugged, but made no reply.

'Well, you said you were "waiting" in the library. What were you waiting for?'

'For whatever was going to happen.'

'Bishop, your contact at the security service must have told you why you and X were going to Lancelot Andrewes?'

'I'm not at liberty to say.'

'They wouldn't have asked you to look after X without telling you what he was getting up to at the school, would they? With all due respect, Bishop, that doesn't make sense.'

'I'm not at liberty to say.'

'All right. Staying with that first time: apart from X and yourself, was anyone else present while you were waiting in the library?'

'Yes. There were two other men.'

'Can you describe those men?'

'I can do better than that, Inspector. I can tell you who they were. They were the men who are now Lord AB and Sir CD. This was much earlier in their careers, obviously.'

Steffie stared at him. 'Are you absolutely sure? Is there any doubt at all in your mind?'

'None whatsoever.'

Both DIs stared at Bishop EF for some time, speechless. Ted recovered first.

'So, you'd come from London all the way to Ely, and there you were in Father Gerrard's library waiting for something to happen; but you weren't sure what, and you were waiting and having a drink of whisky. What did in fact happen?'

'I didn't drink any whisky myself. But I did smoke a cigar. That's my indulgence.'

'What happened, sir?'

'After about ten minutes, Desmond came in with a young girl, about seven or eight years of age, I would say.'

'How was this girl dressed?'

'She was wearing a nightdress of some kind. I can't remember the detail.'

'What happened after Father Gerrard and the girl entered?'

The Bishop sighed deeply and closed his eyes for some seconds.

'Terrible things; unspeakable things.'

Ted shook his head. Steffie took over.

'Bishop, I know this isn't easy for you, but this isn't the time for platitudes. We need to hear exactly what happened.'

'They touched her,' he replied quietly, after a pause.

'In what way?'

Another pause. 'They put their hands under her nightdress and touched her private parts.'

'And you saw this clearly?'

'I did.'

'Who touched her, Bishop?'

'X touched her first, followed by Lord AB and Sir CD – I think in that order, I'm not entirely sure, but I do remember that X was first.'

'Where was Father Gerrard while this was going on?'

'He was standing in the corner, as far as I remember, not playing any part in it, and looking uncomfortable.'

'I'm sorry,' Steffie said, 'but did you say *uncomfortable*?'

'Yes.'

'These men were sexually assaulting his pupil, and he looked *uncomfortable*?'

'That was my impression. He brought the girl into the library, and he did nothing to stop it; so I assumed that he had known what was going to happen, and had brought the girl to the library for that purpose.'

Steffie shook her head. 'You say that you witnessed such a scene on other occasions, approximately once a month?'

'Yes.'

'With the same, or a different girl?'

'There were several different girls, three or four, I think, so we did see the same girls more than once.'

'Did Father Gerrard bring the girl to the library on each occasion?'

'Yes.'

'Did the same things happen on each occasion?'

'Yes. The men were different sometimes. Lord AB and Sir CD were there on most of the occasions, but not always. Sometimes there were other men.'

'How many other men, in total?'

'Five or six.'

'Do you know who any of those other men were?'

'I'm not at liberty to say.'

'Bishop EF, we have two witnesses, Audrey Marshall and a woman we are calling Woman B, who have given evidence that they were molested in Father Gerrard's library during this general period of time on a number of occasions. Both of them say that they were molested by Lord AB and Sir CD, and Woman B speaks of a German man molesting her. Could this man have been X?'

'I'm not at liberty to say.'

'Bishop, I'm going to show you a photograph: if you would look at it, please.'

'Yes.'

'This is the Lancelot Andrewes Girls' School annual photograph for the school year 1942 to 1943. Do you recognise any of these girls as one of those who were molested in the library during the period we're discussing?'

He looked at the photograph vacantly for some time.

'It's difficult to say, you know,' he replied eventually. 'There are so many, and in the picture they're dressed in full school uniform... I can't say.'

'In that case, I direct your attention to two girls: front row, third from left; and the row immediately behind the front row, sixth from right. Look at them carefully, please, Bishop.'

He nodded. 'Yes, quite possibly. I can't be definite after so many years, but it's certainly possible. Are they the two witnesses, Audrey and Woman B?'

'Yes.'

He nodded again. 'Yes, quite possibly.'

'Bishop, do you know whether this abuse continued after the end of the war?'

'I wasn't aware of it after the war. I certainly didn't witness any abuse myself after X stopped his visits to the school during 1945, and I didn't pick up any rumours. I have to say, I was quite surprised to hear that there have been allegations of abuse during the last few years.'

'What happened to X after the war?'

'I have no idea. That's the truth. But even if I did know, I couldn't tell you.'

40

Steffie took a deep breath.

'Bishop, both witnesses also say that you yourself molested them by touching them in the area of their vaginas, and inserting your fingers into their vaginas. Woman B also says that you made her touch your penis and rub it until you climaxed. I must again remind you of the caution. You are not obliged to say anything unless you wish to do so, but what you say may be put into writing and given in evidence. What do you say in response to those allegations?'

'They are completely untrue,' he replied immediately. 'But I understand their error.'

'*Error*?'

'Yes, of course. For a girl to be in that position… well, I saw them at the time. They were terrified, poor things. It's not surprising that they may be mixed up on some of the details. I don't hold it against them.'

'They seem very clear indeed on the details generally, Bishop,' Steffie said. 'They don't strike me as mixed up at all. Are you sure you didn't join in the entertainment your friend Father Gerrard was providing?'

'Certainly not. I am a bishop of the Established Church, and I have been married for more than twenty years.'

'Not then, you weren't,' Steffie replied. 'And Father Gerrard has been in holy orders for the same length of time, but apparently that didn't deter him.'

'I've already told you: he didn't touch the girls.'

'He supplied the girls, though, didn't he?' Ted intervened suddenly. 'So the fact that he didn't touch them himself isn't much to his credit as a man in holy orders, is it? Not to mention that he was supposed to be the headmaster of this school. Was this a part of the interest in education you shared?'

'There's no need for sarcasm,' Singer intervened stiffly.

'All I can say is that I didn't touch them.'

'Are you aware of any reason Mrs Marshall or Woman B may have to hold a grudge against you?'

'No, none at all. As I said before, I don't think they're lying. I'm sure they believe that they are giving an accurate account. It's understandable, but they are mistaken.'

'Bishop,' Steffie said, after a long silence, 'we now have evidence that suggests that eleven girls, including Woman B, had their school fees waived for no apparent reason during the 1940s and 1950s. We have reason to believe that this action may have been taken as a result of their making complaints of having been sexually abused. As a trustee, or former trustee of the school, is there anything you can tell us about that?'

'What evidence?'

He seemed to be taken aback, Steffie thought. 'I'm not at liberty to say,' she replied.

Bishop EF laughed out loud. '*Touché*, Inspector,' he replied. 'But neither am I. I'm sorry. I can't help you.'

'So, you're not denying that it may have happened?'

'I'm not at liberty to say.'

'He's not making any admissions,' Singer commented.

'Yes, thank you, Mr Singer. I think I've got that point.'

'Bishop,' Ted said, after a silence, 'I understand that you say there are certain things you can't tell us. But didn't you at some point speak to your security service contact and make some kind of protest about what was going on?'

'I'm not at liberty to say.'

'Did they know what was going on?'

'I'm not at liberty to say.'

'Well, did you ever speak to Father Gerrard and ask him what he thought he was doing?'

He nodded. 'Yes, of course I did.'

'What did he tell you?'

'He told me that people were putting pressure on him, people high up.'

'Did he say what he meant by that?'

'No. He wouldn't tell me any more. He clammed up.' The bishop paused. 'But he did tell me that what was going on at Lancelot Andrewes was the tip of the iceberg.'

'Again, did he say what he meant by that?'

'No: just that it was the tip of the iceberg, and that if I knew what was good for me, I would swallow my feelings and keep quiet about it.'

He shook his head.

'And that's what I've done, for more than thirty years: swallowed my feelings and kept quiet about it – until today.'

Ted and Steffie looked at each other for some seconds. She gave him the slightest suggestion of a nod.

'Bishop EF,' Ted said, 'would you stand, please? I am arresting you on suspicion of involvement in serious sexual offences against children at Lancelot Andrewes School during the period between 1940 and 1945.'

'Oh, for God's sake,' John Singer protested, climbing to his feet. 'You can't do that. He's come here voluntarily and given you a great deal of information. This isn't going anywhere. You must know that.'

'It's all right, John,' the bishop said, getting to his feet.

'I must caution you that you are not obliged to say anything unless you wish to do so, but what you say may be put into writing and given in evidence.'

'I have nothing more to say,' the Bishop replied, 'except that I am innocent of the charges.'

They booked a conference call with Andrew Pilkington when he came free from court during the lunch hour, and brought him up to date with the events of the morning.

'Where do we go from here, sir?' Ted asked.

'Are AB and CD still refusing to come in voluntarily?' Andrew asked in return.

'Yes, sir.'

'Arrest them both without delay.'

Ted and Steffie looked at each other.

'Sir, you do know that Lord AB's solicitors have issued a statement, saying that he's, how shall I put it…?'

'They implied that he's suffering from some form of dementia,' Andrew replied. 'I know. If they're serious about it, they'll provide us with some medical evidence. Until then, there's no reason not to arrest him. The same goes for CD. One of the newspapers said he had a stroke a few months ago. If so, they'll show us the evidence in due course.'

'There's no problem with immunity from arrest, is there, sir,' Steffie asked, 'with them being members of the House of Lords or the House of Commons?'

'That only applies to civil cases, not criminal,' Andrew replied. 'Go ahead and arrest both of them, and interview them; and I want transcripts of those interviews, and Bishop EF's interview, as soon as possible.'

'Right you are, sir,' Ted said.

'Oh, and call Miss Cathermole and tell her what EF had to say about his wartime employment by the security services. Make sure she gets a copy of the transcript, too.'

'Will do, sir.'

41

Friday 6 September 1974

'I'm glad you could all come,' Andrew began. 'I know it's Friday evening, and I'm sure sitting in my conference room isn't high on the list of things you want to be doing after a busy week. I'll try not to keep you too long. But we start trial on Monday, and I want to make sure that we are all on the same page.'

'Where else would I be on a Friday evening?' Julia asked, as a weary chuckle went around the table. 'I live for this.'

Andrew smiled. 'That's the spirit. When are the Marshalls coming to London?'

'Not until late Sunday afternoon. There's no sense in making them hang around, getting nervous. I've made their hotel arrangements, and I'll make sure they get to court. I can do the same for Mary Forbes, if you like. She has a flight from Toronto into London, arriving tomorrow.'

'That's all right. John's people have been in touch with her, and they'll take it from here,' Andrew said. 'Now: first things first. As you know, Mr Justice Overton granted our application for a voluntary bill of indictment. Ben and I drafted the new indictment, and it's different from the old indictment in a number of ways.'

'It brings in the Three Musketeers at last,' Julia said.

'Yes. We now have four defendants: Father Gerrard, Lord AB, Sir CD, and the Right Reverend EF. We also have a full range of charges, eight counts in all. We have the original four conspiracy charges against Father Gerrard, with the difference that now, the

Three Musketeers are also jointly charged with him in two of those counts – the two relating to the 1940s. Gerrard is charged alone in the 1970s counts involving Emily. Then we have three specimen counts alleging indecent assault against each of the Musketeers individually, and one specimen count of gross indecency with a child against EF only, all relating to the 1940s.'

'And we have a number of new witnesses,' Julia said.

Andrew nodded. 'Audrey and Emily remain our most important witnesses, together with Mary Forbes – Woman B. We will start with Emily, of course, to get her away from court as soon as we can. But we do also have some new evidence. DI Walsh?'

'Ted and I pursued the line of inquiry you suggested, Julia,' Steffie said, 'to find out whether there were cases, in addition to Mary, where families stopped paying school fees as from a particular date, after a daughter complained about having been molested. You were right.'

Julia brought her fist down on the table. 'I knew it.'

'We ransacked the school offices and the storage facility and went through every one of their files. We came up with a total of eleven cases in which payment of fees stopped for no apparent reason: seven in the 1940s, including Mary, and four more in the 1950s. We didn't count Audrey, of course – she was a genuine charity case; and we couldn't find any more recent examples.

'But we interviewed the women involved, and their parents – who are still alive, with two exceptions. As a result, five more women who were molested as girls have agreed to give evidence, as have their parents – or guardian, in one case. Three of those girls identify the German man as one of the molesters, mostly on the basis of his accent; and one identifies Bishop EF. But unfortunately, they don't do so well with the others. Only one identifies Lord AB, and no one identifies Sir CD.'

'So, we know that they weren't asked to pay fees after a certain date,' Ben said. 'But we don't know whether the school waived the fees, or whether they were paid by someone else, do we?'

'Not for sure,' Steffie agreed. 'If the fees were being paid from some outside source, it should have been recorded in the files, and it wasn't.'

'It wouldn't be, if it was all being done under the table,' Ben pointed out.

'Unfortunately, there aren't any bank records from so long ago, so we can't check what payments the school received. All the parents know is that they didn't receive any further invoices for fees, and those who queried it were quietly told not to worry about it. So they're not much help there, and, to be honest, most of them feel a bit guilty about it – they knew they were being bought off.'

'To cover up a case of child sexual abuse,' Julia said.

'Yes.'

'Still,' Ben said, 'it's a remarkable coincidence that the girls who complained were the same girls whose parents weren't asked to pay any more fees. I think that speaks for itself.'

'So do I,' Andrew agreed. 'And I'm not too worried that they can't identify all of the defendants. We've got that from Audrey and Mary. The new witnesses confirm that the abuse was occurring on a regular basis. That should be enough.'

'We've got the statement EF made in interview, too,' Ted Phillips pointed out. 'He puts all four of them right there, in Gerrard's library, and he has AB and CD touching up little girls.'

'Yes,' Ben agreed, 'but he doesn't admit to molesting any of the girls himself, and his statement isn't evidence against the other defendants.'

'But it's evidence against EF,' Andrew said, 'and it's altered the balance of the trial. None of the other defendants has said a word so far, but now that EF has broken rank my guess is that they will all start singing. It's going to be difficult for them to avoid giving evidence. And,' he added with a smile, 'once that happens, the chances are, they will be desperate to lay the blame on each other and they'll end up running cut-throat defences. We can sit back and pick them off, one by one. With any luck we'll nail them all.'

He turned to John Caswell.

'Sounds good to me,' John said. 'The Director's happy to go ahead with the new indictment.'

'Julia, were you able to follow up on EF's story about working for the security forces during the war, and accompanying this strange German man to Lancelot Andrewes?'

Julia sighed audibly. 'I wish I could, Andrew, but that's a door I can't open for you.'

'Understood,' Andrew replied. 'So, that just leaves us with what's likely to happen on Monday. We have a strong case, but there are one or two things that we need to be aware of...'

He paused.

'Go on,' Julia said encouragingly.

'Defence counsel have notified us that they have some preliminary applications,' Andrew said.

'What kind of applications?' Julia asked.

'Applications to stay the proceedings as an abuse of process: in other words, they're going to make an all-out attempt to stop the case in its tracks.'

The others looked at each other.

'How could they do that, sir?' Steffie asked.

'I'm expecting them to argue to the judge that the defendants can't receive a fair trial in the present climate,' Andrew explained, 'because of all the publicity ever since the Three Musketeers were arrested and their names became public knowledge. They may raise some other issues too, for example, health concerns in the cases of AB and CD.'

'There was bound to be publicity when they were arrested,' Julia pointed out. 'And even before the arrests, everyone knew who they were.'

'I know,' Andrew replied. 'But ever since the arrests it's been non-stop – in the papers, on the radio, on television. Wherever you look, you can't avoid it. They will say we couldn't find twelve jurors anywhere in England who haven't been living and breathing it.'

'That's true,' Ben said. 'But it's no reason to stop a trial. It's not unusual to have high profile cases, Andrew. We've both had cases like this before. You just have to rely on the jury to act on what they hear in court, not what they read in the papers.'

'Besides,' Julia added, 'they can't say the publicity has been all bad for them, can they? There's been a lot of cold water poured on recovered memory. *The Times* and the *Telegraph* have even questioned whether it's in the public interest for this kind of prosecution to be brought. The *Express* thinks it's unfair in principle to prosecute anyone thirty years after the event.'

'Perhaps so,' Andrew replied. 'But the Three Musketeers have taken quite a beating in the tabloids.'

'The judge will direct the jury to ignore all that,' Julia said.

'Ah, yes, the judge,' Andrew said. 'I was just coming to that.'

'What about the judge?' Julia asked.

'We're not going to have Delyth Rees this time,' Andrew replied. 'The powers that be have apparently decided that we need a High Court judge to try a peer of the realm and a bishop. I'm sorry, Ben, I was only informed this afternoon, and I haven't had time to tell you. They've given us Mr Justice Evan Roberts.'

'Oh, God,' Ben said, closing his eyes and hanging his head. 'Please tell me you're joking.'

'Unfortunately, I'm not.'

'Why "unfortunately", sir?' Ted asked.

'Well, Ben and I both have – how shall I put it? – something of a history with Evan Roberts,' Andrew said. 'Before his appointment to the bench, he was senior civil Treasury counsel, which meant that he represented ministers and government departments on a regular basis.'

'Including the Home Office,' Julia said quietly. 'He represented the Home Office in the Digby case, which Ben and I were both in, and his only concern was to avoid embarrassing the government at all costs.'

Ben nodded. 'I had an even worse run-in with him in the Welsh nationalist case. This was the case about the people who tried to plant a bomb in Caernarfon Castle at the time of Prince Charles's investiture as Prince of Wales.'

'Oh, God, yes, I remember that one,' Steffie said. 'I was assigned to undercover security work around the Old Bailey for the duration of the trial. You represented the woman, didn't you? She was convicted, but you got her off on appeal?'

Ben nodded. 'Arianwen Finch. Roberts prosecuted her. She was prosecuted on a false basis. Someone on the prosecution team decided to withhold from the jury the rather vital fact that her husband, Trevor, was an undercover police officer. That way, they avoided having to produce him as a witness. If he'd given evidence, she would never have been convicted. Instead, they spun the jury a yarn, telling them that Trevor was a guilty fugitive and they had no idea where he was – when all the time, they were hiding him in London. When that came to light in the Court of Appeal, the court was left with no choice. Andrew had to clean up Roberts's mess for him.'

'He was still trying to salvage the case in the Court of Appeal,' Andrew said, 'even after everyone knew that it was hopelessly compromised. The Director asked me to deal with it. I told the court that I couldn't support the conviction, and that was the end of it. Roberts was hugely embarrassed – as he should have been – and I'm sure he's never forgiven either of us.'

'We never knew whether he was in on the deception,' Ben said, 'or whether he just had no idea what he was doing. It obviously didn't do him any harm, because he was appointed not long afterwards. But, as Andrew said, I don't think he's forgiven us.'

'We've lost Ginny for the time being, as you know,' Andrew said. 'She's got a long civil case in the High Court starting tomorrow. She's been booked for over a year. So, it will be Ben and me, and we're stuck with Roberts whether we like it or not.'

'Couldn't you ask him to recuse himself,' Julia asked, 'hand it over to another judge?'

Andrew shook his head. 'Because we think he might have a grudge against us? Judges are supposed to be above that kind of thing. It would only make things worse.'

'We could remind him that he doesn't know any more about crime now than he did during the Welsh trial,' Ben grinned.

'Be my guest, Ben,' Andrew replied. 'I'll be happy to sit and watch.'

42

Monday 9 September 1974

'May it please your Lordship,' Andrew began. 'I appear to prosecute this case with my learned friend Mr Schroeder.'

They had assembled in court three at the Old Bailey at ten thirty. It had already been a busy morning: checking that arrangements for the witnesses were complete and in place; making sure that all the defence teams had received the papers they needed; ensuring that copies of all the documents had been made for the jury. It was as if they had done half a day's work before the court day even began. In addition, they were apprehensive: approaching unknown territory, a difficult case, now with four defendants, in front of a difficult judge. Until the proceedings finally got underway, Andrew and Ben were nervous. They sat quietly, side by side, in counsel's row, with John Caswell and Julia Cathermole sitting, equally tense, behind them.

'Yes, Mr Pilkington. The Court of Appeal was the last time I had the pleasure of seeing you, wasn't it?'

Andrew bit his lip. 'Yes, my Lord: some considerable time ago.'

'Yes, indeed. Still speaking Welsh, are we, Mr Schroeder?' It was said with a smirk from behind the familiar pince-nez glasses, still held in place by the thin gold chain. The tall, thin figure and the man's superior, patronising manner brought back instant memories of how unpleasant Evan Roberts had been at the bar. His appointment to the High Court bench seemed to have done nothing to improve his demeanour. Something to do with leopards and their spots, Ben thought to himself as he made his way, deliberately, only halfway up to his feet.

'I think your Lordship is confusing me with my head of chambers, Mr Morgan-Davies,' he replied.

The judge smiled thinly, but said nothing. Out of the corner of his eye, Ben saw Geoffrey, the usher, roll his eyes. Evidently what he had just witnessed was not the first display of judicial temperament the court staff had been obliged to put up with since Evan Roberts had come to sit at the Old Bailey.

'This is going to be fun,' Ben muttered to Andrew as he sat down.

'My Lord, the defendants are represented as follows. My learned friend Mr Norris represents Father Desmond Gerrard.

'My learned friends Mr Henderson and Miss Richardson represent Lord –'

'We shall continue to refer to him as Lord AB,' the judge said.

Andrew exchanged glances with Ben. 'My Lord, the defendants are not entitled to anonymity at this stage. The prosecution and the investigating officers used initials as a courtesy until their arrest, but –'

'And we will continue to accord them that courtesy until your opening speech, Mr Pilkington – assuming that the case goes as far as an opening speech.'

Andrew felt every eye in the courtroom on him. He felt a momentary temptation to tell Evan Roberts to make at least some effort to behave like a judge, but he closed his eyes, took a deep breath, and resisted it.

'As your Lordship pleases. My learned friends Mr Henderson and Miss Richardson represent Lord AB.

'My learned friends Mr Wallace QC and Mr Weatherly represent Sir CD.

'My learned friends Mr Moss QC and Mr Laud represent the Right Reverend EF. My Lord, I understand that my learned friends have a number of applications before we proceed to empanel a jury. I will defer to my learned friend Mr Henderson.'

The judge nodded, and smiled graciously in Henderson's direction. Ben shook his head. The sight of Mark Henderson in a criminal court was almost as much a rarity as it had been in his own case, but its significance was not lost on the judge, or on anyone in the courtroom. Henderson was a member of the judge's former chambers, and when Roberts had been appointed to the bench Henderson had in effect taken over his practice as civil Treasury counsel, representing government departments, often in sensitive cases involving classified materials. Given that the judge had only just been assigned to the case, Ben reflected, and that his assignment had not been announced in advance, the choice of Henderson to represent Lord AB was either very fortuitous or very nicely calculated by someone.

'My Lord,' Henderson began, 'I have three applications to make to your Lordship, in all of which I shall suggest that your Lordship should stay these proceedings as an abuse of process. One is concerned specifically with the case of Lord AB, and I propose to begin with that. The other two applications are common to all four defendants, and my learned friends have been good enough to invite me to make those applications on behalf of them all, which if it has no other merit, at least has the merit of saving the court's time to some extent.'

Mr Justice Roberts smiled. 'Very proper, Mr Henderson. Saving time is always something the court appreciates, of course. Please proceed.'

Ben felt a tug on his gown. He turned around, and felt Julia squeeze a folded up scrap of paper into this hand, with a look that said, 'For your eyes only'. The note read: 'Oh God, I hope they don't actually have sex in court. Destroy after reading.' Ben smiled at her, screwed the note up into a tight ball and carefully placed it in his jacket pocket for later destruction. Andrew looked at him inquiringly. He shook his head: nothing.

'I'm much obliged, my Lord. My first application relates to the state of Lord AB's health. Has your Lordship had the opportunity to read the medical reports prepared by Dr Laslo and Dr Frank? My instructing solicitors have served those reports on the Director of Public Prosecutions, so my learned friends for the Crown should have them.'

'We have received them, my Lord,' Andrew confirmed.

'I'm much obliged. 'Your Lordship will see from those reports,' Henderson began, 'that both doctors –'

'Both doctors,' the judge interrupted, 'appear to think that Lord AB is getting older. I'm sure they're right.'

Andrew glanced at Ben, raising his eyebrows.

'My Lord?'

'Lord AB is getting older, Mr Henderson. Isn't that what the reports tell us?'

Henderson seemed momentarily taken aback. 'They tell us rather more than that, my Lord.'

'They speak of a certain physical infirmity, difficulty in getting up and down flights of stairs, and so on.'

'My Lord, they also speak of a rapidly declining memory. They provide numerous examples of –'

'Of Lord AB forgetting appointments, having to write notes to remind himself of what he has to do today.'

'Exactly, my Lord.'

'Well, we all get to that stage eventually, don't we?'

Henderson hesitated. 'My Lord, perhaps we do. But it gives rise to concern about his ability to remember, and, in the context of this case, it puts him at a significant disadvantage. The case against him calls into question his conduct more than thirty years ago, in the 1940s. If his memory is unreliable, he is at a great disadvantage in the eyes of the jury when he is asked to account for the evidence of witnesses who say that they remember. I daresay many of us would struggle to remember what we were doing on a particular day in 1941 in any degree of detail.'

'I think most of us would remember whether or not we had sexually molested a schoolgirl, Mr Henderson, even in the 1940s, wouldn't we? That's the kind of thing that might well stick in one's memory, isn't it?'

Henderson again seemed taken aback. 'Lord AB denies that he ever behaved in that way.'

'In that case, he must remember perfectly well, mustn't he, at least for the purposes of this trial?'

'With respect, my Lord, it's not just a matter of remembering whether or not he molested girls. Of course, he remembers that. But to deal with the evidence, he has to account for his movements in some detail, when he went to Lancelot Andrewes School, and for what purpose.'

'Mr Henderson, are you saying that he doesn't remember whether he went to Lancelot Andrewes School?'

'No, my Lord. Lord AB did go to the school from time to time, in connection with the work of the school. He was one of the school's trustees. But as to the dates when he went there, his memory is understandably vague.'

'As I read the medical reports,' the judge said, 'especially Dr Laslo, it seems to me that any problem Lord AB has is with his short-term memory. He can't remember what he is supposed to be doing today, what he had for breakfast, why he went into a particular room of his house, and all the rest of it.'

'Yes, my Lord.'

'Yet, here he is at court today, having answered to his bail.'

'I'm sure this is one appointment his solicitors reminded him of, my Lord.'

'I'm sure they did. But that's quite different from his long-term memory isn't it? I don't see anything in the reports to suggest that he has any difficulty in remembering the distant past. Of course, we all have some difficulty in remembering the distant past, but that's a different thing, isn't it?'

'Dr Frank's report also suggests that he has some difficulty in concentrating for any great period of time – something which, if your Lordship will allow me to mention it, my instructing solicitors had also noticed. That, of course, will also cause him considerable difficulty in defending himself against a criminal charge in your Lordship's court.'

'In what way, Mr Henderson?'

'It's unlikely that he will be able to focus on the evidence throughout the court day, and give me proper instructions about it.' He paused. 'My Lord, Lord AB is in court, and he hears me say this, but say it I must. The reports do not suggest that Lord AB is senile at this point, but sadly, they do suggest that his mind has made a certain degree of progress down that road.'

Mr Justice Roberts leaned back in his chair.

'I daresay we've all made some progress in that direction, Mr Henderson, certainly those of us who are getting older.'

'My Lord…'

'I take it, Mr Henderson, that you read The Times, as we all do?'

'Yes, my Lord.'

'In which case, you may well have noticed a report, two or three weeks ago, of a speech made by your client in the House of Lords on the subject of trade union rights, the right to strike, the question of picket lines, and so on. Of course, I make no comment from the bench on the merits of what Lord AB said, but it was referred to in The Times's leader for the day; and if the report was accurate, I have to say that his speech seemed to me to be the very model of lucidity.'

Henderson took a deep breath. 'I regret to say that your Lordship has the advantage of me. I did not read that particular report.'

'And I should have thought that a man who is capable of making such a lucid and persuasive speech in the House of Lords is well capable of following the proceedings in this court.'

'My Lord –'

'Shall we move on to your next point, Mr Henderson?'

Andrew scribbled in his notebook and pushed it towards Ben. 'Do I detect a shift in the wind?' Ben scribbled two question marks underneath the note, and pushed the book back.

43

'My next point, my Lord,' Henderson continued, 'is made on behalf of all four defendants. The point is that the prosecution has already tried the case once with only one defendant, namely Father Gerrard. They failed to prove the case then, and there is no reason to suppose that the evidence is any better now that they have four to contend with.'

The judge looked puzzled. 'But retrials happen all the time, don't they, Mr Henderson? The prosecution is allowed a second bite at the cherry, surely.'

'The prosecution is taking several bites of the cherry, not just one. They could have proceeded against all four defendants in the first trial, but they elected not to. That's a decision they must live with. It's not right for them to add three defendants now in the hope that the numbers will make up for the lack of evidence. The evidence is the same now as it was in the first trial. The prosecution failed to prove the case against Father Gerrard last time, and the difficulties standing in their way – the need for corroboration and their reliance on this so-called recovered memory evidence – makes it almost certain that they will fail again.'

My Justice Roberts glanced at Andrew, who stood immediately.

'My Lord, in the first place, as your Lordship rightly says, the prosecution is entitled to a retrial. It's something that happens all the time in these courts. In the second place, the prosecution was fully entitled to proceed against Father Gerrard alone in the first trial, and is fully entitled to proceed against all four defendants now.'

'Mr Henderson says that you can't succeed because you're relying on the same evidence again, and it was found wanting in the first trial,' the judge said.

Andrew smiled. 'That's the whole idea of a retrial,' he observed. 'Otherwise, it wouldn't be a second bite at the cherry. But in addition, my Lord, while we do have all the evidence we adduced at the first trial, we now also have a number of additional witnesses, one of whom identifies my learned friend's client as one of the men who molested her.

'We also have several witnesses who will give evidence that Lancelot Andrewes School engaged in a systematic attempt to sweep the abuse under the carpet in the 1940s and 1950s, by waiving school fees in the case of any girl who complained of the abuse for the remainder of that girl's time at the school. That evidence has come to light since the first trial, and I venture to say that if the jury in the first trial had known about it, the result would have been very different. We fully expect it to be different this time.

'There can't be any prejudice to the defendants in any of this. They are represented; they will have the opportunity to challenge the evidence; and they will have the opportunity to address your Lordship on any points of law that may arise.'

The judge nodded.

'Next point, Mr Henderson, please.'

Henderson exchanged frustrated looks with his colleagues on the defence side.

'Finally, my Lord, I say that your Lordship should stay these proceedings as an abuse of process because it is impossible for these defendants to receive a fair trial, given the level of publicity the case has attracted. The press coverage began long before the first trial, when the rumour mill began its work, and the names of Lancelot Andrewes School and Father Gerrard began to be whispered abroad. Even at that early stage the names of the other three defendants were being bandied about in some quarters. It's all been an open secret ever since.'

He paused.

'That was alleviated to some extent, I concede, by the official use of initials instead of their real names. I understand that my learned friend Mr Pilkington not only agreed to the use of initials, but actually instigated it, and I express my appreciation to him for that.'

He turned to nod to Andrew, who returned the gesture.

'But even before the first trial, the names of the other three defendants were mentioned in certain sections of the press – including the press in other countries – and when the first trial began, they were mentioned by their initials in evidence, in connection with the allegations they now face. My Lord, if they had been prosecuted in the first trial, they would have had the right to challenge the evidence against them. But as it is, the evidence in the first trial has been widely reported, without any challenge to it by three of the four defendants.

'Given the saturation level of the press coverage, which continues even today – I'm sure your Lordship has seen the headlines this morning, as I have – it would be impossible to find a jury of twelve people who have not been following the case in all its gory detail for months. Anyone who has been exposed to the press coverage will inevitably have known the identity of all the defendants, and will inevitably have formed a view against them. The case has already been tried in the press, and it simply isn't possible now to empanel a jury capable of giving the defendants a fair trial in your Lordship's courtroom.'

Again, the judge turned to Andrew.

'The publicity is a matter of some concern, Mr Pilkington, isn't it?'

'Yes, my Lord, it is,' Andrew replied immediately. 'But we often have high-profile cases in our courts, and we have protocols for managing them. It will be important for your Lordship to direct the jury firmly, at the outset of the trial, that they must put out of their minds whatever they may have read or heard about the case, and concentrate on the evidence given in court to the exclusion of everything else. Your Lordship must also warn them repeatedly, throughout the trial, not to follow coverage of the proceedings in the press, on the radio, or on television.'

'That's all very well in theory,' Henderson interrupted, 'but in practice you can't expect a group of twelve people with no legal training to take that on board. They're bound to be affected by what's going on all around them.'

'My learned friend seems to have little faith in juries,' Andrew said.

'That's quite correct, my Lord,' Henderson smiled. 'I don't. Jurors are only human. Even for those of us with the training, putting information one is exposed to out of one's mind is a difficult exercise – as your Lordship, I'm sure, knows only too well. For those without training, I venture to say it's effectively impossible.'

'*I* venture to say,' Andrew replied, 'that if my learned friend's practice had brought him into contact with the criminal courts more often, he might have a more enlightened view. Jurors do this all the time, both in very serious cases such as this and in less serious cases throughout the country, in which there may have been local press coverage. Our experience over the years has been that jurors, almost without exception, are extremely conscientious men and women, who take their responsibilities seriously and listen carefully to directions from the bench.

'Mr Schroeder and I have dealt with any number of high-profile criminal cases – as have some other learned counsel on the defence side in this case – and in each of those cases, the trial judge gave the jury the directions I have suggested. In each case, the jury followed those directions and returned verdicts in accordance with the evidence. I've had a number of such cases in which the jury returned verdicts of not guilty, so I have every confidence in the ability of jurors to be fair and impartial, even in high-profile cases.'

The judge nodded. 'They certainly were in the Welsh case,' he observed.

'In this case, it would be very dangerous,' Henderson protested.

Andrew shook his head. 'If my learned friend is right, paradoxically, it would prevent any prosecution in the most serious cases of all; because the more serious a case is, the more attention it attracts from the press. It can't be right that the most serious cases can never be prosecuted because of press coverage.'

He paused.

'Frankly, my Lord, if we can't trust juries, it brings our system of criminal justice to a standstill. If that were the case, I submit that Parliament would have noticed before now, and there would have been a radical change in the way in which we try criminal cases. That has not happened, and I'm not aware of any plans to make any such change.'

The judge considered for some time.

'I agree, Mr Pilkington. Mr Henderson, are there any other submissions you wish to make?'

Henderson stared at the judge for some seconds, and then glanced questioningly across at the other defence counsel, who, with one exception, shook their heads in unison. Anthony Norris tried to get his attention, but without success.

'No, my Lord.' He sat down, apparently deflated.

'Does anyone else wish to be heard on the defence side?'

Norris stood. 'Yes, my Lord,' he said. 'I do.' He looked dismissively at Mark Henderson. 'Since no one else has mentioned it, I suppose I will have to.'

'What is your point, Mr Norris?' the judge asked.

'My point, my Lord, is that there is one aspect of this trial no one has yet mentioned which will make it entirely impossible for my client to receive a fair trial, and, I suspect, may do so in the cases of Lord AB and Sir CD also – though that's a matter for my learned friends who represent them: for whatever reason, the point hasn't been raised on their behalf.'

'Then you'd better enlighten us, Mr Norris, hadn't you?' the judge said, to smiles around the courtroom.

'I fully intend to do so, my Lord,' Norris replied. He picked up a document he had in front of him on the bench.

'My Lord, following the usual procedure, all four defendants were interviewed by the police. Three chose to exercise their right to remain silent, but one – the Right Reverend EF – treated the police to a detailed account of what he claimed to have been going on in Father Gerrard's library during the war years, between 1940 and 1945. Much of his statement confirms accounts given by the prosecution witnesses, and if true, directly incriminates Lord AB, Sir CD and Father Gerrard – and, indirectly, EF himself. I understand that the prosecution intend to place this statement in front of the jury as evidence.'

'We certainly do, my Lord,' Andrew said, smiling and rising halfway to his feet.

'In that case, my Lord,' Norris said, 'I invite your Lordship to stay the proceedings unless my learned friend gives a clear undertaking not to do so.'

'But why?' the judge asked. 'Are you saying it's inadmissible for some reason?'

'It's a point of law that arises every day in the criminal courts, my Lord – which, I assume, is why it didn't occur to my learned friend Mr Henderson...'

'Oh, really, my Lord...' Henderson protested.

'That will do, Mr Norris,' the judge said. 'Please avoid personal slights on other counsel, and make your submission as succinctly as you can.'

'As your Lordship pleases. The rules of evidence are quite clear. A statement made to the police by one defendant, in the absence of the others, may be admissible as evidence against the defendant who makes the statement, but it is not evidence against any other defendant who may be implicated by it. I can show your Lordship the authorities in *Archbold*.'

Andrew stood.

'That's not necessary, as far as we're concerned,' he said. 'The prosecution accepts that is the law, of course. As my learned friend rightly says, it's a point that arises in criminal courts, day in, day out.'

'Yes,' the judge agreed.

'And what happens in criminal courts day in, day out, is that the judge explains that rule to the jury and directs them to regard the statement as evidence only against the defendant who made it. It all works perfectly well. As I said in reply to my learned friend Mr Henderson a few minutes ago, it is something juries are perfectly able to cope with.'

'In general, that may be true,' Norris replied. 'But there are cases in which the prejudice to other defendants is such that the court shouldn't allow it. One can hardly overstate the impact this statement will make on the jury. But Bishop EF is not obliged to give evidence, and unless he does, we can't cross-examine him. Father Gerrard is entitled to confront his accuser, but if your Lordship allows this evidence, he can't.'

'He has other witnesses he can cross-examine,' the judge pointed out.

'Perhaps so, my Lord, but he's entitled to cross-examine all the witnesses.'

Andrew shook his head. 'Father Gerrard has had every opportunity to defend himself, my Lord, but so far he has chosen not to do so. He could have given the police his account of events, and he could have given evidence at the first trial. He did neither of those things. But he will have a further opportunity to give evidence in this trial.'

'He can't be compelled to give evidence,' Norris retorted.

'I didn't suggest otherwise,' Andrew insisted.

'But you did. In effect, you're compelling him to give evidence because of the overwhelming prejudice of a statement that isn't even admissible evidence against him.'

'My Lord,' Andrew said, 'I don't deny that there are cases in which the strength of the prosecution case makes it advisable for a defendant to give evidence. This may be one of them, it may not. That's a matter for my learned friends to consider with their clients. It's not a matter for the prosecution.'

'Then, I apply for Father Gerrard to be tried separately from the Right Reverend EF,' Norris said.

'The Crown strenuously opposes that application,' Andrew replied firmly. 'The Crown's case is that all four were involved together in conspiracies and the commission of acts of sexual abuse, and it is right that they should be tried together. Your Lordship will explain to the jury that the statement is only evidence against EF, and not against the others, and the jury will deal with it accordingly.'

'That's an exercise in wishful thinking,' Norris complained.

'I don't regard the rules of evidence as involving wishful thinking,' Andrew replied.

The judge held up a hand.

'All right. I've heard enough.'

He consulted his notes.

'I haven't heard anything which leads me to think that this trial can't proceed in a manner which is fair to all four defendants. They will have every opportunity to challenge the evidence, and to draw the jury's attention to any weaknesses in the evidence, and I am sure they will do so very effectively. I will direct the jury very carefully about all the matters counsel have raised, and as Mr Pilkington has said, I have every confidence that the jury will follow my directions. If anything arises during trial that casts doubt on the view I have formed, then I will reconsider, but for now, I'm quite sure that this trial can, and should proceed. The prosecution's applications for a stay of the proceedings as an abuse of process are dismissed, as is the application that Father Gerrard should be tried separately.

'If Lord AB – or Sir CD, who I believe suffered a stroke recently – need to take breaks during the trial, either for medical reasons or to consult with counsel, then of course, I will afford them every consideration.

'Mr Pilkington, I understand that you propose to arrange for the young girl, Emily, to give evidence tomorrow, in view of the uncertainty about how long we would need for legal submissions today?'

'Yes, my Lord. She gave evidence within half a day in the first trial, and it is our view that she should be allowed to do so again, so as to reduce the strain on her as far as possible.'

The judge nodded. 'She will give evidence tomorrow morning, and we will finish with her before lunch.'

'I'm much obliged.'

'My Lord, I can't guarantee to finish with her in that time,' Henderson protested, rising to his feet.

'We will finish with her before lunch,' the judge repeated. 'You'll have overnight to prepare, Mr Henderson, and I expect you to confer with other counsel, to avoid any repetition. I don't want to have her answering the same questions more than once. I'm sure, given the experience of counsel, it won't be a problem.'

The judge conferred briefly with his clerk, Lewis.

'I will rise for a few minutes until a jury panel can be brought down to court. We will empanel a jury and have the Crown's opening, and we will then adjourn until tomorrow morning.'

After the judge had left the bench and returned to his chambers, Andrew and Ben stood and turned to John Caswell and Julia Cathermole, who were shaking their heads.

'Well, it just goes to show,' Andrew said with a broad smile. 'I may have to take back everything I said about Evan Roberts. He started out as if he meant to give us a hard time, but in the end, he went with us on everything.'

'I couldn't believe my ears,' Julia agreed. 'What on earth has come over him?'

John shrugged. 'People do change when they go on the bench.'

'Perhaps so,' Ben said, 'but I'm going to wait to see how he handles the trial before I start singing his praises.'

'You've been burned before,' Andrew said, smiling.

'Yes, I have.'

44

Ben and Julia left the secure witness room, where they had been talking with Emily and Audrey. Emily seemed cheerful and in good spirits, and not at all intimidated. She had brought some school work to do, and was apparently quite happy to sit and do it until she was needed. Audrey, too, was composed, though she was pale and looked tired. Ben had calculated that they would not get beyond Emily and Audrey that day, and indeed, it was unlikely that Audrey's evidence would be concluded. He had advised John Caswell not to ask any other witnesses to attend, though Mary Forbes was on call at her hotel, in case the evidence planned for the day did not last as long as anticipated. They arrived in court just before ten thirty.

'The judge wants to see us in chambers – counsel only,' Andrew said as they were about to take their places.

Ben was taken aback. 'What about?'

'Lewis didn't say: just that we were to let him know when everyone was here. We're just waiting for Norris; I think I've seen everyone else. You haven't seen John, have you?'

'No. He wasn't with us when we went to see Emily. We assumed he was getting the evidence together. I wonder what the judge wants?'

'Let's hope he hasn't had second thoughts about abuse of process overnight,' Julia said.

'I wouldn't have thought so,' Ben replied. 'Roberts has always struck me as the kind of man who doesn't budge once he's made his mind up.'

'Perhaps he wants to warn everyone to behave themselves when Emily's in the box,' Andrew suggested. 'It's the kind of thing most judges would say in open court with the jury present, but he hasn't been in the job all that long, so perhaps he thinks it's better said outside court.'

'Well, we'll soon know,' Ben said. 'Here comes Norris now. I'll tell Geoffrey, and he can tell Lewis we're ready.' He walked away to where the tall silver-haired usher was standing by the jury box. Geoffrey nodded and walked away towards the judge's chambers. He returned a few moments later with the court clerk.

'Come with me, please,' Lewis said grandly.

Andrew and Ben led the way, defence counsel following closely behind. Lewis knocked on the door of the judge's chambers. They heard a 'come in' from inside. Lewis opened the door, stood back as they entered, and took a seat near the door. Ben noticed the judge's face immediately, and stared at him. The cheeks were red, the eyes dark, and the lips were drawn angrily together. It was an expression Ben had seen before, and the reminder was uncomfortable. It was the expression he had seen on Evan Roberts's face when he and Gareth Morgan-Davies had first confronted him about the deception of the jury in the Welsh case; and in the Court of Appeal, when Ben had told the judges that it was their duty to consider the possible involvement of everyone involved with the prosecution. It was an expression that didn't bode well. The judge was obviously not in the mood for pleasantries. There were not enough chairs for everyone to sit down: most judges would have made some light comment about it, perhaps promising not to take too much time over whatever he had to say to them. Evan Roberts said nothing, and left it up to counsel to find a place to sit or stand. Most of the barristers remained standing.

'I've called you in this morning,' he began tersely, 'because within the last half hour I have received some information which calls into question the future of this case. Pilkington, have you received any word from the Director's office?'

Andrew looked at the judge blankly. 'Word, Judge? No. Word about what?'

'Word about this,' Evan Roberts replied, extending a hand in Andrew's direction. The hand contained a document. Andrew took it from him. He read it, and sat down abruptly in a chair that happened to be vacant to his left.

'What is it?' Ben asked. Andrew handed the document to him.

'For the benefit of those who can't see it,' the judge said, 'I have received an order of *nolle prosequi* from the office of the Attorney General. I'm no expert in criminal law, as yet. But unless I'm very much mistaken, this means that he is ordering me not to allow the case to proceed.'

Andrew nodded. '*Nolle prosequi* is an order made by the Attorney General prohibiting the court from proceeding with a particular case. It's an order which can be issued at any time before judgment – in other words, before the passing of sentence.'

'Andrew, since we can't all see it, would you mind reading it?' Henderson asked. Andrew nodded. He took the document back from Ben.

Order of Nolle Prosequi *relating to the case against Desmond Gerrard and three other defendants known as Lord AB, Sir CD, and the Right Reverend EF, now proceeding in the Central Criminal Court.*

Having regard to the powers and discretion vested in me as Her Majesty's Attorney General; and

Having regard to the duty imposed on me to protect the national interest and to ensure fairness to defendants charged in criminal proceedings; and

Having considered representations made to me by learned counsel on behalf of Lord AB and Sir CD, and certain medical reports referred to in those representations; and

Having considered representations made to me on behalf of

Her Majesty's Government; and
 Having considered all the facts and circumstances of the above case:
 I find that –

(1) *Lord AB is physically or mentally unfit to stand trial;*
(2) *Sir CD is physically or mentally unfit to stand trial;*
(3) *In the case of the Right Reverend EF, it would be against the national interest to allow the case against him to proceed;*
(4) *In the case of Desmond Gerrard, having regard to the decisions I have reached in the case of the other three defendants, and to the fact that he has been tried on indictment in respect of the alleged offences on an earlier occasion, on which the jury were unable to agree on verdicts, it would be unfair to proceed against him further.*

In the light of the above findings, I have concluded that the right course is to exercise my discretion and to issue an order of Nolle Prosequi, *requiring the Central Criminal Court and the Prosecution not to proceed further against the said defendants.*

'It's signed on behalf of the Attorney,' Andrew concluded.

Glances were exchanged, but no one spoke for a full minute.

'I think you might have told me you were asking the Attorney to intervene, Mark,' Andrew said quietly.

'We sent you the medical reports, Andrew,' Henderson replied.

'That's hardly the same thing.'

'I'm sorry, Andrew, but frankly, I assumed the Attorney would have consulted the Director before making a decision. That's the usual practice, isn't it?'

Andrew stood, making a massive effort to recover from the shock he felt. 'Judge, I'm taken completely by surprise. I haven't been able to speak with the Deputy Director this morning. I'd like the chance to see him and find out what's going on. I'm going to ask you to adjourn for the day, and to order that the case be listed again at ten thirty tomorrow morning.'

'There's no need for that, Judge,' Anthony Norris objected, sensing blood in the water, and anxious to pounce before his prey could escape. 'Once a *nolle prosequi* is entered, that's the end of the case. The court has no further power to deal with it. You should dismiss the indictment forthwith, and let us tell the defendants they're free to go home.'

'I agree,' Henderson added. 'There's nothing the court can do about it.'

'You don't have to take that action today, Judge, if you have any ground for requesting further information,' Andrew insisted. 'Yesterday, you ruled that there is no reason to stay this case as an abuse of process; so you have every reason to question why today, a government minister is giving you instructions which go against that ruling. And what does the Attorney mean by the national interest? There's no obvious public interest to justify governmental interference in this case. It goes, not only against your ruling, but against the independence of the judiciary. It would be perfectly reasonable for you to inquire further before dismissing the indictment.'

'There's nothing to inquire into,' Norris replied, with a smile. 'The Attorney General has acted within his authority, and it's not for the court to defy him.'

'I'm not asking you to defy him, Judge,' Andrew said. 'All I'm suggesting is that it's important for the court to have all available information before it, to exclude any possibility of error, before taking a step such as dismissing an indictment.'

'I agree,' Mr Justice Roberts said. 'This has a very unpleasant taste to it.'

'With all due respect, Judge,' Henderson replied, 'I'm not sure what you mean by that. There's nothing improper in the defence asking the Attorney to intervene. I hope you're not implying that Wallace or I have…'

'Enough, Mr Henderson,' the judge said angrily. 'I will not

hear any more. This case is adjourned until ten thirty tomorrow morning, when everyone, including the defendants, will attend. Mr Pilkington, I expect you to keep me informed about the progress of your inquiries.'

'Yes, of course, Judge.'

'I'm sorry, Andrew,' John Caswell said when they emerged from the judge's chambers into the courtroom. 'Everyone in the office is running around like headless chickens. The Director has been trying to find out what's going on, and he kept me on the phone. By the time I got to court, you'd already gone into chambers.'

Andrew nodded. 'What did the Director have to say?'

John considered carefully. 'The Director is profoundly shocked.'

'Aren't we all?' Ben asked quietly.

'He's not aware of any compelling public interest which would prevent the case from going ahead, and the Attorney's office didn't say anything to enlighten him.'

'It's an attack on the independence of the judiciary,' Andrew said.

'I suspect the Director would agree,' John said. 'But he has to be very careful. You must understand that, at present, he doesn't know any more than you or I. We don't even know whether the Attorney is going to make a statement in the House, or call a press conference, to explain himself. On the face of it, the Attorney is within his rights.'

'On the face of it,' Andrew commented, 'it's a blatant political intervention, without any justification, designed to prevent the prosecution of four men prominent in public life who have almost certainly committed very serious offences.'

'The Director can't jump to conclusions like that, Andrew. You know that as well as I do. His hands are tied.'

'Surely there must be something he can do?' Ben asked incredulously. 'The Attorney is trespassing on the Director's territory just as much as the court's.'

'The Director reports to the Attorney, Ben,' John replied. 'He has no power to question the Attorney's decision. If you want to get the Attorney overruled, you have to get the ear of the Home Secretary, maybe even the Prime Minister.'

'All roads lead back to the Home Office,' Julia whispered. She had been watching as the defence counsel explained to their clients why they were likely to walk from court free of all charges the following morning, a message she noted bitterly, that Lord AB appeared to understand without any difficulty. A visible mood of exuberance and relief was sweeping through the dock as the defendants were released for the day.

'What?'

'Nothing,' she replied. She forced her attention away from the festivities at the back of the court. 'John, Andrew, this means you're out of it, doesn't it, unless the Attorney changes his mind?'

John nodded. 'I'm afraid so.'

'All right. I suppose Ben and I will have to go and tell Audrey and Emily what's happened. God only knows what we're going to say to them.'

'I'll come with you,' Andrew volunteered.

'Thank you: because before I send them home to Ely, yet again, without any resolution, we need to work out whether we have anywhere left to go.'

Julia returned after finding Audrey and Emily a taxi.

'She has every right to be upset,' Andrew said. 'I wish there was more I could do.'

'You and John have done all you could,' Julia replied. 'You couldn't have anticipated this. But it's all fallen apart, and now we have to pick up the pieces and see if we can glue them together.'

'We should meet later in the day,' Ben suggested. 'If necessary, we may have to make a night of it. Do you want to come to chambers?'

'No, Ben. Let's not rush it. We've taken a body blow. There's no way around that. Nothing's going to change tomorrow, is it?'

'I'm afraid not.'

'Then let's give ourselves a day or two to get our breath back and let our minds start working again.' She smiled. 'Besides, chambers is no place for a wake – which is what it may turn into. Let's leave it until Friday. Come to my place around seven for supper and a couple of drinks.' She paused. 'Bring Jess. Call Ginny and ask if she and Michael can join us. The more the merrier. One or two fresh minds wouldn't hurt at this point, would they?'

'Nothing can hurt very much now,' Ben replied.

45

It's getting to be a familiar feeling: the taxi to King's Cross, the train home to Ely, fretting, feeling the knots in my stomach, feeling beaten down, hopeless, feeling like a victim all over again, nothing decided, everything floating uncertainly in the air, with failure the only likely outcome; this time with Emily sitting silently by my side, practising her nine-year-old's gentle diplomacy by immersing herself in her book, bravely pretending that nothing is wrong, when she knows that everything is as wrong as it could be.

There is one thing that's not wrong, and I must find a way to make sure she knows that. The one thing that's not wrong is that we are alive. We have survived. We have survived everything Father Gerrard, and those paedophiles, and those jurors, and the Attorney General have done to us. Ken and Emily and I are alive; we have survived. We are a family, and we're still here, and we will still be here, tomorrow, and the next day, and the day after that.

Until now, I've been alternating between anger and self-pity, with flashes of guilt that I can't match Emily's courage: her courage, which shames and humiliates me when I compare it to my own incessant state of fear. It breaks my heart when she reminds me so much of Joan, as she does more and more, as every day goes by, with her patience and her quiet stoicism. But now, my anger seems to have turned inwards. It's not on the surface any more. I'm aware of it, and I know I can harness it at any time. But another feeling has come over me now. I'm not sure quite how to describe it. It's not resignation, exactly, because I still want to fight these people tooth and nail, if Julia and Ben can find a way to do it. It's more like a feeling of waking up to reality, of becoming aware of what I'm up against. John Singer and the Ely mafia were the least of our worries, if only we had known it. I don't even know what forces are arrayed against us now, and I can't imagine their strength; and I confess to a certain cynicism creeping into my mind. I'm thinking, for the first time, that there may be forces too strong for people like me to challenge. I'm thinking, for the first time, that it may really be true, what people say: that there's one law for the powerful and well connected in this world, and one law for the rest of us.

46

'This has nothing to do with Six, Julia,' Baxter said.

They were walking slowly through Green Park in an early onset of cool autumnal air, having emerged from the underground station via different exits, in conformity with Baxter's aging classical notions of tradecraft: another well-tried venue, another well-honed method: another promise to answer any questions he could, but no guarantees.

'I wish I could believe that,' she replied.

'It's true,' he insisted. 'We didn't approach the Attorney General. I found out about this from the lunchtime news on the Home Service, or whatever they call it now. I told you before, we have no interest in interfering with the trial.'

'What you told me before was that you didn't have any interest in Father Gerrard. You seemed to have quite a lot of interest in Bishop EF.'

'We've seen the statement he made to the police. It doesn't concern us. It surprised us, to be honest. He kept our secrets better than we'd expected.'

'He talked about the service's involvement with Lancelot Andrewes during the war, and the word is already out about a German man being involved.'

'Yes, but he didn't name Six, and he didn't name Father Köhler. There's no reason for us to try to suppress it. Frankly, it would probably only make things worse if we did. Anyway, we didn't. I know that because if we had, I would have been the one to arrange it.' He smiled. 'C always saves jobs like that for me.'

'Then, who did?' she asked, with a sudden flash of anger.

He stopped; she also stopped and turned to face him.

'You really should come and work for us, Julia. You have all the necessary paranoia already in place. Why do you think someone has been prowling around backstage here? According to the news, it was defence counsel who applied for the *nolle prosequi*, which, apparently, they're entitled to do. It sounded to me as though the Attorney General had his reasons for what he did. I'm sure you don't agree with him – I wouldn't expect you to – but he had his reasons. Why does there have to be something sinister in it?'

'Mark Henderson is virtually standing counsel to the Home Office. You don't think he could prowl around backstage if he wanted to?'

'In that case, why aren't you talking to the Home Office, instead of me?'

She took a copy of the order from her purse and held it out towards him. He took it and read it quickly.

'Two defendants not up to the strain of standing trial, heavy publicity, legal concerns about the evidence. I'm not seeing the service's fingerprints here.'

She moved closer to him and used her thumb to point on the paper. She read the sentence she had pointed to. '"In the case of the Right Reverend EF, it would be against the national interest to allow the case against him to proceed." What does that mean, for God's sake, if it doesn't mean that someone is worried about EF shooting his mouth off? What else about this trial could conceivably harm the national interest? And exactly what representations was Her Majesty's government making to the Attorney?'

'I don't know, Julia. I told you: we're not worried about EF's statement.'

'You really weren't worried about what he might say if he gave evidence? He probably would have, you know. I have three witnesses who identify him as an abuser. He would have had to come up with something.'

Baxter thought for some time. 'All I can tell you is that we're not responsible for this. We've known each other a long time, and I hope you know by now that I wouldn't lie to you.'

'Unless it was in the national interest?'

He smiled. 'Unless it was in the national interest. The rest of the time, I might refuse to answer your questions, but I wouldn't lie to you.'

She returned the smile, and they resumed their walk.

'Who else might have done this, Baxter?' she asked, her voice quieter now.

He shook his head. 'I honestly don't know, Julia. Five, possibly? They've had an interest in EF for longer than we have. But if it was Five, I'd expect them to mention it to us. They know we're an interested party when it comes to EF. I'd be very surprised – and very annoyed, frankly – if they kept us in the dark.' He paused. 'Why aren't you looking at the Home Office? You said their counsel was involved, and there is a connection, isn't there – the waiver of fees in Woman B's case? Are there other examples?'

She nodded. 'Yes, eleven in all. But we have no direct evidence of Home Office involvement except in Woman B's case.' She paused. 'Would they do something like this without telling you?'

'Why would they tell us?'

They resumed their walk.

'What are you going to do?' he asked, after a prolonged silence.

'I don't know. I'm not sure there's anything we can do. We're meeting tomorrow to talk about it.'

'Is it possible,' Baxter asked, 'that by "national interest" the Attorney General meant that any prosecution must be fair to the defendants, nothing more than that?'

'He used the word "unfair" in referring to Gerrard,' Julia pointed out. 'With EF, he talks about the "national interest". I would expect the Attorney General to use some precision of language. So in his mind, there's a difference.'

Baxter laughed. 'If he wrote it himself –'

'Whether or not he wrote it, one would hope he read it before he signed off on it.'

'If whoever wrote it gave sufficient thought to the wording, then you might have a point. But you should read some of the memos that circulate in our office. Not that I'd let you, of course, but if I did, precision of language isn't the first thing that would spring to mind.'

He stopped again.

'Julia, the Attorney General has the reputation of being incorruptible, and we certainly think of him as a straight arrow.'

'I know. But any mention of the "national interest" has a way of influencing people's judgement.'

'If I were you,' Baxter said, 'I would try to entertain the idea that the defence got the better of you.'

'I don't think they did,' she insisted.

'Even so…' Baxter replied.

47

Friday 13 September 1974

'I like your idea of supper and a couple of drinks, Julia,' Ben said, with a grin. He and Jess had just arrived at Julia's luxurious town house, which was secreted away in a quiet, elegant street in a prestigious quarter of Knightsbridge. On being shown into the dining room by a young woman in a smart black and white maid's outfit, they had been met by the sight of a large table standing against the wall, on which were displayed a whole salmon, dishes of caviar, bowls of green salad and potato salad, and heaped plates of sliced fresh French bread. Three bottles of Veuve Clicquot champagne on ice, and the same number of bottles of Evian water, were carefully positioned behind the food. A man in evening dress and another woman in the same black and white uniform were standing nearby, one at each end of the table.

'I leave the details to Jean-Claude and his merry men and women,' she replied, with a nod to the man, who returned it respectfully. 'Cater in, that's what I say. It's the only way for a girl on the go.'

'It's magnificent,' Jess said.

Julia hugged her. 'Ben told me your news, Jess. It's great. I'm so pleased for you.'

Jess kissed her on the cheek. 'Thank you.'

'And, of course, you know Ginny and Michael.'

'Of course.'

Ginny hugged and kissed Jess in turn. 'Our congratulations

too, Jess. I don't know why I haven't seen you since Ben told me, but we're very happy for you both.'

'Thank you, Ginny. How's your case in the High Court going?'

'Settled yesterday,' Ginny replied, 'halfway through trial, on very good terms. I'm in a very, very good mood.'

'Michael,' Ben said, shaking hands. 'It's been a while. How are you? How's practice?'

'Flourishing, thank you, Ben. The inhabitants of Walthamstow are as litigious as ever, especially in the family courts, I'm glad to say. Long may it continue.'

The man and the young woman moved among them, he with the champagne, she with the Evian and orange juice. Everyone except Jess took champagne. They stood as a group in the centre of the room and raised their glasses.

'I'd like to propose one or two toasts,' Julia said. 'First, to Ben and Jess, and their forthcoming new arrival. Every happiness.'

They drank.

'And to Audrey, Ken, and Emily. May they prosper: and confusion to all their enemies.'

'Audrey, Ken, and Emily,' the others responded in unison.

'Well, we have some talking to do,' Julia said, 'so let's take our seats. The protocol is that you all help yourselves, and please don't leave anything because I won't know what to do with it.' She turned to the man. 'Jean-Claude, darling, we have things to discuss: would you and Valérie excuse us, please?'

Jean-Claude nodded. 'Of course, Miss Cathermole. We'll be in the kitchen. Ring when you're ready for dessert.' He ushered Valérie discreetly out of the room and followed, closing the door quietly behind him.

'Dessert? After all this?' Michael asked.

'I find there's always room for a chocolate tarte, Michael, or there's some Camembert, if you prefer.'

At her signal, they eagerly raided the salmon and accompanying dishes, and took their seats at the dinner table.

'So,' Julia said, 'who wants to start?'

Ben replaced his champagne flute on the table. 'Andrew and I talked at some length this afternoon. Neither of us sees any way around the *nolle prosequi*. The Attorney General has the discretion to make the order, and he's given what appear to be logical reasons for it. The High Court won't help us. If he gets up and screams about the national interest, that's all it would take for the Court to uphold him.'

'He made a statement in the House yesterday,' Ginny added. 'It was reported in the *Standard*, and in all the nationals today: there's nothing new. He didn't even mention the national interest. He said he was concerned with the fairness of the proceedings to the defendants.'

'What about fairness to the victims?' Jess asked. 'Whatever happened to that? I don't get it.'

'Neither do I,' Julia replied. 'And I don't buy it. But I think Ben's right. We have no legal basis to challenge it. What's done is done. We have to lick our wounds and move on.'

'How do you move on from this?' Jess asked.

'By changing direction,' Ginny said. 'It hasn't worked out in the criminal courts. Fine, let's follow Norris's advice and sue them in the civil courts. Let's take them to the High Court. That way, we can sue the school as well.'

'Much easier,' Michael commented, 'no jury to worry about – you'd have a judge sitting alone; and you don't have to prove anything beyond reasonable doubt – all you need to prove is that your case is more likely than not to be true.'

'And the rules of evidence are more flexible,' Ben added. 'They don't take corroboration as seriously, and they bend the hearsay rule in ways you couldn't with a jury.'

Jess shook her head. 'That works for Emily, Ginny, but not for Audrey. The statute of limitations ran on her claim long ago. What would it be in this kind of case, six years? If the abuse ended in 1944, 1945, and she didn't sue by, let's say, sometime in 1950, 1951, the suit is time-barred.'

'Not necessarily,' Michael said. 'The statute doesn't begin to run unless you know that you have a claim; and if you're a minor, it doesn't start to run until you attain your majority – so that would be, what, at the earliest 1954 or thereabouts? In any case, Audrey had no memory of the abuse until Emily spoke up, so you could argue that she had no knowledge of the abuse until then: and in that case, the period doesn't begin until 1972.'

Ben sat back with a smile. 'That's a great argument, Michael.'

'But recovered memory is already suspect,' Jess pointed out. 'How likely is it that the court would allow her to rely on it to defer the period?'

'It doesn't matter,' Julia replied. 'If the judge doesn't accept recovered memory, her claim is gone anyway. She has no case without it – forget about the statute of limitations. But if the judge is prepared to give her memory some weight, it prevents the defendants from pouring her out on a technicality.'

'It's worth a try,' Ben said.

'It works for Audrey and Emily,' Julia said, 'but not for Mary, or the other women who came forward, I'm afraid. They have no case. I hope they will give evidence anyway.'

'I'm sure Mary will,' Ben replied. 'I don't know about the others.'

'I'll talk to them,' Julia said. 'Let's hope it won't be a problem.'

'Are we agreed, then?' Ginny asked.

No one replied immediately, but there were smiles around the table.

'It seems we are,' Ben replied.

'The Attorney can't issue *nolle prosequi* in a civil case, can he?' Michael asked.

'He can, actually,' Ginny replied, 'but it would be a hard road to hold. With no criminal penalties at stake and no jury, he would be hard-pressed to argue that a High Court judge couldn't try the case fairly. I doubt he would try to interfere.'

After dessert and coffee, as Ben and Jess were leaving, close on the heels of Ginny and Michael, Julia held them at the door for a moment.

'Are you wishing I hadn't come to you now, Ben?' she asked with a smile. 'I wouldn't blame you.'

'No,' Ben replied. 'We were right about having a fight on our hands, weren't we? But no, I've never regretted it, not even for a moment.'

'I appreciate everything you've done.'

'It's changed for me since Jess told me she was expecting,' Ben replied. 'I'm going to be a father soon myself, and I can really identify with Audrey now. I can feel what she's going through. I'm beginning to understand how careful you have to be – and even then, it may not be enough.'

'It seems it's getting more and more difficult to protect children,' Jess added, taking Ben's hand. 'But at least we're going to make careful inquiries about any school we send him, or her, to.'

'It's made me think about my own family, too.' Ben said. 'I grew up in the East End, just like Audrey. I was too young to be evacuated – I was born after the Blitz. But I know my family spent nights in underground stations, and had friends who died in air raids, and I can't imagine what it must have been like to be a child, with all the bombing going on, and all the devastation – places you'd known all your life just gone, totally obliterated. I suppose my heart went out to Audrey when she told me her story. I'd love to find a way to make things better for her.'

'It's been a lovely evening, Julia,' Jess said, kissing her on the cheek. 'Thank you.'

'I'd love to find a way too,' Julia said out loud when she had closed the door behind them.

PART FOUR

48

The phone on the small table beside Ted Phillips's bed rang insistently. He woke abruptly, sat up, then lowered himself down on to his back and listened to the relentless tone wearily for some seconds. He glanced at his alarm clock: just before six. A call at this hour on a Monday morning could only mean one thing: something serious had happened, and they were going to ask him to get dressed, go out into the cold, and deal with it. He hid his head briefly under his pillow, wishing the phone would stop ringing. But it remained insistent. Besides, he was wide awake now and he knew there was no alternative. If he ignored it, he would have to answer to Superintendent Walker later; might as well get on with it and find out what was going on. He forced himself slowly up on to one elbow, and picked up the receiver. DC Bristow sounded excited, and Ted had to tell him several times to slow down. But less than a minute later, he was giving the younger officer urgent instructions, and promising to be there within the hour.

There was a groan from beside him in the bed.

'I thought you said you were off today?' Steffie complained.

He leaned over and kissed her, feeling his desire for her rising again, and sighing at the thought that it would have to wait till later.

'I was,' he said, kissing her again. 'Sorry.'

'Typical,' she said with a grin. 'At last, after years of trying, I find a divorced man with similar interests, and what happens? I take a day's leave, I go to his place because he tells me he's got a long weekend off, and he runs out of the door to go to work at God knows what time on Monday morning.'

He laughed. 'I know. Next time, I'll come to you.'

She pulled him down on top of her so that their bodies touched from head to toe. 'Are you sure you have to go?'

The desire was almost too much for him. They kissed and touched for a moment.

'I don't want to.'

She nodded and sighed. 'How long do you think you'll be gone? Can we pick up where we left off when you get back?'

'I can do better than that,' he replied. 'Why don't you come with me? And yes, we can start up again when we get back.'

She pushed up on his chest so that she could see his face. 'Come with you? You want to get me involved in some case in Cambridge? I'm out of my jurisdiction, remember?'

'You're already involved in this one,' he replied.

Agnes Reilly, personal secretary to Father Desmond Gerrard, showed the two officers into the headmaster's private living room on the sixth floor of Lancelot Andrewes School. She was weeping copiously and holding a handkerchief to her eyes.

'I found him just before five o'clock this morning,' she whispered through her tears. 'I bring him a cup of tea every morning when he gets up. He doesn't usually get up until six, but he wanted to be up early this morning. He has to go to London – for his case in the High Court, you know.'

Ted and Steffie entered the room quietly and looked around. To their right, with his hands folded in front of him, stood DC Bristow, who nodded respectfully. Beyond Bristow, John Singer, solicitor to the school, was sitting on a sofa in front of a low coffee table, surrounded by files and loose pieces of paper, two brown cardboard boxes at his feet. Beyond Singer, sprawled in the chair behind his desk, was the lifeless body of Father Desmond

Gerrard. On the desk were several empty medicine bottles, a large bottle of whisky, more than half empty, and a heavy cut glass tumbler, bearing the initials DG, remnants of the whisky lying flat and lifeless at the bottom. Ted quickly made his way to the desk, checked for a pulse, and turned back to Steffie, shaking his head.

'I thought I should let the police know,' Agnes whispered from behind them.

'You did the right thing,' Steffie reassured her.

'You also let Mr Singer know, I see,' Ted commented.

'Those were Desmond's instructions,' Singer protested. 'He always insisted that I should be informed without delay in the event of his death.'

Ted turned his gaze to the mass of papers surrounding Singer.

'So that you can go through his files, and what, remove anything that might embarrass the school?'

'So that I can call a meeting of the trustees to appoint a caretaker headmaster, and make sure that the school's affairs continue to be managed as they should be until he is in place.'

'Did you find a note?' Steffie asked, looking at Agnes and Singer in turn. Singer shook his head.

'No,' Agnes whispered. 'But surely he can't have taken his own life, can he? Not a man like Father Gerrard. I mean... well, it's such a grave sin. I'm sure he couldn't...'

Ted shrugged. 'Well, there will have to be an inquest, and we won't know anything for certain until the post-mortem. But I'm not seeing any signs of violence on the body. Is there any sign of anyone breaking into the building, or into Father Gerrard's rooms?'

'No,' Agnes replied. 'Everything seemed normal. He always locks the door to his rooms at night. I open it with my key when I come in with his tea in the morning. It was just the same today as it always is, except that...' She started weeping again, and sat down abruptly in an armchair.

'I had a good look round, here and on the ground floor, sir,' DC Bristow volunteered. 'I couldn't see any sign of a break-in, or disturbance.'

Ted nodded. 'All right. But I'd like to have the pathologist look at the body before they take it away.'

'I understand the school's regular doctor is on his way, sir,' Bristow said. Agnes nodded.

'Good,' Ted said. 'But I still want our pathologist here. Meanwhile, Mr Singer, why don't you explain to us what these files are that you've been going through, and what they have to do with the trustees appointing a caretaker headmaster?'

'That's none of your business, Detective Inspector. There is no criminal investigation pending against Father Gerrard. The Attorney General ruled that he wasn't guilty of anything.'

'The Attorney General stopped the prosecution. That's not the same thing as a finding of not guilty,' Steffie pointed out.

'Either way, you're off the case,' Singer replied. 'And now, if you don't mind, I'm going to pack these papers into these boxes and get them to my office, so that I can start making some calls.'

Ted shook his head. 'I don't think so, Mr Singer. This is a potential crime scene, and you're not removing anything from this room without my permission.'

'Crime scene? What the hell are you talking about? Desmond killed himself. That's not a crime these days, to my knowledge.'

'I don't feel sure about that yet,' Ted replied. 'I need to make further inquiries before I jump to any conclusions. Until I do, the evidence remains here. You will take nothing from this room.'

'You can't stop me,' Singer protested. 'You have done your best to hinder and harass me ever since this started, and you've been totally disrespectful. I'll have you –'

'Detective Constable Bristow,' Ted interrupted, 'borrow the phone over there and call the station. Get the pathologist lined up and, after you've done that, tell them to get a search warrant for Father Gerrard's private rooms here, and his study and private library on the ground floor. Mr Singer is free to leave if he wishes, but make sure he doesn't remove a single piece of paper until the warrant arrives – and if he obstructs you in the execution of your duty, arrest him.'

Bristow nodded. 'Very good, sir.'

49

'May it please your Lordship,' Ben began, 'I appear for the plaintiffs, Audrey Marshall and Emily Marshall, with my learned friend Miss Castle. Mrs Marshall sits behind me with our instructing solicitor, Miss Julia Cathermole. Mrs Marshall also represents her daughter Emily as her next friend for the purposes of these proceedings. The representation on the defence side is exactly as it was before your Lordship in the criminal trial.

'My learned friends Mr Henderson and Miss Richardson represent Lord AB.

'My learned friends Mr Wallace QC and Mr Weatherly represent Sir CD.

'My learned friends Mr Moss QC and Mr Laud represent the Right Reverend EF.

'My learned friend Mr Norris represents Father Gerrard, but today he also appears for Lancelot Andrewes School. Your Lordship will have noticed that Father Gerrard is not present this morning.'

'I had noticed that,' Mr Justice Roberts confirmed. 'Where is he, Mr Norris?'

'My Lord, I'm afraid I don't know,' Norris replied. 'My instructing solicitors are trying to find him as we speak. They reminded Father Gerrard that he was due at court today. Indeed, they spoke to him on Saturday morning and arranged to meet him in the crypt café at nine o'clock this morning, but so far he hasn't appeared. My Lord, it is not yet eleven o'clock. It's possible that he has been delayed while travelling, or there may have been some emergency at the school. As I say, those instructing me are making inquiries, and I will let your Lordship know what they find out as soon as I know myself.'

'It's very frustrating to have to wait for him, when apparently, he can't even be bothered to send a message,' the judge replied. 'I've been sitting in my chambers waiting to start the proceedings.'

'There's no reason why your Lordship shouldn't begin,' Norris replied soothingly. 'I'm sure there's a good explanation for Father Gerrard's absence. I'm here to represent his interests, and those of the school, as is Mr Dixon, the chairman of the school's board of trustees. My learned friend Mr Henderson will be making some preliminary submissions on behalf of all the defendants, submissions which are bound to take some time. I have no objection to your Lordship making a start.'

'Yes, very well,' the judge replied reluctantly after some thought. 'I will hear from you now, Mr Henderson.'

'I'm much obliged, my Lord,' Henderson said.

'I do hope you're not going to tell me that you have another *nolle prosequi*, Mr Henderson. I think we've had enough of those for one case, haven't we?'

Henderson smiled ingratiatingly. 'I'm hoping it won't come to that, my Lord. In common with all my learned friends, I am quite sure that, now that your Lordship will be sitting alone, without a jury, you will be able to take account of any difficulties my client or Sir CD may have, and take steps to ensure that the proceedings are fair to them. But I have two other matters to raise.

'The first was raised in our pleadings, and it is this. We say that Audrey Marshall's case is barred by the statute of limitations. As your Lordship knows, all civil actions must be brought within a certain time of the claim becoming due, or they become time-barred. Your Lordship understands the reasons for the rule, I'm sure, but since we are in open court, it may be proper for me to explain it briefly.

'The more time elapses since the events the court has to inquire into, the more likely it is that witnesses will have died, or become unavailable; the more likely it is that documents and other pieces of evidence will have been lost, misplaced, or destroyed; and the more likely it is that the memories of those witnesses who are available will have faded. In short: the more difficult it becomes for the court to reconstruct the facts of the case with any confidence that it is doing so accurately. That, of course, has the potential to prejudice all the parties, but particularly the defendants, who may find it difficult to defend themselves – and all because of the plaintiff's failure to start proceedings within the very reasonable period allowed by the law.'

'Yes,' the judge replied.

'In this case, the period allowed by the law is six years. My Lord, I concede at once, of course, that my point doesn't apply to Emily Marshall's case, which is still well within the limitation period. But Audrey Marshall complains of events she says occurred during the period between 1940 and 1945. She is clearly out of time – and her case illustrates the importance of the limitation rule perfectly. It is unfair to ask any defendant to defend himself against allegations based on what he is said to have done more than thirty years ago; and it is especially difficult for defendants such as Lord AB and Sir CD when there are medical reasons for their inability to remember such remote times in the necessary detail.'

'I think I indicated during the criminal proceedings that I wasn't unduly impressed by the medical reports,' Mr Justice Roberts replied.

'Your Lordship made that very clear. But with respect, that doesn't matter now, because this is a civil case, and if the case is time-barred, then it's time-barred. I mention the medical reports again only to emphasise the fact that the period of limitation is not a mere technicality, but a rule of law that serves a very worthwhile and important purpose.'

The judge nodded. 'What do you say about that, Mr Schroeder?'

Ben stood slowly.

'My Lord, I'm afraid my learned friend omitted to mention the most important point about the limitation period, namely the point from which the period starts to run. He assumes that the period runs from the moment when the wrongful act is committed. But that's not what the law says. The law says that the period begins to run when the plaintiff is aware that a wrongful act has been committed, and aware that she has a cause of action because of that wrongful act. In most cases, of course, the plaintiff is aware of all that immediately – but not necessarily. There are many cases where that's not true.

'The classic case is where the defendant destroys or conceals evidence of his wrongful act, for example in a case of fraud, so that the plaintiff has no opportunity to find out about it until it's too late. There are cases where the plaintiff is abroad and out of touch when an act of fraud is committed against her in England. There are cases where the defendant assaults the plaintiff so severely that she's in a coma for many years, or where the full extent of the injury she has sustained doesn't reveal itself for many years. And my learned friend failed entirely to mention one very important point: that in the case of a minor, the period doesn't begin to run until she achieves her majority. That's especially important where the minor is also an orphan. So in Audrey Marshall's case, the period couldn't possibly have begun to run until she turned twenty-one, in October 1954.'

'That's still longer than six years, Mr Schroeder,' the judge pointed out. Henderson was smiling and nodding.

'Yes, I'm aware of that, my Lord. But it is an important point, nonetheless. During the first criminal trial, my learned friend Mr Norris went to great pains, when he cross-examined Mrs Marshall, to suggest that she must have remembered what happened to her during her remaining time in school. But when she left school in 1951, the period had not even begun to run. What happened between 1940 and 1954 is irrelevant. If your Lordship accepts Mrs Marshall's evidence, then she was unaware of any claim against the school or the other defendants until 1972, which is within the period of six years.'

The judge turned inquiringly to Henderson.

'My Lord,' he replied, 'that doesn't follow at all. If Mrs Marshall had some memory at that earlier time, between 1940 and 1954, it makes it very hard to accept that she then forgot all about it until 1972. But in any case, in my submission, none of that matters.'

'Not even if she had no memory at all of the events until 1972?' the judge asked.

'Not even then, my Lord: not in this case.'

'That would be rather a harsh rule, wouldn't it?'

'There are those who believe that the statute of limitations is always a harsh rule, my Lord,' Henderson said. 'But it's equally harsh to a defendant to make him liable when the facts of the case can't be determined with any certainty. When Mrs Marshall says that she "recovered" her memory in 1972, what she's really saying is that her memory had faded – faded in a particularly serious way, of course – but faded nonetheless: which is exactly why we have the limitation rule.

'In addition to that, my Lord – as my learned friend Mr Norris said in the criminal proceedings – the defence doesn't accept the premise. We don't accept the validity of this so-called "recovered memory", and if your Lordship is against me today, I would invite your Lordship to adjourn the proceedings so that we can retain an expert witness to deal with that question.'

Ben sprang to his feet immediately.

'That would simply cause further delay and further unnecessary costs,' he protested. 'If my learned friend had wanted to consult an expert, he's had ample opportunity already.'

'My Lord, it's not my practice to advise my clients to pay for expensive expert witnesses in cases which are clearly time-barred,' Henderson replied. 'That wouldn't be a responsible use of their funds, and frankly, I'm surprised that I have to argue the point. But if your Lordship were to have any doubt about the limitation period, you would first have to resolve the question of whether Mrs Marshall's claim of "recovered memory" is a proper basis for excusing her failure to bring her action in a timely fashion. That means that she will have to give evidence, so that we can all cross-examine her –'

'She gave evidence in front of Judge Rees,' Ben intervened, 'and was ably cross-examined by my learned friend Mr Norris. Your Lordship and my learned friends have the transcript of her evidence. There is no need to put her through it again.'

'That's not acceptable, my Lord,' Henderson replied at once. 'This is a different case. My client wasn't involved in that trial, and neither was Sir CD or Bishop EF. We are all entitled to cross-examine her in this case, and in addition, we are entitled to call an expert witness to prove that what she's claiming is, in scientific terms, pure nonsense.'

The judge nodded. 'You said you had a second point, Mr Henderson?'

'Yes, my Lord.'

Anthony Norris stood. Ben glanced in his direction and noted that his face was white.

'I'm terribly sorry to interrupt, my Lord,' Norris said quietly. 'But before my learned friend continues, I must tell your Lordship that I have just received some very bad news.'

50

Ben glanced at Ginny and then turned to look behind him. Julia was staring grimly ahead. Audrey was pale, and was holding her face in her hands.

'I must ask for an adjournment, my Lord,' Norris was saying. 'This is an action that can be continued against Father Gerrard's estate, and of course, the school's position is directly affected by his death. I need some time to advise my instructing solicitors, and Mr Dixon, on where we go from here.'

Ben and Ginny exchanged looks. She nodded.

'I can't object to that, my Lord,' he said, 'as long as my learned friend is not proposing a lengthy adjournment.'

'I would ask for two weeks, my Lord,' Norris said.

'If I may, my Lord,' Henderson intervened, 'we will need longer than that. My learned junior, Miss Richardson, has just pointed out to me that, even if your Lordship is with me about the statute of limitations, Audrey Marshall will still have to give evidence – in support of Emily Marshall's case. We will be obliged to discredit Mrs Marshall's evidence in any event. We're going to need an expert witness, whichever way your Lordship rules.'

'That just goes to show that my learned friend should have anticipated the need for such a witness much earlier,' Ben replied. 'It's not right for him to keep the plaintiffs waiting for their day in court at this late stage, when he should have acted before. The plaintiffs have been kept waiting quite long enough. This is their third attempt to go to trial. It's not good enough.'

'I'm surprised that my learned friend was prepared to go to trial without an expert of his own,' Henderson said. 'It must be clear now, even to him, that he can't. He needs time, just as much as I do.'

'I don't accept that,' Ben replied at once.

'I think we should all take some time, in the circumstances,' the judge replied, holding up a hand. 'I haven't decided how to rule on the matter of the statute of limitations, but it may well be that scientific evidence would assist me: and I agree that it would be helpful when we go to trial – as we will in Emily's case, whichever way I rule.'

He paused for some time.

'I will adjourn the case for four weeks. That will have to be enough for both sides to instruct their experts. I'm sure one expert witness will do for all the defendants. That expert must confer with the plaintiff's expert, and they must provide the court with a statement indicating the matters on which they agree, and on which they disagree, not less than seven days before the adjourned date.'

'I'm obliged to your Lordship,' Henderson replied. 'I'm sure my learned friend Mr Norris is anxious to confer with his instructing solicitors and with Mr Dixon. But if your Lordship will indulge me, I did mention that I have a second point to make, and it may be convenient to make it now, so that your Lordship can consider everything together during the coming four weeks.'

'Yes, very well,' Mr Justice Roberts said.

'My Lord, before I proceed, I must do two things. First of all, I must invite my learned friend Mr Chapman to come into court; he is waiting outside, I believe. Secondly, I must invite your Lordship to close the court to the public.'

Ben turned around quickly. Julia was scribbling him a note. It read, 'Harry Chapman? He is standing counsel for MI5, sometimes acts for MI6.'

'May we know why, my Lord?' Ben asked.

'I will explain, once the court has been closed to the public,'

Henderson replied. 'There are matters of national security involved.'

The judge shook his head. 'In a case involving sexual abuse, Mr Henderson? That's a bit far-fetched, isn't it?'

'No, my Lord. If I may remind your Lordship, the Attorney General based one part of his *nolle prosequi* in the criminal proceedings, the part relating to Bishop EF, on the national interest. That remains true, and Father Gerrard's unfortunate death – although my learned friend Mr Chapman doesn't know about it yet, as far as I'm aware – makes it all the more important.'

'You've lost me completely, Mr Henderson,' the judge replied. 'But I suppose I will have to try to get to the bottom of it.'

'I'm sure my learned friend and I can assist with that,' Henderson replied evenly. 'Perhaps your Lordship would be good enough to rise for five minutes, to allow me to bring Mr Chapman up to date?'

'Very well,' Mr Justice Roberts replied. 'But let's not take too long about it, shall we?' He stood and left the bench abruptly.

'So now,' Julia said, 'we have counsel for the Home Office and counsel for the security services putting their heads together. I have a bad feeling about this.'

'Would someone please explain to me what's going on?' Audrey asked.

No one replied immediately.

'Your cue, Julia, I think,' Ben said.

Julia nodded. 'It's all to do with the German man. But it's all nonsense.'

'The man who molested Mary?'

'Yes.'

'The government was involved with him in some way?' Ginny asked. 'How?'

'I'm sorry. I can't tell you any more –'

'Julia…'

'I'm sorry. I can't. But I will say this: in my mind, it's got nothing to do with the case, or certainly shouldn't have anything to do with it. At least, I assume that's what they're talking about. There's no other connection I know of. If it's anything else, we will have to wait to find out about it from Chapman.'

Audrey shook her head.

'How do we fight these people?' she asked. 'How does anyone ever find the strength?'

51

'My Lord,' Harry Chapman began, after Henderson had introduced him to the court, 'it has come as something of a shock to hear of the death of Father Gerrard. I didn't know about it before I came to court. I've taken the time your Lordship kindly gave me to consider very carefully. I've concluded that it doesn't affect the submissions I have to make to your Lordship.

'I propose to provide your Lordship with a general account of the matter that concerns the security services. I propose to do so in closed court, so that the parties and their counsel will be able to hear everything I am going to say, although the public will not.' He paused. 'I am also going to take an additional step, a step I take reluctantly when I take it at all. I'm going to ask your Lordship to read an affidavit from a senior officer of the domestic intelligence service, MI5. I regret that it will not be made available to the parties, or to their counsel. It provides your Lordship with further information of an extremely sensitive nature, the disclosure of which the heads of the security services, and the relevant minister, would see as damaging to the national interest.'

Ben stood at once. 'My Lord, I must object in the strongest terms. It's not the practice in this country to hold secret trials. If my learned friend is going to make submissions that affect my clients' rights, he should do so openly, so that we can all understand what the minister and the security services are worried about, and have the chance to respond.'

The judge held up a hand.

'I'm not going to permit any secret trials, Mr Schroeder. But I do have some experience in representing the government in sensitive matters, and during my time at the bar I had to make submissions to the court similar to those Mr Chapman is making. I have a duty to allow the government to say whatever they wish to say. That doesn't mean I'm going to agree with them. I'm afraid you will have to trust me on that, Mr Schroeder.'

''I have every confidence in your Lordship's sense of fairness,' Ben replied, surprised to find himself speaking those words to Mr Justice Roberts, 'but the principle on which the courts work in England is that justice must not only be done, but must be seen to be done. That principle is meaningless if part of the proceedings takes place in secret, behind closed doors.'

'I have every intention of ensuring that justice is seen to be done,' the judge replied. 'Your point, please, Mr Chapman.'

'May the court be closed to the public for a short time, my Lord?'

The judge nodded. Chapman waited for the usher to ask the several journalists and members of the public to leave court, which they did with a show of reluctance, and to place a notice in the door of the court indicating that access to the public was temporarily restricted.

'My Lord, when the Attorney General referred to the national interest in relation to Bishop EF, he was referring to the fact that, during the war, the security services had an interest in the Bishop, and indeed in Father Gerrard – which is why I've had to consider my submission to your Lordship very carefully since learning of his death. The services also had an interest in a German man, who was known to Bishop EF, and who was seen with the Bishop and Father Gerrard at Lancelot Andrewes School – among other places.'

Ben turned around to glance at Julia, who raised her eyebrows. 'Other places?' she mouthed silently.

'As your Lordship knows, when Bishop EF was interviewed by the police, he gave a partial account of his activities at that time – I think everyone here has copies of the transcript. I say a partial account, because the Bishop declined to answer a number of questions, saying that he was not at liberty to do so. He was right to take that course. If his statement were to be used as evidence, or if Bishop EF were to be advised to give evidence himself in these proceedings, questions might well be asked about the subjects he was not at liberty to disclose to the police. My Lord, although much of this material is now of purely historical interest, there are some aspects of it which might bring to light the detailed activities of the secret services, and the identities of certain persons whose personal safety might, even now, be compromised. It might, in certain circumstances even lead to the loss of life: and I will tell your Lordship frankly that I am concerned, in addition to being shocked, by the death of Father Gerrard, for exactly that reason.'

'But Mr Norris indicated that Father Gerrard had taken his own life,' the judge replied. He, too, sounded shocked.

Anthony Norris stood. 'My Lord, that is the information my instructing solicitors received from the police. But there will be a post-mortem and an inquest, and it's not beyond the realm of possibility that the police's initial conclusion might be called into question. One simply doesn't know at this stage.'

'If I may, my Lord,' Chapman added, 'I will hand up the affidavit I referred to and ask your Lordship to retire to chambers to read it. Your Lordship understands that I will have to take it back immediately afterwards?'

'Yes, very well,' the judge replied. 'I will read it now.' He left the bench abruptly.

When the judge had gone, Chapman approached, his hand extended.

'Hello, Julia. Nice to see you again. How are you?'

She took his hand. 'Hello, Harry. I didn't expect to see you here in this case.'

'I didn't expect to be here. I was consulted about the Attorney General's order in the criminal case, of course, and I thought that had put an end to it all.'

'That's what people like you always think,' Audrey said. 'Does it make it easier to sleep at night?'

'Audrey...' Julia whispered, touching her hand.

Chapman smiled. 'You would be Mrs Marshall, I suppose?' He offered his hand. She took it reluctantly. 'I understand how you feel.'

'Do you?'

'Yes. I do, as a matter of fact. We're not all quite as evil as you seem to think. We have a duty to uphold the national interest – someone has to. But that doesn't mean we don't care about people. Knowing what I do about your case, I have every sympathy with you, and, of course, with your daughter. Don't quote me on this,' he added quietly, glancing towards the defendants, 'but personally, I wish you every success.'

'You have a strange way of showing it,' Audrey replied.

Chapman nodded. 'I understand.' He turned to Ben and Ginny. 'I'm glad to meet you, Schroeder, Miss Castle. I heard all kinds of good things about you during the Digby case. Baxter was very impressed with you both. He approved.'

'Did Baxter approve of this?' Julia asked.

Chapman stared without answering. 'Do excuse me, Julia. I think the judge is coming back to court,' he said, walking quickly away.

Mr Justice Roberts took his seat, handing the affidavit to his clerk, from whom it made its way quickly back to Harry Chapman.

'Mr Chapman,' the judge said, 'I have listened carefully to your submission, and I've read the affidavit you handed up, which I have now returned to you. What exactly are you asking me to do?'

'I'm asking your Lordship not to allow Bishop EF's statement to the police to be used in evidence, and to order that no reference to it be made in these proceedings, or indeed, outside court, for any purpose whatsoever.

'I'm also inviting your Lordship to dismiss the case against Bishop EF, on the ground that if it continues, he may feel obliged to give evidence. If he has to give evidence, he may be unable to defend himself without disclosing facts which may jeopardise the national interest, and perhaps put the safety of certain individuals, including himself, at risk.'

'My Lord,' Ben protested, rising quickly to his feet, 'this is outrageous. The affidavit my learned friend gave your Lordship must have read like the script for a James Bond film. I wouldn't know, of course, because in this secret proceeding, I haven't been allowed to see it. But nothing my learned friend has said in court comes close to justifying the orders he's asking your Lordship to make. Frankly, I'm not sure how such orders could even be legally proper.'

Mr Justice Roberts smiled. 'You needn't be concerned, Mr Schroeder. Mr Chapman, I have no intention whatsoever of making the orders you invite me to make. Without disclosing the matters dealt with in the affidavit, they are matters that would have no real relevance to the action I am asked to try. I'm not sitting with a jury. I'm perfectly capable of confining this case to relevant evidence. I've read Bishop EF's police interview, so there will be no need to refer to it in detail during the trial. If the Bishop decides to give evidence, I will not allow him to be asked irrelevant questions. I have every confidence that I can conduct the trial fairly in the interests of all the parties, while at the same time not compromising the national interest, or anyone's personal safety.'

'As your Lordship pleases,' Chapman replied quietly.

'As I indicated earlier,' the judge said, 'I shall now adjourn this case for four weeks, to consider the statute of limitations, and to allow the parties to present further evidence, in the form of expert opinions, if they wish to do so.'

'You can't win them all, Mark,' Julia smiled as Henderson passed her on his way out of court with Harry Chapman.

They stopped and turned to look at her. 'You know how this works, Julia,' Henderson replied. 'This was just round one. We lost this round, but we're still in the fight. You know that.' He got close enough to whisper in her ear. 'Take my advice. If your girl gets the chance to settle this case, she should take it.'

'Is that a chance someone is going to offer her?' Julia asked.

'You never know,' Henderson replied.

'Mark's giving you very good advice, Julia,' Chapman added.

'Give my best regards to Baxter, Harry,' Julia said, walking away.

52

Andrew Pilkington was relaxing in his room in chambers in Temple Gardens, nursing a large mug of strong tea made for him by his clerk, Lawrence. Compared to other barristers, Andrew spent relatively little time in chambers. As Treasury counsel, he was based at the Old Bailey, where he and his colleagues had their own work rooms, and where they kept their often highly sensitive case papers away from the risk of prying eyes. But tonight there was to be a dinner in honour of a long-standing member of chambers who had recently retired. Andrew kept his evening dress in chambers for such occasions. He had an hour in which to dress and make his way to the Reform Club in Pall Mall, where the dinner was to be held. He gulped the tea gratefully; as it went down, he felt the warm liquid revive his body, infusing a welcome burst of fresh energy. It had been a long day, spent poring over papers for a forthcoming case of municipal corruption. He was also pondering a strange phone call he had received earlier in the afternoon from a civil servant, who seemed to be inquiring, in the most oblique manner imaginable, whether he might be interested in a vacancy on the Old Bailey bench which was expected to arise during the next year or two. Lawrence interrupted his reverie with a discreet knock on the door.

'Sorry to disturb, Mr Pilkington, but there's a DI Steffie Walsh on the line, asking if she could have a word. She says it's urgent, sir.'

'DI Walsh? Yes, of course, Lawrence. Put her through.'

'Hello, sir,' Steffie said. She sounded slightly breathless. 'It's been a while since we last spoke. I hope you remember me.'

Andrew laughed. 'Of course, I remember you.'

'I'm sure you're busy, sir, but do you have a few minutes to talk?'

'Yes,' Andrew replied. 'What is it?'

She hesitated. 'I don't know whether you've heard the news, sir... about Father Gerrard – the headmaster in the Lancelot Andrewes case?'

'Father Gerrard? No. What's going on?'

'He's dead, sir.'

Andrew sat upright in his chair. 'Dead? How? When? What happened?'

'Well, sir, Ted – DI Phillips, that is – and I were called to Lancelot Andrewes School early this morning by a DC Bristow from Cambridge CID. Agnes Reilly, Father Gerrard's personal secretary, went into his rooms as usual to give him his morning cup of tea, and found him dead in the chair behind his desk. Apparently, he was supposed to be at the High Court today for the civil case.'

'That's right,' Andrew said. 'I remember, it was due to start today.'

'Yes, sir. When we arrived, we noticed that there were five medicine bottles on the desk. The labels said that they were prescription pain killers and sleeping pills. There was also a bottle of whisky – with a lot of the whisky gone.'

Andrew sat back again in his chair, and looked down from his window out on to the Middle Temple gardens.

'So, he committed suicide?'

Steffie hesitated. 'That's the way it seemed to us, sir. There was no sign of violence, and DC Bristow didn't find any indications of forcible entry, or anything out of place. But...'

'Go on...'

'Well, sir, he didn't leave a note – or at least, there was no note to be found when we arrived. Now, Agnes seems to be a very religious woman, and she was obviously very shocked at the idea of a priest taking his own life, so at the risk of being unfair to her, it's not out of the question that she disposed of it before she called the police: you never know. But as I say, she told us there was no note, and we didn't find one.'

'He might well have been feeling some pressure because of the case,' Andrew suggested. 'After all, he'd already been through the strain of being arrested and going through a trial – and he was very nearly put on trial a second time, wasn't he? And now it was all about to happen again. That's a lot of stress. Perhaps it was too much for him.'

'That's what we thought, sir – at first. But this afternoon, the pathologist hinted that it might not quite so straightforward.'

'What did he mean by that?'

'She, sir, actually.'

Andrew smiled. 'She. Sorry.'

'She's not saying. Everyone's being a bit tight-lipped about it at the moment, but some question has come up about the cause of death. They're doing a post-mortem, of course, and there will be an inquest. We've made it clear that we need to know what's going on as soon as possible. We should hear back in a day or two.'

'Well, let me know,' Andrew said.

'I will, sir. But… there's more.'

'All right.'

'When DI…'

'"Ted" is fine,' Andrew said, smiling again.

'Yes, sir. When Ted and I arrived, John Singer was there – you remember him?'

'The school's solicitor?'

'Yes, sir. He'd been going through Father Gerrard's papers, and he was getting ready to remove a large quantity of documents from the room.'

'What, with Father Gerrard's body still there?'

'Yes, sir. Agnes told DC Bristow the doctor was on the way, but there was no sign of him, and we eventually had to call him ourselves. Anyway, DC Bristow saw what was happening, and he didn't let Singer out of his sight until we arrived. Singer told us that it was all to do with the trustees appointing an interim headmaster, but we weren't convinced: so we arranged for a search warrant, and made Singer leave the documents in place until it arrived. I hope we weren't out of line, sir. We were aware of the Attorney General's order, but... well, there was just something about it that didn't feel right.'

'I don't think you were out of line at all,' Andrew reassured her. 'If anyone questions it, I'm sure you'd say you had reason to believe that further offences had been committed, or were about to be committed: wouldn't you?'

'Yes, sir: and I'm pretty sure we would be right.'

'Go on.'

'We executed the search warrant, and took the documents Singer had collected, plus a few more, back to Parkside nick. Ted and I have spent the afternoon going through them, or making a start, anyway: we still have a long way to go, and it looks like it's going to be a long night. But we've already turned up some interesting stuff. Gerrard kept a personal file, which is obviously concerned with the abuse at Lancelot Andrewes School.'

'In what way?'

'It has copies of the records belonging to some of the girls who were abused. It has a list of names and addresses – in a kind of code, just a first name, an initial for the last name, and a phone number. It wasn't hard to crack. The Three Musketeers were listed, and there was a Father K. There was no number for Father K, so we don't yet know who he might have been. But there were a number of men we haven't come across before. Some we've already identified, and a couple of them have a high public profile – Parliament and the Church. We expect to identify the others without too much trouble.'

Andrew thought for some time. 'I'm not sure that would be enough to persuade the Attorney General to let us go ahead. But we could try.'

'Oh, that's not the best part, sir,' Steffie said. He could almost see her smiling. 'The Lancelot Andrewes file is only the beginning.'

'Oh?'

'We also found a number of other files, containing much the same kind of material – pupils' records, names and phone numbers. But these files relate to five other schools in different parts of the country. We haven't delved into them very far yet, but we believe we will find the names of a considerable number of men, some of them very much in the public eye.'

'My God,' Andrew whispered into the phone.

'Ted is arranging for a copy to be made of everything we seized,' Steffie continued. 'We would like to bring the papers to you, so that you can see for yourself. I don't want to seem pushy, sir, but how would tomorrow afternoon be? If we burn the midnight oil we should have a provisional list of names for you by tomorrow; and I can't really give you a reason, but I have a gut feeling that it wouldn't be a good idea to let the grass grow on this.'

'Yes, all right,' Andrew replied. 'I'm not in court tomorrow. Bring the papers to the Old Bailey, and we'll keep them there for now.'

'Thank you, sir,' she said. 'That's a load off my mind.'

Andrew smiled. 'If you don't mind my asking,' he said, 'how did you come to be up in Cambridge this morning? Were you working on another inquiry?'

There was a silence for a few seconds. 'Oh, no, sir: I just... happened to be here for a... long weekend,' she replied.

'Right. Well, see you tomorrow, then.'

After some minutes of contemplation, Andrew called Julia Cathermole. He repeated to her what Steffie Walsh had said.

'We found out about Gerrard this morning,' Julia replied. 'Norris informed the court as soon as the news came through. The case had to be adjourned.'

'How did Audrey take another adjournment?'

'I think "resignation" is probably the best word to describe it. It's almost as though she's got used to these continual disappointments, but she's still got plenty of fight left in her. Harry Chapman turned up to represent the security services, and she gave him a piece of her mind while the judge was off the bench.' She laughed. 'For a moment, I thought she might actually land one on him.'

'Has she gone back to Ely?'

'Yes, there's nothing she can do here for the moment.'

Andrew was silent for several moments.

'What did Harry Chapman want?'

'He wanted the judge to order that we couldn't use Bishop EF's police interview as evidence, or refer to it in any way.'

'What? Don't tell me Evan Roberts went with that.'

'No, not at all. He told Chapman to get stuffed, almost in so many words. But even so, I'm…'

'Yes. I have a bad feeling about this, Julia.'

'So do I. What do we do?'

'Get in touch with Ben and Ginny and tell them about the new files, but make sure they understand they're not to talk to anyone else. I will need your input on this before I decide what to do next. Can you be with us when Steffie brings the papers tomorrow?'

'No problem,' Julia replied.

She paused, then chuckled. 'So that's what our good Musketeer Bishop EF meant.'

'Come again?'

'In his interview, remember? EF said Gerrard told him that Lancelot Andrewes was the tip of the iceberg. Perhaps, now, we know what he meant.'

53

Tuesday 4 March 1975

When her secretary put the call through, Julia was about to leave her office for the Old Bailey. She was running late because of a frustrating morning meeting that had dragged on and on without any resolution, and she was anxious not to keep Andrew waiting: but something told her it was a call she ought to take.

'Hello, Julia,' Mary Forbes said. 'How are you?'

'I'm well, Mary, thank you. How are you? How is Toronto?'

'We're both doing fine,' Mary replied.

'Still working on the same case?'

She laughed. 'Oh, yes, I'm afraid so. It's like *War and Peace*. I'm beginning to think it will never end.'

'So, what can I do for you?'

She sensed a hesitation in Mary's reply.

'I'm sure you know all about this already. But I thought I ought to call, just to let you know that I received one, too.'

Julia stared blankly at her phone.

'One of what? Mary, what are you talking about?'

There was a silence.

'Oh, God, don't tell me you don't know. I'm talking about the letter from Lancelot Andrewes School. It arrived yesterday, by telecopier.'

Julia suddenly felt a cold chill run up her spine. 'Letter?'

'It's a letter from the trustees of Lancelot Andrewes School, marked, "Strictly private and confidential". It's signed by the chairman, a Mr Dixon, and by John Singer, the school's solicitor. It's what you and I would call a "without prejudice" letter. They're offering to settle all claims for child sexual abuse at the school, even in historic cases that would be barred by the statute of limitations. It says they've set up a settlement fund – though it doesn't say how much. It's all without prejudice: the school makes no admission that anyone was abused, or that it has any liability to anyone. They invite us all to submit a short statement about what happened, and to sign a form, agreeing that we will not disclose the facts of our cases, or the fact that we have received a settlement. If we ever disclose it, the whole agreement becomes void, and they can sue to recover the amount of the settlement. Offer valid for one month, after which it lapses. You know the kind of thing, Julia. It's the usual stuff: we see it all the time.' She paused. 'You have a telecopier, don't you? I'll send it over to your office.'

Julia recovered, with an effort. 'Yes. That would be very helpful, Mary. Thank you.'

'You didn't know about this? I can't believe they would send this out without letting you know.'

'Neither can I,' Julia said. She hesitated. 'Look, Mary, strictly speaking, it's none of my business, but do you mind if I ask whether...'

Mary laughed. 'Good God, no. I know what's going on here, as well as you do. They're trying to buy off your witnesses. Well, you've got to admire their consistency: it is in the best Lancelot Andrewes tradition, isn't it? But they're not going to buy me off. I was going to write back, telling them where they could stuff it, but on mature reflection, I think I'll probably just ignore it. You've still got me, Julia. You know that.'

'Thank you, Mary. I really appreciate it.'

'How many other witnesses you still have is another question.'

'Yes,' Julia agreed quietly.

'Well, chin up, Julia. Don't let the bastards get you down. Warm up your telecopier. It's on its way.'

Julia stood, seething, her hand gripping the receiver she had replaced in its hook, for several minutes. Eventually, she picked it up again and dialled a number.

'Mr Singer, please,' she said, when a woman's voice answered.

'Just a minute, please. May I tell him who's calling?'

'Julia Cathermole.'

After some moments, a male voice came on the line.

'Julia, to what do I owe the pleasure?'

'It's Miss Cathermole to you, Mr Singer, and I'm calling to ask how much it costs to buy off a witness in a child sexual assault case? Is it still the value of their school fees, or does it take more than that these days?'

At first there was a silence. Then she heard him splutter on the other end of the line.

'I don't know what you mean. The letter we sent out is a good faith attempt to settle current or anticipated proceedings.'

'My clients Audrey and Emily Marshall are the only people suing Lancelot Andrewes School, as far as I'm aware.'

'There may be other cases in the pipeline.'

'According to you, they're all time-barred.'

'So we've argued to the judge, but we have no means of knowing how he will rule. If we have to go to trial with numerous plaintiffs, it could turn into a very expensive exercise. Naturally, I advised my clients, the trustees, that it might be prudent to consider an overall settlement before it gets out of hand. They agreed with me.'

'Some of the women you've approached have been listed as witnesses for the plaintiffs.'

'They're also potential plaintiffs themselves. As far as I know, Miss Cathermole, there's no property in a witness. I don't know of any reason why I shouldn't contact them.'

'Have you contacted my clients? You see, I only found out about this a few minutes ago, from a witness abroad who received your letter yesterday. I practice in London, and I haven't received it. I do hope you haven't sent it directly to my clients, Mr Singer. As they are legally represented in the proceedings, that would be a grave breach of professional conduct, and I give you my assurance that, if you've done that, I will haul you in front of the Law Society and do my damnedest to have you struck off.'

'I'm sorry, Miss Cathermole,' Singer replied, insincerely. 'Haven't you got it yet? I assumed we'd sent it to you, of course. I'll speak to my secretary and make sure you have it.'

'That's not the point. In case you didn't know, it's a criminal offence to bribe a witness not to give evidence.'

'I would advise you to moderate your language, Miss Cathermole,' Singer replied. 'It's not against the law to offer a settlement to a potential plaintiff. That's all I've done.' He paused. 'What would your clients say about it, do you think? I assume you will advise them that an offer of settlement has been made?'

'If I receive such an offer,' Julia replied, 'I have a duty to advise them of it, and I will. I anticipate that they will tell you exactly what you can do with your offer. But I will advise them of it.'

'Well, that's their prerogative, of course,' Singer said. 'But I'm bound to say, it might be in their best interests to at least consider the offer: it has all sorts of advantages. They can put this whole thing behind them, have some closure, move on with their lives, you know. The little girl won't have to face the ordeal of giving evidence again. You really should think about taking the offer while it's still on the table.'

'It's funny you should say that, Mr Singer,' Julia said. 'You're the second person to give me that advice in the last twenty-four hours.'

'Then, perhaps you ought to give it some consideration, don't you think, rather than just turning it down out of hand?'

'I'll be taking counsel's opinion,' Julia replied, 'and you will hear from me when I've received her advice.'

'As you wish.'

'Oh, and while I've got you on the phone, Mr Singer – just as a matter of interest – is the offer limited to pupils of Lancelot Andrewes, or does it apply to pupils of the other five schools?'

Julia sensed shock in the silence that followed.

'What? What five schools? What are you talking about?'

'We'll speak again soon, Mr Singer,' Julia replied, hanging up.

54

The files had filled four large brown cardboard boxes. Ted Phillips and Steffie Walsh had carried them from the car they had parked nearby into Andrew's office at the Old Bailey, and, with the help of the staff, deposited them on his table. Both officers looked tired, and Andrew made sure they had an ample supply of strong coffee in front of them before asking them any questions. Julia had arrived at the same time, also looking tired and tense.

'I contacted Ben and Ginny yesterday,' she said quietly to Andrew. 'They couldn't be here this afternoon, but they said to call them later if we needed to talk.'

'That's fine.'

'And... can I whisper in your ear for a moment?'

She ushered him into a corner of the room, away from where Ted and Steffie were helping themselves to more coffee.

'I may have been a bit indiscreet this afternoon with John Singer,' she confessed.

'What do you mean, indiscreet?'

'He's sent out a letter to the victims, offering a financial settlement, on condition that it all remains confidential. As a result, I probably don't have any witnesses left, except for Mary Forbes, God bless her. I only found about it when she called me from Canada, just after lunch.'

Andrew thought for some moments. 'Did he approach Audrey?'

'No. He would have to approach her through me; and now that

he has, I will have to tell her about it. But I called Singer just before I came over here, to let him know what I thought, and I'm afraid I lost my temper.'

'I can't say I blame you. Is he allowed to do that?'

'I have a call in to Ginny for an urgent opinion. But I think I know what she's going to say. Once I cooled down, and my instinct kicked back in, it occurred to me that he's probably all right as long as he doesn't make it a condition that they not give evidence against the school. I haven't read the letter yet – Mary's sending it to me – but I doubt he was stupid enough to do that.'

Andrew shook his head. 'Don't be too concerned about it for now. Let's see what happens. I'm not sure he's done any real harm. You can still subpoena the witnesses if you have to. Frankly, I'm not sure the judge would hold it against them if they settled for some money, in the circumstances. I think the school would look pretty silly if they tried to criticise them for it.'

She took a deep breath. 'While I was losing my temper, I asked Singer whether the offer was limited to Lancelot Andrewes or whether it extended to the other five schools.'

'Ah,' Andrew said. 'I see. So, he knows that we know.'

'I'm sorry, Andrew.'

He shook his head. 'No. Don't worry. I'm sure it would have occurred to him sooner or later that the police were bound to tell me, and it would be very surprising if I didn't tell you.'

'All the same...'

'Don't worry about it.'

They walked back to Andrew's desk, and took their seats. Andrew turned to Ted and Steffie, who were still gratefully imbibing the coffee.

'Is this everything?'

'Yes, sir,' Ted replied.

'Any further word on Father Gerrard?'

The two officers looked at each other.

'The pathologist now believes that the cause of death was

a lethal dose of potassium cyanide,' Steffie said.

'What?'

'We have officers going through his rooms again,' Ted added. 'They haven't come up with anything yet. It could have been delivered through the pills he swallowed, or in the whisky, I suppose. They will have to test everything.'

'So, this could well be a murder case?' Andrew asked.

'Could be,' Steffie replied.

'Cyanide does show up sometimes as a method of suicide,' Julia said.

'It's going to be a long inquiry,' Steffie replied.

Andrew nodded. 'All right. Tell us what's in the files.'

Steffie placed a hand on top of one of the boxes, and selected a file folder.

'This is a good example. It's for St Edgar's School in Yorkshire, near Boroughbridge. It's a Church of England girls' boarding school, not unlike Lancelot Andrewes in some ways.' She handed the folder to Andrew, who placed it between Julia and himself. 'You will see about twenty pages from records for pupils during the 1960s, noting that they have been excused payment of fees. There are also – believe it or not – some notes of calls from parents making complaints, and some notes made by Father Gerrard as a record of a conversation he had with the headmaster, a Father Wilkinson. It's hard to believe that they would keep stuff like this, but they did. Then you have several pages of different notes, again in Father Gerrard's handwriting –'

'Can we verify that?' Andrew asked.

'Oh, yes. We have numerous samples of his handwriting. We'll run them by our questioned documents expert, but there's no doubt about it. As you can see, there's a list of names, all first names, with initials in place of surnames. But there are phone numbers, too. We have reverse directories – that's how we're able to get to them. There are instances where phone numbers have changed, and some of the numbers are quite old, so we've had to work with old directories, and there are a few we haven't tracked down yet. But we'll get there.'

'And these names are all men?' Andrew asked.

'So far, yes.'

'What kind of breakdown?'

'I'm talking about all the files together, now. The men are overwhelmingly from the professional classes: doctors, lawyers, engineers...'

'Police officers,' Ted added quietly.

'Seriously?' Andrew asked.

'Including one or two who outrank us,' Steffie added. 'Then we come to the really interesting ones: two current and three former government ministers, seven Members of Parliament, two judges – one High Court, one Crown Court – eighteen ministers of various denominations, including Church of England, Roman Catholic, and Methodist: and assorted mayors, local councillors, business leaders, and other men who should know better.'

Andrew bit his lip and turned to Julia.

'Welcome to the rest of the iceberg,' he said.

'Yes,' she replied.

The phone rang. He answered. 'Andrew Pilkington... yes... what? Yes, he's here.' He offered the phone to Ted. 'It's for you, Superintendent Walker.'

Surprised, Ted stood and took the phone. 'This is DI Phillips... oh, yes, sir... yes, we're with Mr Pilkington now... what? You're joking, sir... no, sir, you're not joking, obviously... I understand, sir... No, that must have been after we left to come down here... Sir, did they say why?... All right, sir, I understand... Will do, sir.'

He was looking pale as he handed the receiver back to Andrew.

'Are you all right, Ted?' Steffie asked. 'What's going on?'

'They're going to cover it all up,' Ted replied.

55

'Tell me exactly what Superintendent Walker said,' Julia said quietly.

Ted looked shaken. With a huge effort, he recovered his composure. 'He said that about an hour after we left to come down here, four officers came to Parkside nick. They identified themselves as a detective inspector, a detective sergeant, and two detective constables attached to Special Branch.'

'The security service's police enforcers,' Steffie added.

Ted nodded. 'They demanded that the Super hand over the documents we'd taken from Father Gerrard's rooms, and in addition, all copies of Bishop EF's interview.'

Julia looked at Andrew. 'What did the Superintendent do?'

'He handed them over,' Ted replied. 'You don't argue with Special Branch.'

They were silent for some time.

Andrew reached out his hand towards his phone. 'I'll find out what's going on,' he offered.

Julia put a hand over his. 'No. Andrew, there isn't time,' she said decisively.

'What do you mean?'

'My guess is, we have thirty minutes or less before they come through that door. They know you two are down here to see Andrew, and they'll want to know why.' She leaned forward and looked Ted directly in the eye. 'I'm going to ask you a very important question, Ted. Think very carefully before you answer.

Did you tell Superintendent Walker that you were bringing a copy of the documents to Mr Pilkington?'

Ted closed his eyes and tried to focus. 'I can't…'

'I don't think we did, in so many words,' Steffie said. 'But he knew where we were going, and he probably assumed that's what we were doing.'

'All right. Did he say anything on the phone just now, anything at all, about the fact that you'd made a copy?'

'No,' Ted replied. 'He just told me we should get ourselves back to Parkside as soon as we can.'

'Are you absolutely sure?'

'I'm sure.'

'So, I can be confident that Special Branch doesn't know about it?'

Ted looked at Steffie and shook his head. 'They may or may not know, but they're bound to guess. Special Branch aren't fools, Miss Cathermole. It won't take them long to put two and two together. Why else would we be here this afternoon?'

Julia shook her head. 'I don't care about what they guess, only about what they know. Andrew, am I correct in thinking that when Special Branch get here, you will have to hand these papers over to them?'

Andrew thought for some time. 'If they demand them, yes. I would have no choice. But I could hold them off for a while. I could insist on consulting the Director first.'

'How long would that buy us?'

'Not long. The Director is at the bottom of a direct chain of command which leads up to the Home Secretary. In the end, I'd have to give them up.'

Julia held her head in her hands for a few moments. 'If you needed to make copies of these papers, how would you do it? Would you copy them in-house, or would you send them out?'

'With this many? We'd send them out,' Andrew replied immediately. 'There's a firm on Fleet Street we use for all our heavy-document cases.'

'So, I'm guessing they're discreet, reliable?'

'Yes, I'm sure they are.'

Julia stood. 'Good. You're sending them out now. I'm going to need a trolley, and some help getting them to my car.'

'I can get you a trolley,' Andrew said, 'but –'

'Ted, Steffie, I'm going to need your help with these.'

'Our pleasure,' Steffie said, with a grin.

'Julia,' Andrew said, 'what are you doing?'

'When Special Branch get here, tell them you need to consult the Director. Buy us as much time as you can.'

'And when the time runs out…?'

'Tell them the truth – you've sent them out for copying and you'll hand them over as soon as Ted and Steffie bring them back.'

Andrew stood and shook his head. 'But that doesn't make sense. Why did I have them copied?'

Steffie was smiling broadly. 'Because Miss Cathermole asked you to, sir.'

Julia returned the smile. 'Exactly. I have clients suing Lancelot Andrewes School and the Three Musketeers. These files are like gold dust. We were working together on the criminal prosecution until recently. Why shouldn't you copy them for me if I ask?'

'But then, they're going to ask what happened to your copy,' Andrew insisted.

'Yes, of course they will. Again, tell them the truth. Ted and Steffie helped me load my copy into my car before bringing the papers back to you.'

'But then they'll come after you.'

'Yes,' Julia said, smiling towards Steffie again. 'And when they do, I'll hand over my copy like a good girl.' Steffie returned the smile, nodding.

'But –'

She touched his arm. 'Better you not know any more, Andrew. I'm going to have to ask you to trust me. I know exactly what I'm doing. I've played this game before.'

Andrew raised his eyebrows quizzically.

'If you must know, the first time was for my father, in Vienna, when I was twelve,' she said. 'I'll tell you more some day when we have time.' She turned to the two DIs. 'But I do need to know that you're both on board with me. They're not going to harass Andrew, but they might give the two of you a hard time. I won't do this if it puts you at any risk, so if you have any doubts, or concerns, or moral objections at all, tell me and we'll drop the idea now.'

'None from me,' Steffie replied at once.

'Let's get moving,' Ted said. 'Where's the trolley?'

56

'It was nothing to do with us, Julia. I keep telling you.'

On this occasion, to Baxter's private amusement, Julia had imposed her own tradecraft on the meeting. At her insistence, they had met on Hampstead Heath, ignoring the odd spot of rain falling from cloudy skies. It was a good choice, he noted, with professional satisfaction. In this weather they had the Heath almost to themselves.

'Well, who was it then? Five?'

'No. For God's sake, Julia, times have changed. We're not at war any more. We don't go around knocking people off because it seems like a good idea. I'd be the one for the chop if I even suggested it. C would throw me off the roof personally – not to mention that we have the minister and his minions following every move we make. I'm sure the same applies over at Five.'

'Well: who, then?'

'I don't know. Perhaps nobody. Perhaps the police got it right the first time. He took his own life. God knows, he had enough on his conscience.'

Julia shook her head. 'So, what you're telling me is that Gerrard commits suicide using potassium cyanide. Potassium cyanide, Baxter? It's one of the oldest service clichés in the book.'

'Yes, it is. But for suicide, too. We've had many agents take that way out over the years. You know that. Besides, Desmond Gerrard had a wide range of contacts, Julia. If he wanted it, he would have had access to any poison you care to name.'

'And within an hour John Singer is in his rooms, sorting through his papers and getting ready to have them away and make a bonfire of them.'

'Singer would have done that if Gerrard had been run over by a bus. He must have known that there was material there he wouldn't want to see the light of day.'

'And then, when the police take custody of the papers, Special Branch are at Parkside police station within hours to remove them; and not content with that, they raid the offices of Treasury counsel, and my office, in case anyone else may happen to have a copy. Who set Special Branch on us, Baxter?'

'Well, it wasn't us, Julia. I know that, because if we had, we wouldn't be having this conversation.'

She stopped in her tracks and looked him in the eye without speaking.

'If I had to guess,' he continued, turning his eyes away from her gaze, 'some high-level amateur panicked and went off the reservation.'

'Panicked?'

Baxter shrugged. 'You've seen the documents, Julia: I haven't. But from what I hear, they could cause a number of people high up in government some serious embarrassment, and these are people who have the power to pull certain strings. It's not the wisest thing to do, because the strings will have their fingerprints all over them, and in the end it will come back to haunt them. In the end they'll give themselves away. But amateurs don't think like that, and I could give you a long list of people who could get Special Branch mobilised if they put their minds to it.'

They resumed their walk. Baxter smiled.

'But why bother? I'm sure you'll put the copy you still have to good use.'

She couldn't resist returning the smile. 'I hope you're not implying that I haven't cooperated fully with Special Branch.'

'Come off it, Julia. You're forgetting: I spent more than enough time in Vienna working with your dad. I know exactly what you're capable of.'

They laughed together.

'Seriously, though: what are you going to do with it? I can't see any easy way.'

'Neither can I,' she replied.

57

Tuesday 1 April 1975

'The parties having been unable to come to any resolution,' Mr Justice Evan Roberts began, 'I now have to decide whether I should allow the case to proceed to trial, or whether I should find that it is time-barred because of the statute of limitations. I have not found it an easy question. The allegations made against the defendants are extremely serious, and they are men prominent in public life; but on the other hand, if there is any truth to these allegations at all, both plaintiffs, one of whom is not yet ten years of age, have suffered terrible abuse. One of the parties to the case has died in mysterious circumstances, though the action continues against his estate. The stakes are very high for all the parties. I am very grateful to Mr Schroeder and to Mr Henderson, who have made the question I have to decide as clear as it could be. It remains, nonetheless, a difficult one.

'It is well known that the statute of limitations serves an important purpose in civil cases. The more time elapses between a cause of action arising and the plaintiff commencing proceedings, the more danger there is that the court will be unable to reconstruct the facts of the case with any degree of confidence. Witnesses may have died, or become unavailable; documents and other evidence may have been lost or destroyed. The dangers are obvious. The limitation period for actions for intentional wrongful conduct in the nature of sexual assault is, and has at all times material to this case been, a period of six years. In the case of Audrey Marshall, that is obviously a live issue, because in her case the abuse is said to have occurred during the period between1940 and 1945.

'In the case of Emily Marshall, no such issue arises, because any abuse that occurred in her case must have occurred in or after the year 1972. But there is another issue in her case, which may or may not arise, depending on my decision in her mother's case; I shall return to that matter later.

'Mr Schroeder submits that the statute of limitations can't apply to Audrey Marshall's case. He points out, quite correctly, that the period does not begin to run, firstly, until a plaintiff attains her majority – which in Mrs Marshall's case would have been in 1954 – and secondly, until she is aware of the facts and circumstances giving rise to her claim – which, Mr Schroeder says, would have been in 1972, when she recovered her memory of the abuse. Mr Henderson agrees with that statement of the law in principle, but he argues that it breaks down because it would not be safe for the court to rely on evidence of recovered memory.

'It is an odd – and in my view, unsatisfactory – feature of this case, that until I adjourned the case a month ago, no one appears to have thought it necessary to enlist the help of the experts in trying to determine whether or not a court can safely rely on recovered memory as evidence. I observe in passing that an entire criminal trial at the Central Criminal Court before Her Honour Judge Rees took place without any reference to expert opinion: not surprisingly, the jury proved unable to agree on a verdict. At the same time, having now received the report of the two experts, Dr Sutherland for the plaintiffs and Dr Howlett for the defendants, I must say that the question seems almost as impenetrable as it did without their report. That is not meant as a criticism of the doctors: apparently, this is a matter in its infancy in scientific terms, and one on which the experts find it difficult to reach any meaningful common ground. So I must do my best with what I have.

'It is very much in Mrs Marshall's favour that her evidence in the criminal trial was precise and detailed, and that much of it is so similar to the evidence of her daughter, and to that of an independent witness referred to as Woman B, that it is difficult to write it off as a coincidence. It is also true, however, as Mr Henderson points out, that on their own account of it, Mrs Marshall and Woman B talked about what had happened at the time, with each other and with other pupils of the same age. Mr Henderson also says that any similarity to Emily's evidence is concerning, for the same reasons. Despite that, the similarity is compelling.

'On the other hand, there is much force in Mr Henderson's argument, reflecting Mr Norris's cross-examination in the criminal trial on behalf of Father Gerrard, that it is difficult to see how Mrs Marshall could have spent a further six years at Lancelot Andrewes School after the alleged abuse stopped, without being reminded of it continually – by the walk up and down the staircases, passing by Farther Gerrard's private library, and by the continuing scenes in her dormitory when a girl was taken away at night. Those matters, and the tragic event of her sister's death, Mr Henderson argues, could not have failed to act as a constant reminder. I confess that I find that argument a difficult one to refute.

'Turning to the experts, both agree that in theory, there is no scientific reason why memory should not be lost and later recovered. Indeed, both experts were aware of cases in which that had happened: for example, a person involved in a serious accident may suffer from retrograde amnesia for some time, and may recover his memory when he is exposed to a photograph, or something said by another person involved in the accident. Both experts were also aware of cases in which soldiers returning from war appear to have suffered very prolonged bouts of amnesia, only for memories to return years later. Both doctors agree, therefore, that Mrs Marshall's account of her recovered memory is not scientifically impossible. Indeed, Dr Sutherland would go further. He believes it to be inherently credible. Dr Howlett, though he is sceptical, believes that, even if her evidence is inaccurate, it is not necessarily dishonest in any way: it may simply be her imagination taking the place of a failed memory of the relevant years.

'Both doctors, however, have some hesitation in saying the court should rely on Mrs Marshall's evidence in legal proceedings. That, of course, is quite a different matter from believing her account for normal social purposes, when there are no consequences. In any legal proceedings, accepting evidence has very clear consequences for other parties, and this case is no different. Dr Howlett counsels against accepting evidence of this kind in any legal proceedings in the present state of scientific knowledge, and urges the courts to wait until there have been further scientific developments suggesting that it is sufficiently reliable. Dr Sutherland, on the other hand, believes that evidence of recovered memory can safely be left to the judgment and common sense of a judge or jury; he points out that the failure of the jury in the criminal trial to agree on a verdict is not necessarily logically related to the evidence of Mrs Marshall. In Dr Sutherland's view, many kinds of evidence pose problems for judges and juries, and this is just one more example: the evidence should be scrutinised with the utmost care, but not rejected out of hand. He adds that the evidence should be considered on a case-by-case basis; and that the presence or absence of corroborative evidence may be an important factor.

'These arguments have caused me considerable anxiety. At the end of the day, I have reluctantly concluded that I must err on the side of caution. In the present state of scientific opinion, I am not persuaded that it would be safe to rely on recovered memory in legal proceedings, or at least that it would be safe to do so in this case. I stress that I do not find that Audrey Marshall's evidence is in any way dishonest. There is nothing to suggest that she has not acted throughout in the utmost good faith, sincerely believing her recovered memory to be an accurate recollection of what went on at Lancelot Andrewes School in the 1940s. I have considered carefully to what extent the evidence of Woman B and that of Emily corroborate her memory. In my judgment, the discussions that took place at the time make it dangerous to rely on them for that purpose.

'The irony is that, but for the statute of limitations, Woman B would undoubtedly have been entitled to maintain an action against each of these defendants. Although that does not help Woman B – or Mrs Marshall – I hope it will be enough to deter any of the defendants from thinking, or saying, that they are leaving court without a stain on their character. But for the reasons I have given, the action brought by Mrs Marshall must be dismissed as being time-barred, and judgment entered for the defendants accordingly.

'Emily's case has also caused me great anxiety. While there is no issue as to the statute of limitations in her case, there is a question of corroboration. In a civil case, in which the judge sits without a jury, issues of corroboration play a far less significant role than in a criminal case, in which the judge must direct a jury of lay people about matters of law. In civil cases, a judge can take into account the presence or absence of corroboration, among all the other relevant factors, in deciding whether the evidence of any given witness is sufficiently reliable. I am quite satisfied that I will be able to do so in this case. For that reason, I have concluded that there is no reason why the case on behalf of Emily Marshall cannot proceed to trial. I order that her case be fixed for trial accordingly. I emphasise that if Mrs Marshall and Woman B wish to give evidence in that trial, in addition to any other witnesses, there is no reason why they should not do so.'

The judge quickly left the bench.

'I told you they should settle while they had the chance,' Mark Henderson whispered to Julia on his way out of court. 'The offer is still open for Emily.'

'Oh, do fuck off, Mark,' she whispered back.

Audrey, standing nearby, heard. Julia was about to say something, but Audrey gently placed a finger over her lips. Without saying a word, she hugged Julia, Ben, and Ginny, and turned to go.

'We'll take the offer,' she said as she left.

PART FIVE

58

Audrey Marshall
When I received Julia's invitation to dinner, my first reaction was to find a polite excuse for declining. The sense of numbness and hopelessness I've felt ever since my case was dismissed has taken over my life. Our GP, Linda Gallagher, is prescribing me anti-depressants. The settlement we received in Emily's case hasn't helped. It wasn't ungenerous: in fact, we won't have to worry about school fees for the rest of her career at the excellent boarding school in Norwich she's now happily attending. But our voices have been stopped. Our lips have been sewn tightly together. We're not allowed to disclose the amount we received, and the settlement was made on the express basis that neither Lancelot Andrewes School, nor its board of trustees, nor the estate of Father Desmond Gerrard, nor Lord AB, nor Sir CD, nor the Right Reverend EF makes any admission of guilt or liability. It's all without prejudice. We, on the other hand, have been prejudiced to our core. I hated to accept it. Deep inside me I longed to emulate Julia, and just tell Mark Henderson to fuck off. But that would have made it be all about me. It would have been an indulgence that made me feel better for five minutes: but it wouldn't have been fair to Emily. I've put Emily through enough. It was time to let it go.

Now that I've thought it through, I realise that I've never really said thank you to Julia, or to Ben and Ginny: I mean, I have, but I didn't thank them right at the end, not when it really mattered. Once again, I have to stop it being all about me. I will go and have dinner with them, because I owe it to them to thank them properly. But it's not just that. Almost without my knowing it, they've become my friends as well as my trusted advisers. I've come to know them. Julia, with her exotic background, her manic social persona, her occasional need for isolation; and her special friends, always younger, and really beautiful and really clever and really funny, like Julia herself. Ben and Jess, so happy with their new son. They've called him Joshua, after Ben's grandfather, whom they both adore and who's very fragile now. Jess is fretting about whether to continue practice or take a break until he starts school. Ginny is sad that she can't be like Jess: she told me so tearfully, one afternoon, when we were waiting for something to happen at court – I forget what, and it doesn't matter; so she and Michael are thinking about adopting. In a strange way, I've had a window into their families, just as they've had a window into mine; and we've looked into each other's lives compassionately, and affectionately. We've walked a long, hard road together.

So yes, of course I will go, to say thank you and tell them in my own way that I love them, and will always love them, very much. The dinner will be a wake: I know that. But wakes have their purpose. Perhaps this one will lift the cloud hanging over my head, and help move my process of grieving along, towards its completion.

59

Julia welcomed Audrey and Ken into her dining room. They were the last to arrive. The circular oak dining table was formally set with Julia's best green and white Wedgwood dinner service and Waterford crystal wine glasses. Jean-Claude and several helpers were putting the final touches to the candelabras and floral arrangements, and a delicious aroma of French country chicken in gravy was wafting into the room from the kitchen. On the far side of the room, Ben and Ginny were talking to two men Audrey didn't recognise.

'Sorry we're late, Julia: trains, you know.'

Julia kissed both visitors on the cheek.

'You're not late. You've timed it just right. Make yourselves at home. How's Emily?'

Audrey smiled. 'Feeling left out. She wanted to know why she couldn't come with us, and have dinner with the grown-ups. She said it wasn't fair because we're always telling her she's a big girl now, so why shouldn't she?'

'Why indeed?' Julia said, laughing. 'Of course. Look out, Ken, you may have another lawyer in the family.'

'It wouldn't surprise me,' Ken replied. 'She's growing up so fast.'

'Well, next time, I'm going to invite her as well,' Julia said. 'Come through.' As they did, Valérie, wearing her black suit and white apron, stepped forward smartly and offered glasses of champagne and orange juice. They chose the champagne.

'Come on, I'd like you to meet two American friends of mine,' Julia said, ushering them forward with an arm gently around Audrey's waist.

'Ken and Audrey Marshall, this is Simon Lester.'

'Nice to meet you.' He was thirty-five, with a friendly face, but keen, inquiring eyes, self-assured in a dark blue jacket and a white open-necked shirt. His accent was unmistakably New York, but softened by an extra layer, the result of wide travel and exposure to people in many different places.

'Simon Lester,' Audrey said, looking at Julia. 'I've heard your name before, haven't I?'

'I would certainly hope so,' the older, and much larger man standing next to Simon said, 'after all the dough I've spent promoting him.' The accent this time was unrefined New York.

Simon laughed. 'This is my publisher, Ed Rafferty, managing director of Fulbourn and McIntyre, out of New York.'

They shook hands.

'Simon wrote a book called *Lifting the Lid: A Legislature in Crisis*,' Julia said. 'It went to the top of the *New York Times* non-fiction best seller list within a week of publication.'

'Of course,' Ken said. 'You're the author who exposed that prostitution racket in Washington, the one involving those senators and congressmen: the one that wasn't supposed to exist, according to the FBI.'

Simon nodded. 'I'm interested in things the authorities say don't exist.'

Jean-Claude entered discreetly from the kitchen.

'Dinner is ready, Miss Cathermole, if you'd like us to serve?'

'Yes, of course, Jean-Claude. Let's all take our seats, shall we? Simon, I've put you next to Audrey. Ed, why don't you sit here next to Ginny? Ken you're on Ginny's other side, and Ben, you're here, next to me.'

She took Jean-Claude aside.

'Jean-Claude, we have things to discuss. You understand…'

'Of course, Miss Cathermole.' He turned to the guests. 'Ladies and gentlemen, welcome. To start, we have a simple tomato salad with French bread. We'll serve that with the main course, a Languedoc roast chicken with onions and garlic in a red-wine gravy sauce. To accompany it, I've selected a red Burgundy. It's been breathing on the sideboard; it will be ready now. As long as you don't mind pouring yourselves, we won't need to disturb you. Just ring when you're ready for us to clear away.'

He rang the bell, and almost at once, four black-suited waiters, two men, two women, entered silently bearing the wonderfully aromatic dishes, which they proceeded to distribute. As Julia poured the Burgundy, Jean-Claude hovered around the table, directing operations with a touch here, the pointing of a finger there. The whole process seemed to take no more than a few seconds, and once their service was complete, he waved his staff discreetly into the kitchen. The door closed silently behind them.

When dinner had ended, and they had poured coffee, Audrey raised her wine glass.

'I don't know quite how to say this, Julia. But Ken and I want to thank you, and you too, Ben, Ginny, from the bottom of our hearts for everything you've done for us, and for Emily. I understand that we've reached the end of the road now. I understand that this is a wake – and I couldn't imagine a more elegant and delicious one. I know this is the end. But I'm glad we came as far as we could. I'm glad we tried. So I want to propose a toast to you – and of course, to Andrew, and John, and the officers, Steffie and Ted. We are humbled that you would do so much for us. Thank you.'

They drank.

'We are the ones who are humbled, Audrey,' Ginny replied, choking back a tear. 'Your fighting spirit, your love and support for Emily – and yourself – you've been an inspiration.'

'You've touched Jess and me too,' Ben added quietly. 'We're parents now, and – well, you've set the standard for us.'

'Goddamn it, Julia, what is it with you Limeys?' Ed demanded suddenly. 'What's all this talk about a wake? This isn't a goddamn wake – not if I have anything to do with it.'

'What do you mean?' Ben asked.

'I think,' Julia said, holding up a hand before Ed could reply, 'that the moment has come to adjourn upstairs.' She rang her bell and Jean-Claude appeared as if by magic.

'Jean-Claude, dinner was wonderful.'

There was a hearty round of applause, which the chef acknowledged with a brief bow of the head.

'We're going upstairs for a brandy. We won't need anything else. Can you let yourselves out if you finish clearing up before we come back down?'

'Of course, Miss Cathermole. Good night.'

60

Upstairs was the large attic at the very top of Julia's townhouse. It was a special place, to which only special guests were invited, on special occasions. The chairs and sofas were comfortable, the lighting subdued, and the room's old, dark wooden beams ran along the ceiling and curved seductively at its corners, down into the walls. Bottles of water and an excellent old brandy were arrayed on a side table.

'Why did we have to wait till we got up here?' Ed asked. 'Why all the fuss?'

'Because it's the only part of the house I keep swept,' she replied.

'Come again?'

'Somehow, I don't think you're talking about how clean your house is,' Simon said, smiling.

'No. I'm talking about sweeping against bugs,' Julia replied, matter-of-factly. 'I do it every month, just to be on the safe side. I know it sounds exotic, but you don't see it as exotic if you were raised in a service family in a residence abroad. It's just a fact of life. When I was growing up in Vienna, my father had the house swept every week. I still have contacts with the service; I've done some work with them, and I've never lost the habit.'

'Do you think they may be trying to listen in?' Ben asked.

'It's possible. I thought so during the Digby case. I'm not sure, to tell you the truth, but there are times when I prefer to err on the safe side.' She paused. 'So, everyone grab a drink: the protocol upstairs is, help yourselves and make yourselves at home.'

She waited for everyone to be seated. 'OK. Audrey, I do have an ulterior motive in inviting you and Ken here tonight. I invited you because it's possible that we may still have another chapter to write – in the literal sense, as well as the figurative. That's why Ed and Simon are here. Simon, the floor is yours.'

Simon sat forward in his chair and looked straight into Audrey's eyes.

'Audrey, you and I have only just met tonight,' he said. 'But I know from Julia that you have an incredible story to tell. I want to write it.'

'It's a helluva story,' Ed added, 'and when's he's written it, I intend to publish it.'

Audrey and Ken looked at Julia, and then at each other.

'You want to write our story? You mean, as a book?'

'You bet,' Simon replied. 'Look, Audrey, you've been abused, your daughter has been abused, God only knows how many other girls have been abused in schools up and down this country for more than thirty years: and what happens? The schools try to buy their way out of trouble, and the government buries its head in the sand and tries to cover it up.'

'And comes damn close to doing it,' Ed added. 'I'm getting angry just thinking about it.'

'I believe it's going to make a lot of people angry,' Simon said. 'This is a major scandal, and we can't let your government get away with sweeping it under the carpet.'

'Heads are going to roll, Audrey,' Ed said with a smile. 'Believe me. We're going to bring some people down, just like we did in Washington. And it couldn't happen to a nicer bunch of guys. And even better,' he added contentedly, 'it's going to be a big, big, seller: huge.' He paused. 'So, what do you think? Are you ready to stand up and fight another round, or do you still want sit back and enjoy the wake?'

Audrey laughed. 'I don't know what to say.'

She turned to Ken, who shook his head. 'Neither do I. It's something that never occurred to me.'

'I'm sorry we've taken you by surprise,' Julia said, smiling. 'Perhaps I should have warned you in advance, but I have a weakness for the dramatic moment.'

'Well you've certainly succeeded there,' Ken said.

'I think this gives us one last chance to turn things around,' Julia said, 'and you can trust them to do a good job. I've known Ed for years. He's an old family friend, and once it became obvious that the powers that be were intent on burying us six feet under, I called him in New York. It was Ed who suggested Simon – and his track record speaks for itself. We think this would be the perfect sequel to *Lifting the Lid.*' She smiled. 'But of course, I would like counsel's opinion.'

Ginny shook her head. 'Obviously, my main concern would be an action for libel. Libel is an expensive business.'

'What libel?' Simon asked. 'We're going to be telling the truth, the whole truth, and nothing but the truth.'

'Yes, but you have to be able to back the story up. I don't know what the libel laws are like in America. I seem to remember reading somewhere that you make it very hard for public figures to sue, because of the emphasis you put on freedom of speech.'

'That's exactly right,' Ed replied.

'But that's not the case in this country. You have to be able to dot every "I" and cross every "T" if you're challenged.'

'That's the way I always work,' Simon replied, 'but not because I'm afraid of the law. I don't worry about the law. I worry about my personal standard. My background is in journalism, and my personal standard is that I don't write a word unless I believe one hundred per cent in my sources, and I'm one hundred per cent convinced that I'm writing a true story – a story I can back up every step of the way.'

'You can't do that in this case, Simon,' Ginny said. 'The government has put an embargo on all the documents you'd need, under the Official Secrets Act.'

'On you maybe,' Simon said, 'but not on me. I haven't signed any official secrets forms, and I'm not going to be doing my writing here. I'll be writing this in my apartment on East Seventy-Second Street, enjoying my great view over the Park. I can look at any documents and quote from any documents I want.'

'But we don't have them,' Ginny insisted. 'The government seized whatever they could, and we had to give an undertaking to destroy the rest.'

Julia coughed. 'Yes, well, actually, Ginny...'

'What are you saying, Julia?' Ginny asked, genuinely startled.

'I'm something of a – what is it you Americans call people who hoard things, Ed?'

'Pack-rats.'

'Pack-rats: that's it. I've always been a bit of a pack-rat; and because of my family connections over the years, I have access to secure methods of keeping documents that might turn out to be useful somewhere down the road – methods most people don't have access to. You'll understand if I don't elaborate on that – even if the room has been swept. But if certain documents need to find their way into Simon's hands, that can be arranged without our fingerprints being on them.' She paused. 'I'm not worried. It's the government that's going to be embarrassed by this, not any of us.'

'That sounds like a dangerous game, Julia.'

She smiled. 'Not if you have the right people playing it with you.' Seeing Ginny about to protest, she added, 'That's all I'm going to say about that.'

Ginny shook her head, and there was a long silence.

'Can you tell us what documents might be stashed away in your secure places?' Ben asked.

'Everything,' Julia replied.

Ben's draw dropped. 'Everything?'

'The court transcripts, EF's police interview, the documents they found in Father Gerrard's rooms... everything.'

Ed smiled. 'See what I mean? It's going to be a great book.'

'The government will ask for an injunction to prevent publication, once they get wind of it,' Ben said.

Ed laughed. 'Good luck to them. No disrespect to your Queen, Ben, she's a fine lady: but the royal writ hasn't run in the State of New York since 1776. F and M will publish this book in New York, and there's nothing your government can do to stop us. Not only that, we will sell the book world-wide, and we have unofficial ways of making sure that anyone in Great Britain who wants a copy can get one. It's not hard, and, don't forget, it's going to attract a lot of publicity. This book will be reviewed in all the major papers, in Europe and stateside. What are they going to do here, ban *Le Monde* and *Frankfurter Allgemeine*? Ban the *New York Times*? I don't think so.' He laughed again. 'They'll get tired of the charade before long, Ben. They'll abandon the injunction. But it won't matter. There'll be plenty of copies in circulation here, even before we can legally give it to our British subsidiary.'

Ben turned to Audrey. 'If you do this, it will mean a lot of publicity for you all, Audrey – including publicity for Emily. Are you ready for that?'

'And they may come after you for breach of the settlement agreement,' Ginny added.

Audrey and Ken looked into each other's eyes silently for a long time. Then they smiled, and Audrey turned to Simon.

'Do you have a title in mind, Simon?' she asked.

'I sure do,' he replied. 'I'm planning to call it *One Law for the Rest of Us*. That has a certain ring to it, don't you think?'

61

'May I have your attention, please?' Ben almost shouted, after he had tapped on his glass with a fingernail for almost a minute, to call those assembled to order. 'I've been asked to do the honours this evening.'

The occasion was a celebratory chambers party. At the end of a hard-working week, and in the light of good news, the wine was flowing freely. The last two heads of chambers to leave for the High Court bench, Duncan Furnival and Bernard Wesley, were in attendance, and every member and pupil had made sure to return from court in good time.

'The first order of business,' Ben continued, 'of course, is to congratulate Mr Justice Gareth Morgan-Davies on his appointment to the High Court bench, and his assignment to the Queen's Bench Division. In that division he can devote himself, at least some of the time, to criminal work: and judging by my recent experience, that's an area in which he will be able to bring about some much-needed improvement.'

He waited for the applause and laughter to subside.

'As you all know, Gareth was my pupil-master. Technically, pupillage lasts for six months or a year, and in that time, the master is supposed to instruct the pupil thoroughly in the ways of our profession. But a real pupillage doesn't last six months or a year: it lasts a lifetime; and that has been my experience with Gareth. Yes, during my pupillage I learned as much as I could have ever dreamed of about advocacy, about how to behave in court, about how to behave in chambers, about the way we do things at the bar, and about the ways we don't do them: and that knowledge has served me well in the years I've been in practice. But long after my pupillage officially came to an end, I knew that Gareth's door was always open to me. His advice was always at my disposal, however long it took, and however inconvenient it was to dispense. He regarded it as a lifetime relationship, and so do I. And in the cases we did together after my pupillage ended – both as colleagues and adversaries – he stood up for me and supported me. I've never been without his advice and wise counsel.

'I've been asked to take a pupil myself in the near future, and I don't mind admitting that I'm feeling apprehensive about it. I'm sure it's going to be nerve-wracking, having a pupil at my side the whole time, watching everything I do, and asking awkward questions. Gareth, that never occurred to me while I was a pupil, but I'm beginning to see now what you went through.'

'At last,' Gareth commented, to chuckles around the room.

'But I have Gareth's model of being a pupil-master to guide me, and that will be more than enough.

'Everything comes at a price, of course, and in my case the price was having to listen to frequent imprecations in Welsh, and learn to follow the fortunes of Wales in that strange sport, the name of which escapes me, the one they play with that odd-shaped ball.'

There was loud laughter.

'After all I taught you, Ben,' Gareth said, shaking his head. 'How could you?'

More laughter.

'But even that proved to be helpful,' Ben continued. 'During the Welsh investiture case, Gareth took me to Wales and helped me to understand the forces at work there, the way people thought about Wales, and about independence from England, and about the nation's pride in itself. He took me to an international at Cardiff Arms Park – you remember, Donald, you were there too – and although the rules of the game remain a mystery to me, the feeling I had, being in the stadium, listening to the singing and the cheering, soaking up the passion, helped me to understand so much about my client and the others involved in the case.

'Quite apart from the benefit I had of being his pupil, Gareth's leadership of chambers over the last few years, after Bernard left us for the bench, has been outstanding. His calmness, his vision, and his hospitality in his room after hours, have been an inspiration. Ladies and gentlemen, please raise your glasses: I give you the toast: Mr Justice Morgan-Davies.'

The toast was drunk and greeted with a prolonged round of applause.

'Don't be a stranger, Gareth. Come back and see us when you can.'

'I will,' Gareth promised.

'This means, of course,' Ben said, 'that Aubrey Smith-Gurney ascends to the exalted rank of head of chambers, and in just a moment, I will ask him to say a few words. Aubrey, congratulations to you, if that's the right word.'

'Commiserations would be more like it, Ben,' Aubrey replied.

'And last, but not least, congratulations to Kenneth Gaskell on getting Silk, and to my dear friend and room-mate Harriet Fisk on being asked to sit as a special master in a commercial case. Well deserved, both of you. That's enough from me. Gareth, would you like to say a word or two?'

'I won't keep you for more than a moment,' Gareth replied. 'It is traditional for the outgoing head to propose a toast to chambers, which I now do. I just want to say that I've enjoyed every moment of my years in chambers. There are a few moments in any career when you look at yourself in the mirror one day and ask, "Why did I ever get myself involved in all this?" There have been several such moments in my career, especially since I took over from Bernard as head of chambers; and it was probably on those occasions that Ben heard most of the Welsh imprecations. But on the whole it's been a delight, and I can promise Aubrey that being in charge is not as bad as he thinks – well, not quite, anyway. The reason for that is the friendship and support you can count on from every member of chambers. You couldn't ask for a better group of colleagues. Please raise your glasses again, ladies and gentlemen. The toast is: chambers.'

Some minutes later, as Gareth and Ben were chatting, Anthony Norris approached.

'Anthony,' Gareth said. 'I'm sorry we can't congratulate you on Silk today, but I'm sure it won't be long delayed.'

Norris lit a cigarette. 'It's that bloody case,' he replied, 'the one that started all this fuss about sexual abuse. If I hadn't represented that bloody priest, I'd have my silk gown too, just like Kenneth.'

Gareth smiled. 'It does seem to have caused a bit of a furore, doesn't it?'

'A furore? The whole country is up in arms, Gareth. Women are coming forward in their thousands. Sexual abuse is becoming an industry, and the name of Desmond Gerrard is anathema.' He turned to Ben. 'I told you this would happen. Just wait till it's your turn.'

'You told me that they would stop appointing our heads of chambers to the bench, Anthony,' Ben pointed out, 'and that Kenneth wouldn't get Silk. But both of those things have happened.'

'That's all very well,' Norris replied. 'It's my career that's suffered. There's a black mark against my name.' He turned back to Gareth. 'Couldn't you look into it for me, Gareth? I'm sure you know the people to talk to.'

Gareth placed a hand on Norris' shoulder. 'Anthony, this was your first time of asking, wasn't it? It's not unusual to be turned down the first time. I'm sure you'll get it next time. It's just the way these things work. You have to be patient.'

'I'm the first one in chambers it's ever happened to,' Norris protested.

Gareth nodded. 'Yes… well, I'm sure there's a reason, but I can't imagine it has anything to do with the case. Quite the contrary, really. They like to see that you've been involved in some important high-profile cases. It gives them confidence that you can handle more complicated work – the kind of work you would expect to be doing as a Silk. I honestly can't see that case doing you any harm, Anthony.'

'So, what should I do about it?'

Gareth shrugged. 'There's nothing you can do, except carry on, and try not to let it get you down. That would be my advice.'

Norris shook his head and walked away to refill his glass.

'Do you think he'll get it next time?' Ben asked.

'I don't know, Ben,' Gareth replied, 'but if he doesn't, I assure you, it will have nothing to do with Father Desmond Gerrard.' He took a sip of his champagne. 'If I were you,' he added, 'I would start work on your own application. Make sure you put me down as a referee.'

62

Monday 3 October 1977

As the lengthy filmed segment drew to a close, the veteran presenter tweaked his trademark bow tie once again and made a final adjustment to his spectacles before looking into the camera.

'Good evening. In this special edition of *Panorama*, we have two guests live in our studio. They are the author Simon Lester, and Audrey Marshall, the woman whose stand against some people in high places appears to have shaken the British establishment to its foundations in recent days. Welcome, to both of you.

'Mr Lester, let me start with you. Ever since your book *One Law for the Rest of Us* was published, we've had a wave of reaction from almost every section of society, from the very highest in the land to the man and woman in the street. And of course, even before your book was published, it was one of the most badly kept secrets of all time.'

Simon laughed. 'Yes, your government did its best to keep us quiet; but when people are ready to speak out, you can't silence them forever. Eventually, the dam was bound to burst: it was just a matter of time.'

'I've had my copy for months,' the presenter said, smiling. 'I'm not going to say how I got it, but I will say that it wasn't particularly difficult.'

'No. I think many people in Great Britain had copies before the injunction was lifted and we published officially. Even for those who didn't have the book, it wasn't hard to find out what was in it.'

'Mr Lester, let's go over the fall-out, as we understand it to be today: although we know that whatever we say today may be overtaken by events even before this programme ends. As our filmed report just now showed, it's all been moving at a breath-taking speed.'

'It has, indeed. It's hard to know where to start. We know that the Attorney General has rescinded the order he made preventing the prosecution of Lord AB, Sir CD and the Right Reverend EF. We now expect that they will be going to trial at the Old Bailey in the near future.'

'Yes,' the presenter said, 'and before we go any further, it's only fair to note that in your book, you make no criticism of the Attorney General personally for the order he made originally, preventing the trial from going ahead?'

'That's correct. The Attorney received representations from the defence lawyers; they made reasonable arguments to him on behalf of their clients, and he acted properly at the time. It's right to say also that he acted immediately to revoke his order once it became clear that he hadn't been given the full picture, shall we say.'

'He's now given the green light to the Director of Public Prosecutions to conduct a comprehensive investigation, hasn't he?'

'Yes, and the expectation is that the Director will proceed, not only against those three men, but against any others who may be identified in connection with child sexual abuse in other schools.'

'Yes: and in fact, the BBC understands that the Director is already examining the records of a number of schools, including the five other schools named in the papers found in the rooms of Father Desmond Gerrard, the headmaster of Lancelot Andrewes School.'

He paused.

'And on the subject of Father Gerrard: according to who you ask, he either committed suicide or was murdered, on the eve of the trial of the civil action brought against him in the High Court. His death has become one of the darkest of all the many dark aspects of all this, hasn't it? Do you have any thoughts about it?'

Simon shrugged. 'We may never know for sure. The inquest remains open in case further evidence comes to light. The case has some strange features: no suicide note was ever found, and the police haven't been able to trace the source of the cyanide. But I'm picking up some hints from one of my sources that further evidence may come to light, suggesting that Gerrard was in fact murdered.'

The presenter smiled. 'Would this be the famous Source X-ray, as you call him in your book, who, you say, is highly placed in one of our security services?'

Simon returned the smile enigmatically. 'No comment.'

'Fair enough. But if Gerrard was murdered: why?'

'In my opinion? He knew too much. He knew all the men who were abusing those girls, and his world was crumbling. He was going down, one way or the other, and if he'd been tempted to speak out in an attempt to save himself, he would have taken them down with him.'

'So, if Gerrard was murdered, there must be a lot of suspects?'

'Yes, there are, and maybe we will never know who did it.' Simon smiled again. 'On the other hand, we live in a strange world, don't we? Who knows? We may not have heard the end of the story yet.'

'And – I can tell from looking at your face – that's all you're going to say about that tonight, isn't it?'

Simon laughed. 'That's correct, sir.'

'Fair enough,' the presenter said. 'Let's move on to the victims of the abuse. A growing number of women have now come forward to complain of having been victims of sexual abuse at as many as nine schools. In some cases, the complaints go back for many years, and they have been naming the men they say abused them.'

'Yes. The latest figure I have is in excess of eighty, and I don't think the list is anywhere near being closed yet. I also understand that they implicate a large number of men, many prominent in public life, particularly in churches of several denominations, but also in

Parliament, government, the courts, and – to an increasing extent – show business. They haven't all been named as yet, of course.'

'We're still using initials, are we?' the presenter asked, smiling.

'Apparently, and we may have enough to use up the alphabet several times over. We may need to go to three or four initials instead of just two.'

'One intriguing fact,' the presenter continued, 'is that the papers found in Father Gerrard's rooms seem to suggest at least one link between the various schools, other than Gerrard himself.'

'Yes. A man called John Singer, who I mention in my book, was acting as a solicitor on behalf of all the schools. What his exact role was in all this isn't clear as yet, but, as you reported in your news programmes on the BBC last week, Singer has been arrested and his offices searched.'

'Last Wednesday, if I remember rightly.'

'Yes. And I have a source – not Source X-ray, but a source I believe to be highly reliable – who tells me that Singer has been interviewed by the police, and has offered to cooperate with them and give evidence, in return for immunity. If that is confirmed, we can expect to see a whole series of criminal trials lasting for some considerable time.'

'Extraordinary,' the presenter said. 'This saga is going to run and run, isn't it?

'It certainly seems so, sir.'

The presenter shook his head. 'You've been working on this story for a long time now, Mr Lester, beginning with your meetings with Audrey Marshall, interviewing other witnesses, including her young daughter Emily, trawling through thousands of pages of documents. Looking back on it all now, how do you see your role in the story?'

Simon smiled. 'That's an interesting question. I haven't really given much thought to it; I've been so busy with the story, and with the book.'

He thought for a moment or two.

'I guess I would see my role as a modest one, but no less important for that. I've always felt that every democracy needs several layers of protection. If you only have one layer, it's too easy for the powerful and the unscrupulous to override it, to cover up their wrongdoing and that of their friends. In the States, we have several safeguards written into our Constitution, with our separation of powers between the different branches of government. Here in Great Britain, you also have safeguards, but they're not as easy to see because you don't have a written constitution.'

'We still have them, though, don't we?'

'Yes. The law is, and must be, the first line of defence; and in most cases the law is enough. But this case shows that even the law can be manipulated sometimes. After the law, the next line of defence is the press. But the press doesn't always get to the truth. They may not have the means, or they may not have the will, because of their allegiances, or those of their publishers.'

'So, who do you turn to when the law and the press fail you?' the presenter asked.

Simon smiled. 'I guess you turn to a guy with a typewriter on East Seventy-Second Street.'

The presenter laughed.

'Mrs Marshall, let me turn to you. How do you feel about all of this?'

63

Audrey Marshall

How do I feel about all this? Good question. During my appearance on *Panorama*, I gave it a fairly anodyne answer. I wasn't being intentionally evasive. I've never been very comfortable talking to large numbers of people; and although in the glare of the studio lights I was only directly aware of the presenter, Simon, and the camera operators, I knew that there were a lot of people listening to me and watching me out there, and the knowledge inhibited me. And quite apart from that, it's a complicated question: one I'm not sure I could answer fully in a week of talking, never mind a minute or two of one edition of *Panorama*. But it is an important question: and I'll do my best to answer it now.

Looking back over my life, and especially my life since Emily confided in me in January 1972, I remember feeling, in no particular order: distress, anxiety, fear, horror, hopelessness, despair, anger, rage, vengefulness, and an enveloping blackness that never seemed to lift. Sometimes I felt them in combination; sometimes they lasted for months, or even years, on end; sometimes they succeeded each other in rapid succession; and sometimes they ran together, like paints from an artist's palette left out in the rain, until they merged, and I could no longer distinguish one from another.

In the end, they would have destroyed me: I can see that clearly now. If I hadn't come to the realisation that I couldn't let this be about me anymore, I would eventually have given up. I would probably have gone the same way as Joan: hanged myself in the quiet of an ordinary afternoon: or fallen as if by mishap under a train; or hoarded the pills Linda Gallagher gave me until I had enough for an accidental overdose. But when I decided not to let it be about me anymore, a remarkable thing happened. I was able to open my heart back up, and let in others who had also suffered: and as I started to open myself up, as I began to focus on the suffering of others, I saw something so incredible that it stopped me in my tracks. I saw that I was actually one of the lucky ones.

Once people got to know about Simon's book, so many victims began to find the courage to come out, and to speak their pain and anger, and to demand redress for their suffering: at first one or two here and there; then a trickle, then a stream; and finally a flood – not only women who had been pupils at the schools we knew about, but victims of other schools, and of churches, and of doctors, and of youth leaders, and of show business celebrities, and of employers, and of members of their own families. Often, they wrote to me, because my name was already out there, and they felt I was someone they could talk to. At first, I shied away from them: I didn't want to know. I'd had enough. I wanted to hide away with my family: I wanted to avert my eyes from horror on such a scale. I wanted to pretend that I could ignore it and get on with my life. But that didn't last long: it was impossible for me to turn my eyes away when I had already seen so much, and when these women knew my story from the book. They knew I was one of them. I was already present in their lives. I'd played a part in enabling them to come forward for help, and for justice. I couldn't turn my eyes away from them now.

So, I decided to make my presence count. I replied to everyone who wrote, and it was then that I began to see how lucky I was. There were women out there who had tried to take their own lives; women who had turned to drink or drugs; women who had fallen victim over and over again to a series of abusers posing as lovers; women whose sex lives had become terminally dysfunctional; women whose husbands and lovers, unable to understand what was going on with them, had turned against them and abandoned them; women whose children had done the same; women whose lives had been torn apart as they looked helplessly on.

My own nightmares have never completely gone away, but they have subsided. I've made peace with my loss of Joan, and with the loss of so much of my childhood and my young life. I have my family. We are safe and well. Ken and I are strong together. Emily is strong, too. She gives every appearance of having come out of it unscathed. She hasn't, of course: her demons are going to surface sooner or later. But we're prepared. We talk frankly to her about sex, and love, and men to avoid, and men to embrace, and although she knows more about the mechanics of sex than she should at her age, at least now, she's learning about it from those who love her, not from men who are abusing her. When her demons surface, she will have the tools to confront them, and loving parents to confront them with her. Compared to many women I've spoken to, we're living a dream.

So, I've made my life about reaching out, as much as I can. I've started a network of women who can help and support each other. I'd known for a long time that I would eventually have to leave my position with the diocese: Bill Hollis has remained a good friend, but the job held too many memories, too many bad feelings. I couldn't stay there. So, I gave notice, and now I'm working on the network full time. The spare bedroom at home has become our office, where, with Emily's help, I keep files so that I can keep in touch with every woman who contacts me. I also put them in touch with each other, and with men and women who can help them. Julia is putting together a list of lawyers up and down the country who are willing to represent them. A friend of Ginny's, a clinical psychologist, is putting together a list of colleagues who will offer crisis counselling. The Bishop of Ely has offered to become our patron. Ken is setting the network up as a registered charity. We're calling it the One Law Foundation.

Returning to my feelings, I'd always imagined that when the abusers were finally put on trial, when they were finally called to account and sentenced for their crimes, and when their victims were finally vindicated and received justice, I would feel elation, and I would revel in their downfall. I wanted them locked up, and I wanted to be the one entrusted with the task of throwing away the key. I know many women who feel that way, and they're fully entitled to their feelings. Their abusers are going to fall a long way down, and they're going to fall hard. They will have a long time to reflect on the damage they did to so many young lives, and on the insult they added to injury by covering up such a long history of calculated, cynical wrongdoing. Their victims are entitled to rejoice in their richly deserved fate. But I can't join in. I just can't find satisfaction in such a colossal waste of human potential.

Perhaps it's because I've moved on from my own pain, or perhaps I'm just tired: I don't know. Whatever the reason, I simply feel sad that it had to come to this: and that the cycle of abuse, injury, concealment, discovery, and retribution will probably continue long after this particular drama, and those actors who have featured in it, have left the stage. But at the same time, I also feel hopeful. I feel hopeful when I think how many heroes I have in my life: when I think about Ed Rafferty, and the guy with the typewriter on East Seventy-Second Street; and about Andrew Pilkington, John Caswell, Ted Phillips, Steffie Walsh, Julia Cathermole, Ginny Castle, and Ben Schroeder; and about the people at the centre of my world, Ken and Emily. Because when I think of them, I know that I'm not alone: I know that there are others who care, and who won't let the cycle repeat itself unopposed.

That's the best feeling of all.

Author's Note

This is a novel. The events and characters depicted in it are fictitious, as is Lancelot Andrewes School; and any resemblance to any persons, living or dead, is entirely coincidental. All authors say that, and mean it, routinely. But in this case, I want to go a bit farther, because any author who sets a novel in a particular time in the past, such as 1974, inevitably encounters, in the course of writing about it, real people who lived and played their part in the real history of that time. It is never a comfortable encounter, and certainly not in this book; and for that reason, I want to ensure that I distinguish fact from fiction more particularly in one or two cases. Any of my readers who wishes to do so can easily discover the identity of the Attorney General in 1974. He was a man of ability and integrity, who served in public life for many years with great distinction. In case I haven't made it clear in the book, as I intended, no suspicion of misconduct of any kind falls on his shoulders. Similarly, there is also no suggestion that the Diocese of Ely, or any of its employees or agents at the time, was guilty of any misconduct. I had the honour of knowing the then Bishop of Ely personally, and I know that he would never have been party to covering up any scandal, much less the kind of scandal I describe in this book.

But while an author may say that his work is fictitious, he may equally say that the story he tells is intended to represent some truth about the human condition; and in that case, he may fairly describe his story as a myth. Howard Sasportas once defined a myth as something that never happened, but happens all the time. He meant, I think, that the essence of a myth is that it reveals recurring human archetypes in the comforting garb of fiction, and so illuminates those archetypes for us when we encounter them in our lives. In that context, for me, the story I tell is a myth: I point no finger at any individual in public life in 1974, yet I point the finger at many such throughout the course of history.

Child sexual abuse is an archetype that has always been with us, but it has come into particular focus in recent times. In the UK, we have set in motion a public inquiry on a vast scale – so vast that its very ability to carry out its mandate is in question, even leaving aside its ill-starred beginnings, during which it has lost, not only its first leaders, but also the trust of many victims. The scale of the abuse under inquiry is almost too great to credit. The horrific revelations of clerical abuse, across a wide spectrum of churches and clerical educational establishments, are as remarkable for the systematic and cynical attempts by the churches to cover them up, and to protect predatory priests and ministers from investigation, as for the casual obscenity and disregard for the most basic of human dignities they permitted to flourish for so long. Not far behind in this sickening history is the prevalence of familial abuse, and the chilling reality of the horrors that lay hidden under the casting couch, and behind cheerful phrases such as 'Jim fixed it for me'.

One of the more encouraging signs in more recent times is the extent to which we have enabled victims to come forward in the expectation that they will be believed, and that action will be taken to investigate their complaints, and to prosecute those against whom there is evidence of sexual offences. The system is still far from perfect, but we have come a long way from 1974. Those of my readers who are not lawyers may be surprised by the fact that, historically, children were not automatically regarded as competent witnesses; and by the extent to which the rules of corroboration were then capable of rendering prosecution cases untenable. Children are now subject to the same test of competence as other witnesses, and the corroboration rules have since been abolished almost in their entirety: arguably, a swing of the pendulum too far. The rules of corroboration were unduly technical, and far too restrictive, but the concepts underlying them were neither illogical nor unreasonable. Sadly, there are cases of deliberately false allegations, of childish hysteria, and of misguided and mistaken allegations, and these realities must also be addressed in any balanced system of law. But almost everyone, myself included, agrees that the law today is a vast improvement on the law of 1974.

The courts are also far more open to evidence of recovered memory. In 1974, the subject was by no means as well understood as I have depicted it in this book. Until the sudden focus on such evidence in the 1980s and 1990s, as the result of the long-running series of satanic ritual accusations – which overshadowed even the Salem witch trials in their subjugation of scientific principle to naked superstition – relatively little attention had been paid to it. In an attempt to make the issues comprehensible, I have allowed my judges and lawyers to sound knowledgeable about it – vastly more so than they would have sounded in 1974. The truth is that in 1974, claims of recovered memory would have been regarded by most lawyers as just another example of unreliable memory, and would have been attacked as such in the course of a trial. Many judges would have refused to allow such evidence even to go to a jury. Today, while expert opinion on the subject remains divided, and while it must be treated with appropriate caution, judges are far more likely to leave evidence of recorded memory to the common sense of juries, which, subject to proper judicial oversight, is the appropriate test for evidence in criminal cases.

Victims of sexual abuse still have much to fear; and the fear of not being believed, and of having their claims ridiculed and dismissed out of hand, is one of the most terrible injustices our legal system has tolerated in our relatively recent history. We deal with such fears much more compassionately and effectively than we used to, and we show much greater ambition to bring perpetrators to justice, whoever they may be, and behind whatever religious, political, or establishment façades they may seek to hide. All that is good. But there is still a long way to go, and the problem is enormous. I am not presumptuous enough to suggest that this book should play any major part in taking it further. But mythology has a proven track record in attracting people's attention, and if my myth can do that to any small extent, I will be glad.

As ever, my thanks: to my friends at No Exit Press, especially Ion Mills and Claire Watts, for their confidence in my writing; to my editor, Sally Partington; to my agent, Guy Rose; and above all, to my wife Chris. As I write this, we are days away from our silver anniversary, and throughout that time, she has been my rock and my unfailing support in all I do.